Better than Revenge

EJ Blaise is an Irish author of all things romance. When she's not creating unrealistically perfect men, she can be found travelling, reading and dreaming of running a bookstore café.

By EJ Blaise:

The Sun Valley Series
Unexpected
Bide
Curveball

The Serenity Ranch Series
Bloom
Chaos

Better Than Revenge

PRAISE FOR BETTER THAN REVENGE!

'*Better Than Revenge* is full of wit, charm and delicious tension. EJ Blaise delivered everything readers could ever want from a fake dating romance and so much more'
Hannah Bonam-Young, *New York Times* bestseller

'Fake dating has never been hotter . . . or deliciously messy. Blaise delivers a sharp, addictive college romance that's packed with rippling banter and delicious chemistry. From a fiery female protagonist you'll immediately adore to the golden retriever you'll want to root for, *Better Than Revenge* is, through and through, the book of the summer'
Elena Armas, *Sunday Times* bestseller

'EJ Blaise is the queen of wit, banter, and romance. *Better Than Revenge* is funny, sexy, and heart wrenching. Heath and Daniela will have you kicking your feet and giggling all the way through. Don't miss this one!'
Becka Mack, *New York Times* bestseller

'EJ Blaise is an immensely talented author who knows how to captivate her readers with the perfect mix of hot, witty, and emotion'
Hannah Grace, *New York Times* bestseller

'Buzzy and addicting, *Better Than Revenge* is a witty and emotionally brilliant romance that hits all the right spots with fake-dating, a toxic ex, and a golden-retriever boyfriend. I couldn't put this one down!'

Aamna Qureshi, author of *The Baby Dragon Café*

'BETTER THAN REVENGE is a fun, hot, beachy read packed with sharp humor, sexy tension, and just the right amount of angst. A boy obsessed and a perfectly prickly girl make for an irresistible pairing. Delightfully funny with real depth, it's another standout from E.J. Blaise'

Ki Stephens, author of *Game On*

'The black cat x golden retriever romance of my dreams! *Better Than Revenge* is punchy, witty, and full of so much heart. Not to mention utterly delicious banter! A pitch-perfect college romance – I dare you not to fall for Heath and Dani from the very first page'

Grace Reilly, *USA Today* bestseller

'Sexy, funny, pacy, and a little emotional, I absolutely devoured this read. Dani is such a wonderfully multifaceted character, you can't help but root for her, and Heath - the walking, talking green flag - has officially been added to my roster of blond kings!'

Anise Starre, author of *Just a Taste*

'*Better Than Revenge* is a tension-filled romance full of amazing banter and steamy moments!'

E. Salvador, bestselling author of *Please Don't Go*

'Witty, emotionally rich, and unputdownable – *Better Than Revenge* captivates from its opening line to its unforgettable final moments. EJ Blaise delivers once again!'
Kanitha P., author of the *Full Throttle* series & *All You Need is Gloves*

'*Better Than Revenge* is the perfect summer romp full of personality and, of course, a touch of revenge. Witty banter, loads of tension, heaps of drama, and hints of self-discovery as Dani finds her path with Heath by her side (both for the bit, and for real) made this one a read to remember!'
Esha Patel, author of the *Offtrack Series*

'Watching a spiky woman fall for a man who loves her edges will never get old, and *Better Than Revenge* did it perfectly. Delicious prose, complex, relatable characters, and some of the best banter I've ever read; it's actually annoying how good this is. I can't wait to watch EJ Blaise soar'
Georgia Stone, author of *The Friendship Fling*

'EJ has perfected the art of writing romance. Every interaction between Dani and Heath only left me wanting more. Full of witty banter, relatable characters, and a love story of two perfectly matched people, *Better Than Revenge* has easily solidified itself as one of my top romance reads'
Zarin Madiyha, author of the *Coates Academy* series

'Readers are bound to be swept away with Dani and Heath. *Better Than Revenge* had me kicking my feet and spinning around in my chair in absolute glee from chapter one. An instant favourite'

Meg Jones, author of the *Game, Set and Match* series

Better than Revenge

E J BLAISE

HEADLINE ETERNAL

First published in 2026 by Headline Eternal
An imprint of Headline Publishing Group Limited

This paperback edition published in 2026

3

Cataloguing in Publication Data is available from the British Library

Paperback ISBN 978 1 0354 3800 6

Typeset in 10.35/16pt ITC Clearface Std
by Six Red Marbles UK, Thetford, Norfolk

Printed and bound in Great Britain by Clays Ltd, Elcograf S.p.A.

FSC www.fsc.org
MIX
Paper | Supporting responsible forestry
FSC® C104740

Headline's policy is to use papers that are natural, renewable and recyclable products and made from wood grown in well-managed forests and other controlled sources. The logging and manufacturing processes are expected to conform to the environmental regulations of the country of origin.

Headline Publishing Group Limited
An Hachette UK Company
Carmelite House
50 Victoria Embankment
London EC4Y 0DZ

The authorised representative in the EEA is Hachette Ireland, 8 Castlecourt Centre, Dublin 15, D15 XTP3, Ireland (email: info@hbgi.ie)

www.headlineeternal.com
www.headline.co.uk
www.hachette.co.uk

For a very lost, very lonely twenty-year-old.
Look what you did!

Content Warning

This story contains explicit sexual content, profanity, reference to parental loss, minor reference to past disordered eating habits, and mild violence.

If these are sensitive topics for you, please take that into consideration. If they aren't, please exercise compassion.

ONE

ANY MINUTE NOW, I'M GOING TO COMMIT A CRIME.

Because if I hear my name whispered in a scandalized tone one more time, somebody's getting murdered.

Hoisting myself out of the pool and ripping off my goggles and swim cap, I just about manage to resist the urge to ping them both at the gaggle of people lingering nearby, sneering at me like I'm the devil incarnate. Like *I've* done something wrong. Like *I* cheated on my boyfriend, on my partner of almost two fucking years, on the only person I've ever been with. Like *I* left *him* for *my* side piece – not the other way around.

Unbelievable. It's un-fucking-believable to them that the tall, raven-haired *dickhead* right there amongst them could possibly be the villain. Ben is the dirty bastard here, yet I'm the one with metaphorical daggers slashing my skin while he holds court, his little posse all one pathetic move away from dropping to their knees and kissing his feet.

Snagging my towel from the bench I dropped it on at the beginning of practice, I dry myself off with a little more vigor than necessary, tangled wet hair falling in my face as I bend over to scrub at my legs until light brown skin blushes red. It's not like I was best friends with anyone on the team to begin with – hell, it's not like I was really *friends* with anyone. I'm not heartbroken to lose their oh-so-dear companionship, but come the fuck on. How has Ben managed to shit all over our relationship and still come out smelling like roses?

And *her*. Jesus Christ, how is *she* not the antichrist? Sienna is petite and blonde, and she smiles with all of her shiny white teeth without looking like a predator, so that makes it okay that she slept with my boyfriend? Repeatedly? How the hell does that work?

I don't get it. I really, really don't get it. I'm utterly baffled, but I'd rather pull out my own teeth than ask for an explanation. It already physically pains me that I care, that I spent half of this first practice of the season glowering about Ben and pretty, perfect Sienna. So much so that I almost let a girl whose personal best I could swim while dead asleep – I could swim it *dead*, full stop – beat me in a practice race.

Distracted, I practically hear my dad hissing from beyond the grave. *Not good enough, Daniela. Not you.*

He wouldn't be wrong. It *isn't* good enough. It *isn't* me. Shit, didn't Ben demolish our relationship a few months ago – on the very last day of sophomore year, to be precise – specifically because of my hyper-focus on swimming? As much as I would get off on proving him wrong, the sacrifice wouldn't be worth it. *Ben* isn't worth it.

Slinging my towel over my shoulder, I tilt my chin upwards, readying myself to march past my teammates as if their subtly veiled disparaging doesn't make me want to jump back in the pool and take some frustration out on the water. But I only make it a handful of steps before the doors to the pool complex fly open and a cacophony of noise suddenly floods the building.

'What the hell are they doing here?' someone murmurs, just as I think it. As tension throbs between my shoulder blades and tightens my posture, a groan brews low in my throat, and something between a scowl and a grimace contorts my face as I watch the Cove College swim team – our closest, fiercest rivals – strut inside.

And I do mean *strut*. They're all big, tangible energy, loud and rambunctious, their young coach not doing all that much to keep them in line – a stark contrast to Haven Cove University's very own drill sergeant, who turns up his nose at the intruders and audibly scoffs.

And at the center of it all, there's him.

Heath Belfort.

Six feet and a neck-breaking amount of inches of tan, tattooed, infuriatingly attractive *presence*. Unavoidable. Unignorable. Against my will, my eyes track him as he saunters toward the pool, laughing and smiling and messing around with his teammates in a way that makes me think *Oh! That's what camaraderie looks like!*

Because unlikeable he is not. And, sometimes, I wonder if that's why my ex hates him so much. If it infuriates Ben not only that his sworn rival is so well-liked, but that he is infinitely *more* well-liked. Probably. That, and the whole him-being-a-better-swimmer thing. Like, a lot better. Like, has beat him in every race they've ever swum kind of better. Like, so good even I can't help but be impressed – and a little irritated, because I'm not sure he even knows how good he is. And I'm not sure he cares. I can't claim to know him – our interactions have rarely gone beyond me trying not to laugh whenever he and Ben traded silly, oh-so-*manly* barbs – but I know he doesn't really act like a competitive swimmer. He doesn't have that drive. He doesn't—

'What the fuck is this?'

Oh, here we go.

See, before, when I was still playing the painstakingly perfected role of the dutiful girlfriend, I would've rushed over and stood stoically at a simmering Ben's side. I would've listened to him snap at Heath, would've watched Heath playfully retort, would've listened somewhat intently to Ben's bitching when it was all over and feigned sympathy for his poor, fragile ego being wounded once again by someone with more talent, more personality, *and* more wit.

For a split second, habit drives me forward a step. Moves me closer until reality – until common sense – kicks in and I remember that Prince freaking Charming has a new doting damsel by his side.

Sienna doesn't look like she's feigning anything. She looks genuinely distraught as she pouts and rubs Ben's back soothingly, so supportive as he faces the man I genuinely, unironically heard him call his *worst enemy* more than once.

A stark contrast to all the glowering happening on the HCU side of this odd little stand-off, the Cove College contingent only smile – smirk, really – at my teammates and at each other, exchanging looks like they know something we don't.

It's Heath who explains their unexpected presence, *self-satisfied* not even close to correctly describing his tone. 'Didn't you hear, Pullman? We're moving in.'

Despite the weather outside doing its very best to hang on to summer, the temperature indoors suddenly plummets. '*Excuse me?*'

'Our pool filter broke,' the brunet, just-as-smarmy guy beside Heath chimes in – Kai Shen: I recognize him almost as easily as I do his golden best friend. The second-best swimmer at Cove College and, consequently, public enemy number two for Ben. 'So, I guess we're sharing for a while.'

'*What?*' Ben splutters, all but stomping his feet like a disgruntled toddler. 'No!'

'Don't cry, Benny.' One corner of his full mouth curling upwards, Heath adds, '*Again*.'

Before I manage to stifle it, a snicker escapes me. I can't help it. I've been holding one in since Heath decimated Ben's time in a relay a year or so ago, and my then-boyfriend damn near burst into tears, never mind the fact his team still won.

Yet *my* dedication to the sport was the problem. *Okay*.

Like he did all those months ago when I gently – okay, maybe not-so-gently – told him it wasn't that big of a deal, Ben swings a scowl my way.

Heath, on the other hand, flashes me a smile. A wide, bright smile that I imagine has sent many a girl to her knees.

Mine, obviously, remain steady.

'Hey, Dani.'

I crook a brow – a silent *why are you talking to me?* that doesn't actually do anything to deter him. In fact, it seems to spur him on, that ever-present grin stretching wider, and it definitely, unintentionally draws him an inch closer.

'Been meaning to congratulate you.'

Up goes the second brow, though this one is marginally more intrigued than sarcastic.

Blue-green eyes shimmer with pure mischief, reminiscent of the sun catching on a piece of sea glass, and then he winks. 'Heard you lost some dead weight recently.'

Another snicker tickles the back of my throat. *Lost, stolen. Potato, potato-h.*

'Freedom looks good on you,' Heath continues, and I swear those eyes light up even brighter when, finally, I bite.

'Nice to know I looked like shit before.'

'You?' Heath blows out a breath, looking startlingly sincere for someone who never seems to stop kidding round. '*Never.*'

Yeah, okay. I get it. The charm, the smile, the pretty words – I can see why half the town is in love with this guy. If I were *that* kind of person – soft and loving and susceptible to flattery – I'm not sure I'd be able to resist either.

But I'm not. I'm . . . well, according to the general populace, I'm a mean, heartless viper who drives men into the arms of other women with the sheer power of my bitterness. So, when Heath sidles closer and croons suggestively about some party on the beach tonight, I'm more than capable of maintaining my usual blank, uncaring stare. 'Have fun.'

That pretty, close-shaven head cocks to one side. 'You don't wanna come?'

This time, the snicker doesn't come from me. 'Daniela doesn't party,' someone on my team quips, and I'd be grateful for the back-up, if it didn't feel more like a knife in the back.

Before I can say anything, Heath fires back, 'Maybe Daniela just doesn't party with you.'

'Daniela can speak for herself.' I roll my eyes. *Oh, handsome knight, how shiny your armor looks.* 'Thanks, but no thanks.'

Heath pouts a little, but he doesn't push. Not really. Just suggests that I 'think about it'.

'Yeah,' I drone, non-committal, as I start toward the changing rooms, my parting wave dismissive. 'I'll think real hard.'

'Help,' I yell half-heartedly as I let myself into the apartment I live in alone, yet for some reason I don't find empty. 'Call 911. There's an overgrown manchild stealing my chips.'

Slightly older, only a few inches taller, and a hell of a lot less mature, the man sprawled on *my* couch like it's *his* couch barely spares me a cursory glance, too focused on the shitty reality show playing on the laptop screen in front of him. 'Stealing?' my brother scoffs, waving a hand coated in barbecue seasoning dismissively. '*Please*. More like *saving*. We both know these weren't getting eaten any time soon.'

Not true. I had grand plans for kicking off the season by demolishing the entire bag – before my coach's nose properly attunes to the scent of trans fats and excessive sodium.

Kicking off my flip-flops by the front door, I drop my bag and pad into the kitchen. One hand undoing the crude braid I'd hastily fixed my damp hair in for the walk home, I grab a kombucha from the fridge with the other, and one more too, because I know that even though Sebastian swears they taste like straight vinegar, his aforementioned manchild energy means he always wants whatever I have. 'What're you doing here?'

Between mouthfuls of my chips, he explains, 'Wellness check. Mother Dearest says you're not answering her calls.'

'She's not my mother.' I cluck my tongue as I hip-check the fridge door closed, hard enough to make the contents rattle. 'And I've been busy.'

'You're always busy.'

God, have I heard that one before. 'Yeah, it's called having a life.'

Another snort echoes around my studio. 'You don't have a life, Dani. You have structure.'

Even though Sebastian easily catches the can I chuck at him, he still swears at me shrilly, shaking out his hand like the big drama queen he is. '*Pendeja*. For that, I'm *telling* you to come to dinner tonight instead of asking.'

An honest-to-God chill runs down my spine. There are a whole list of things I would rather do than spend the evening sandwiched between my stepmother and my brother, fielding questions I don't want to answer and defending my life choices.

Sandwiching myself between my cheating ex and his mistress, for example. Or re-taking Intro to Anthropology with Mr Henson, the professor from hell. Or swimming in the ocean.

All hard nos in my day-to-day life, but akin to a spa day in comparison to a Williams family dinner.

'Sorry.' I shrug as I crack open my drink. 'I don't think that fits my *structure*.'

My brother groans as he drops his head back against the arm of my sofa. '*Daniela*.'

'*Sebastian*.' I mimic his childish tone. 'I'm busy.'

'Doing what?'

'Stuff.'

'What stuff?' he presses. 'Drinking protein shakes? Doing homework? Throwing darts at a picture of Ben?'

'*Actually*,' I set a hand on my hip, fingers drumming against the denim shorts covering a yellow swimsuit, mouth moving before common sense can catch up with it. 'I'm going to a party.'

Sebastian blinks. 'A party.'

I swallow, and, fuck, if it doesn't taste like desperation. 'Uh-huh.'

Eyes the same shade of chocolate-brown as mine narrow. 'Where?'

'The Inlet.' I quickly name the stretch of sand nestled along the craggy coastline that I know college kids frequent whenever the temperamental Pacific Northwest weather is just right.

My brother remains unconvinced. 'With who?'

'Some people from the team.'

Now *that* makes him laugh, deep and snarky. 'Yeah fuckin' right.'

'Not *my* team,' I correct, clearing my throat before digging my hole just a little deeper. 'Heath Belfort invited me.'

A pair of dark brows meet a darker hairline. 'Excuse me?'

'You heard me.' My thumb repeatedly flicking the tab of my can, I round the tiny island separating the kitchen from the living room and make a beeline for the even tinier bathroom. 'Done interrogating me yet? Because I need to shower.'

'Wait.' With far more grace than such a long body should be capable of, Sebastian scrambles over the back of the sofa. Genuine wonder lighting up his entire face, he manages to jam his foot between the bathroom door and the doorframe before I can lock myself away. 'Are you being serious?'

'Yes,' I technically don't lie. He did invite me, I guess. Loosely. The only lie is me having any intention of actually going.

Except the look on my brother's face makes my gut sink – evokes a whiney *fuck my life, how am I getting out of this?* too.

'Heath Belfort,' he repeats, whistling as he leans a shoulder against the doorframe. 'Wow. How'd you manage that?'

Something in his tone makes my eye twitch. *Right*. How could the Wicked Witch of the Cove *possibly* attract the attention of the human equivalent of a golden unicorn? *Unfathomable*. 'Charmed him, obviously.'

'Scared him, more like.' Elbowing his way further into the bathroom, Sebastian drops a hand on each of my shoulders, squeezing in a disconcertingly affectionate way. 'This is good, Dani. You need to have some fun.'

I have fun, I want to insist, but the ensuing argument wouldn't be worth it. 'If you're satisfied with my social calendar, can you leave now?'

Sebastian laughs, and that sunken feeling in my gut? It multiplies.

'Oh, *mi hermanita*.' He clutches me even tighter, giving me a shake for good measure. 'You think I'm gonna miss a chance to watch Ben watch you get all cozy with fuckin' Belfort?'

My chest itches, a sure-fire sign of the pesky stress rashes that've been plaguing me since, oh, I don't know, *birth*. 'Aren't you a little old for a college party?'

My twenty-five-year-old, fully-fucking-grown brother actually *hisses* at me in mock outrage. 'Bite your tongue. I'm still a student at heart.'

He still *drinks* like a student, he means.

'Besides,' Seba continues, patting my cheek. 'The Inlet isn't a frat house, Dani. God knows I won't be the oldest person there.'

But he *will* be there.

Yeah. Fuck my life.

TWO

I CHANGED MY MIND.

There *is* something less enjoyable than spending time with my stepmother – descending a freaking cliff in search of a college beach party teeming with people I don't particularly care for, and who don't particularly care for me either, as the setting sun casts my impending death scene in pretty, golden light.

'*Seba*,' I hiss in my brother's wake, as he skips down the sketchy path like a freaking mountain goat. Meanwhile, I struggle like a dumbass, rocks scraping my bare feet as the Birkenstocks dangling from one hand severely impede my ability to balance. 'Slow the fuck down.'

Like the show-off he's always been, Sebastian turns to walk backwards, flashing me a smirk. '*Por qué*? Nervous?

I scowl. 'To break my neck? *Yeah*.'

'To see your new man,' he corrects, in an irritating sing-song tone. 'God, this is gonna be good.'

I disagree. Wholeheartedly. I have the distinct feeling that this is going to be an absolute nightmare. I'm going to eventually reach the bottom of this godforsaken cliff, people are going to notice me and wonder what the hell I'm doing here, and . . . well, shit, I'm not easily embarrassed, not by a long shot, but this might be too much, even for me.

Contrary to popular belief, I'm not a robot. I have the capacity to feel real, human emotions – other than rage and irritation, of course. Like trepidation. And unease. Both of which I feel right now, with a little nausea added to the mix as I anticipate the looks of pure and utter shock I'm about to be on the receiving end of.

And Sebastian is going to witness everything. He's going to know I was lying, because Heath fucking Belfort is not going to come bounding up to me, delighted by my presence. He invited me as a joke, as a way to rile up Ben, I know that, but it won't look like I know that. It will look like I took it seriously. Like I showed up here expecting . . . God knows what. 'Listen, Seba—'

Too late. It's too goddamn late. His feet have already hit sand, he's already scurrying toward the group of twenty-something-year-olds sprawled across the shoreline, each of them toting an alcoholic beverage of some description – each of them looking in my direction, because my loud-ass brother easily captures their attention with his arrival.

Unlike me, Seba is extremely likeable. Like, chronically. He was on the cusp of his final year of college when we moved here, an entirely shitty position to land yourself in, yet he had zero trouble falling in with the popular crowd. Just like he has zero trouble finding them now. He's swept up before I even make it to the sand, a drink shoved at him and a phone screen turned his way as he's commanded to add to the playlist being whipped along the beach by a coastal wind.

No such thing happens to me. Unsurprising, but still a little . . . I don't know. Demoralizing, I guess. I'm a big girl, a tough girl – *chingona,* my mom used to proudly call me – but still. Fuck. Talk about uncomfortable.

Seba doesn't even look back at me, and I guess that's kind of the way our relationship has always been. That's the kind of hold I've always had in his life. Fleeting and loose.

I don't let it get to me. Never have, and certainly not now, when I'm the center of freaking attention.

It takes no more than five seconds to find a pair of familiar dark blue eyes, squinting as they train themselves on me, blatantly confused and a little pissed. Which is, once again, unsurprising. Even when our relationship was actually good, I never wanted to party with Ben. I rarely let him force me to go out, and on the rare occasions I did, it was only when his pleading started giving me a migraine. I bet me being here – at Heath's request, no less – is killing him.

I wonder if it's killing Sienna, how intently her boyfriend peers at me while she frowns up at him.

God, I hope it is.

Karma, bitch.

Flicking my hair over my shoulder, I smile. My version of a smile, at least. Terrifying, I've heard it described as more than once, and that suits me just fine. That's what I'm going for. That's—

'You came.'

Head swinging abruptly to the side, I reel back just a little when I find turquoise eyes far closer than I anticipated. 'Jesus.' My hand flies to my chest, my smile already gone. 'You need a bell.'

'Kinky.' Mouth stuck in that perpetual grin, Heath winks

before smoothing out his expression – softening it. 'Guess all that "thinking" worked in my favor.'

I cross my arms with a huff, brows knitting together in a forced frown. 'You think I'm here for you?'

Heath glances over one broad, muscular shoulder, then the other, before fixing those damn ridiculous eyes back on me. 'Who else, Daniela?'

Jesus. I shift as something that's not quite discomfort wiggles in my belly. 'I'm here with my brother, actually.'

When I nod in his direction, Heath follows my gaze and lets out a soft, unconvinced, slightly smarmy, *'ah.'* 'You joining him?'

Eyeing Sebastian as he chugs a beer while single-handedly cracking open another, I repress a grimace. 'You got a better offer?'

Heath snorts. 'Oh, Dani. Do I ever.'

Except he doesn't offer. He doesn't give me much of a choice at all. Before I can really protest, he cups my elbow and guides me toward the small group gathered around a makeshift firepit. More people I vaguely recognize greet me – a softly smiling Black girl with braids down to her waist and a vintage-looking camera slung around her neck, two near-identical redheads sitting side-by-side, and, obviously, the infamous Kai. He's the one who hands me a drink: a cup filled to the brim with something dark that smells like cola, but I know better.

'It's rum,' Heath tells me, as he drags me down to the sand, settling right beside me, almost too close for comfort. 'That okay? We've got plain soda and water and stuff if you prefer. I know you don't really drink.'

I tap my pointer finger against my cup in an offbeat rhythm, huffing a humorless laugh. 'Oh, you know that, do you?'

Resting his forearms against his bent knees, Heath shrugs, but there's nothing casual about the way he looks me dead in the eye. 'I pay attention.'

Unnerved, I look away, bringing the cup to my lips just to give myself something to do, something else to focus on. 'I drink.' Not often, but I do. I'm partial to rum, actually, and I can't help but wonder if the one in my grip is simply a coincidence, or another display of *attention*. 'Thanks.'

Out of the corner of my eye, I see Heath lean forward, trying to catch my gaze. 'Be honest. It hurt you to say that?'

'Yes. Deeply. I believe I'll burst into flames at any moment now.'

A melodic chuckle floats toward me. 'You're funny.'

'Don't sound so surprised.'

'I'm not.' Heath shifts, rocking ever-so-slightly to one side so our shoulders brush. 'I already knew you were funny.'

'You know a lot about someone you've never spoken to.'

'We've spoken.'

'We've interacted through a third party.'

'Hmm. Sounds so *sexy* when you put it like that.'

Now it's my turn to laugh. I'm not sure I've ever made anything sound sexy in my life – I believe that was among Ben's complaints. Not sexy.

Not sexual.

'Hey.' Once again the side of Heath's body brushes against mine. 'What's that face for?'

'Nothing.' I kiss my teeth. 'Nothing at all.'

I'm unsure how, exactly, I get so drunk so quickly.

I just know that it happens. I just know that I'm drunk. Obscenely so. So much that I've started to anthropomorphize the fire in front of me, my rum-addled brain convincing me that the flames are smiling.

I smile back. I laugh quietly beneath my breath as I wonder if fire is my only friend, as a snippet of my dad likening me to it scratches the far corners of my memory, as I sag against the person beside me – the person who hasn't left my side. Who hasn't pushed me into conversation. No one around me has. They've just let me exist in their presence – out of pity, I think, but I'll take it.

For now. Tomorrow, I'm sure I'll kick my own ass for not just getting up and leaving, but, for now, I don't have the wherewithal.

So I sit and I listen and I don't listen too as I get lost in my own thoughts, and every so often, I sneak a glance at Heath. Leaning into me as much as I do him. Freaking gleaming in the firelight, sculpted features cast in shadows, flames dancing in those pretty, pretty eyes and reflecting off buzzed golden hair. He catches me more than once, always cracking a smile, sometimes bumping his shoulder against mine. One time, he yanks a strand of my hair, and I actually laugh – I like it. It's playful. Fun. Casual. Things I don't get to be, things I'm not. Things my last relationship wasn't.

God, I can't even count how many times my emotions around

that doomed coupling derived from stress and tension and *pressure*. If I'm honest, when I realized Ben was breaking up with me – before I got the sordid details of it all – I was *grateful*. Genuinely. Before the words *'I slept with someone else'* left his mouth, I breathed an actual sigh of relief.

Relief. Honestly. Briefly, I wondered if I really was a robot like people say. I wondered why I wasn't heartbroken, wondered what was wrong with me, before coming to my senses and concluding there wasn't anything wrong with *me*. There *isn't* anything wrong with me.

'Didn't say there was.'

I jolt, my head heavy as I lift it to frown at Heath. 'What?'

'I don't think there's anything wrong with you.'

'Oh.' Shit. I said that out loud? 'Thanks.'

'Two thanks in one night?' A long, low whistle makes me shiver. 'I think I deserve a prize for that.'

'Such a man,' I drawl – slur, really. 'Wanting a reward for someone else's accomplishments. *I'm* the one being polite.'

'Oh, so *you* want a reward?'

Something about his tone makes me gulp. Something about the way he dips his head, bringing us eye-to-eye, almost forehead-to-forehead, makes my stomach twist.

'Tell me,' he croons, eyes flicking between both of mine. 'What's your reward, Dani?'

I have an idea. A wild, rum-fueled idea that does not align with reality, that can't possibly be something I'd actually want. A slightly spiteful notion that I quickly swat away, shaking my head as I draw backwards. 'Stop that.'

Heath follows my retreat, refusing to relinquish our close proximity. 'Stop what?'

'*That.*' I flick my hand at him. 'Being all . . . Heath.'

'Being all Heath,' he repeats, with a laugh, crooking a brow. 'What does that mean?'

I shoot him a dry look. 'You know exactly what it means.'

'Humor me.'

'Listen, pretty boy. I'm not the one, okay? All that,' I gesture to . . . well, all of him, 'is wasted on me. I'm a waste.'

Heath simply stares for a moment, silent until one corner of his mouth lifts smugly. 'You think I'm pretty?'

Of course that's what he took from that.

'Okay.' Huffing another laugh, and shaking my head again too, I plant both palms in the sand. 'I'm gonna go now.'

Or at least I intend to. I try to, but the moment I push upright, gravity yanks me back down. In a true feat of grace, I topple onto Heath, get caught with a grunt and an exhale that brushes . . . my mouth.

His breath brushes my mouth.

Because that's how close we suddenly are. So close that when his tongue darts out to trace his bottom lip, I practically feel it on mine. I certainly feel his gaze, bouncing from my eyes to my mouth and back up again, as tangible as the steadying fingers that graze my bicep on an upwards path until a thumb traces the protrusion of my collarbone.

Head tilting to one side, Heath drawls, 'A waste, huh?'

I swallow thickly, unsettled by the sudden . . . *energy* floating around us. 'Uh-huh.'

'Hmm.' He nods slowly, thoughtfully. 'Better try harder, then.'

I have to look away.

Except my quest for turquoise-free peace only grants me a different kind of torture.

At some point, Ben has found his way to the firepit. Settled directly across from me, the new love of his life relaxes in his embrace, but he watches me intently. With his mouth set in a rigid line, he wears an expression I know all too well, one I've been on the receiving end of so many times.

Somehow, the jackass thinks he still has a right to be pissed at me. He thinks he can be mad that I'm talking to someone he doesn't like. He thinks I give a flying fuck about what he thinks.

Frustration itches beneath my skin. Averting my gaze, I'm once again bombarded by unnaturally bright irises that suck me in, draw me forward, make that itchy feeling calm down just a little.

Vaguely, like muffled noise in the background of a phone call, I register a voice abruptly getting louder, seeking attention.

A voice I recognize because I heard it every day for almost two years.

A voice that, only a few months ago, worked so damn hard to rip me apart.

A voice that showers me in spite and spurs me to lean forward and press my lips to Heath's.

Part of me – the deeply insecure part that I mostly manage to keep under lock and key – expects him to push me away. To yell or laugh or quip something mocking, or do some combination of all three.

Except he doesn't. He hesitates for a moment, an awful, mortifying moment, and then . . . fuck, he kisses me. He *really* kisses me. Like, one hand cupping my neck, the other gliding across my cheek before burrowing in the hair at my nape kind of kissing. Using his grip to tilt my head back and grant himself better access kind of kissing. Dizzying, discombobulating kind of kissing that makes me forget who I'm kissing, where I'm kissing him, *why* I'm kissing him.

Even if I remembered, I don't think I'd care. I only care about the mouth on mine, the tongue tangling with mine, the groan that rips from his throat that I answer in kind as greedy fingers drag me closer.

Until, suddenly, they don't.

'Fuck.' Reeling backwards, Heath blinks rapidly, chest heaving with panting breaths that match mine. 'You're drunk, Daniela.'

'So are you.'

He doesn't deny it, just like I can't deny it, because, yes, I am drunk. Jesus Christ, I really am. Drunk and stupid and *oh my fucking God, what did I just do?*

This time, when I attempt to get up, I succeed. Swaying a little, I press a hand to my forehead, squinting in the direction I abruptly start walking, unsure if it's the right way and not caring – I just need to get away.

When someone shouts my name, I ignore it. When someone abruptly grabs me, I stumble and spin around, expecting to find

Heath, only to be faced with Ben. A furious Ben. *Two* furious Bens because I'm seeing double, I'm *hearing* double – I hear Ben ask what the fuck is wrong with me so many times it makes me feel even dizzier, and I'm suddenly really nauseous, and I'm really, really not okay, and . . . 'I think I'm gonna be sick.'

And then, I am.

THREE

'HERE YOU GO, *TORMENTITA*.'

Dropping into my brother's passenger seat with a groan, I snatch the iced latte he holds out toward me like I'm a starved animal, drowning my mutter of gratitude with a greedy gulp of caramel goodness.

I can't remember the last time I saw Sebastian two days in a row, but if it involves a ride home from practice and coffee, I'm more than fine with it. I guess it's his guilt manifesting. After all, if he hadn't ditched me in five seconds flat, I never would've found myself hammered and vomiting on the sand with my ex barking in my ear about what an embarrassment I am.

That is, until someone promptly told him to go fuck himself. Not me, unfortunately. My brother, I think. It's all a bit foggy, really. I vaguely recall someone getting rid of Ben. And someone – the same person? – twisting my hair away from my face, rubbing my back, crooning something comforting. The only thing I really remember is getting home and crawling into bed, where I proceeded to rot for a meager few hours before my alarm went off.

'Y'know,' Seba pats my thigh with one hand and drops a breakfast croissant on the dashboard with another, 'I think Coach Bell would've forgiven you for skipping practice just this once.'

'I don't skip practice.'

I never have. I swam a meet with the flu once, for God's sake – and won, though I didn't beat my personal best, so my dad made me jog the mile-ish home. If I can do that, I can push through one hangover. I *did* push through a hangover.

The drastic increase in snarky, derogatory comments were a little harder to wade through – turns out, the only thing more heinous than me getting cheated on is me daring to move on. Shock horror. Call the village freaking elders – but I survived that too. I made it out unscathed. And, more importantly, I literally made it out before the Cove College crowd turned up. Now, I want to make it out of this parking lot, so I can be alone with my croissant. 'Can we go, please?'

Seba starts to nod, but when a headache-inducingly loud ringtone suddenly echoes around the car's interior, I groan again. 'Two minutes,' he promises, despite the fact no one has ever exited a vehicle for a simple two-freaking-minute conversation.

As he rounds the corner of the pool complex and disappears from sight, I slump in my seat. Propping my forearm against the open window, I tilt my head toward the sky and close my eyes, settling in for what'll likely be a long wait.

Only a minute passes before knuckles rap against the roof, making me jump.

I open my eyes, and the urge to retch suddenly strikes me again.

Nope.

Huffing, I stab at the button to roll the window up, but begrudgingly stop when fingers curl around the top of the glass. I'm not opposed to a little dismemberment, and especially not when it comes to *him*, but perhaps not in the light of day with witnesses lurking.

'Get out of the car, Daniela.'

Maybe just the pinkie.

Scowling at my ex, I don't do what he so brusquely demands. Let him rave at me through the crack in the window. Whatever. I don't give a shit.

'Seriously? You can't even talk to me now?'

'Oh, I can.' I bare my teeth in a loose interpretation of a smile. 'I just *really* don't want to.'

In the blink of an eye, the car door opens and Ben drags me outside, practically growling as he snatches my sunglasses off my face. 'Grow the fuck up, Dani.'

Just as quickly, I rip my arm from his grasp, my glasses too, and plant both hands on his chest so I can shove him away. 'Grab me like that again and see what fucking happens.'

Like the frisbee of my nightmares, he rebounds, ending up even closer. 'What the hell were you doing last night?'

Folding my arms, I silently crook a brow. *Whatever do you mean, dickhead?*

'If you're trying to make me jealous . . .'

Then it worked, I can't help but think, with no small amount of glee, of *exhilaration*. Because that's what he looks right now – jealous. He looks like a pathetic, jealous boyfriend, no matter how much he tries to huff and puff and portray all this forced exasperation, no matter how snidely he says, 'Shit, then that's really pathetic, Dan.'

I blink slowly. 'Sorry, did you say something? I wasn't listening.'

'You—'

I cut him off with a tut. '*Rude*. I wasn't finished.' Slumping against the car, I take a long second to survey the hangnail plaguing my middle finger – just because I know the perceived nonchalance will piss him off – before cutting him a mild glare. 'I wasn't listening because I don't give a fuck about anything that comes out of your mouth. Not one thing. I'm done with you, Ben. I really, really wish you could actually be done with me too.'

He barks a haughty laugh. 'I *am* done. I've moved on. I have a girlfriend, babe. *You* are throwing yourself at fuckboys to try to get my attention.'

'Not throwing myself at anyone right now, yet here you are.'

Two hands lift in frustration, one of them raking through wet hair as Ben backs up a step while the other gestures erratically at me. 'This is exactly why I left you, you know that? If you could stop being such a fucking bitch for five seconds—'

'One.' Fixing a saccharine smile into place, I hold up a finger. 'Two.' Up goes another. And then another, and another, and another, while I count aloud until I reach five. 'Look at that. Five seconds. Bet you can't stop being a prick for one.'

Ben opens his mouth.

'*Oops*.' I sigh with mock disappointment. 'Big fail.'

'Fuck you, Daniela.'

'Fuck *off*, Ben.'

'Hey.'

As a third, unfamiliar voice unexpectedly intervenes, my anger at Ben channels itself into a fresh scowl for the girl suddenly lingering a handful of steps away. '*What?*'

'Excuse her.' Not for the first time, Ben apologizes on my behalf. Not for the first time, he sets a scolding hand on my shoulder, squeezing. Not for the first time, I shrug it off. 'Can we help you?'

'Yeah,' the girl replies, two deep divots dimpling dark skin as full lips part to make room for a wide grin that only makes the next words out of her mouth all the more shocking. 'You mind fucking off so I can talk to Daniela?'

While Ben physically recoils, I laugh aloud. 'Yes, Ben,' I practically cackle, all but rubbing my hands together in evil glee. 'You mind?'

He does. Deeply. He would love to stay and gripe some more, I can read it on his face, but he doesn't. Throat bobbing as he swallows his pride, he reluctantly backs off, tossing one last threat my way before he turns around and jogs over to his awaiting entourage. 'This isn't over.'

'I'm shaking in my flip-flops.' I roll my eyes to the sky. When they come back down, they land on my new hero. 'Do I know you?'

Twisting the end of a braid around her finger, the girl chuckles quietly. 'Yes, actually. We've met. Several times.'

As a teeny tiny little fragment of guilt turns my stomach, a ring-adorned hand dismisses it. 'Imani Jones,' she introduces herself, and the name definitely rings a bell. As does her face.

At the very moment I remember – with no small amount of cringe-inducing dread – that she was one of the few gathered around the firepit last night, Imani cocks her head at me, onyx eyes narrowing ever-so-slightly. 'I'm friends with Heath.'

Jesus. Even hearing his name kind of makes me want to be sick. 'Ah.'

'I know Ben has probably tainted your perception of him—'

'No more so than he has the rest of the male species.'

That draws a laugh out of her. 'Right. Anyway. I'm shooting some promo pics for the team today and I saw you over here, and I just wanted to tell you that Heath is a really good guy.'

I wait for the punchline, for it to become clear why she's looking at me like *that*. 'Okay?'

Imani sighs. 'What you did last night wasn't cool.'

'Okay,' I repeat, no less confused. 'If you have a crush on him or something, that's not really my—'

'Jesus, *no*.' With a scoff, she emphatically shakes her head from side to side, practically gagging before composing herself and hitting me with, 'You used him to make Ben jealous.'

Something defensive licks a path up my spine. 'That's not what I was doing.'

In some sense, maybe, but jealousy wasn't my prime objective. Rage and mortification were. And it worked like a charm, obviously, but I can't even enjoy it without the guilt trip? Seriously unfair.

As Imani eyes me skeptically, my own gaze narrows. 'I'm sorry,' I half-laugh, half-scoff, 'but did you have this same conversation with Heath?'

Dark brows pull together. 'What?'

I run my tongue over my teeth and drop one hand to my hip, the other drumming against the top of my brother's car. 'Did you scold *him* for using *me*? Or is it different because he's a sweet little boy and I'm an evil witch?'

'I don't think you're an evil witch,' she's so quick to clarify, yet

I still find it hard to believe her. Equally hard to believe is: 'And he wasn't using you.'

'Right,' I snicker, as I slide my sunglasses back into place, shielding another eye roll, though I suspect Imani senses it anyway. 'He kissed me because he's madly in love with me, not because I'm his rival's ex.'

For a second, Imani is quiet. And then she smiles again, shaking her head as she chuckles. 'Y'know, I think there's a reality somewhere in between those two.'

'Unlikely.' Hauling the car door open again, I duck back inside. As I slam the door behind me, I reach for my now-tepid coffee whilst waggling my fingers dismissively. 'Anyway. *So* lovely chatting.'

Briefly looking almost . . . shell-shocked, Imani starts slowly walking backwards, still wearing that odd, sort of surprised smile. 'Let's do it again sometime.'

Yeah, right. 'Boy talk over cocktails?'

With a laugh, she turns around, lifting one hand in a blind wave. 'Bye, Dani.'

Calling a goodbye in her wake, I let my head hit the headrest with a thump.

And at some point as I watch her through the windshield as she walks away, as I think about what she said, as I catch sight of fucking Ben glowering in the distance, a wild, ridiculous light-bulb pings above my head.

The first time I entered Barefoot Joe's, I was an eighteen-year-old from out of state and so completely ignorant of the deep-seated rivalry that all but splits this college town in half. I had no idea back then that the boardwalk diner was Cove College territory, and that, as an HCU student, I was essentially forbidden from entering. I learned pretty quickly, though – nothing like a little *friendly* hazing to put the new freshman in her place – and I never came here again.

Until today.

As a bell tolls above my head and announces my entrance, my hackles rise, my head on a swivel like I'm freaking prey on the lookout for a threat. Though, I guess I'm actually the predator. *I'm* on the hunt. And it doesn't take me all that long to track down exactly what I'm looking for – *who*.

Stationed at the opposite end of the counter taking orders, Heath does a double take when he spots me sliding onto a stool. When I wave stiffly, he glances over his shoulder, laughably dorky as he points to himself and mouths, *'Me?'*

Lips pressing together, I nod sharply.

Jesus, that smile. *Put it away*, I almost command. I don't need it right now. I don't need the unfamiliar, somewhat daunted way it makes me feel, not when what I'm about to do – God, I can't believe I'm about to do it – is plenty daunting all on its own.

'Well, well, well.' The very image of smug, Heath glides in my direction, snagging a plated slice of apple pie on his way and dropping it in front of me, and I guess it's a really bad time, considering I'm about to ask for a pretty major favor, to gloat that he clearly doesn't know me as well as he thinks he does – I fucking hate cooked fruit. 'You come all the way out here just to see me?'

'My place is, like, five minutes away.' *Not exactly a detour.* 'But, yeah. Guess I did.'

Surprise paints his features, like he didn't think that was actually the case – or maybe he just didn't think I'd actually admit it.

'Okay.' Palms flat against the counter, he looms over me, making my five-foot-nine frame feel more like five-foot-nothing. 'I'll bite. What's up, pretty girl?'

Well, shit. Here goes nothing.

'I wanna get him back,' I blurt out, well and truly ripping off the Band-Aid. 'Ben, I mean.'

Heath's expression drops. 'Seriously?' He huffs incredulously, briefly dropping his head as it rocks from side to side stiffly. 'Shit, Dani, *why*? You know you could do a lot better.'

It takes me a second to realize my mistake, and a lot less to splutter a hasty clarification. 'No. *No*. God, no. I mean, I wanna get him back. Like, revenge.'

His soft 'ah' sounds oddly . . . relieved.

'So, what?' Heath drops his forearms to the counter, regarding me quizzically as he settles at eye-level. 'Want me to slash his tires or something? You strike me as someone who'd know how to do that all on her own.'

'Thank you,' I say, pressing a hand to my chest in a touched gesture that isn't really all that sarcastic. 'But no. I . . . I think we should date.'

There. I did it. I got it out. The utterly outrageous scheme that came to me in some kind of demented waking nightmare, founded quite simply and solely on the vicious need to make Ben squirm, has been sufficiently verbalized.

To Heath's credit, he doesn't even flinch.

He does, however, seem to malfunction for a long moment – a *minute*, really. 'I'm sorry,' he eventually drawls, voice a low rasp. 'I think I just hallucinated. You *what*?'

'I think we should date,' I repeat – and abruptly realize that I've done that misspeaking thing again. 'Or *pretend* to date.'

'*Or?*' Heath raises his brows, the corners of his mouth lifting too. 'Which one is it, Daniela? Kind of a big difference.'

'Pretend,' I clarify firmly. 'Obviously.'

'Obviously? *Ouch.*'

'You know what I mean.'

'Don't think I do. Why is it so obvious?'

Something akin to a stifled scream scratches my throat. 'It's a yes or no question, Heath.'

'Honey, I don't remember hearing a question.'

Briefly dropping my head back, I take a moment to sigh at the ceiling before looking at the smirking man intent on driving me insane again. 'Will you pretend to date me, or not?'

'*Why?*'

Did I not just say? 'To piss off Ben.'

To make him jealous, if we're getting into the technicalities of it all. Seethingly, debilitatingly jealous. Even more, to *embarrass* him. If I managed to do it without even trying, if everyone thinks that was what I was doing anyways, then, *God,* imagine what I could do with a little effort. It's . . . well, it might not be *perfect*, but it's something.

Heath hums thoughtfully, leaning forward until I have no

choice but to remember the last time we were this close, until I'm squirming and fisting my hands in my lap to stop from spinning myself around and hauling ass out of here. 'And what's in it for me, exactly?'

'You get to piss off Ben.' I frown. 'I thought that was obvious.'

Kissing his teeth, Heath props his chin in his hand. 'Tempting, but not good enough.'

Deadpan, I offer, 'You get to pretend to date me.'

'Oh, well, then I'm sold.'

For some reason, that doesn't sound quite as sarcastic as I think it's meant to. 'Well, what do you want?'

'Hmm.' He leans back a little, the quirk of his mouth promising something I don't think I want to hear. 'Loaded question.'

'Say something dirty and see what happens.'

'Don't worry, Wednesday. Not interested in my next swim being piranha-infested.'

'Might make you swim faster.' I raise a hand, my pointer and middle fingers crossed. 'Here's hoping.'

'Is this how you get people to do things for you? Insult them?'

'Is it working?'

He pauses to think about it, white teeth tugging on his lower lip. 'Little bit.'

'Okay, then. We have a deal?'

'Hang on a second. Jesus. You don't do anything at human pace, do you?'

My spine straightens, my fingernails digging into my palms. 'I'm not a robot.'

'I didn't say that.' A tiny frown creases a sun-kissed forehead. 'I know you're not. Robots can't kiss.'

God knows I'm not a blusher, but I can't deny the heat that burns my cheeks. 'We're not talking about that.'

'No? You just barged into my work, begging me to be your boyfriend, but you won't talk about a little kiss.'

'*Little*. Thanks.'

'I have a couple better descriptors, but I'm not allowed to talk about it.'

'Fine. If you pretend to date me, we can talk about it. We can even do it again. Congratulations.'

Heath laughs, he smiles, but he still doesn't agree, and now I'm really getting frustrated. 'C'mon, Belfort. You're seriously gonna miss a chance to get under Ben's skin?'

Still chuckling a little, he sighs at me. He stares at me. He thinks about me, I think, and my offer, and his eyes get this weird, blown-out, freaking *sparkly* quality to them. And then he leans forward again, even freaking closer, the concept of personal space clearly lost on the man. 'You're a history major, right?'

'Minor.' My frown returns with a vengeance. 'How do you know that?'

'Me too,' he replies, without answering my question. Before I can press further, he distracts me, dangling a freaking carrot right in front of my nose. 'I gotta retake a class I failed last year. Help me pass it, and I'll do whatever you want.'

'You failed a class?' On instinct, I reach out, tapping him on the forearm as I tut quietly. 'It's your senior year, Heath. You can't fail anything.'

As uncomfortable as I've ever seen him, he shifts, dismissing the concern that catches me off-guard as much as it seemingly does him. 'I won't fail it again. Right?'

Even though I brought this up, even though this is my dumb-ass idea, I hesitate. I think about it, even though it's all I've thought about since it popped into my head this morning, even though I've driven myself half mad thinking about it. I wonder if it actually is the great idea I think it is. If it's truly a genius stab at revenge. I watch Heath's hand extend toward me, and I pause before grasping it.

I do, however, grasp it.

I shake it.

I agree, 'Right.'

FOUR

AS MY GAZE DRIFTS AROUND THE DIM, CRAMPED storage room of Barefoot Joe's, I can't help but wonder how many girls Heath has enticed back here in his time.

Without meaning to, I ask just that aloud, and a low, teasing laugh makes the hairs on the back of my neck stand up. 'You're getting a jump on the jealous girlfriend thing, huh?'

My snort is incredulous. 'I'm not *jealous.*'

Slumped against the wall opposite me, Heath pouts. He really looks like he means it when he croons, 'How disappointing.'

'Stop that.'

'What?'

'*That.*' The same way I did last night – God, was that really only last night? – I gesture at all of him. Specifically, that cockily quirked mouth and the fucking twinkle in his eyes. 'I told you, I'm not the one.'

'No? It worked pretty well before.'

I open my mouth, if only to insist on him shutting his.

'Ah-ah-ah,' Heath tuts, head shaking playfully. 'You forget our deal already? We're allowed to talk about it now.'

We're supposed to be talking about something else. Something more important, more important than a drunken kiss at least. Something that would implode before it even began if any inquisitive ears overheard, hence why we're trapped in a room with the same square footage as a fucking bathroom stall.

When I remind Heath of that, he sighs dramatically. 'Fine. Go on. Lay the details on me.'

I shift awkwardly, my thumbnail finding its way to my mouth.

Heath raises an insistent brow.

A glower creasing my forehead, I huff. 'I'm thinking, okay?'

'Shouldn't you have done that before you begged—'

'There was no *begging*.'

'—me to be your boyfriend?'

'*Fake* boyfriend. Important distinction, *I think*.'

The corner of his mouth lifts, but I wouldn't exactly call it a smile. It's a little tight, like the uncharacteristically clipped way he probes the details out of me. 'How long are we doing this for?'

I take a second to think about it – I need a second to swallow what's not quite panic, but something close, because, God, putting a timeline on this thing make it feel real. 'Until the end of the semester?'

'I don't know,' Heath muses playfully, and I blink at the sudden change in his demeanor, the whiplash-quick shift back to his usual self. 'Don't wanna be nursing a broken heart for the NCAA championships next spring.'

'You are not gonna break my heart.'

Ask around, I add silently, scornfully, *I don't have one.*

'I was talking about mine,' Heath claims, and I roll my eyes. *Yeah, fucking right.*

'March is too far away.'

'End of the semester it is,' he concedes . . . begrudgingly? Am I imagining that? He's disappointed that our fake relationship doesn't have a longer expiration date? Surely not. 'What're the rules?'

My nose scrunches.

His head cocks to one side. 'No rules?'

'*Rules* makes it sound so . . . formal.'

'No rules,' he repeats, tongue tracing his upper teeth. 'Dangerous game, Daniela.'

I huff as I chew on my nail. 'Well, what *rules* do you want?'

Heath thinks about it for a moment. Clicking his tongue thoughtfully, he pushes off the wall, one hand brushing over the stubble of his buzz cut, the other slipping into his pocket. 'Can I touch you?'

Right now? I stop myself from asking, literally right before the question falls off my tongue, more hopeful than I have any right being. 'Do you usually touch your girlfriends?'

Something dark and heady twists his expression.

I look away. Amend, '*Publicly*. Safe-for-work-ly.'

'I've never had a girlfriend.'

'That's a lie.'

'Nope.'

My gaze flicks back to him, narrowed and knowing. 'Tracey Bellingham.'

'What about her?'

'You were dating. I heard her crying in a locker room after a meet once. I thought it was because she came second—' *to me*, I don't mention, but I think Heath knows anyway. '—but it was because you hadn't texted her good luck or something.'

'We were *dating*,' Heath corrects, as he sidles a little closer. 'She wasn't my girlfriend.'

An important distinction. Hm. 'Why didn't you text her?'

'Because I had a meet too. I was trying to focus.'

The parallel of that isn't lost on me; how many times has Ben bitched me out for being unsupportive, for daring to pour all my focus into myself and not reserving any for him? 'So, technically, I'm your first girlfriend.'

'Technically.'

'I'm gonna get shanked if I ever step foot on Cove College territory, aren't I?'

'I'll protect you.' Another inch between us gets obliterated. 'You didn't answer the question.'

I forgot the question. I keep forgetting it. He's standing too close for me to remember menial things like *questions*. Only when I side-step, move out of his orbit, out of his eyeline, does it come back to me. 'You can touch me.'

The noise he makes is incredibly, inexplicably pleased. 'Where?'

'Why do I get the feeling you're angling for an explicit answer?'

'Because I'm a man and you are an outstandingly beautiful woman.' He ducks into my line of sight again, his smile a little teasing, a whole lot more serious. 'Just wanna know what you're comfortable with.'

I shrug. It's not like it matters. It's just touching. Intimacy in all its forms has always been a somewhat blasé concept to me, so why should this be any different? 'Anywhere.'

Again with that noise. Blown pupils and a clenched jaw and a quick, almost imperceptible shake of his head, a stiff body as he backs up like he's forcing himself to. Slouching against the wall again, he crosses his arms over his chest, his fingertips digging into his forearms. 'Kissing?'

Before I can stop myself, I quip, 'Not like we haven't done that before.'

'Oh, so *you* can bring it up.'

'Jesus, Heath. What, you want me to rate it? Full marks, congratulations.'

Another noise. A different noise. A low, satisfied hum that would make my knees tremble, if I were the kind of girl to develop trembling knees when faced with humming, satisfied men. Which I'm not. Definitely not. I'm lock-kneed and steady, and not at all croaky when I quietly, oh-so-nonchalantly, completely professionally, let him know, 'You can kiss me.'

His lips part.

'Ask where, and I will punch you in the throat.'

They press shut again, twitching like they're trying not smile. *Jackass.*

'Anything else?'

Chewing on my bottom lip, I pretend to think about it some more. Stall a little because, honestly, one thing did immediately come to mind. A can of worms that I'm not entirely willing to open, but I force myself to anyway. 'If you, uh, don't wanna do this anymore, can you tell me before you . . . y'know.'

Heath crooks a brow. 'Before I . . .?'

Fuck my life. 'Before you . . . *move on.*'

He blinks. 'Are you asking me not to cheat on you?'

'Well, it wouldn't be cheating. I know that. But no one else does. I just don't wanna do that . . .' I swallow, my throat almost too tight to add a quiet, *'again.'*

Like freaking clouds covering the sun, Heath's expression darkens. 'So Ben *did* cheat. Fuck, I didn't think he was actually that dumb.'

My chin drops. Absently pulling at my fingertips, I admit, 'I always figured you didn't know it was happening.'

'Why?'

'You never threw it in Ben's face. But sometimes I kinda also thought maybe you did know and you didn't say anything because you liked holding something over him. Over me too.'

Heath clears his throat. Shifts, sneakers scuffing against the tiled floor. 'I didn't know, Daniela,' he insists, so adamantly it's like convincing me is the single most important thing in the world.

I hum again. Fiddle some more. Find myself saying, for some reason, 'Everyone on my team knew.'

'Seriously?'

'I'm pretty sure they encouraged it. Helped them. Shit,' I laugh and it's only a little humorous, a lot humor*less,* so bitter and embarrassed. 'I keep thinking of all these times that someone held me up for some silly reason, like they wanted to know what pre-workouts I take or if I'd had a certain professor before, and I just wonder now if they were stalling me because Sienna and Ben were banging around the corner or something.'

'That's really fucked up, Dani.'

'They didn't owe me the truth. We're not friends.'

Heath says nothing.

Clearing my throat, I straighten up. Shift the subject elsewhere before this one kills me. 'Speaking of friends. What do we tell yours?'

'That we're dating.'

'Like, really?'

'Uh-huh.'

'And they'll believe it?'

A small smile curls his mouth, wry for reasons I don't understand. 'They'll believe it.'

How ominous. And unsettling. Prompting a question that I'm not sure I want the answer to. 'So, how do we do this? How do we start?'

Heath smiles.

Ominous.

Unsettling.

Prompting a question that I know I don't want the answer to, but I get one anyway.

'You've got to be fucking kidding me.'

'What?' Brows high and lips parted, Heath paints his face with aghast confusion so fake my eyes damn near roll out of my head. 'You don't like this?'

I cast my gaze around the pier, brimming with people and noise and bright, flashing lights that are already giving me a headache. 'Why the hell would I like this?'

He laughs like I'm joking. Which I'm not. Genuinely, I'm

baffled as to why he thinks I would enjoy somewhere this loud and busy and reeking of grease and ripe bodies. God, if this is what the boardwalk is like on its last legs at the very end of the season, when the tourists have cleared out and kids are back in school, I dread to think what it's like at the peak of the season. I literally *shiver*. 'If you try to get me to eat a corn dog, I'm gonna punch you in the balls.'

'Tempting.' His mouth quirks briefly before flattening. 'You've never been here?'

'Shockingly, this isn't my scene.'

'But Ben comes here a lot.'

'Impossible, considering we were surgically attached and all.'

Heath tugs on my hair, his turn for an eye roll. 'We want people to see us together, darling. This is a good place.'

There's nothing good about this place, in my opinion, but I can admit he has a point. I can concede – slightly. 'You get an hour.'

'So generous,' Heath croons. 'You really don't like corn dogs?'

'They're disgusting.'

'They're an American staple.'

When my face clearly disagrees, Heath barks a laugh. Pushing off the railing we're leaning against, he hovers a hand near the small of my back – not quite touching, just guiding me further into the fray. 'What *do* you like?'

'Things that aren't fried.'

'What a sad little life.'

I cut him a dry look. 'I'm an athlete.'

'I know. I'm kidding. I don't eat this shit either.'

With a will of their own, my eyes trace the lean, honed muscles bared by a loose tank and tight shorts – emphasis on the *short*. No. I'm sure he doesn't. 'So what do we do?'

'You're gonna watch me adoringly while I win you something pretty.'

'What if I wanna be the winner?'

'How shockingly out of character.'

My knuckles find a hard sternum and punch out a huffed laugh.

'Fine. *I'll* adore *you*.'

And he does. He really does. He drags me through the crowd, past half a dozen food stalls and arcade stalls, until he finds one he likes and stations us in front of it, swinging an arm out toward the ring toss game as he commands me to *show him what I've got*.

And as I show him that what I've got is absolutely zero prowess outside of a swimming pool, he fixes those pretty freaking cartoon prince eyes on me and smiles like I'm the apple of them.

Four fucking rings, I toss and completely miss the narrow-necked bottles I aim for. I huff with irritation, clenching the final ring with one hand, scratching at my forearm as the itch of incompetence wreaks havoc on my skin. Tossing it haphazardly, I stifle a frustrated noise when it hits the rim.

'Look at that,' Heath nudges his shoulder against mine. 'You're not good at everything.'

I stiffen, trying not to scowl. Logically, I can recognize that it's completely ridiculous for me to be annoyed right now. It's a fucking carnival game.

Illogically, I want to crack one of those bottles over Heath's head.

Rolling my shoulders back, I turn to him, feigning a bored, unbothered expression. 'What next?'

Heath doesn't answer. Uncharacteristically silent, he stares me down for a long moment, those eyes flicking over every curve, crease, and freckle of my face. He makes a noise in the back of his throat before handing the guy manning the stand another five-dollar bill.

I cross my arms over my chest, trying not to huff, trying even harder not to shove him off the goddamn pier as he accepts a new set of rings with a grin, clearly gearing up to show off – to show me up.

Except he doesn't.

He holds out a ring, jiggling it when I hesitate to take it. Once I do, he plants both hands on my shoulders and gently turns me to face the bottles again before moving to stand behind me.

'Here.' Breath tickling my temple, Heath slides one hand down my arm. Covering my grip with his own, he gently guides me through a practice toss. 'Like this.'

I swallow. Shift a little, a minute shuffle forward so the heat of his body isn't quite so scalding. My fingers twitch beneath his, flexing before curling around the plastic again, and when he gives me a little squeeze before retreating, I take the cue. Moving like he showed me, I throw the ring at the rows of bottles lined up a foot away.

And because Heath is the fucking Midas of the cove, it lands exactly where it should.

'Good girl.' He drops a hand to my hip, squeezing gently, and I chose to blame the unexpected touch for why I shiver instead of the low, rumbling praise. 'Do it again.'

I do. Four more times, and, every time, they catch the bottleneck with a loud, relieving clink. Every time, my chest puffs up just a little more, the corners of my mouth rise, and the urge to punch myself in the face for being so damn *pathetic* amplifies.

Though not quite enough to drown out the addictive buzz of success.

Lips brushing my hairline have me malfunctioning for a second, and it takes me another one too long to accept my stuffed animal prize the guy manning the booth hands over – I don't snap out of it until Heath haughtily snatches the fuzzy blue whale for himself.

Lovingly cradling it to his chest, his knuckles graze the underside of my chin. 'My winner.'

Though part of me begs to reject the idea of being *his* anything – I don't even acknowledge the much smaller, much sillier, much more *deprived* part that simpers, just a little – I lock that instinct down. It would be counter-intuitive to the point of this whole outing.

It would confuse the many, many people I suddenly become very, very aware of. Mostly because they seem very, very aware of us.

Swallowing around a sudden lump of anxiety, I resist yet another knee-jerk reaction. The one that urges me to lock my fingers around Heath's wrist and hold tight, ground myself as what's meant to be a public display of affection is actually publicly displayed. 'People are watching us.'

'That is the prime objective.' Smoothly, without hesitation, as if we do this all the time, Heath interlocks his fingers with mine. Raising both to his mouth, he kisses the back of my hand tenderly before tugging gently. 'C'mon.'

'Where are we going?'

He answers with another yank, dragging me out of the crowd and off the boardwalk, and down a set of sand-encrusted stairs to the beach below, and then back in the direction of the boardwalk again, except, instead, we go under it.

'Is this where the cool kids hang out?'

'This is where they fuck.'

Choking on an inhale, I trip over my own damn feet, only narrowly saved from diving head-first into the grotty sand by Heath's tight grip. Bemused, bewildered, and honestly deeply fucking concerned, I gape at him. 'You're kidding.'

'Nope.'

As a particularly rancid gust of sea air assaults my nostrils, I choke again. 'People have *sex* under here?'

'My, my,' Heath croons teasingly, flashing a row of white teeth that aren't quite perfect. A couple of gaps, a crooked incisor and a chipped canine that prove even he is capable of imperfection. 'Aren't we prudish.'

'God forbid a girl doesn't wanna roll around in dirty sand that smells like sewer.'

Heath hums a mocking, pitying noise as he whips off his shirt and lays it on the damp sand. Bare-fucking-chested, he gestures dramatically to the makeshift picnic blanket. 'M'lady.'

I roll my eyes so they don't linger on certain sculpted aspects of a bronzed, tattooed body. 'Fuck you.'

'Was that in the rules?'

My mouth twitches, but I don't indulge the laugh sitting heavy in the back of my throat – I don't give those twinkling eyes the satisfaction. I just lift my chin and drop onto the thin tee that does very little to protect me from the sand, but, hey, I still appreciate the thought. I even mutter some barely intelligible gratitude, followed by a much more audible 'If we're not . . . ' Jesus, I can't even say it. 'Then what are we doing down here?'

'Letting people think we are.'

Something warms zip down my spine. Just another bout of humiliation, I'm sure. 'Ah.'

Legs kicked out in front of him and crossed at the ankles, Heath settles that freaking plushy whale on his lap, leans back on his palms, and hits me with one of those fucking smiles. 'What's your favorite color?'

'Don't you know that already, oh wise one?'

'Probably. Test me. Count of three.'

To my mental eye-roll tally, I add another strike, but I oblige. We count down in unison, and, at the same time, we bark, 'Blue.'

Damn it. 'Lucky guess.'

'Guess mine.'

'Why?'

'Because we're *bonding*, baby.'

'I don't know. Blue.'

God, that *laugh* again. 'No. Brown.'

'Brown? Like mud?'

'Like coffee,' he corrects, the gaze fixed so intently on me, as if we're discussing something far more important than colors. 'Espresso. Real dark.'

'Odd.'

'Beautiful.'

'I meant *you're* odd.'

'It's endearing, huh?'

'Not the word that comes to mind.'

'It's something dirty, isn't it?'

'Jesus Christ.' Choking on a laugh, I tip my gaze up, shaking my head at the pier's grimy underside. 'I don't think I can do this.'

'Daniela Marina Maldonado Williams admitting defeat? Did hell just freeze over?'

I don't even question how he knows my full fucking government name. I don't have the energy for it. A single outing and I'm mentally wiped. God, how am I ever going to keep this charade up? How am I ever going to keep up with him? Why did I ever—

'Hey, Dani?'

'What?'

Long fingers curl around my bent knee and squeeze. 'Breathe.'

'Can't,' I claim, though my lungs certainly seem pretty freaking willing to oblige. 'Might get pregnant.'

He laughs so loud, I'm sure the throng above us can hear it.

Staring at the hand still cupping my knee, at the thumb tracing the curve of it, I toy with the borrowed t-shirt separating me from . . . y'know what, I'm not going to think about it. 'How long do we have to stay down here?'

'At least an hour. Won't be very believable otherwise.'

'Ambitious.'

'I'm selling myself short, actually.'

I resist the urge to admit that anything longer than ninety seconds would be pretty damn impressive to me, if only because I think he'd find it more pitiful than humorous. 'So we just . . . sit here?'

'We could—'

'Don't even say it.'

Practically cherubic, Heath blinks innocently. 'I was gonna suggest a friendly round of twenty questions.'

I snort – I frown some more, just a little, at that one word. Friendly. 'Is that what we're gonna be?' I ask slowly, the very epitome of awkward. 'Friends?'

'Oh, baby.' He pats my knee, freaking *beaming*. 'We already are.'

FIVE

PHASE ONE, ACT TWO – THAT'S WHAT HEATH CALLS our next outing, a couple of days later.

The objective is the same as Phase One, Act One: be seen together. Get noticed. Ease the general populous of our little cove into the idea of a Belfort–Williams union before shoving it in their faces – it's more believable that way, he claims. We're laying the groundwork, he says.

I'm not entirely sure what our groundwork is doing in Salt & Sound Records, but I'll bite. I won't complain either. I like this place. It's busy, but not in the people kind of way – more like physically, with every inch of the walls holding racks of old records and CDs, the tables cutting the store down the middle stacked with full crates. It's quiet, except for the low drone of *Nevermind*.

I'm humming along to 'Come As You Are' and sifting through a box of Fleetwood Mac records when warmth envelops me from behind. A chin drops to my shoulder. Breath sears my collarbone. Gone as quickly as it descended, like Heath just wanted to remind me he's there, just wanted to get my attention.

And, oh, the fingers hooked through my belt loops, the knuckles grazing my bare waist, certainly do that. 'Favorite song?'

'Ever?' I shift and his hand dutifully falls away. As does he, moving a safe distance away, hip propped against the table, arms crossed over his chest. 'Or right now?'

'Both. You've intrigued me.'

'I can't think of any.'

'You can't think of a single song?'

Lips pursed, I shoot him a dry look. Sliding further down the aisle, my fingers trail over vinyl after vinyl as I think – I freeze when I find one that's almost painful to recognize. I start to pick it up only to drop it a second later, before Heath can notice me looking at it and get curious. I don't want to talk about Natalia Lafourcade, my mother's favorite artist – I don't want to talk about my mother. I want to leave her where she is, safely tucked away in a soft, neat corner of my mind, perfect and kind and teaching me to dance in the kitchen of our childhood home.

Instead, I keep looking. Like some stroke of fate, I find another I recognize. Snagging the Darkness record that was, at one point, the soundtrack to my childhood because a tape of it lived in my dad's car, I flip it toward Heath.

He takes it with an approving hum. 'Good choice.'

'"I Believe In A Thing Called Love"'.

'You do, do you?'

Cheeks heating, I hip-check him on my way back down the aisle. 'My favorite song, dumbass. Always.'

He makes another soft noise as he puts the record back and searches for a different one. As he holds up a Jets album and he hums 'Are You Gonna Be My Girl' beneath his breath, I roll my eyes, and he makes another noise. A sweet, pleased sigh that makes my heart do something very odd in my chest.

He steps forward, damn near suffocating me as he leans around me to drop the record back in its box. 'Gonna have to learn those.'

The edge of the table digs into the curve of my ass as I reel back, inching out of his orbit. 'What?'

'Your eye rolls. What they mean.'

'They mean you're annoying.'

'Sometimes.' He cocks his head, mouth quirking. 'Sometimes not.'

My eyeballs do a quarter revolution before I catch them.

A puff of laughter warms my skin. A second later, before I even register him moving, Heath kisses me. Quick and chaste, gone without really being there at all, but still, I jerk away instinctively.

'Shit.' Heath retreats too, eyes wide, cheeks suddenly a rosy red. 'Sorry. Too much?'

'No. You just surprised me.'

This is what we're supposed to be doing, right? This is good. We need the practice. *I* need the practice, clearly. And it's perfect, practicing right here, right now, right this very second, actually – the bell above the entrance chimes, and the tinkling noise shepherds in a group of girls I'm sure must go to Cove College.

The drool gathering at the corners of their mouths and the knowing glances they shoot each other as their gazes rake up and down the length of Heath give them away.

Gripping the table's edge, I straighten up. When he doesn't move, I drop my head to one side inquisitively. 'Go on. I'm ready now.'

With a quiet laugh, he slowly leans in again. Barely an inch away from my mouth, he suddenly detours. He kisses one cheek. Then the opposite. One corner of my mouth gets the same fleeting attention, and the other isn't left neglected for too long. His nose nudges mine, and my breath catches as his lips brush my Cupid's bow before finally – God, did I really just say *finally*? – dipping lower. Really kissing me.

Still chaste. Not quick. Long enough that my heart starts to pound and my skin starts to crawl – no, not crawl. Heat. *Tingle*, fuck my life, and it's that completely alien sensation that has me wrenching myself away.

Not very far, though. For some reason, I can't separate us more than an inch. We're almost at eye-level. I'm on my tiptoes, though I don't remember rising.

Slowly, I lower myself back down to solid ground. 'What's yours?'

Eyelids drooping heavily, Heath practically slurs, 'What?'

'Your favorite song.'

A flurry of blinks, and then he clears his throat. With practiced nonchalance, he walks away, rattling off an answer followed by another question, and I answer that, and offer a question too, and we go on like that for a while. We leave the record store and linger in the flower shop across the street. We're in the bookstore when he asks, 'Why anthropology?'

Flipping through a weathered bodice ripper, I answer easily. 'My favorite character in my favorite TV show was a forensic anthropologist. Thought it sounded cool when I was younger—' I don't specify that it was *her* I was really fixated on for a long while.

'—and then when I got old enough to actually understand everything, the interest kinda just . . . stuck.'

Heath hums, intrigued, another question loudly brewing, but I beat him to it.

'Why history?' I ask, frowning a beat later and adding, 'Wait, what's your major?'

'Business. I want to open a surf shop, but I always liked history, so . . .'

'You don't wanna swim professionally?'

He shrugs. 'Not really.'

My frown must worsen because he laughs, flicking my crumpled forehead affectionately. 'I take it you *do* wanna swim professionally?'

'Why else would I be doing it?'

'That is a very sad question, Daniela,' he says quietly, moving on too quickly for the statement to really hit home, for it to hurt. 'Then why go to college at all? Why not just go straight into it?'

'My mom wanted me to go.' I couldn't have been older than seven, but I so vividly remember her waxing poetic about the wonders of higher education, the privilege of it all, how the single year she attended was one of the best years of her life. 'Felt kind of disrespectful to ignore a dead woman's wishes.'

I swear to God, I hear Heath's heart fucking drop. 'Your mom died?'

An echo of my ex-boyfriend's voice rings in my ear, snidely wondering aloud if it would kill me to be a little more sensitive. 'Sorry. Too blunt.'

'*I'm* sorry. I didn't know that.'

'It was a long time ago,' I offer, an attempt to alleviate the pity flooding his features. I don't need it, I don't want it. The concept of grief is kind of a gray, fuzzy area for me, and I don't need the punch of guilt I always get when someone else feels it more potently on my behalf than I do myself. 'If it makes you feel any better, my dad died a lot more recently.'

'Why would that make me feel *better*?'

My mouth opens only to promptly shut. My frown reigns supreme once more. I have no idea. I don't know why I even said that. If anything, Dad's death was worse – I was older. I remember it more. I was *there*. Watched him from the deep end of the pool in our apartment complex as he clutched his chest and just . . . dropped.

The longer my silence persists, the softer Heath's expression gets. 'So it's just you and your brother?'

'And our stepmom.' Who I really would rather not discuss right now, so I slide the forgotten book back onto its shelf and start toward the exit. 'Can we be done with twenty questions?'

He's got more than twenty now, I can tell. I can hear at least a hundred rattling around in his brain, and I don't know where the fuck he finds the control to keep them all in.

Long legs overtaking me, he beats me to the double doors and pushes them open, ushering me outside with a dramatic gesture, and, God, do I always roll my fucking eyes this often or does he just bring it out in me?

Am I really so clueless as to how the hell to act around him that a single snarky gesture is pretty much all I can manage?

Shaking that thought right out of my head before it takes

root and festers, I start down the sidewalk in the vague direction of my apartment. I only make it a few steps before his hand catches mine and starts to drag me the other away. 'What are you doing?'

Half a stride ahead of me, Heath tosses a smile over his shoulder – briefly, I wonder if he really does that so often or if I bring it out in him, before dismissing the idea as idiotic.

'Didn't I tell you?' he muses, oh-so-innocently, and oh-so-*dreadful* is how I suddenly feel. 'We have dinner plans.'

'I don't think this is a good idea.'

Plastic bags full of takeout hanging from his crooked fingertips, Heath tosses me a grin over his shoulder. 'It'll be fine.'

Fine. I snicker. How *Not* to Inspire Confidence 101.

'Maybe this escaped your notice,' I snark, as we amble toward a front door I don't recognize, 'but I'm not exactly a people person.'

'*What?*' Looking back at me with wide eyes, Heath tries and fails to fight the amused twitch of his mouth. 'I had no idea.'

My expression remains unimpressed. 'Heath, this is a bad idea.'

'We don't have to stay long, okay? Just come in and eat, and I'll drive you home in an hour.' Shifting both bags of food to one hand, Heath holds his free one out to me, pinky extended. 'Promise.'

I stare blankly at the little finger wrapped in a thin, gold ring and marked with a tiny crescent moon. 'What am I supposed to do with that?'

'Jesus.' The tan digit wiggles pointedly. 'Were you ever let outside as a child?'

I bristle. I try not to, but I do. Just like I try not to snap, but I do that anyway too.

'I was joking.' Rougher than necessary, I loop my pinky around his pinky and grant him his stupid promise. 'You get forty-five minutes.'

As if sensing the clock starts the very minute the words leave my mouth, Heath wastes no time dragging me inside.

The noise hits me immediately. Loud music first, and then, once my ears have attuned to the unsettling volume, I pick out voices. Laughter. A hollered round of greetings when Heath calls out, 'We're here.'

'We?' someone answers, and my stomach just about falls out of my ass.

I swing a glare on Heath. 'They don't know I'm coming?'

At least he has the decency to look mildly sheepish – however, he does not have the decency to stifle a smile. 'They like surprises.'

'*Heath*.' Fuck our deal. Fuck him. I'm going to kill him. I'm going to kill him and then I'm going to get the hell out of here and I'm going to chalk this whole dumbass idea up to delusion, and—

'Holy shit.'

Briefly, my eyes close. My heart pounds. I feel, for a moment, like a little girl. Scared and small and completely out of my depth. And then I open my eyes, pin them on the group crowding the doorway at the end of the hall, gaping at me, and I smile as evenly, as *nicely*, as I'm capable of. 'Hi.'

'Holy shit,' someone repeats. The same voice as the first time – Kai. Kai, who shoulders his way around his friends to stride down the hall and punch his best friend on the shoulder. 'Fucking hell, Belfort. You actually *finally* did it.'

I get a millisecond to be confused, to be curious, before my attention is stolen by a squeal and a flurry of red hair and bright blue eyes an inch away from my face, belonging to the girl who clasps me by the biceps and gives me a shake. 'It's you!'

'Easy, Matty,' Heath chides gently, playfully, his hand landing on the small of my back. 'Don't scare her away.'

Matty – *Matilda,* she introduces herself in a high-pitched flurry of words – loosens her grip, channeling a little of that over-excitement into another squeal instead. 'It's so nice to finally meet you. Officially.'

'Yeah,' I force myself to smile, and I really try to mean it. 'You too.'

Hooking an arm through the crook of my elbow, Matilda drags me further into the house. 'This is my brother, Brendan,' she gestures to the quiet redhead we brush past on our way into the kitchen – *her* kitchen, this is Matilda and Brendan's place, I quickly discover, and Imani's too. Kai doesn't live here, but he might as well, and Heath has spent more than a couple of nights on their sofa, and they like hanging out here because it's the nicest and the quietest and equidistant from Cove College and the local strip of bars, of which the old pub, Salt Lane, is their universal favorite. The over-priced cocktail bar next door is their secret, pretentious favorite, but, really, they prefer drinking at home, where they can control the music and the company, and Kai, for some fucking reason, took a bartending course and mixes a mean mojito.

I learn that they've known each other pretty much their entire lives. That Imani grew up next door to Heath, and his mom used to babysit Matilda and Brendan, and they met Kai in grade school and never got rid of him. They went to high school together, graduated together, started college together – they have always been together.

I learn some things that aren't told, but observed, too. Like how Brendan watches Imani when he thinks no one is looking. And how Imani seems to expend a whole lot of effort *not* watching him. Matilda checks her phone every five minutes, but she angles the screen discreetly, like she doesn't want anyone to know who she's texting. Kai's voice rings in my ears, because Kai is the catalyst of all conversation, Kai is the killer of any lulls, Kai is entirely averse to silence, and the mere concept of it too.

And Heath likes to stare. At me. He likes to stare and he likes to *look*, to *really look*. To check on me as I'm bombarded with a torrent of information before I've even sat down, as everyone flutters around the kitchen island preparing drinks and dishing up food, and once I finally do take a seat at the kitchen table, I'm so damn overwhelmed, I chug one of those famous mojitos without a single thought for tomorrow's early start.

The chair beside me creaks as Imani drops into it, and the very second my glass runs dry, she tops it off, eyeing me wryly. 'Boy talk so soon?'

I mimic her smirk, though I'm not sure mine is quite as steady. 'I work quick.'

'Hm.' Dark eyes flit to where Heath stands at the kitchen counter, sifting through takeout boxes with the others. 'Clearly.'

More defensive than I have any right being, I snip, 'Problem?'

'Concern,' she corrects. 'But Heath's a big boy. And he has excellent taste in women.'

'Yes, I do.'

A bowl lands in front of me with a clunk as a body settles to my left, an arm slinks around my shoulders, a mouth presses to my temple – a move that almost makes me jerk away, but I catch myself at the last second. Instead of flinching, I force myself to lean into Heath. And I turn to him to . . . I don't know, exhibit some kind of loving behavior, but my gaze gets caught on that bowl instead.

Earlier, when Heath was abusing his employee discount and ordering the mountains of food we toted here from Barefoot Joe's, I had literally shivered at the long list of things that are most definitely not swim-season-diet approved.

None of which have ended up in front of me.

So busy wondering where the hell Heath found brown rice, sweet potatoes, and fucking *tofu* in that greasepit of a diner, it takes me longer than it should to realize he's staring at me again. Intently. Nervously, I dare say – I dare say his quiet 'Okay?' is a little damn nervous too.

'Yeah.' I clear my throat, and clear my face too, because I guess I shouldn't be so affronted at my boyfriend accommodating my dietary needs. Especially not when his plate is heaped with the same thing. 'Thanks.'

'You're welcome, baby.'

I jolt, and I pray our audience attributes the reaction to yet another ear-splitting squeal.

'Sorry.' Looking not all that sorry, Matilda props an elbow on the table, chin in her palm, eyes wide and inquisitive and *excited*, as she gazes across the mahogany at us. 'I need to know how this happened.'

Beside her, Kai lets loose something pretty close to a cackle. 'Pretty sure we saw exactly how this happened.'

And then he makes a slew of obnoxious kissing noises.

And then he grunts and frowns, and stoops beneath the table a little to rub what I imagine is an aching shin. 'Who the hell just kicked me?'

I smile innocently. 'Oops. My bad.'

The group erupts into snickers. Glaring, Kai brandishes his fork threateningly and promises retribution, which makes Heath grunt a warning that makes everyone laugh some more, and then they dissolve into chatter again, and, internally, I thank Kai for his childish antics, because no one asks about me and Heath again. They just . . . accept it. Act like nothing is amiss.

They eat and they drink and they laugh as they talk a million miles a minute about everything and anything, and my head is spinning. I can't keep up. I am so far out of my comfort zone, I don't even know where I am. I don't know what to do, and I hate that. I hate that this is so normal for them and so *not* for me, and probably so damn obvious. It must be, because, otherwise, I don't think Heath would be clutching my upper thigh so tightly. I don't think his thumb would be drawing circles on my shoulder.

I don't think he would sporadically, throughout our allocated forty-five minutes and long after, because I can't quite bring myself to be the monster and break this up, keep dropping his head to the curve of my neck, kissing it as a guise for a soft whisper. 'Okay?'

I could say no. I could say yes, but insist we leave anyway. Time is up, after all.

Yet I don't.

SIX

A PALE BLUE VINTAGE FORD BRONCO THAT LOOKS exactly like the type of thing a tan, blond surfer named Heath would drive idles outside my apartment – the vehicular equivalent of a flashing neon sign that the tan, blond surfer in question leans against. Arms crossed. Sunglasses shielding his eyes from the last of the year's sun. Loose shorts and a cropped white shirt working together to show off sun-kissed skin and a trim, muscled midriff and the waistband of a dark blue Speedo.

A girl on my team lives upstairs. The guy right next door is in at least one of my ex-boyfriend's classes – I vividly remember many a time spent lingering in my open doorway, waiting for the pair of them to run out of things to say about economics. Pretty much this entire apartment block is taken up by HCU students. I imagine that, by the time I make it downstairs, the whole university will know that Heath Belfort picked me up this morning. No less than five people will have texted Ben.

Which, I suppose, is good. It's the whole point. It's what this ridiculous, foolish plan is all about.

Stepping away from my living-room window, I sigh. Adjust the duffel bag hanging off my shoulder. Flex my fingers before curling them into a ball, clenched tight like the rest of me.

'Suck it up,' I chastise myself gruffly, as anxiety pulses beneath my skin, making me all clammy and twitchy. 'This was your damn idea.'

This was your damn idea, I repeat, as I wrench open my front door. And again as I hustle down the steps, flip-flops slapping loudly, the bag full of my regular practice gear smacking into my hip. And once more for good luck as I get too close to my new fake boyfriend to ignore the deep grooves dimpling each of his cheeks, the dazzling smile he flashes, those damn sea-glass-colored eyes that sparkle as he slides off his sunglasses.

'Morning, gorgeous,' Heath hollers, and I'm caught between a wince, a blush, and a scowl. I edge a little more toward the middle one when he brushes his lips against my cheek, quick and unhesitant and so damn casual, so natural, as nonchalant as the way he sets a hand on my lower back, guides me around the hood of his truck, and opens the passenger door for me. 'Sleep okay?'

No. I slept like shit. Alternated between tossing and turning and not sleeping at all, and tossing and turning and half-dreaming, half-remembering a much less chaste kiss. 'Uh-huh.'

That warm palm remains flush to my skin as I climb inside the Bronco, though it moves to squeeze my thigh, just below the hem of my shorts. 'Are you ready for this?'

I bristle. I don't like his tone, the softness to it. Don't like how he's looking at me, that softness neither. 'It was my idea, wasn't it?'

'Just saying.' God, I don't even like his shrug. Not soft at all. A little tense. Like he doesn't much like my tone either. 'You look a little nervous.'

I huff, and Heath smiles. He pats my thigh once more before closing the door and jogging around to the driver's side. I watch him through the salt-stained windshield, wincing as he lifts a hand and waves at someone I can't see, at someone who surely saw me, at someone whose fingers are likely flying across a phone screen right now, desperate to be the first source of this tasty morsel of gossip.

As Heath settles behind the wheel, I turn to him. 'Run through the plan again.'

Clicking his seatbelt into place – and refusing to start the car until I've done the same – he adjusts the rear-view mirror so the only view he has is of me. 'It's your plan.'

'And I want to make sure you remember it.'

'It's not exactly armed robbery, Dani. You think I'm an idiot?'

'I mean, you are failing a class.'

'Ouch, baby.'

I purse my lips. 'Plan. Go.'

Heath sighs, pure drama, but he obliges. 'I drive you to practice. Walk you inside. Hold your hand. Kiss you a little. Watch you, lovestruck and adoring, as you reduce your teammates to tears with all that talent. We kiss some more. Ben falls to his knees in despair. You cackle over his crumpled form.'

I flush from my hairline to the tips of my toes. 'Ad-lib, much?'

'Tell me, my love. How long did it take you to come up with that?'

I roll my eyes, batting him away when he pinches my chin playfully.

With an eye roll of his own, Heath sighs. 'No one's gonna

believe you're madly in love with me if you scowl every time I touch you.'

'No one's gonna believe I'm madly in love, full stop. You have nothing to do with it.'

'Darling, you say the sweetest things.'

'Stop calling me names.'

'Why? It's what couples do.'

I ignore him in favor of flipping down the sun visor and using the tiny, ineffectual mirror to fix my hair into twin French braids.

'You should probably call me one.'

'No, thanks.'

'C'mon.'

'No.

'One name. That's all I'm asking for. Give a man a little joy.'

I blink, frowning. 'Why would I ever want to do that?'

'Daniela,' he laughs my name, shaking his head, *smiling*. 'What did you used to call Ben?'

'Ben.'

Another husky laugh echoes around the Bronco's interior. 'Exactly. Think how much it'll piss him off when you strut in there, calling me the love of your life.'

'I'm not doing that,' I scoff, though I do pause. Think – mentally flick through the terms of endearment that don't inspire my gag reflex. Hover over a vague memory of my mom and my dad, one doting on the other. '*Cariño*. Happy?'

'Very.' Lifting one hand from the steering wheel, he grabs one of the reusable mugs in the cupholder between us and extends it in my direction, giving it a shake so the contents clink. 'Earned yourself a prize.'

Accepting the mug skeptically, I peel off the lid, peer inside and . . . crack, just a little, when I find ice cubes floating in what smells like green tea and lemon and coconut water. 'How did you know?'

'I told you. I pay attention.'

I try to come up with a single scenario where Heath would be in the position to pay attention to the drink I make every morning, in the peace of my own home, before practice, and I come up blank. 'Is *paying attention* a synonym for stalking?'

Another laugh. A wide smile and bright eyes that completely focus on me as we pull up to a red light. 'Is it stalking if I'm just incredibly observant, and you are just incredibly not?'

'What does that have to do with anything?'

'I can think of, like, eight times we've been in the same room and you haven't noticed.'

My eyes narrow. 'That's an exaggeration.'

Except it isn't. Not at all. Because he names, with ease, eight different instances when he was lurking in my general vicinity and I had no idea. Stints in the gym and study sessions in the library and post-practice caffeine boosts at The Siren Pod – he spends a solid minute ragging on my ex's preference for an espresso sunrise. He flicks up a finger for each one and he keeps his eyes on the road as the light turns green, and he turns a little pinker with each admission, though his voice remains steady and honest and uncaring. Like it's a natural instinct to be embarrassed, but he denies it. He won't let himself.

'And I'm being nice,' he says, once he's done, and he chuckles like I'm not speechless and gaping in his passenger seat. 'I'm not counting almost every meet you've ever competed in.'

'I know you're at those. You're competing too.'

He hesitates. Seems to think twice about admitting something else, but goes ahead anyway, 'Not all of them.'

'Then why do you come?'

Again, hesitation. A thought mulled over twice. Another admission that doesn't sound entirely as truthful as the first. 'I have friends who compete in your bracket.'

'Oh.'

Clearing his throat, he reaches for his own mug. 'Yeah.'

'What're you drinking?'

'Oat milk salted-caramel matcha.'

I commit that to memory. And then, because I can't resist, I quip, 'And that's supposed to be better than an espresso sunrise?'

'Bite your tongue, vicious woman.'

A sharply cleared throat stops me in my tracks as I start toward the front entrance of HCU's natatorium.

Glancing over my shoulder, I frown at Heath, standing still a couple of steps behind me, two light brows raised and a hand held out in my direction. When I stare at it for a second too long, he chuckles lowly and wiggles his fingers. 'You're supposed to hold it, Daniela.'

'Is that necessary?'

Evidently, it isn't.

Because instead of holding my hand, Heath closes the distance between us and loops an arm around my shoulders, practically strangling me with the thick, veined forearm that locks across my upper chest.

'You're right.' Tattooed fingers tickle my collarbone. 'This is much better.'

I can't say I agree. Although, it doesn't feel bad, exactly. Just different. A little awkward because while Heath seems perfectly comfortable, I'm stiff, hands hanging limply at my sides.

With a dramatic sigh, Heath lifts one of them. Guides my fingers so they wrap around his wrist. 'Are you against PDA or do you just have no idea how to do it?'

My grip tightens as his words strike something sensitive, but fuck if I'll admit how big of a sore spot that is. 'Let's just get this over with.'

'Enough with the sweet nothings.'

My face fixes in a glare, but it's half-hearted. The closer we get to those big double doors, the more my nerves kick into overdrive, and the less I can remember why the hell I'm doing this. My heart hammers in time with our footsteps, the building looming before us getting bigger and bigger, scarier and scarier, and I'm flustered and flushed and, Jesus, shaking as I reach for the door handle.

Only to be stopped by Heath. Turned to the side. Assessed.

Offered, 'Last chance to change your mind.'

I almost do.

Except I tilt my head up to look at Heath – I revel, for a

minute, in him being so much taller than me – and find his expression calm. Unbothered.

He's not freaking out, so why the hell am I?

I swallow hard and straighten my shoulders. 'Scared, Belfort?'

'Of you? Terrified.'

Yet he takes my hand and drags me inside anyway.

Pretty damn quickly, I remember why I'm doing this.

I'm rewarded for my nerves and trepidation. Rewarded with dropped jaws and wide eyes, and my ex-boyfriend turning a particularly glorious shade of red, my new favorite fucking color, as every eye in the building lands on me.

And the hand holding mine.

'What the fuck?' more than one person voices aloud. Quietly, sure, but audible all the same. As audible as the surprise, the *shock*, that stains the atmosphere, steadily increasing as Heath tugs me a little closer.

He pecks my temple, and someone chokes.

His mouth drags a long, affectionate path to the curve of my jaw, and I hear someone ask if this is real life.

My smile comes easily. My smile is very real. My smile is my finest attempt at lovestruck, and it has something in the near distance clattering to the tiled floor.

It makes Heath jerk. Those eyes, those stupid, hypnotizing eyes, widen. The rise and fall of his chest suddenly ceases, and he doesn't move a muscle as I rise onto the tips of my toes and brush a nervous, clumsy kiss on a warm, freckled cheek. 'I gotta go change.'

A deep, ragged noise rumbles in his throat. 'Okay.'

I drop to my soles again. For the benefit of our audience, I raise my voice, just loud enough to be overheard, not quite so loud that it's obvious I want to be. 'You ready to see what real swimming looks like, *cariño*?'

Heath blinks. Nods slowly, like he's in some kind of trance of his own. Says nothing, no sharp quippy comeback, and I temper my disappointment with a hefty dose of *this is fake this is fake this is so fucking fake.*

With a wonky smile, I start toward the changing rooms, only making it a couple of steps before I abruptly come up short – before I'm *made* to come up short. By a long, strong body darting in my path. By fingers interlocking with mine once more. By sparkling eyes and a rough, throaty noise, and hot mouth brushing the corner of mine.

My ears ring a little. I definitely flush. My gaze fixates on the lips hovering an inch from my own, and my mind fixates on what would happen if I leaned forward just a little.

I lean back just a little instead, and common sense comes rushing back to me like a slap to the face.

Because Heath isn't looking at me. He's looking just beyond me. I don't have to follow his gaze to know exactly who he's looking at because he tells me. 'I think Ben just passed away.'

Fake, I remind myself sternly. *Focus*. 'Excellent.'

SEVEN

WE SPEND TWO HOURS DOING INDIVIDUAL MEDLEY drills, yet I find none of the regular joy in practicing my specialty.

I prove *why* it's my specialty, and I find no joy in that either. I'm joyless. I'm distracted. I'm . . .

Fuck me. I'm *nervous*.

No. I don't think that's the right word for it. I don't exactly know the word for the feeling encompassing me, inhibiting my natural ability to get the hell out of my head when I'm in the water. I don't know if there actually is a word for the infuriatingly off-putting sensation of wondering whether or not the fake boyfriend you're using to get back at your ex-boyfriend is impressed by your aquatic prowess. If he's really watching me as I cut smoothly through the water, or if he's sitting on the sidelines, fiddling with his phone like Ben used to do. If he's bored. Uninterested. Counting down the minutes until practice is over and our charade can end for the day.

I don't glance over to find out. I want to so fucking bad, but I deny myself. I won't. It's bad enough that I care – I can't go a mortifying step further by being so obvious about it.

By the time Coach calls an end to practice, I'm wound up tight, too tight. Hauling myself out of the pool, I don't head for Heath like I know I should, like I'm supposed to. It looks bad, I'm aware, but I think it would look worse if I went over there and . . . I don't know. Flinched away from any advances he might make. Couldn't look him in the eye. Punched him in the face if he joked about my form.

Disintegrated if he complimented it.

Instead, I make a beeline for the changing rooms, busting through the door like a bull in a china shop, like I just had a really shit practice, not a really good one.

The girls already in there startle. Eye me like I am, in fact, an enraged beast ready to charge. Which honestly isn't all that different from how they usually look at me, but there's a certain level of . . . *curiosity* accompanying it today. A lot of it.

And, oh, they are so very *subtle* about it.

The first couple of whispers, I brush off. Ignore. Focus on wrenching off my swim cap and unravelling two wet braids, carefully combing my fingers through the knots.

But then they get louder. Even less subtle. Whispers become chat and snickers and a handful of burning glances, and fuck, I can't just sit here and take that disrespect, can I?

'If you're gonna have a conversation about me, in front of me, do you think you could include me?'

Silence. A couple of coughs. And a quiet, cautious, wildly doubtful, 'You're dating Heath Belfort?'

Disguising a sharp breath behind a grunt, I brace my hands on my hips, head cocked at Erica, my ex-boyfriend's new girlfriend's best, bitchiest pal. A butterfly stroke enthusiast, like me. Not good like me, though. 'What do you think?'

Erica flicks a glance at her pretty, blonde friend. 'Since when?'

'Why do you care?'

'You and Ben only just broke up.'

'Well,' I laugh, my towel snapping as I shake it out. 'Considering Ben moved on *before* we broke up, I think I'm allowed to do the same.'

Pitying eyes flit to Sienna, like she's the victim, like I'm the bad guy for bringing up *her* indiscretions.

I scoff. Forgoing my usual post-practice routine, I drag a pair of shorts up my still-damp legs, throw my towel over one shoulder and my bag over the other, and march out of the changing room before I literally murder the next person to open their mouth.

I wonder, briefly, if it's some kind of cosmic permission that the next voice I hear belongs to the person I really want to murder the most.

'What the fuck, Daniela?'

As the changing-room door slams shut behind me, I suck in a deep, centering breath before fixing my face into an expression of perfect impassivity, the exact kind I know will infuriate my ex. 'What the fuck, Ben?'

He's bright red. Like, real scarlet. Practically foaming at the mouth. Furious.

I smile.

I don't think he's ever looked so handsome.

'This is a joke, right?'

I purse my lips, feigning confusion. 'I'm not following, Benjamin.'

Too quick for me to evade, fingers lock around my wrist. Squeeze hard enough to hurt. Curl into tight, furious fists when

I use a combination of shaking, threatening, and pinching to free myself from their grasp. 'Heath?' he spits. 'Are you fucking kidding me?'

'What?' My eyes widen, *so* innocent. 'You don't approve?'

'Heath?' Ben repeats, and I glance at the man in question, finding him lingering on the far side of the building, surrounded by his teammates, practically out of sight. 'No one else would be your rebound, so you had to fuck *him*?'

'Didn't *have* to. Just wanted to.'

Ben sputters and swears and rakes a hand through his hair, and déjà vu slaps me in the face – déjà vu of a *past* damn déjà vu makes me wonder if it's always going to be like this. Me pissing him off, followed by a public confrontation where he spits vitriol and tries to tear me down.

Oh, fuck. Who am I kidding?

It's *been* like this. For longer than I ever should've put up with.

'Were you fucking him the whole time?'

'God, I wish,' I sigh wistfully, staring longingly into the distance, batting my lashes dreamily. 'Boy, was I missing out.'

'Real nice, Dani.'

'Why do you care?'

'I don't.'

'That vein in your forehead sure says otherwise.' Sighing, I let my face fall into an expression that mimics the one he flashed me only . . . Jesus, was it really just a few days ago? When he cornered me in the parking lot and spat the exact words that I relay back to him now. 'You're not jealous, are you? Because that would be pretty pathetic.'

In a feat I didn't think possible, Ben turns even redder. '*I'm* pathetic? He's using you. You have to know that. You have to know that no one could ever—'

Like me? Want me? Love me?

I don't get to find out.

A pointedly clearing throat cuts my ex off.

A soft 'Baby' makes that temper visibly soar.

Lips press to my temple, and I'm surprised the pool water doesn't start bubbling, boiled by the ferocity of Ben's anger.

'Baby,' Heath says again, his smirk hot against my skin. 'Good practice.'

When I shift to face him, his mouth drags a hot line across my forehead. Reeling back, I fix a smile into place. '*Gracias, cariño.*'

Out of the corner of my eye, I see Ben flinch.

Right in front of me, I see the corner of Heath's mouth lift even higher.

A warm hand slips into mine and squeezes. 'C'mon. The team wants to say hi.'

I doubt that, but I'll go with it, considering being around Ben is more tiring than two hours of pushing myself to the physical limit.

Heath tugs and I follow – or I try to, at least.

Ben makes another grab at me, he spits my name again, and when I rip my hand away and jab a finger against his chest, he has the audacity to look *surprised* by my fury. 'That's the last time you grab me. This is the last time you talk to me like shit. Get the fuck over yourself, get the fuck over me, and leave me alone.'

Ben scoffs, lips parting as he prepares to drop some more sweet nothings, I'm sure, but, again, he doesn't get the chance. Again, Heath cuts him off – by dragging me away, out of earshot, out of reach, and it's as he silently guides me toward his team that I realize he didn't say a single thing to Ben. No jibes nor comments. None of the usual taunting.

'You're very tame today.'

'What could I possibly say to him,' he drawls, stopping so abruptly that I almost ram straight into his back. Turning so slowly, a warning shiver tickles my skin. Stepping so close, I have no choice but to breathe in that salty, smoky scent that somehow drowns out the stench of chlorine. He continues, 'that would beat me doing this?'

I wonder if he does it quickly on purpose. If he presses his lips to mine without warning so I don't have time to brace, to react, to flinch or retreat or give us away completely.

It's a chaste kiss. Barely a kiss at all. There and then gone in the same breath, in one smooth movement, in so little time that it really shouldn't affect me at all.

Yet my breath catches.

My lips tingle.

A shiver traces a long, languid path down my spine and pools near the base, right below where Heath's hand rests.

His thumb strokes the divot just above where my back dips and becomes an entirely different part of my anatomy. 'Okay?' he murmurs quietly, for my ears only.

Slowly, I nod. Silent. Slightly stunned.

Heath grins. Like he can tell how off-kilter he's made me, and he likes it. He kisses me again like he likes doing that too, and, shit, who am I kidding? *I* like it.

I like it so much, I don't register we have company until someone is socking me semi-gently on the shoulder, crooning something that snaps me back to reality. 'Nice practice, Lola.'

I squint at Kai, who smiles at me like we're best fucking friends. 'Lola?'

Heath tugs on my damp hair. 'The hot fish from *Shark Tale*.'

I laugh, and at least three people do a double take in my direction. 'Thanks, I think.'

'The siren lives up to her reputation.'

'The *siren*?' I laugh again, a real cackle this time. 'Do any of you actually know my name or do you just prefer to make ones up?'

'We know who you are, Daniela,' some guy I maybe vaguely recognize chimes in as he saunters up beside Kai. Unfurling the arms crossed over a hoodie stamped with the Cove College Swim insignia, he flicks me a greeting salute as he introduces himself. 'Ryan.'

I nod with some semblance of politeness, my eyes narrowing as his rake over me in a way that even someone as socially inept as me can decipher – he's interested. In me. Or in what I look like, at least. I grit my teeth to stop from snapping them at him, one inhale away from letting loose something suitably scathing when a clearing throat again snags my attention.

A hand curls around my waist, and my gaze shifts to the man it belongs to – the man who's looking at me a little weird too. 'See you later?'

The dismissal doesn't *sting*, exactly. It more . . . catches me by surprise. Knocks an inch off my height and a decibel off my voice, so I'm a little hunched and a lot mumbling when I admit, 'I thought I could stay. Watch you swim.'

Obviously, the same thought hadn't crossed his mind – obviously, my willingness to linger amongst my mortal aquatic enemies has taken him by surprise. 'Yeah?'

I contemplate taking it back. Just for a second. For the single, quick second it takes me to recognize not just surprise in Heath's expression, but hope. Like he wants me to stay. 'Yeah.'

He beams like this is the best thing that's ever happened to him.

I . . . well, internally, I might just beam a little too.

Legs crossed at the knees, I balance an open notebook on the curve of one. A pen poised between my lips, I chew on the end of it thoughtfully, brows pulling together as I watch the Cove College co-ed team run relays, and try to decipher what I'm seeing.

Try to figure out why, exactly, Heath is leisurely swimming lengths like he has nowhere at all in the world to be, like he doesn't care, like this whole practice is a waste of his time – and how, exactly, he stills wins every damn leg.

He's laughing. Bobbing around in the water like he's in a wave pool on vacation. More than once, he ducks beneath the lane rope separating him from Kai and the two of them roll around like little kids, splashing and ducking and laughing, so much *laughing*.

I've never laughed during practice, not once in my life. I try to imagine how my dad would've reacted if, in the middle of a lap, I just burst out into giggles, and I can't because it never would've happened. That was not the training environment Dad fostered. That isn't the environment *I* foster. I don't find joy in training; I find joy in winning. In succeeding. In dedication.

I don't like that sitting here, watching Cove College clearly adopt a very different attitude, makes my own feel wrong.

Wincing as I bite down a little too hard and taste ink, I swipe at my mouth and toss the ruined pen into my bag. I dog-ear the page I've been scribbling on before closing my notebook and putting that away too, standing just in time for Coach Keller to call time on practice.

Heath is still in the water when I make it poolside. I hover on the edge, towering over him, brows high. 'Are you always like this?'

'Dashingly handsome?'

'Unfocused.'

'It's just practice.'

I quite literally look down my nose at him. 'Practice is how you get good.'

Like butter wouldn't fucking melt, Heath grins. 'I'm already good.'

'Practice is how you get better.'

'I'm already better.'

My eyes roll before narrowing on the wet hand that wraps around my ankle, the other beckoning me closer. With a sigh,

I drop to my haunches, forearms stacked on my thighs, spine curved, voice a low grumble. 'Pull me in and I'll drown you.'

A wicked smile curves his mouth. He tugs teasingly, but he lets me go. Both palms braced against the concrete on either side of me, he pushes himself up out of the water like some kind of merman god. His muscles strain as he brings his face an inch away from mine, one bicep bulging when he shifts his weight entirely to one hand so he can lift the other. His thumb swipes the corner of my mouth and comes away ink-stained. 'You were writing notes for me, weren't you?'

'No.' *Just made a few mental ones.* 'I made a study plan.'

'For me?'

'No, for Coach Keller.' I wind a wet strand of his hair around my forefinger and tug. 'Yes, for you. That's the deal, right?'

'Right.' Heath drops a little, chin lifted as he gazes up at me. His eyes go a little glazed for a moment, pupils blowing wide, and I'm about to ask if he's having a stroke when he abruptly cuts me off.

Surging upwards again, he brushes his mouth against mine. That same lazy, chaste way he seems to prefer. Nose dragging against mine, wet hair tracking droplets down my face, the rest of him dripping all over the rest of me.

'You're getting me wet.'

'*Daniela*,' he scolds playfully, flicking water at me. 'We're in public.'

Against my will, my cheeks flush. I try to shove him away, but, apparently, he's been doing upper-body workouts since the womb, so he goes approximately fucking nowhere.

So I do instead.

'Get out.' I slap my hands against my thighs before standing up. 'We've got work to do.'

I'm not sure where I imagined Heath to live – I'm not sure that I ever actually have imagined it. I am sure, however, that it wouldn't have been the quaint, sun-bleached bungalow nestled so close to the waves crashing on the nearby shore that I smell salt with every inhale.

Well, that last part, I could've guessed. Not the ivy-covered exterior nor the wind chime providing a gentle, ringing soundtrack, nor the neatly kept garden speckled with flowers every shade of the rainbow, but the proximity to the sea, yes. The surfboards propped against one side of the modest home, yes.

The child that comes tearing out a pale blue front door?

Not so much.

'*Uncle Heath!*' the little girl screeches, blonde curls bouncing as she throws herself at the man who drops to a crouch, only a few steps ahead of me, in order to catch the niece I didn't even know he had. 'You're late.'

'Late?' Heath scoffs. 'To do what?'

'To see me.' The little girl blinks, deadpan. 'Did you bring Kiki?'

Heath chuckles. 'Not today.'

His niece pouts. Pouts at *me*, as if I'm the reason this *Kiki* isn't here, as if I've taken their place. 'Who's that?'

A palm running down the back of her curls, Heath squeezes

her shoulder. 'This is Daniela.' He pauses, and I wonder if I imagine the way his grip tightens, the flash of discomfort on that handsome, sun-baked face. 'My girlfriend.'

Boy, does he sound *delighted* to admit that.

The little girl doesn't notice his tone. She's too busy gasping in . . . surprise? Disbelief? Is even she, at her young age, astounded that her uncle would date me? Bring me home? Introduce me to his family?

I've never been introduced to anyone's family. Not really. Ben's parents are hardly ever in town, and when they are, when they meet him for dinner, I'm never invited. I only met his mother once, by accident, when I bumped into her at a meet, but I'm not entirely sure she knew who I was. When I introduced myself, said *I'm Daniela* and stuck my hand out politely, she only replied *that's nice.*

I guess that just wasn't the nature of that relationship.

Apparently, it is the nature of this one.

Swiping my clammy hands down the sides of my shorts, I lift one of them in an awkward wave. 'Hi.'

The girl dips her chin, squinting up at me from beneath the long lashes that must be a Belfort family trait. 'Hello.'

'Dani,' Heath calls my attention to him, the reservation he wore only moments ago replaced with soft amusement. 'This is Lyla.'

'I'm five,' the girl, *Lyla*, adds, clearly proud of what she must deem pivotal information.

'Cool.' I nod, stiff, unsure. 'I'm twenty-one.'

'Cool,' Lyla parrots, before turning to her uncle. 'Is she the girl you and Mommy and Aunty June talk about when you think I'm not listening?'

Heath clears his throat, and it's only later, much later, when I'm lying in bed, mentally replaying the day, that I'll notice how he ducks his head to hide a blush. How his chuckle is a little abashed, his insisted, 'You're delusional, little one,' is a little choked.

As it is, in the moment, I don't notice. I'm distracted. Surprised all over again when a blonde, curvy figure appears in the doorway of that adorable house. Barefoot, hands on her full hips, mischievous curiosity lighting up the face that, even from a distance, I can tell is ridiculously beautiful.

A face, I realize as she saunters across the sand-speckled, grassy front yard, that is the carbon copy of my fake boyfriend's.

Tanned, freckled, and with long locks the same shade of blonde as the girl lingering between Heath and I, the woman comes to a stop a couple of steps away from us, and graces me with the full brunt of her attention. 'Who's this?'

A young voice grumbles, 'Not Kiki.'

The woman chuckles. 'Lala, honey, you saw him last night.'

Heath's head snaps to her – to his sister, I quickly gather, because there's no way that shared eye color is pure coincidence. 'Kai was here last night?'

Kai. Kiki. I rein in a laugh, only managing it because I'm rather intrigued by the way the sister I didn't know Heath had ducks her head to hide a soft, secret grin. The way she mindlessly, girlishly ruffles the curls of what has to be her daughter. 'He dropped by.'

Heath, on the other hand, is not smiling. 'Why?'

'Brought us dinner.'

'Why?'

'Because we're friends, Heath. Jesus.' With a huff, she shakes her head, shakes off her brother's inquisition, and focuses her own on me. 'It's Daniela, right?'

'Right,' I slowly confirm, fighting a frown, oddly put-off by her knowing who I am even though it's not really that weird. We live in a small town, my ex is her brother's mortal enemy – it's not exactly surprising that I would come up in conversation. Except something, call it gut instinct or self-consciousness or delusion, tells me that I don't just come up in context to Ben. 'It's nice to meet you . . .'

'Saylor.'

Saylor. Right. Fuck, I should know that, shouldn't I? God, I might be an even worse fake girlfriend than I was a real one. 'It's nice to meet you,' I repeat, like a dumbass, because I can't think of anything else to say. God. What's wrong with me? I'm not the queen of extroverts or anything, but, fuck, I've interacted with living, human beings before. I know how to function like one. So why am I all nervous and bumbling and fucking weird?

'It's nice to meet you too,' Saylor replies, smiling sweetly, either kind enough to ignore my conversational inadequacies, or just not noticing them. 'You hungry? We were just making lunch.'

'We're good,' Heath answers for me, patting the duffel bag where he stored the takeout we got on the way here, guiding me toward the front door with the other. He pushes me across the threshold – my stiff hesitance earns me a quipped *you need an invitation, Carmilla?* – and through the house. We leave Lyla and Saylor in a kitchen that looks like something straight out of a beachy boho-chic Pinterest board, and Heath warns them to leave us alone – I say nothing at all.

I am too busy acting like there's nothing weird about being shepherded into Heath's bedroom. I do not give into the baser instincts demanding a snooping session. After a quick, cursory glance around the surprisingly neat room, I oh-so-casually remark, 'Lyla's cute.'

'She is.'

'Saylor's pretty young.'

'A year younger than us.'

'So she was . . . seventeen when she got pregnant?'

Heath clucks his tongue. 'Sixteen.'

Jesus. When I was sixteen, I was . . . well, I wasn't getting pregnant. Wasn't even thinking about boys. Certainly wasn't attracting any. Wasn't trying to. I was swimming. Training.

Grieving.

Thankfully, a disgruntled noise cuts off that train of thought before it can really grow legs. 'Got a problem with that?'

I start to frown, only to realize I'm already frowning, and quickly, I realize what Heath's own dourness must be about. Even quicker, I clarify, 'I'm not judging.'

'Sounds like you are.'

'I think that's just my default tone.'

He laughs. A reluctant but real sound.

I sigh. A quiet, relieved exhale.

'Sorry.' I fiddle with the strap of my bag, shifting from one foot to the other. 'I really wasn't judging.'

I was just curious. Not trying to pry. Although, is it really prying if it's something I should already know? Something others would expect a girlfriend to know? Not that I think someone is ever going to quiz me on Heath's sister's pregnancy timeline, but it could come up in conversation. Based on Heath's reaction to talking about it, it has before, and not in a great light. If it did again . . . well, I'd like to be informed. Educated. Capable of a suitably eloquent defense, one beyond *shut the fuck up*.

I could explain that to Heath, but I don't. I don't want to press the conversation any further, and I'm pretty sure he doesn't either, considering a nod is his only response. A nod, and dropping to sit on the floor at the foot of his bed, rooting through his bag for his own lunch, patting the space beside him. 'C'mon. Let's eat.'

Topic dismissed, I guess.

As I do what he urges and take a seat beside him, legs folded beneath me and a takeout box of salad balanced on my thighs, I take a stab at a different topic. I'm not sure why. I have a certain affinity for silence, but something about Heath's is . . . unsettling. 'You have another sister, right?' His niece mentioned another aunt. 'June.'

Heath nods. 'She went to college out-of-state. My parents moved with her.'

'Let me guess. She's the youngest?'

With a wry laugh, he nods again.

'You guys are close?'

'People used to think we were triplets.'

Which is a yes, I guess. Smiling faintly, my gaze drops to my salad. 'That's nice.'

'You and your brother aren't?'

My shoulders lift and fall vaguely. I don't know how to explain that we're not *not* close, but we're not exactly friends either. We have our moments. Fleeting, infrequent moments that usually come about when Sebastian is bored.

Correction – I *do* know how to explain that. I just don't particularly want to.

'Anyway.' One hand shovelling a forkful of kale into my mouth lest I accidentally put my foot in there again, the other reaches into my bag and plucks out my notebook. Opening it to the page covered in my most recent scribbles, I slide it toward Heath, letting him mull over it for a minute while I chew. After swiping my tongue over my teeth in a search for stray leafy greens, I cautiously ask, 'This sound okay?'

'Sounds thorough.' He looks up from beneath his lashes, one brow high. 'And specific. Do you, like, lurk in the back of my lecture hall or something?'

'The curriculum is online.' *Thank God.* Something tells me that the hardest part of our entire agreement isn't going to be the whole dating aspect, but the studying. Heath kind of strikes me as one of those guys who fails classes because they can't be bothered to do the work, not because they actually can't do it. 'You know you have an essay due the first week of December, right?'

'I do?'

God, I really can't tell if he's joking or not. 'It's worth more than half of your grade, Heath.'

He hisses a breath through his teeth. 'Damn. Sounds important.'

'*Heath*.'

'I'm kidding.' Playful fingers pinch my fucking cheek. 'You're adorable when you're all serious.'

'You're infuriating when you're not serious at all.'

'So, all the time, then.'

My head drops back, a sigh wracking my entire body. 'This is going to kill me, isn't it?'

A sparkling gaze seeks mine. 'Oh, but what a fun way to die.'

EIGHT

'DO YOU DO ALL THAT EVERY DAY?'

With a bottle of rosemary oil poised halfway to my damp roots, I shift my gaze from my own face, reflected in the mirror propped in front of me, to the man sprawled on my sofa. Snorting quietly, I tip a few drops loose and use a scalp brush to massage them in. 'Let me guess. You use eight-in-one shower gel on your entire body and call it a day?'

'Excuse *you*.' A decorative cushion sails through the air, and I just about dodge it in time to avoid an oily catastrophe. 'I condition.'

I cast a pointed look at his near-bald head. 'You condition *what*, exactly?'

Another pillow assault has me ducking and chuckling – a glance over my shoulder has me sobering up fast.

Heath only sauntered into my apartment a couple of hours ago, yet he already looks like he belongs here. Like he's part of the damn furniture. Lounging casually with an arm propped behind his head, the other resting on his stomach, long fingers lazily scratching the patch of hair-dusted lower stomach that's revealed by a short tee and a low waistband, he ignores the textbooks strewn across the coffee table. The stacks of notes, *my* notes, don't hold his interest much either.

I do. Unwaveringly. I'm not entirely sure he's taken his eyes off me once since he arrived bearing dinner from my favorite restaurant and a bookbag that I don't think he would've even opened if I hadn't demanded it. A demand he only met after we ate, after he yapped my ear off about his day, and extracted reluctant, bland information about mine, after I literally dragged his ass to the sofa and threw a book at his head and told him I wouldn't speak to him again until he was at least halfway through his assigned reading for the week.

With the way he's been intently watching me slather on skincare and hair serums and soothing oils made for aching, athletic muscles, I'd be surprised if he was halfway through a sentence. 'You're supposed to be studying history, not my grooming habits.'

The hand on his stomach flexes. 'One is infinitely more interesting than the other.'

Ignoring the way my stomach flutters just a little at that, I push to my feet. Eyes linger on my bare legs, burning my calves as I round the sofa. In the kitchen, I bypass the takeout littering the counter and open the fridge, snagging a couple kombuchas before returning to the living room and dropping to the floor in front of the coffee table.

Tossing one cold can to Heath, I pick up the neatly stapled wad of paper lined with my handwriting and throw that over too. 'Here. I made some notes.'

'You did my reading?'

'I like reading.' I like studying, and I like taking notes too, but before I can insist anymore, Heath shakes his head.

At first, I think it's disbelief guiding the slow movement.

When he returns my notes and brandishes a notebook cluttered with his own scrawl, I realize it's refusal. 'I have my own.'

Two fingers stabbing the stack, I push them over again. 'Mine are better.'

'I don't need them.'

'Evidently, you do.'

'I can't use your notes.'

'Why not?'

Tanned cheeks turn ever-so-slightly ruddy. 'I can't read your handwriting.'

Squinting at my perfectly legible flowing strokes, I ask again, 'Why not?'

'Because I can't.' Heath shifts, body slanted in my direction even as he steadfastly avoids my gaze. 'I'm dyslexic. Cursive is harder to read.'

'Oh.' My own cheeks flush, my voice a raw croak as it struggles to be heard around the foot currently wedged in my mouth. 'I didn't know that.'

'Why would you?'

There's no accusation, no snark nor bite, but I flinch anyway, guilt socking me in the stomach because I should know. It's been a week of this, of daily study sessions fit in around daily flaunting our fake relationship, and I just . . . haven't noticed? God, I can think of at least a dozen gripes aimed at his spelling, at his handwriting, and he just laughed, brushed it off, and *I am an asshole*. 'I'm sorry.'

He doesn't wave off my apology so much as pretend I didn't even say it. 'So I've been thinking about the next phase—'

'Heath—'

'—and we need to up the ante a little. Really dig our heels in. Make Ben sweat.'

Resting an elbow on the table and my temple against my knuckles, I sigh my defeat. If he really doesn't want to talk about it, I'll drop it. *For now*. 'I'm pretty sure he's *been* sweating.'

'He's been jealous,' Heath corrects, a little of the tension leaking out of him as I oblige his subject change. 'We want him inconsolable. Regretting life choices. Punching walls.'

'Nix the last one. I think he gets a kick out of it.'

Heath stiffens. His gaze flits around my apartment, taking stock of the walls, like he's searching for telltale holes hidden behind the paint. 'He seriously does that?'

Once. After a particularly lackluster out-of-state meet. 'He doesn't like losing.'

'Neither do you. You don't get violent.'

'Because I don't lose.'

'Jesus.' With a low huff, Heath slumps against the sofa, fingers curling into tight balls where they rest on his upper thighs. 'He's such a fucking child.'

'Toddler is more accurate, I think.'

That strong jaw works as Heath clenches it, as his brain works too, as some thought bounces around in that pretty head of his – one that makes him look at me with hard, cautious eyes. 'Just walls?'

It takes me a second to get what he's asking. When I do, my spine snaps straight, my head just about snapping off my neck with how fervently I nod. 'Just walls.'

Heath swallows. Slowly nodding too, his fists unfurl just as leisurely. Swallowing again, he clears his throat. 'Phase Two. Time to really rub us in his face.'

'Right. What's the plan?'

'What do you think would hurt him the most? What's a sore spot?'

Where do I start? 'He used to complain a lot about me not going out with him. Like to parties and bars and stuff.'

'We can definitely work with that.'

'Good.'

Restless, charged energy swirls around us, making me squirm. Grabbing my laptop, I pull open a new document, something to engage my interest, something for my hands to do, something I should've done already. One set of fingers flying across the keyboard, the other reaches for my useless notes. I feel Heath watching me, and I glance up to find him frowning, lips parted, but I butt in before he can ask what I'm doing. 'You got a plan?'

'Oh, honey.' Just like that, his frown melts away to make room for a grin. 'I always have a plan.'

It's two days later when my phone chimes – and provides zero clarification, just the ambiguity I've quickly learned my fake boyfriend has a penchant for.

Salt Lane at eight.

I'm sighing at the time – and cursing my narrow window to get ready – when another text comes through.

Need you in blue, baby.

I stare at my screen for ten minutes too long before I force myself to put my phone down and leave its general vicinity. I'm behind the ornate vintage screen that separates my bed from the rest of my studio, ripping into my wardrobe in search of everything blue I own and cursing Heath for not specifying a shade when my doorbell rings. Once, then again a moment later, followed by a flurry of impatient knocking that has me grumbling curses beneath my breath and answering the incessant summons with a hard yank and a brusque 'Jesus, *what?*'

Two sets of wide eyes, one dark brown and one bright blue, blink at me. 'Is that how you always answer the door?'

'I wasn't expecting anyone.' Least of all the duo dancing on my doorstep, shimmying like a pair of overexcited puppies. 'How do you guys know where I live?'

'Magic.' Curling a hand around my doorframe, Imani cocks her head like she can't fathom why I'm confused. 'Heath texted you, right?'

'He did.' My gaze flits to Matilda and narrows when her megawatt smile threatens to scald my eyeballs. 'Didn't realize it was gonna be a group affair.'

Both girls only smile brighter. 'We tend to come as a package. You've been getting off easy lately.'

A mercy that ends tonight, apparently.

Without waiting for an invitation, the girls push inside my apartment, filling it with chatter and laughter and, after digging out a portable speaker from the small backpacks they each have hanging off a shoulder, the soft crooning of an indie playlist. Bottles of wine appear on my coffee table, mugs are snatched from the kitchen cabinet, make-up bags and hair tools and clothing is strewn across my living room, and though I wince at the mess, my proclivity for order is overshadowed by confusion. 'You still haven't told me what you're doing here.'

Clustered around my mirror, they look at me like it's obvious. 'Getting ready.'

'Is that a group activity?'

Now they look at me like I'm stupid, a silent *duh* echoing off the walls. But they don't let my obvious cluelessness hang in the air – Imani just finishes gathering her braids into a chunky claw clip while Matilda keeps smoothing moisturiser on her pale skin. 'Do you know what you're wearing?'

I don't even know what's happening. 'Something blue, apparently.'

A pair of matching grins are exchanged so quickly I almost wonder if I imagined them. They move on so quickly, I decide I must've. 'You want some wine?'

I nod, if only because a nice Pinot Noir might do something about the ringing in my ears. Accepting the mug Matilda offers, I tap the ring on my middle finger against the ceramic as I try to figure this out. 'So Heath sent you to make sure I actually come out tonight?'

'No.' Imani twists to face me, holding up a burgundy eyeliner with one hand, beckoning me over with the other. 'C'mere, I wanna try this on you.'

Tentatively, I cross the living room and sit cross-legged on the floor across from Imani, Matilda's elbow brushing between my shoulder blades as she twists her vibrant hair around a curling iron. 'Eyes closed,' the former commands, and I obey just as long fingers adorned with pretty rings and prettier nails crook beneath my chin, holding me in place as she sweeps liner across my lash-line. 'Okay, open.'

As I do, I find Imani sitting back, surveying me, apparently pleased.

'Pretty,' she compliments with a wide, sincere smile. 'You want me to do the rest of your make-up too?'

I nod, partly because I'm god-awful at make-up anyway, mostly because I get the feeling refusing isn't really an option. I sit quietly and I sip my wine, and I let Imani do as she pleases – which could very well be some interpretation of a clown, I consider, when the possibility of this all being one big elaborate prank briefly crosses my mind because I can't quite fathom why else they would be here.

'Heath really didn't tell you to come over?'

Finishing styling her own hair and moving onto mine, Matilda yanks on a strand. 'We already said no.'

'Then why—'

'Y'know,' Imani cuts me off with a dramatic noise, 'I'm starting to think that everyone who says you're so smart has never actually had a conversation with you.'

'*Rude.*'

'We just wanted to hang out with you. Is that really so hard to believe?'

Rolling my lipgloss-slicked lips together, I refrain from answering.

I glance at my reflection just in time to catch the girls exchanging a look that isn't quite as smiley as the last one.

Matilda sighs, one hand curling around my shoulder while the other sets her mug down on the coffee table. If there's a follow-up to her long, breathy drawl of my name, I never get to hear it – I cut it off with a sharp '*Careful*.'

'Sorry!' Cringing, she snatches up her mug again, revealing the dark red ring left behind on the stack of papers she'd set it on. As she dabs at the stain with the hem of her shirt, she stoops to get a better look at the now-smudged writing. 'What is it?'

I pray that the man-made blush carefully swept onto my cheeks hides the real one beneath it. 'Just some notes for Heath.'

Cooing noises escape both girls, but the smile curling Matilda's mouth doesn't last long – it fades into a frown when, as she sets down the wine-stained pages, her gaze catches on a different pile. A furrow forms between her brows as she scans the handwritten text again, then its printed twin. 'These are the same.'

'My, uh, handwriting didn't work for him.'

That frown deepens for another second before realization wipes it clean. Lips parting, a soft noise escapes them as Matilda shuffles on her knees over to me, a lithe, freckled arm wrapping around my shoulders and squeezing gently. 'I knew I liked you.'

NINE

IN MY ENTIRE COLLEGE CAREER, I'VE FREQUENTED the local watering holes of the cove exactly five times – every single one of them involved peeling my drunk ex-boyfriend off the sidewalk.

Salt Lane was almost always the scene of the crime. Something of a neutral ground in our town, Cove College and Haven Cove University students co-exist there peacefully. Somewhat. Or at least that's what I've heard. I've been here, but I've never *been* here. I've never sauntered past the bustling outdoor area and into the pale green building for the pure pleasure of having a drink with friends. I've never been all dolled-up with a girlfriend hanging off either arm – I've never had girlfriends, full stop. And God knows my boyfriend has never been lounging in a booth waiting for me, never lit up at the sight of me, never clambered over the back of the leather seat and elbowed his way through the crowd to get to me.

For a second, just before Heath reaches us, as Imani and Matilda coo in my ears, as I get my first glimpse of a student night out, I feel something like grief. Loss. Not quite regret for missing out on the typical college experience – how can I regret something self-inflicted, something I know I didn't actually want, that I wouldn't enjoy? – but *something*. Something that makes me sad, for all of five seconds, before eyes the strangest, deepest, most oddly calming shade of cyan distract me.

The girls melt away as strong hands bracket my hips. Both throw me winks that I barely see, that are eclipsed by the smile that sears my cheek.

'Wow.' Thumbs trace the curve of my ribcage, digging in just barely as Heath reels back to rake an appreciative glance down my body. 'You actually listened.'

'Curiosity got the better of me.' My fingers flex at my sides before fingering the navy A-line dress I finally settled on – that the girls finally settled on, I should say, after making me try on every blue item of clothing in my wardrobe. And, now, I guess I know why this little number was the chosen one. Coasting a hand up his chest, I tug on the collar of an indecently unbuttoned shirt the exact shade of my dress. 'So we're *that* couple, hm?'

'You're lucky I didn't wear a dress too.' Flashing a goofy grin, Heath leans in close enough to completely envelop me in the scent of salt, sea, and something purely him. 'Like this one a lot, by the way.'

'You wanna borrow it?'

'Do I get to take it off you first?'

The basest, most pathetic facets of my psyche squeal, just a little. 'Down, boy.'

'Can't help it.' He tugs on one thick shoulder strap, his thumb scraping my collarbone. 'You look beautiful.'

'As opposed to usual?'

'Take the compliment, witch.'

'Now *that's* a compliment.'

Heath laughs, shaking his head as he leans in to kiss my cheek again. 'C'mon. Let's get you a drink.'

Nodding eagerly enough to drag another chuckle out of him, he takes my hand and maneuvers me through the crowd. We reach the bar and he moves to stand behind me, arms wrapped around my waist, forearms stacked across my ribcage, a chin digging into my shoulder as I lean over the sticky counter to yell a non-alcoholic order. Heath flashes two fingers to indicate he wants the same, and I start to tell him it's okay, he can drink if he wants to, but warm lips dragging along the slope of my neck dry the words right up.

They travel across my skin, mapping a route from the curve of my shoulder to the nape of my neck. While fingers sweep my hair away, a nose brushes my hairline, an inhale makes me shiver, a low groan and a husky murmur accomplishing the same. 'You smell so fucking good.'

Do I normally stink? I start to quip, but a grunt and a tightening grip cut me off.

'Compliments,' he sighs, mouth moving to where my pulse flutters. 'Need to work on those.'

'No one's even listening.'

Heath stiffens. His breath misses a beat before releasing in a sigh. 'Don't look, but Ben is watching.'

'He's here?' I start to turn only for teeth to catch my earlobe, to catch my breath too.

'I said don't look.'

'I wasn't looking at him.' Lifting my chin, I tilt my head to the side until I find Heath's warm gaze. 'So is this your big plan? Matching outfits?'

'Think you're underestimating your ex's possessive streak. And no. Not all of it.'

'The suspense is killing me.'

A dry smile. A warning pinch. 'An article came out today. *Collegiate Swimmers to Watch*. Guess who was in it?'

'Seriously?' I pull back a little further. Smile a little harder. 'Heath, that's amazing.'

'More importantly,' he quickly brushes off my compliments – *how ironic*. 'Guess who *wasn't* on it?'

'Ah.' I risk a glance at my ex. 'You gonna show him?'

'Messaged him a link approximately forty-five seconds after it came out.'

'Evil.'

'Thank you.'

'So we're celebrating while he's drowning his sorrows?'

'Exactly.'

'Double evil.'

A hot hum ruffles my hair. 'Think you're rubbing off on me.'

Snorting, I snag the soda bottle the busy bartender finally slides my way and turn in Heath's arms. 'Anything else? A subsection to this phase, perhaps?'

'Just one.'

How odd, I find myself thinking, *that the little things he does right before he kisses me already feel familiar.*

I already know his little tricks and habits, I can already anticipate them. Before his hands even move, I know they're on a path to cup my face, that fingers will follow the contours of it, like he's memorizing every indentation, each freckle. I know that, at his own fucking leisure, he'll use that grip to drag me closer, keep me an inch away before lowering his mouth to mine.

I know he kisses slow and sweet and firm, completely unrushed, as if kissing is the destination rather than just part of the ride. I know he likes to finish by drawing my bottom lip between his teeth, dragging it with him as he pulls away.

I know I don't want him to pull away at all.

My hand is halfway to Heath's mouth before I even realize it's moving. Throat tight, I swipe my thumb along the reddened, swollen outline, smiling faintly when the pad comes away glistening pink and a little sparkly. 'Not quite your color.'

He laughs, head shaking as he scrubs at his mouth too 'This shit burns.'

'It's plumping.'

'It's masochism.'

'Sorry.'

The corners of that plump mouth droop – not quite flat, not a smile either. 'Worth it.'

How odd, my inner monologue repeats, *that two flippant words might be the most romantic thing anyone's ever said to me.*

I clear my throat – clear my mind of such a depressing thought. 'We should go find your friends.'

'Right.' Heath blinks as he draws further away, dragging a hand over his head before jerking it toward the booth he vacated earlier. 'They're over here.'

His hand slipping into mine again, he guides me to his friends, who hoot and holler and shift to make room for us. We end up huddled in the corner of the booth, my thigh plastered against Heath's, warmed by his hand. Kai boxes me in from the other side, his side flush to mine and his voice reverberating through my fucking bones as he leans across me to yell something at Imani, who lounges on the other side of the booth. Everyone's yelling, everyone's *loud*, music and voices and clinking glasses, and, fuck, my skin is crawling. I'm remembering why I don't go to bars, I'm twitching and uncomfortable and my throat—

The hand on my thigh squeezes gently. 'You okay?'

I stare at it, mentally tracing the outline of all those pretty little tattoos speckling tanned knuckles. 'It's loud in here.'

Heath shifts closer, and I groan internally until I realize he's just angling himself to dig around in his back pocket. Moving away again, he holds out his hand, palm to the ceiling, a little cube sitting in the center, the lid of which he thumbs open to reveal a set of earplugs. Plucking them out, one hand tucks my hair behind my ears while the other slots the soft silicone into place. An instinctive sigh of relief escapes me as the pulsing noise abruptly settles to a dull throb.

The throbbing in my chest, however, isn't quite so dismissible. It only gets worse when, smiling softly, Heath fixes my hair, giving one long strand a tug. 'Better?'

Swallowing, I nod.

He hums, satisfied, sweet as he kisses my cheek before retreating. As if he was never interrupted, he goes back to his conversation.

As if it's never beaten properly before, my heart finds a new rhythm.

*

The People's Prince.

I've heard the nickname before. Rolled my eyes at it. Never got it, really, beyond as a joke, but now, as Heath floats around Salt Lane, I can see it. That invisible crown slanted jauntily atop his shorn hair, glinting in the low overhead lighting, as bright and glittering as the personality that attracts damn near every person in here.

Chin in my palm, I drum my fingernails against the side of a wine glass half-full with the dregs of the bottle the girls convinced me to split. I'm not drunk, I'm barely even tipsy, but I feel oddly . . . high. Floaty. *Relaxed*, though I barely recognize the feeling.

Me. Relaxed in a busy bar, sipping cheap wine, socially worn out from chatting with friends who've started calling themselves *my* friends, guarding the booth whilst everyone else replenishes their drinks, watching my *boyfriend* charm the ever-loving shit out of anything with a pulse.

I wonder if he even has it in him to be rude. He smiles at everyone who smiles at him, talks to everyone who talks to him, looks like he's actually listening, like he actually cares. He leaves Imani and Brendan at the bar to dance with Matilda near the live band tucked away in the corner, and as some girls mosey on over, my stomach clenches. I wait for it to go a little beyond friendly, for hands to wander, for that smile to turn slick, for all the signs I dismissed in Ben because . . . well, I don't actually know why. I just did. Over-confidence, maybe. Disbelief that he would actually cheat on me.

I wait and I wait and I wait, but it never happens. Heath doesn't so much as touch another girl. Jesus, more than once, I watch his lips form my name, while he jabs a finger in my direction.

I don't know what else to do but laugh. Gaze. Sit here with stars in my fucking eyes, burning up from the inside out.

'You like him.'

I glance at Kai as he flops into the booth – and brings the stench of the cigarettes a D1 athlete should most definitely not be smoking – with raised brows and a faintly amused smile. 'I do tend to like the people I date.'

A boisterous laugh splutters out of him as his gaze pointedly flicks to where Ben is with his own friends, where he *sulks*, and though I see a million quips flit through Kai's brain, none come out. 'You *really* like him.'

'Is that so shocking?'

'A little. I'm not gonna lie, at first, we really thought this was, like, a game or something. You getting back at Ben.'

My stomach twists uncomfortably. 'Sounds vindictive.'

'If the shoe fits, Cinderella.'

'Am I, like, the boogeyman of Cove College or something?'

'*Siren*,' he reminds me with a wink. 'I'm just trying to say that I'm happy it's real. That you're looking at him like that. God knows he's waited long enough.'

'Yeah, he seems real desperate for female attention.'

'*One* female's attention.'

Something odd slithers around in my gut – something *green*. 'What's that supposed to mean?'

I don't get to find out – Heath appears before his best friend can spill any sordid details, and I forget about the thing I won't dare to call jealousy because Heath, all of that *presence*, chases it away. 'Stop conspiring with my girl,' he demands of his friend, though those pretty eyes remain steadfastly fixed on me.

'*Conspiring?*' Kai huffs, throwing out another wink as he slips a heavy, sweaty arm around my shoulders and squeezes. 'We're bonding. Right, Dani?'

Fighting a grimace, I gingerly pinch his wrist between my thumb and forefinger and peel him off me. 'Practically joined at the hip.'

'I can feel the love.' Snickering, Heath plants both palms on the table and stoops until we're eye-level. 'Come dance with me.'

Faking a frown, I cast a glance over each of my shoulders, humming with mock surprise when I find no one lurking. 'Oh.' I face Heath again, eyes wide. 'You're talking to me? I thought a member of your fanclub was lurking.'

'Ha ha.' Kissing his teeth, he dances his fingers across the tabletop and snags my hand. 'C'mon, smartass.'

'I don't dance, *cariño*.'

'Not even with me?'

My eyes roll away from the adorable pout that I fear might actually have some kind of magical power over me – and they just so happen to land on a different pout, a far more vexed one, right as its owner streaks past us.

And just like that, an idea sparks.

'Actually.' I slip Heath's grip only to assert my own, clutching his wrist as I wriggle out of the booth. 'I have a better idea.'

Leaving Kai cat-calling behind us, I drag Heath in my ex-boyfriend's wake, into the narrow, dark hallway that leads to the smoking area out back. Fresh air still lingers, the door is still swinging, and I guess we have about ten minutes before Ben stomps back inside.

And I waste a whole thirty seconds second-guessing my plan.

'Is this where you seduce me?'

My cheeks flush.

Heath fucking lights up. 'It is, isn't it?'

'You said we need to up the ante, right?'

'I did.'

'We want him inconsolable, right?'

'Uh-huh.'

'So—'

'Jesus, Dani, just kiss me already.'

My eyes narrow. 'You kiss me.'

He doesn't need to be asked twice.

In the blink of an eye, he's all over me. And, for a second, I'm back at the beach. It's that night again, the catalyst for all of this, and I am getting the shit kissed out of me by Heath fucking Belfort. Except, unlike that kiss, this one doesn't end almost as suddenly as it begins. This one doesn't start a crescendo that quickly falls flat, and it isn't drunken and foolish and sloppy.

Heath kisses me like he's been thinking about it all night. Like all he does is imagine pressing his lips to mine, tangling his hands in my hair, and shoving me up against a wall with the kind of enthusiasm that makes a girl tremble. My mouth opens on a gasp, and his groan is nothing short of stark relief as he takes advantage of my parted lips, slips his tongue between them, and I briefly, madly wonder if this whole deal was actually orchestrated by some deprived, depraved part of me who simply wanted to make out with him again.

He's just making it look real, I remind myself. That's why I'm kissing him back so emphatically too. We're committing to the bit. Just extremely dedicated in our efforts to cause Ben severe psychological—

'Oh, *fuck*.' He bites my fucking neck, right above my fluttering pulse, soothing the sting with a wet lick. I didn't know I liked that. Jesus, who am I kidding? I didn't know I liked *kissing,* not this much. He only abandons my mouth for a second and I whine, I drag him back up, I'm *greedy*.

His smirk is scalding. His forehead too, burning where it touches mine. 'The kiss and touch clause is still anywhere?'

'That's what I said, isn't it?'

'Just checking,' he mutters hoarsely, along with a *thank fucking God* that makes my breath catch almost as much as another kiss does.

A hard kiss. A sure kiss. The complete opposite to touches that remain hesitant and light and *frustrating*.

'C'mon, Belfort.' I nip his bottom lip. 'Commit.'

Something akin to a growl rumbles in the back of his throat, and then, *fuck,* is he committing. He's all over me, everywhere, nibbling my jawline and the notch of my throat and my collarbone, skimming over my chest until his teeth catch the neckline of my dress. Eyes flick up to meet mine, like he's checking for further permission that I give with a jerky nod.

And then, those teeth are sinking into the swell of my breast instead. Leaving a mark.

A claim.

It feels a little too damn good so I close my eyes, I try to get a damn grip – Heath gets a fucking grip, a grip on my thigh and my ass, and, suddenly, my leg is hooked around his waist, his thigh has slotted between mine, and I gasp at the pressure. I gasp as it hits me with startling, wet, hot clarity how turned on I am. I gasp so loud, it echoes off the fucking walls.

Abruptly, Heath pulls away.

'Fuck.' His eyes seal shut, his head shaking, his breath coming in broken pants – my breath comes in broken pants too, we pant into each other's mouths. We're still close enough to share breath. '*Fuck*, sorry.'

I don't say anything. I don't quite have the capacity for words, nor do I actually know what to say when a man apologizes for kissing you. For kissing you in a way that most definitely does not require apologies. Maybe I should be apologizing. Maybe I did something wrong. Maybe something really eloquent was about to leave my parted lips, but I guess we'll never know because someone else's parted lips beat me to it.

'What the fuck?'

TEN

HEATH BACKS AWAY FROM ME SO ABRUPTLY, HE practically leaves a man-shaped dent in the wall behind him.

I almost laugh. Scratch that – I do laugh. Though I press my knuckles to my swollen lips to try to stem the noise, I can't restrain a quiet snort at the sight of my fake boyfriend, flushed bright red for reasons that have nothing to do with where his mouth just was, gaping like a fish at my very real brother.

'Belfort,' comes out as a low croon, just as evil as the fucking glint in Sebastian's eyes. 'Having fun?'

Heath practically blurs with how hard he shakes his head. 'No.'

My hand flicks out in a mildly offended, questioning gesture. '*No?*'

'*Yes.*' That poor, startled deer-like expression briefly swings my way before hastily returning to my brother. 'I mean, no. I was—'

'Defiling my sister in a dark hallway?' Sebastian tuts, as if his sensibilities are anywhere close to being delicate. '*For shame.*'

As Heath starts to turn purple, I take pity on him. 'Enough, Seba.'

'Kidding.' He holds his hands up, brandishing an innocence he does not possess. 'Defile away. God knows she needs it.'

I don't give him the satisfaction of rising to that. 'What're you doing here?'

'What am *I* doing here?' Eyes wide, Sebastian sidles closer so he can coil my hair around his forefinger and yank. 'What are *you* doing here, my little recluse? Besides getting pregnant.'

I bat him away with a choked huff. 'I'm just . . . y'know. Hanging with friends.'

'*Disculpa.*' Seba fakes confusion, but he is completely honest in his depiction of a massive asshole. In Spanish, he continues, 'I think there's a language barrier. Repeat that for me?'

'Fuck you.'

His grin is pure wicked. 'That's Heath's job, apparently.'

Mine is pure warning. 'You're gonna give him a heart attack.'

'Karma, for the extensive eye-washing session I'm now in need of.' He chucks me gently upside the chin before shifting his saccharine expression to the unusually pale man watching us cautiously. 'Relax, Belfort. I'm just fucking with you. Not the way *she's* fuck—'

'You have five seconds to get out of here before I kill you.'

My threats only make my brother snicker, and my attempts to shove him back into the bar only have him rebounding. 'Seriously, Dani. What're you doing here?'

'*Seriously*, I'm here with friends. Heath got mentioned in this big sports article so we're celebrating.'

'You couldn't celebrate in a bed?'

'*Seba.*'

'I'm *kidding*. Jesus.' Losing at least a little of that sarcastic edge, he lifts his chin at Heath. 'Congrats, man.'

'Thanks,' Heath croaks, and I take one little selfish, unreasonable second to revel in rattling such an unflappable man.

'Carry on.' Blowing a cheesy kiss that makes me groan, Sebastian finally grants us mercy and moves toward the back door. Right as his fingers graze the wood, it starts to swing inwards.

And in walks something else straight out of my nightmares.

Ben comes up so short, the door almost smacks him in the face – I lament the moment he saves it. Clutching the edge with a white-knuckled grip, his nostrils flare as he realizes he's walked into what I'm pretty sure is a trio straight out of his nightmares too.

He never did like my brother.

'Oh.' The brother in question gasps, the noise quickly dissolving into a laugh – a knee-slapping, belly-aching, certifiable cackle. 'Oh, this is *amazing*.'

Ben is nowhere near as amused. 'What's so funny?'

'I'm just imagining what would've happened if you walked in on what I just did.' That cackle reaches witchy levels. 'Damn. Need to work on my timing, huh?'

'For fuck's sake, Seba.' *For fuck's sake, universe. 'Basta,'* I hiss, shoving the doubled-over bane of my fucking existence toward the back exit. '*Vete. Por favor.*'

Finally, Sebastian disappears, though I'd bet everything in my bank account that he's on the other side of that door, ear pressed to the wood.

Not that there's anything to hear. Just a whole lot of heavy breathing. Not me, not Heath, just Ben and his rage as his tiny drunken mind slowly pieces together what, exactly, he almost walked in on.

I think it's the hickey on my chest that really slots the puzzle pieces into place for him.

His nostrils flare wide enough to flash brain. With an incensed grunt, Ben stumbles in my direction only to be cut off by Heath moving in front of me, blocking me from sight, muttering a vaguely threatening 'Don't even think about it.'

I hear another enraged exhale. More unsteady footsteps stomping down the hall.

And, right before my ex disappears, an oh-so-subtly coughed *slut*.

'Excuse me?' someone else beats me to hissing.

Someone else beats me to slapping down the dismissive middle finger Ben flashes. Grabbing him by the shoulder, Heath yanks him to a stop, and my drunken ex wobbles as his sober-ish fake successor forces him to turn around. 'You wanna say that again?'

Ben shrugs him off, shoves him back. 'Fuck off, Belfort.'

'Hey.' Heath clamps a hand around my ex's forearm. 'Apologize.'

'Suck my dick,' Ben snarls, as he rips himself free. 'God knows your girlfriend's done that enough.'

I snort. God knows that's a *lie*. As soon as I learned he wasn't all that fond of reciprocation, my mouth closed for business. But if he's going to get dirty, then, hey, who am I not to join in? 'Worst five seconds of my life, every time.'

A strangled noise leaves Heath. He faces me just long enough to fix me with a pleading look. 'Baby, don't make laugh right now.'

I mouth an apology I don't really mean, but it's okay. It's not me he's really seeking one from anyway. It's Ben who he looks down his nose at, Ben whose sternum he jabs at sharply, Ben who he once again demands to, '*Apologize*. Right now.'

'Fine,' Ben snaps, but I was with the guy for almost two years – I know what he sounds like when he's being a shitty little weasel, and God knows he sounds like that right now. 'I'm sorry,' he starts, and I'm already prepared for the very opposite of an apology that follows, 'that I didn't dump you sooner. And I'm *so* sorry,' he shifts that manic gaze to Heath, 'that you're stuck with *that* now.'

'I'm fucking warning you—'

I lift a hand, halting Heath's chivalry. I don't need it. Dealing with Ben and his hissy fits is a particularly well-honed skill of mine. 'Y'know,' I drawl, my face perfectly, infuriatingly blank. 'One of these days, your insults might actually hurt.'

'One of these days, you might stop being a raging bitch.'

'Wouldn't bet on it.'

'Slut,' he slurs.

Faking a yawn, I grab Heath's waistband to keep that tightly wound, practically vibrating body from pouncing. 'Real original, Benjamin.'

'You're desperate.'

'For you to piss off? True.'

'Frigid freak.'

Now *that* has me flinching. Only a little. I catch myself, and I can only pray Ben doesn't notice the slip. Hurriedly releasing Heath, I curl my hands into fists and focus on the bite of my nails into my palms instead of the panicked thumping behind my ribcage. 'Don't you have someone else to bother? Your current girlfriend, maybe?'

Ben's mouth quirks, and I know, without a doubt, that my prayers have gone unanswered. 'Y'know what, yeah. I *will* go find her. I think I'll bring her home. Let her know she's worth more than a quick fuck in a hallway.'

Don't I silently get as close to begging as I'm likely to get. *Don't fucking do it.*

'Gotta say,' he drawls, and I hate him, I hate myself for ever being with someone who could look so satisfied at my impending fucking doom. 'It's pretty nice having a girlfriend who doesn't need to choke me to get off.'

My entire body goes up in flames. 'Shut the fuck up.'

'What?' Blue eyes widen, but they don't even attempt to look innocent. 'You don't want your boyfriend to know you're a little freak? Jesus, man, the shit she wanted to do to—'

The crack of knuckles colliding with a jaw ends that sentence for him.

My knuckles. His jaw. Smarting cartilage that I cradle as I curse. Hard bone that Ben palms. Fingertips that come away bloody as they find a lip that a tooth must've caught as collateral. 'What the *fuck*, Daniela?'

Beyond vicious bilingual profanity, I'm incapable of a real response. Of detailing how despicable I find him, how much I hate him in this moment, how he deserves so much worse than a fist to the face. I'm too angry, too mortified, and when he opens that fucking bleeding mouth again, my eyes brim with burning, frustrated tears.

'What was that?' Ben questions, shrieks, and mocks, all at once. 'Foreplay? You wet now, babe?'

With a shriek of my own, I lunge at him again, almost managing to snag a fistful of his shirt before an arm hooks around my waist and yanks me away.

'Enough,' a low voice croons in my ear, and my throat clogs with bile, with so much more than embarrassment. 'He's not worth it.'

He's dead, is what he is. I think I might actually kill him. I promise, in every language I know, that I will. And I must really look unhinged right now, I must sound really fucking serious, because as the grip holding me back tightens, I swear my ex pales.

So lost in pure rage, so busy trying to escape strong, imprisoning arms, I barely register the back door swinging open again. 'What the hell is going on in here?'

As if he's likely to find any kind of sympathy from anyone in this hallway, Ben fucking tattles, 'Your bitch sister just attacked me.'

'You deserved it,' three voices hiss in unison, and I would laugh at Sebastian's dry, unwavering conviction in Ben's fuckassery, if I wasn't so busy trying to stifle overstimulated sobs.

My brother takes one look at me and winces. 'You got her, Belfort?'

He does. He's got me tight; he's got me fucking airborne. Before I know it, Heath is hauling me out back, and then through a narrow alleyway that spits us out at the front of the building, tucked around a corner, hidden from anyone lingering in the outdoor area.

The second my feet hit the ground, they try to retrace his steps.

Heavy hands on my shoulders keep me in place. 'Nuh-uh.'

I try and fail to shrug him off – try to keep the shrill desperation out of my tone, and fail at that too. 'I need to go back inside.'

'No, you don't.'

'I left my phone in there.'

'Y'know, when you commit murder, you probably shouldn't record it.'

Actually, I was thinking something more along the lines of trawling the internet until I find a witch to curse the ever-loving fuck out of my ex. Mostly, though, I just want to get my stuff and go home. 'Let me go.'

He does – physically, at least. That big body, however, remains a fucking roadblock, preventing my every escape attempt. 'Dani, baby, you would not do well in prison.'

I huff indignantly. 'Yeah, well, you would do worse.'

'It's not a competition, honey.' Daring to back up a whole inch, Heath snags me by the wrists, squinting at the knuckles that I barely notice are throbbing until he pulls a face at them. 'Are you okay?'

Just like that, with one little question, I'm not. The anger or adrenaline or whatever it was that was keeping me upright, fueling my fight, suddenly rushes out of me in a flood.

The stench of humiliation, however, remains perfectly intact.

I can't believe Ben did that. I can't believe that, after everything he's already done to me, I still find myself surprised by the levels he'll stoop to. But what he just did, what he said, how he said it, how he *twisted* it . . . *fuck*. If I wasn't already so sure that I never meant anything to him at all, that he never loved me, that he never so much as *respected* me, I sure am now.

'I need to get out of here.'

Heath nods frantically, a little desperately, looking like he's about to click his damn heels together in the hopes it'll teleport us somewhere else. He takes out his phone, probably to text someone about bringing out mine, but I steal it away, slip it back in his pocket. I can live without it for a night – besides, the only person likely to text me is standing in front of me. Nervously shifting his weight from one foot to the other, hesitating for a moment, mumbling a quiet 'fuck it' before throwing an arm around me, holding me tight. 'I got you.'

'You can stay,' I offer weakly, not really meaning it at all. I can't remember a single time in my recent life when I didn't rejoice at the prospect of being left alone, yet, right now, it makes me shiver.

And it must be really, really obvious, because Heath doesn't even entertain the idea. He just tucks me closer, kisses me on the temple, and mumbles that if he goes back inside, he might be the one committing murder.

And that's when I change my mind – I think *that's* the most romantic thing anyone has ever said to me.

I'm not sure why Heath bothers holding a finger to his lips as he ushers me inside his quiet, dark house – I haven't said a word since we left the bar. I haven't so much as looked at him. Haven't done anything but walk two paces behind him as he leads the way, my arms wrapped tightly around my middle, mortification wrapped tightly around the rest of me.

I should've just gone home. I could've. I don't think Heath would've stopped me. But I didn't. Couldn't. Wouldn't. Didn't want to feel any more alone than I already do, and that rarity caught me so off-guard, I went with it without question.

Question. *Questions*. I can sense them brewing. I know Heath has them, but he doesn't let them spill. He leaves me alone – that is, until we're in his kitchen.

'C'mon, Million Dollar Baby.' He raps his knuckles against the countertop, reminding me of the ache in mine. 'Hop up.'

I start to obey – I must take too long, because Heath decides to hoist me up himself. My ass hits the laminated wood, but he doesn't retreat, he doesn't let me go, his hands linger on my hips, the rest of him between my spread thighs.

He murmurs my name, a clear request to meet his gaze that I deny. He shifts, stooping, searching for it himself only to stop all of a sudden – only for it to get caught elsewhere.

On the ever-darkening bruise half-hidden by the neckline of my dress.

'Sorry.' He clears his throat, backing away, only gone for the few quick moments it takes him to dip into the freezer, and then he's back, pressing a bag of frozen peas to my knuckles, soothing the pain with the cold and my little protesting hiss with another quiet apology. 'Got a little carried away.'

'Did you?' I rasp. 'Barely noticed.'

'Careful, Dani. I love a challenge.'

I cringe at his tone, at the suave sensuality in it that I just can't stomach right now. Shaking off his touch, I rearrange my dress until the mottled skin is hidden. 'It's fine. Least of my worries.'

'I'm sorry.'

'You didn't do anything.'

'Exactly.' Frustrated regret sharpens his features. 'He always talk to you like that?'

'No. It's a new development.'

He doesn't quite look like he believes me. 'How new?'

'I know you guys have been rivals since birth or whatever, but he was really nice to me when I first moved here. He was my first friend. My only friend. He got me. Knew when to leave me alone, was okay with leaving me alone, and then he just . . . I don't know. Got fed up. Bored.'

'You're the least boring person I know.'

I don't know why a sentiment that should be so sweet has my ex's accusations ringing in my ears, but it does. 'What he said—'

'It's none of my business.'

'I didn't . . . I didn't do anything. I asked once if . . . if we could try some stuff. He said no, I said okay, and I never brought it up again. But he did. He thought it was funny. Used to make jokes and send me fucking domme porn.'

'He's an immature piece of shit.'

I stare at my hands, spinning my ring until the skin beneath burns. 'I just wanted to try something different. I thought it might . . . fix things.'

'What do you think is broken, Dani?'

Whatever part of my brain is responsible for my fickle libido. Me, in general. My brain, clearly, because . . . 'I don't know why I'm talking to *you* about this.'

'Because I'm incredibly kind and approachable.' Heath flashes a soft grin. 'It's not a big deal. You think you're the only college student who wants to experiment a little?'

'I feel like I'm the only college student who doesn't really care about sex.'

'I can guarantee that you're not. Dani—'

'I'm tired.' *I can't talk about this anymore*

A long, harsh sigh ruffles my hair. A second later, gentle fingers smooth over it, twirling around the messy ends. 'Okay,' he says, but when I try to hop down, he doesn't let me. He mumbles, 'One more thing,' before beginning a slow approach, and when I don't move, he carefully wraps his arms around me. Hugs me. Whispers, 'There's nothing wrong with you, Daniela. Not a single thing.'

Swallowing around the lump in my throat, I exhale properly for what feels like the first time in hours. Slowly, as my body leaches the warmth from his, the stiffness in my muscles recedes. Inch by inch, my shoulders slacken. The weight sitting heavy on my chest lightens bit by bit until I can breathe, until I can actually feel Heath pressed against me, feel his heart thumping, steady and soothing, and by the time my body completely lets go and slumps into him, his heartbeat is a perfect match to my own.

'I'm sorry,' he mumbles after a while. 'But I gotta make sure you know that if I'm ever making you uncomfortable, you can tell me, okay? I'm not gonna get mad at you.'

Briefly, I think about earlier. Before we were interrupted, before Heath pulled away. I felt lots of things. I feel lots of things when I'm around Heath. Disconcerting, unfamiliar, confusing things, but uncomfortable is never one of them. 'You don't.'

He pulls away, hand rising to stroke a thumb across my forehead, like he senses the frown there before he even sees it. 'Then why the face?'

Because you don't, I answer only in my head, not brave enough to speak it aloud. *And I don't get why.* 'What's wrong with my face?'

'Too pretty. Hurts to look at sometimes. Like staring at the sun.'

'My face causes physical pain. Great.'

'You have the worst case of selective hearing in the history of mankind, you know that?' He pinches my chin. Gives my head a shake. 'You're all frowny again.'

'Default setting,' I claim – I *lie,* and he sees right through it. 'It's nothing. I'm just tired.'

'You wanna sleep over?'

'You can take me home.' *If you want,* I don't verbally add, but, somehow, he hears it anyway – he sighs like the unspoken words piss him off.

He repeats the question, annunciating the *want* of it all, and as bright eyes bore into me, the part of me that's preconditioned to detest being an inconvenience, to assume that I always am one, shuts down. *I* shut down; I slump again, my forehead hitting his collarbone. 'Can I stay here, please?'

'Well, since you're being so polite about it . . .' Fingers skim the ridges of my spine, splay at the base of my back between two dimples. 'Of course you can. You always can.'

Oh, what relief I find from words I didn't even know I needed to hear. Words I believe, even though I probably shouldn't, because it's unhinged, really, to think that I could turn up here, at this house that I've only been to once before, at any time, in any situation, no matter what, and a man I've only really known for less than a month would just . . . let me in.

To *know* that is borderline clinically insane, but I do.

'C'mon.' Guiding me to the edge of the countertop, he eases me off of it, steers me out of the kitchen and down the hallway until he's pushing open the door of a familiar bedroom, and, suddenly, the *bed* aspect of this arrangement registers. One bed that seems to shrink more and more before my very eyes the longer I scrutinize it from where I hover in the doorway.

'I'll sleep on the floor.'

My scrutiny shifts to Heath, hunched at the waist and rifling through the neatly folded laundry stacked at the foot of his bed. It intensifies, and grows a vaguely offended sharp edge. 'That's idiotic.'

'Again with the sweet nothings.'

'Scared to share a bed with me now?'

'Scared isn't the word, honey.'

I don't huff so much as just . . . exhale. Loudly. Not breathy or frustrated or irritated at all. Because that would be dramatic. 'You sleep on the floor when other girls stay over?'

'Funnily enough—' Slinging what looks like a t-shirt and a pair of boxer-briefs over one shoulder, Heath turns to me again.

Starts toward me again. Crowds me as I flatten my spine against the doorjamb, forces a crick into my damn neck as I strain to meet his towering gaze. '—I don't make a habit of bringing hook-ups back to the house I share with my sister and her five-year-old.'

'Dark hallways are your specialty?'

'No.' The curve of his mouth is dangerous. Almost as bad as that low, teasing rumble. 'Dark hallways are *your* specialty.'

'I—' My cheeks flush. I have zero defense. It was me, technically, wasn't it?

'Hey.' The curve of a knuckle lifts my chin before dragging along the line of my shoulder, down my arm, until Heath is holding my hand again, squeezing it. 'I wasn't complaining.'

Just what every girl wants to hear. *You kissed me, and I didn't complain.* 'High praise.'

'You want highly inappropriate instead?'

I almost say yes – I'm sure he sees the consideration bounce around in my brain, sure that's why he smirks, sure he opens his mouth to tease me only to reconsider and cluck his tongue instead. 'C'mon,' he says again, jerking his head toward the ajar en-suite door. 'You wanna shower?'

I shake my head, but he leads me into the bathroom anyway. He tosses me the clothes I guess I'm borrowing, and I laugh quietly when I unfurl the t-shirt and find *The Darkness* stamped in faded white letters. Briefly, I consider revisiting that stalking conversation – quickly, I forget all about it when he drops to a crouch, rummages around beneath the sink, and retrieves what looks like a Tupperware container, neatly packed with . . .

I frown. Snatch the container so I can get a closer look. Confirm that I am, in fact, staring at a secret stash of familiar products. The mini counterparts of the brands I use habitually. Unopened, unused.

'Didn't get everything,' Heath grumbles – *defends*, almost. 'But it's fine, right?'

'Fine,' I repeat in a croak, and it sounds wrong. Like a lie, because this is so beyond *fine*. 'Why did you get all this?'

'Just in case.'

Just in case. I pluck the mini version of the serum I slather on every night, that eats up more of my budget than is sensible, and I almost laugh.

Ben never even bought me a toothbrush.

Heath dropped fifty dollars on a fucking serum *just in case.*

'Thanks' doesn't come out right either. Too pallid, too insignificant. Clutching the container to my chest like it's a rare freaking gem, not a plastic tub of skincare, I clear my throat and try again. 'You don't have to sleep on the floor.'

It's a horrendous display of gratitude. Truly abysmal, even for me.

And yet, Heath grins like I've him offered him a golden medal. Like the offer is a bit of a rare freaking gem too.

ELEVEN

I WAKE UP IN A BED THAT ISN'T MINE, IN CLOTHES that aren't mine either, tucked beneath the arm of a man who's only mine in the most dishonest, fantastical sense of the word.

The tip of my nose is an inch away from a bare, sun-tanned chest. If I moved even slightly, it would brush a well-developed pec, the one detailed with a flowing, fine jellyfish that I suddenly feel compelled to trace. A compulsion that, because of the lingering haze of sleep or the remnants of an emotionally charged night or just the pure artistry of the ink, I can't quite beat. A compulsion that I follow all the way down his torso to where the intricate tentacles wrap around his ribcage. My nail scrapes the sensitive spot where bones stretch skin tight, and Heath twitches.

I freeze.

I try to retreat, to feign sleep, but it's too late. My wrist is already being held hostage, dragged to a warm mouth, lathered in a sleepy breath. 'Well, that's a nice way to be woken up.'

Fuck my life.

Snatching my hand away – and feeling absolutely *nothing* when Heath whines like a poor little puppy being deprived of attention – I roll out of bed. Standing shakily, I rasp an oh-so-casual 'Good morning' like nothing at all is amiss. Like I always wake up in his bed – in anyone's bed but my own.

God knows a night in the glorified frathouse Ben has lived in our entire college lives never quite appealed to me.

'Morning.' Bedsheets rustle. Another yawn echoes around the room. Practically against my own will, I glance over my shoulder and watch as Heath lazily stretches. At the sight of him all rumpled and groggy, I think some things that aren't so much words, but warm, fuzzy noises.

Things that quickly turn impure when he drags a hand down his abdomen, dips it beneath his waistband, and quickly adjusts a very awake part of his anatomy.

If I gasp, I won't admit it.

I'd like to pretend I don't flee the room either, but Heath won't let me get away with that – his rasping humor follows me into the en suite. 'Got somewhere to be, honey?'

Snatching my dress from where I left it strewn across the counter, I rush to change out of my borrowed pajamas. 'Uh-huh.'

I didn't bother to close the door behind me, so another drowsy laugh is loud and clear. 'Where's that?'

Somewhere that isn't here, I answer only in my head. Twisting to get a better look at the back of my dress in the mirror – and steadfastly avoiding looking at the rest of me because, not so shockingly, a night of drinking, punching, and complete humiliation has not done me any favors – I stifle a groan as I struggle to zip myself up.

My silence earns a sigh. Footsteps on floorboards. Knuckles

on wood before the creak of hinges. Warmth and ocean and shivers as Heath fills the doorway. Arms crossed, shoulder resting against the jamb, head at a taunting tilt. 'Have breakfast with me,' he asks, demands, and pleads all at once. 'I make a mean omelet.'

'I'm good.'

'Running doesn't make you hungry?'

I cut him an unamused glare. *'Ha ha.'*

A faint smile curving his mouth, he abandons his post. I stiffen as he finds a new one right behind me, as he steals the zipper from my fumbling fingers and holds it hostage. 'Why, exactly, are you running?'

'It's cardio day.'

The quip earns me a tut, and the purr of a zip moving the wrong way. I forget to be annoyed about that, for a second. I get distracted by the feel of long fingers peeling my dress further apart before splaying wide across the middle of my back.

By the time I collect myself enough to jab an elbow backwards in a *super* polite request for a little personal space, my zipper is kissing the base of my spine, and I am dangerously close to a full frontal slip.

Clutching the sagging fabric to my chest, I turn so I can hit Heath with my real scowl, rather than just a reflection of it. 'What the hell?'

'Is this about last night?'

Beneath my palm, my heart thunders. 'What about last night?'

'You've got my bitemark on your tit, Daniela. Bit late for coy.'

My gaze drops. My nose wrinkles. *Jesus*. 'What, were you hungry?'

'I plead the fifth.' He stares at my chest, *admires* it, licks his goddamn lips, for what I swear is a full minute before lifting his eyes to mine. 'Are you okay?'

'I'm a little concerned about developing a blood clot.'

He chokes on a laughed rendition of my name. 'I meant after last night.'

The most stubborn parts of me rise to the surface and snap, 'Why wouldn't I be?'

His brows raise. Pose a challenge. *Do you really want me to elaborate?*

I kiss my teeth. *No. I really, really do not.*

'My knuckles hurt, I still want to kill my ex, and I'll probably be embarrassed for the next decade or so, but I'm fine. Happy?'

'Could be happier.'

'Enlighten me.'

'Stay for breakfast.'

'Do I *look* susceptible to emotional blackmail?'

'You look very, very pretty.'

'Is it the bed-head, the pillowcase imprint, or the giant mouth-made bruise that's doing it for you?'

'The semi-nudity. The hickey is a close second, though.'

I laugh. God, how does he do that? Turn every moment light, lift every mood, make me forget how supremely shitty I might be feeling – make me guilty and desperate because, shit, I wish I could return the favor.

Shifting from one foot to the other, I clutch my dress a little tighter and sigh. 'I don't like omelets.'

'Shit.' Heath gasps, eyes widening. 'Offer rescinded, then.'

'Fuck you.'

'That's on the table?'

So briefly it barely registers as a real thought, an extremely inappropriate image flashes through my mind. Me, on a table. Him, on his knees in front of it. 'Y'know, I really wish you did have an ex—'

'So you could beat her up?'

Jesus. Maybe *this* is why he doesn't have any. No one can keep up with him – they spontaneously combust, simply trying. 'So I could ask where the fuck your off-button is.'

'That's more of, like, a third-date activity.'

I groan, laugh, make a noise I don't know how to describe. I just know that Heath's chest is very warm where my forehead thuds against it – that his touch is much the same as it coasts down my spine.

'Naked breakfast, on the other hand,' he murmurs, toying with my gaping dress some more, 'is definitely okay after a first date.'

'Great,' I murmur back, and goosebumps sprout beneath my lips. 'Strip.'

Why I'm surprised that he actually moves as if to yank down his sweatpants, I don't know – daring him to do anything is like dangling a fucking bone in front of a dog. He flashes a trail of golden hair that I suspect leads to a very happy destination before I manage to slap his hands to a stop. 'If only last night was a date.'

Heath sighs. 'If only.'

I shiver because I'm cold, I tell myself. Not because of a low timbre and husky yearning I don't entirely believe is forced.

That warm hand takes its sweet time gliding up my back, curling around my shoulder, squeezing before letting me go so slowly, it's as if it takes actual, physical effort to unstick his skin from mine. Just as leisurely, he slopes out of the bathroom. 'Take your time. I'll be in the kitchen.'

'Fully dressed,' I call in his wake, earning a grin and a wink and, Jesus Christ, a purposeful flash of tanned, toned ass-check that I suspect might've become an entire tanned, toned ass if I didn't slam the door shut, blocking the view.

I stare at the light-wash grain for too long to be considered normal before wrenching my gaze away, letting out a low, vaguely humorous, partly pained laugh. I have almost zero idea what just happened. How I went from a panicked escape attempt to *sure, honey, I'll stay for breakfast.*

I don't dwell on it. I fear my brain might actually implode if I do. For now, I'm resigned to it just being one of those things. A phenomenon. Inexplicable. Inevitable. I just have to . . . go with it.

I snort. *Just go with it.*

As if I've *ever* done that in my life.

Showered, slathered in lotion and skincare, and wrapped in a towel that smells suspiciously like the sensitive skin laundry detergent I use, I cautiously ease open the bathroom door.

Part of me expects to find Heath lurking impatiently on the other side – part of me is disappointed that he isn't. Instead, all that waits for me is fresh clothes set on a neatly made bed. And even though I might've stretched the limits of that whole *take your time* declaration – what is a steaming hot shower for, if not to contemplate one's entire life? – I don't get dressed right away.

This might not be my first time in Heath's room, but it is my first time *alone*. No watchful eyes to temper any snoopy urges. A closed door between me and Heath, and some very loud, very moody vocals providing coverage in case I, I don't know, bump into the bookshelf tucked in the corner and knock over a trophy.

Or a hundred.

He uses one of his many first place accolades as a jewelry stand, leather cords and silver chains looped around a wooden plaque. The thinnest, most vertical of the bunch are stacked with rings in every shade of metal. One acts a makeshift bookend to keep a line of records in place.

It's so . . . casual. So *what, this ol' thing?* So unlike my own victorious collection – I don't polish my awards or anything, but they're displayed with neat pride. Or with arrogance, if you're looking at it through my ex's eyes.

This is so Heath; so good, and he doesn't even care.

I look away before I get annoyed.

I look elsewhere and I get . . . something else.

A misshapen spiderweb of string and photographs and little mementos, like movie tickets and receipts, decorates the cream paint of one wall. So many faces stare at me, people I don't recognize and people I do; mostly, some combination of Heath and his four musketeers, though Imani's frequent absence does tip me off as to who took most of them.

Carefully, I thumb a photo of the five of them, huddled together on the beach, wet-haired and smiling. In another, it looks like they're in the stands at a swim meet; only Heath and Kai are wet, but they're all smiling. They smile at me from the bed of that baby blue Bronco too, their legs hanging over the edge, colorful surfboards stacked behind—

My perusal comes to a sudden end. Hand hovering an inch from the wall, I quickly glance over my shoulder. With Heath nowhere to be seen, I carefully unclip a photo with only one person in it.

Me.

Begrudging, frowning me.

I remember Imani taking it – more clearly, I remember how much I didn't want Imani to take it. It was at Barefoot Joe's a few days back, and I was waiting for Heath to get off work so I could force some studying on him, and, instead, I had some socialization forced on me. Like moths to a flame, his friends turned up one by one until the booth was full, I was surrounded, and that camera flashed in my face.

And now here I am. Hanging on Heath's bedroom wall, nestled amongst his nearest and dearest.

God, what am I supposed to do with that?

'I like that one.'

'Jesus.' Half-cursing, half-shrieking, I jerk away from the tall, hard body suddenly stationed right behind me. As heat creeps up my neck, I hurriedly clutch the knot of my towel, ensuring it's secure. 'What the hell?'

The picture of innocence, Heath smiles. 'Making sure you didn't drown.'

I snort, tightening my grip a little. 'What if I'd been naked?'

Making a raspy, wistful noise, he pins me with wide, freaking starry eyes. 'You mean what if dreams really do come true?'

My elbow aims for his ribs – a cupped, calloused hand prevents it from finding its target. Another curls around in front of me, a forefinger adorned with an inky dagger and a thumb marked with a tiny, wonky heart pinching the photo, stealing it back.

'Mine,' Heath grouses playfully as he returns it to its place.

Decidedly less playful, I practically shout, 'I wasn't snooping.'

Sure you weren't, his face silently mocks – his mouth is a lot less subtle. 'You get to my underwear drawer yet?'

'Hm.' I pull a face, feign disgust. 'Had to take another shower.'

Naturally, Heath interprets that the exact opposite way I intended. '*Dirty.*'

'That is *not*—'

'Breakfast is waiting, darling,' he interrupts, before I can set him straight, and strides out of the room before I can try again.

I let loose another curse, bury another shriek in the back of my hand, and quickly change. Plucking at the stretched-out neckline of another borrowed t-shirt, I'm balancing the need to ask where the hell Heath bought such an exceptionally soft pair of sweats and why the hell I feature in that damn friendship shrine when I pad into the kitchen on bare feet, and promptly forget both at the first strong whiff of coffee, and the abrupt reminder that I'm a little hungover.

And starving. So starving that I'd probably eat an omelet, but that's not what slides in front of me.

Deciding that I must be more than a little hungover if a plate of scrambled eggs, sourdough toast topped with avocado and pumpkin seeds, a handful of raspberries and a whole peeled orange is making my throat a little tight, I start stuffing my mouth before I do something heinous like cry. Or ask the universe aloud why it gave me a real boyfriend who bitched and moaned whenever I didn't abandon my eating habits in favor of adhering to his, but a fake one who might as well have crawled inside my brain to download my regular meal plan.

When that turns out to be a particularly hard question to deny myself, I replace it with a different one. 'Is your sister here?'

Stealing a raspberry from my plate despite his own heaping portion, Heath shakes his head. 'She took Lyla to the library already. The kid's like you.'

I spend an entire minute trying to think of a descriptor for myself that's also appropriate to apply to a five-year-old.

'*Smart*,' Heath fills in the blank, thwacking my wrist in a gentle reprimand. 'She's a little nerd.'

'An academic,' I correct.

'A genius.'

I flush. Stuff my mouth some more to prevent anything embarrassing from coming out, avert my gaze in case that does anything funny – find a laptop covered in familiar artsy stickers sitting on the counter, and remember something. 'Can I borrow that?'

He nods, calling out the password as I flip it open. Logging into my email account, I find the draft with that set of rewritten notes attached, and less than a minute later, Heath's phone dings to announce incoming mail.

'What's this?' he asks, but I get the feeling it's rhetorical – I get the feeling he knows exactly what it is because his face does this thing, it morphs and softens and *sweetens*.

'I printed a copy too,' I tell him, the words coming out all croaky. 'Is the font okay? I, uh, googled it, but if there's a better one—'

'It's perfect.' Throat bobbing with a deep swallow, Heath looks at the typed-up version of my notes like I've offered him something a million times more valuable. 'Thank you.'

'That's okay.'

'It's more than okay.'

'It's notes, Heath. Not a kidney.'

'It's really fucking nice, Dani.'

'Okay, well, you don't have to sound so surprised.'

'I'm not. I just . . .' Heath sighs. Oddly exasperated, he drags a palm over his shorn, shaking head, his expression not quite pained, but something awfully close. 'Thank you, Daniela.'

I try to remember the last time someone thanked me so genuinely. I try to remember the last time I did anything to earn it. I come up empty on both fronts. 'You already said that.'

'I really mean it.' He means it so much, he says it again. Mutters it against my temple after hauling my stool closer and throwing an arm around my shoulder. Leaving it there as we eat.

I try to remember ever enjoying a meal so much.

Again, I come up empty.

'I heard she bit him.'

A round of incensed gasps echo around the parking lot. If my hackles weren't already raised, the *barely* whispered suggestion that I attempted to rip out my ex's jugular with my fucking teeth would do it.

'Ignore them,' Heath murmurs against my hairline, but that's easier said than done. *Them* is a vast entity. *Them* is almost every member of my team. *Them* is circling me like fucking vultures, killing time as we wait for an unusually late Coach to show up for early morning practice by squawking about my *little brawl.*

He was minding his own business, and I attacked him.

I was belligerent and yelling, yet somehow also meek and weepy.

The words *vicious* and *jealous* and *fit* are repeat offenders – *I'm* about to be a repeat offender. Jesus, I've never punched anyone in my life before last night, but, right now, I'm seconds from morphing into Katie fucking Taylor.

'Everyone's staring at me.'

'Well, that's what happens when you're so damn beautiful.'

It doesn't *occur* to me that, in a matter of twenty-four hours, I've been casually tossed more compliments than I have in my entire life so much as it *slams* into me like a runaway train. 'You're not funny.'

'I'm not joking.' The bastard is smiling. I can hear it; can feel it against my temple too. 'They don't matter, Dani.'

'Whatever Ben's telling everyone matters.'

'Why?'

'Because it does.'

'For a genius, you're not all that eloquent.'

I pinch the back of the hand cupping my shoulder and Heath chuffs, digging his chin into the top of my head. 'Just know that for every HCU drone spitting at you right now, there are, like, five Cove College students throwing a party in your name.'

'Maybe I should transfer.'

'Again with my dreams coming true.'

I snort a laugh. His own skates across my neck when he drops his face to the slope, breathes in deeply, nudges the neckline of the borrowed hoodie aside like he's trying to crawl beneath it. His other arm locks across my chest too, his whole body wrapped around me like a weighted blanket. It would be so easy to slump against him, to let him swallow me whole, to protect me. I almost do.

And then I hear my name and *psychopath* in the same hushed sentence, and my entire body locks up tight, any comfort I might feel dies a quick death.

Sighing, I twist until my mouth finds the curve of pierced cartilage. 'Where the hell even is he?'

Heath shivers. 'Scouring the drugstore for a perfect foundation match. Heard he has quite the bruise.'

My spine straightens – with intrigue, not gratification. Obviously. 'Really?'

Heath nods. Definitely not at all gratified either.

I don't revel in violence, and I'm not proud of myself, but . . .

well. It certainly perks me up. At least a little bit. For the single second the universe deems it fitting to spare me, and then it knocks me down once more – it conjures up my ex-boyfriend, strutting across the parking lot, wearing a bruise, sure, but also a smile.

A big, shit-eating smirk, fixed right on me.

'Daniela,' I hear, but it doesn't come from Ben – it's our coach who summons me with a jerk of his head. 'A word, please.'

'Ominous,' Heath voices my silent concern. 'Need back-up?'

Inside, I nod nervously. Externally, however, I shake my head as I detangle myself from my human straightjacket, and force myself out of his magnetic orbit, much to the chagrin of my entire fucking body, right down to my damn molecules. Nevertheless, I stride toward Coach, chin up, arms wrapped around myself – a poor substitute for stronger ones.

I skip a step, a breath, and a heartbeat all at once when, before I even reach him, Coach commands me to 'Go home.'

I come to a stop so abrupt, it's as if an invisible wall has suddenly stopped me in my tracks. It feels a bit like it too, like I've slammed into something hard enough to knock the breath out of me. I practically wheeze, 'Excuse me?'

'You're not joining us for practice today.'

I blink. I repeat myself with a quiet laugh, a tentative frown, sure I've misheard.

'We have a zero tolerance for violence, Daniela.'

'For—' Disbelief splutters out of me, staining my skin with a hot flush. 'You've got to be fucking kidding me.'

'I let you get away with not being a team player, Dani, but you're not above the rules. You can't punch your teammates.'

'He—'

'I don't care what he did,' Coach snaps, and it hits me with this weird, jarring clarity how true that is. He doesn't care. I could tell him anything, I could detail the entire conversation, every conversation I've had with Ben since we broke up, and it wouldn't matter. He wouldn't fucking care. 'This hostility, Dani? I'm sick of it. We have a code of conduct. You broke it. You're suspended from the team for a week—'

'A *week*—'

'—but if you stop talking back to me right now, you can join us at the meet this weekend.'

My mouth opens. Nothing comes out. Not because I'm heeding his warning, but because I'm genuinely speechless. Thoughtless too. Emotionless, I wish; a whole lot of emotion clogs my throat as I watch my coach walk away without another word, without a damn care, and herd the rest of my team inside; my parting gift is snickers and smug looks and a complete lack of anything close to sympathy.

I've never missed a practice in my life. Not once. I don't miss anything. I don't get suspended. I am freaking model in everything I do. I . . .

I swallow thickly. Palm the base of my throat like I can pluck the lump there right out, toss it away. Rake my nails across my chest until I find my erratic, sore heart, and spend a moment wishing I could rip that right out too.

'What happened?'

My sharp inhale hurts. My *embarrassment* hurts. I feel teeny-freaking-tiny, too small to possibly meet Heath's gaze, so I evade it. My head hangs low as my unsteady feet carry me toward the parking lot exit, by-passing the car.

'Where are you going?'

The question has me coming up short; I don't know. Hands fisting and flexing repeatedly at my sides, I try to think – I try harder not to burst into fucking tears.

'Baby.' Warm fingers twine with my twitching ones. 'What the hell just happened?'

I sniff. With my free hand, I swipe roughly at my eyes; I'm fucking horrified when my knuckles come away wet, and even more so when my voice breaks as I spit, 'He suspended me.'

Heath goes so still, it's almost alarming. I swear he short-circuits for a moment, expressionless and silent and not even breathing, I don't think, until his lungs empty with a disbelieving, '*What?*'

'Ben told Coach about the other night, so he suspended me.'

'Did you tell him—'

'He doesn't care.'

Still holding my hand, Heath tries to turn around, to storm toward the pool complex. 'I'll tell him I punched him.'

It's my turn to yank him to a stop. 'He *won't* care.'

'How long?'

'A week.' God, my chest hurts. 'But I can swim at the meet.'

'You shouldn't. Teach them a fucking lesson.'

The most resentful parts of me consider it. They beg for it, turn red with glee while the rest of me is scarlet with pure fury. '*Esas son mamadas.*'

'This *is* bullshit.'

I jerk – out of my head, away from the present, toward Heath. 'You speak Spanish?'

'*Claro que sí,*' he croons, like an asshole. 'You didn't know that?'

'Why would I know that?'

'Because I've literally spoken to you in Spanish before.'

He has? I frown, wracking my brain and coming up empty, except for little snippets of *guapa* and *linda* and *mi amor* that were cast out playfully, teasingly, meant-to-inspire-jealousy-ingly, that I thought were the extent of his knowledge, that do not a hispanophone make. Something I start to point out until a different occasion suddenly comes to mind.

It was over a year ago, I think. At a meet. Ben had just lost his heat pretty spectacularly and wanted comforting, but I was trying to get in the zone and he was being a dick – he called me a bitch, so I walked away. I remember him yelling after me, calling me a robot. I remember muttering nonsense to myself as I recited the words to the book my mom read to me the most when I was a kid – I guess *El Principito* imprinted on me as a source of comfort or something, because it's what I've always turned to when I need to self-soothe.

And I remember Heath being there. Appearing out of nowhere. That deep voice lowering to match my mumbling as he asked, '*The Little Prince*?'

I had grunted. Snapped at him, told him to fuck his pretty ass off, not in English, and it didn't register at the time that he had understood. Laughed. Quipped, 'I *knew* you thought I was pretty,' in the same tongue.

It does now. 'I forgot about that.'

'Yeah, well, we've established I'm not particularly memorable to you.'

I open my mouth to argue – if I even have an argument, I don't know, and I don't find out, because Heath hushes me, holds me, guides me back to his car. 'I'll drive you home.'

My body revolts at the mere suggestion. 'I don't wanna go home.'

'Then I'll drive you somewhere else.'

'You have practice.'

'I'll skip it.'

'I don't want you to skip it.'

'Well, as The Rolling Stones once said . . .'

I don't laugh. I don't smile. I don't have the capacity to find him even remotely funny – I don't have the capacity to stop myself from sounding quite so harsh as I grumble, 'Just leave me alone, Heath.'

'I don't wanna.'

'What was that about a song?'

'Compromise – I'll leave you alone if you let me drive you wherever you wanna be alone.'

Even through the stubborn, infuriated lens clouding my senses, I recognize a losing battle. I grumble and I scowl and I pout a little, but I concede. 'You can walk me to the library. And then you go to practice.'

'Yes, ma'am.' Playfully, he salutes me. Sweetly, he lifts our entwined fingers to his mouth and kisses the back of my hand. 'They don't deserve you, Dani.'

I don't know what to say to that. I just sigh. As we walk away from the building where my team happily practices without me, where they freaking celebrate my absence, I feel like I leave a little piece of me behind.

I feel like it isn't the first time I've felt that way.

TWELVE

IT'S BARELY LIGHT OUT WHEN I SLAM MY FRONT DOOR shut the next morning, toting grand plans of running to the shitty public pool on the other side of town.

It's closed, with summer long gone and all, but I know kids hop the fence all the time. I've never heard of anyone contracting some brain-eating amoeba from lapping the barely treated, murky depths; even if I had, I fear I would risk it.

Maybe they'd eat away at the exact right parts. Make me a *team player*. Make me less *hostile*.

It's kind of funny that, as I twiddled my fucking thumbs yesterday and flitted from lecture to lecture, absorbing nothing, then lay on my living-room floor and stared at the cracks in the ceiling as I desperately tried to regulate the flood of emotions making my fucking skin hurt, it was those words that cut me the worst. Not the banishment. If I'm being completely honest – in the rare moments I manage to beat back my frustration enough to make room for coherent thought – I get why he suspended me.

It was *how* Coach did it that fucks me up. I didn't deserve to be whacked down like that, to be dismissed so carelessly. Ben should've copped at least a little shit too.

But no. It was just me. Because I'm me.

Blowing out a harsh breath, I shake the bad attitude right out of my head before slipping my headphones into place, pressing play on a soft rock playlist cranked to the max, and start down the street at too quick a pace, too soon, but, hey, who cares if I injure myself?

I've got all fucking week to recover.

I only make it halfway through a single song before honking penetrates the music. Repeatedly. Unwavering, no matter how steadfastly I try to ignore the baby blue truck that I pretend I don't recognize. The lull between songs arrives, that obnoxious beeping only gets worse, and I quickly lose my grip on my flaring temper. Roughly pushing off my headphones, I just about resist the urge to kick the Ford Bronco trying to crawling up my fucking ass. '*What?*'

Leaning out the open driver's side window, Heath smiles innocently. 'Good morning, my love.'

'Fuck off.'

'That's my girl.' One hand tip-tapping against the steering wheel to the rhythm of a Steely Dan song, he attempts to summon me with a crooked finger of the other. 'Let's go, baby.'

'Busy. Sorry.'

'Don't care. *Sorry*.' Clucking his tongue at me, he slaps the side of the truck. 'Get in or I'll get you in.'

Brows high, I scoff. 'Try me.'

God, it's like he expected me to say that. Like he's prepared to launch himself onto the sidewalk, more prepared than I am to evade his grabby hands. I blink, and I'm already being plopped on the passenger seat. Strapped in. Patted on the head like a freaking dog. 'Was that so hard?'

'This is kidnapping.'

'Yeah,' my kidnapper drawls, as he slides behind the wheel. 'You sure put up a fight.'

I huff, but I can't exactly argue, can I? I might as well have climbed in the damn car myself with how hard I resisted. Like my subconscious was more than happy to go along with whatever Heath has planned. 'Where are we going?'

Brows high, Heath looks at me, then at the surfboards stacked in the bed of his truck, and back to me again. 'Where do you think, honey?'

'I don't surf.'

'*Yet.*'

Slumping with another huff, I try another escape route. 'I'm really not in the mood for company.'

'As opposed to every other day, when you beg for it.'

'Heath.'

He huffs now. Good-natured and teasing, as he so often is, but with a strain of something harsher beneath it. Something close to frustration. As if he's irritated he even has to elaborate on his sudden appearance, as if I should've expected it. 'What kind of boyfriend would I be if I let you wallow all on your lonesome?'

'A fake one.'

His laugh isn't quite that. His voice, a touch deeper as he amends, 'What kind of friend would I be?'

I look down, staring at my twiddling thumbs. 'I have no parameters to judge that, so I guess you're off the hook.'

Silence. A sigh. A warm hand slipping between the headrest and my neck, a thumb circling my pulse. 'I would have to be the literal devil to let you swim in that pool. You'd catch, like, a minimum of five diseases.'

'Yeah, well. I'm a hostile environment. Nothing would survive.'

The grip on my nape tightens. Just barely digging in. Not enough to hurt, but enough to . . . *something*. 'Your coach say that?'

I neither confirm nor deny – Heath comes to his own conclusion anyway.

The noise he makes is bitter and sounds all wrong leaving him. His grip retreats, both hands curling around the steering wheel instead. 'That fucking team is the hostile environment.'

My own hand is halfway to my tingling nape before I catch myself. 'I don't wanna talk about it.'

'Okay.' He gives up easily. Too easily. Jarringly, and I'm caught between suspicion and disappointment – is there some kind of ulterior motive here, or does he just not care enough to push? – when he says, 'The others are meeting us at the beach.'

If he notices the dubious side-eye I throw him, he doesn't acknowledge it. 'Okay.'

'Wanna run drills?'

I picture frolicking through dark, frigid oceanic waters, and I suppress a shiver. 'Pass.'

'*You?*' He gasps dramatically. 'Pass on *swimming*?'

Silently, I plead for the sudden ability to turn back time. I would much rather discuss my shitty team, my shitty coach, anything else shitty in my life, than my disdain for large, tidal bodies of seawater. 'I don't like the ocean.'

'Okay. Well. We have to break up.'

Despite the sudden pulse of anxiety behind my sternum, I manage a snort.

'Are you scared?' he asks.

'Of course not.'

'Of course not,' he repeats, half-smiling. 'Then what is it?'

The term *lightning doesn't strike in the same place twice* comes to mind as I consider side-stepping the subject. Call it gut instinct or common sense or, hey, maybe I just actually know Heath as well as he claims to know me, but something tells me he isn't going to let me get away with two dropped subjects in one car ride.

So, as if it isn't any big deal at all, with a shrug and so much forced nonchalance it makes my head hurt – or maybe that's just from recalling the horrid incident – I casually admit, 'I almost drowned once. Got caught in a rip.'

'Jesus, Dani,' he says, like it is a big deal, not shrugging, definitely not nonchalant, and definitely not smiling anymore. 'I'm sorry that happened.'

'Wasn't your fault.' I state the obvious. No, that blame lies with a different man entirely. One I can't actually blame, because he's nothing but bones in the ground now. But I don't want to talk about that, I don't want to talk about *this*, so I move on and I fucking pray he comes with me. 'Would you really break up with a girl if she didn't like the ocean?'

Heath is silent for so long, I almost think he isn't going to let me get away with it. That he won't push. And then, eventually, 'Would you date someone who didn't like swimming?'

'I don't really wanna date someone, full stop.'

Silence. Assessment. Disappointment, if I were brave enough to recognize it.

'So?' I prompt after a while. 'Are we broken up now?'

Heath laughs. Loud and amused in a way that doesn't match the soft, honest smile he wears.

Nor an even softer, 'For you, I'll make an exception.'

The second we pull into a sand-dusted parking lot, a salty gust of wind carries over not only the scent of the ocean, but also the holler of a familiar voice.

'Oh my God,' Kai screeches like a fucking gull as he leaps off the car hood he's sitting on and peels toward us. 'Is that my hero?'

Heath mutters his friend's name in warning, but it's no use. And it's not just Kai that needs fending off; the truck has barely stopped before my door is ripped open, and my arm just about detached from my body with how intently Imani yanks it toward her so she can peer at my knuckles.

'Shit,' she whistles, elbowing Matilda as she comes up behind her, showing the redhead and her twin brother the mottled skin – lingering proof of my *vicious attack*. 'You actually did it.'

Nudging Brendan out of the way so he can get a better look, Kai whistles too, low and impressed – he smirks, freaking devious. 'Check her teeth.'

I wrench my hand away from their scrutiny just so I can

thwap it against the bare chest that's revealed by a half-on wetsuit. Shaking off Imani, I hop out of the truck, shutting the door behind me with a loud slam that emphasizes a snapped, 'I did not *bite* him.'

'But you did punch him.'

Not a single word passes my lips as I elbow through the group to join Heath where he's hoisting a couple of boards out of the truck bed – not a single word, yet Kai reacts as if I whipped out my phone and played a high-definition video of the whole thing.

'Oh my God,' he hoots again, and the next thing I know, he's wrapped himself around me from behind. He's hugging me. He's jumping up and fucking down, and consequently, so the fuck am I. 'Your bar tab is on me for the rest of your life.'

'That's hardly a reward,' Matilda snickers, as she yanks Kai off of me, smirking at an unusually stoney-faced Heath as she does. 'Means she's stuck with you for the rest of her life.'

Feigning dry laughter, Kai shifts his affections to his be-freckled friend instead, and I spend a moment being grateful that I wasn't subjected to a freaking head-lock, like Matilda is, before a brush against my arm draws my attention sideways.

Voice low and her face a sympathetic scrunch, Imani pats my shoulder gently. 'Heard about the suspension.'

I stiffen, even though I'm not surprised. The news had completely circulated HCU before I even finished my first class of the day. For God's sake, I swear even a few of my professors were looking at me funny. 'That skywriter Ben hired wasn't exactly subtle, was it?'

'He's a dick. Your coach is a dick. Your entire team is a whole bag of dicks.'

'It's fine.'

She doesn't look like she agrees, but she lets it go. 'Are you going to the meet on Saturday?'

'Course I am.'

'We'll be there too, y'know. If you wanna sit with us.'

'I'll look for you. If I have time.'

'Find some. Heath'll put on a real good show if he knows you're in the stands watching.'

My mouth quirks against my will.

'You've seen him swim before, right?'

I nod again. At least *that* I remember. One time specifically rather vividly. Because, God, did I get in trouble when Ben, in all his jealous glory, scoffed that his rival wasn't nearly as good as him, and I, without thinking, laughed so very loud. And then, thinking very clearly, snickered, *in your dreams, maybe.*

He didn't speak to me for a week after that.

I'm pretty sure that was the week he started boning Sienna behind my back.

And there's something kinda serendipitous about that, I think.

'You seen Heath surf before?'

At that, I shake my head.

'He's probably embarrassed,' Kai calls out, one arm stretched behind him as he tugs up the zip of his wetsuit, 'because he's really not as good at me.'

'Gotta let you have something.'

'Your boyfriend, the white knight.' All conspiratorial, Kai nudges me. 'You joining us?'

I barely even shake my head before he groans, head thrown back dramatically. 'Oh, c'mon. Might even have some fun, Elsa.'

'Don't call her that.'

As Heath's fist connects with his best friend's shoulder a little too hard to be considered friendly, a memory comes to mind. Being at some party that Ben dragged me to, and a group of Cove College dipshits crooning the lyrics to that song from *Frozen* when I walked past. Heath socking the ringleader in the gut, telling him to shut the fuck up.

Cold, they were calling me.

Frigid, Ben called me.

Knowing is how Heath looks at me, like he's remembering the same thing, and it has a familiar vein of frustration bubbling and building and threatening to spill over. And while my favorite avenue of venting is undoubtedly submerging myself in a body of water, the ocean is *not* my body of choice.

The ocean makes me shiver and squirm and shake my head emphatically, brows pulling together as I curl my fingertips around the lip of the truck bed and hoist myself up onto it. 'I'm good right here, Kiki.'

Chimes of laughter ring out across the lot, whipped up by the wind so it's almost dancing around me. Flipping me off with one hand, Kai picks up his board with the other and jogs toward the shoreline. Brendan, ever the silent introvert, bids me the same head tilt goodbye he used as a greeting before following his friend.

Heath, however, lingers. Sidles closer until my knees press

against the wetsuit he wriggled into at some point during the chatter. Crooks a finger beneath my chin and lifts, guiding my face to where he wants it so he can drop a kiss to the corner of my mouth. 'Okay?'

I nod, resisting the urge to bat his hand away because I don't like how my mind stills at the contact. How some of that frustration eases. How I fucking *yearn* to lean into his touch.

Eyes almost exactly the same shade as where the dim sun catches the shallower water and turns it a little green search my face for a long second before Heath rises again. He looks like he wants to say something, but he must decide against it, it must not be important, because, without another word – with another ruffle of my goddamn hair – he follows the boys into the water.

Refusing to watch him go like some pathetic romantic, I stare at my swinging feet instead as I wait for the girls to do the same.

I frown something fierce when, instead, metal creaks as two bodies hoist themselves up to sit on either side of me. 'You guys don't surf?'

Matilda hums as she shifts to get comfortable, a freckled shoulder nudging mine. 'We like to let the boys get out some of their testosterone before we go in and show them up.'

'Exactly,' Imani agrees, shivering as a particularly strong gust of wind assaults us. 'I don't know if you've noticed, but Heath is, like, dangerously competitive.'

At that, I frown. Internally, at least. Externally, I nod as if I can imagine Heath being dangerous in any capacity. As if I can imagine him being really, truly competitive. Yeah, he competes. He likes winning. Obviously, he likes competing with Ben. But it's not, like . . . urgent. Not like me. Not like a lot of other swimmers, like most of the other swimmers on my team, and on his. I've always gotten the impression he does it for fun, not because he wants to be the best, or beat the best. 'Right.'

'Besides.' Leaning back on her hands, Imani cocks her head as she gazes toward the water, at the three bodies quickly getting lost in the big, blue swells. 'It's kinda fun to watch.'

In the moment, I scoff quietly. I can't imagine how it could be fun to sit on cold metal in a cold parking lot, and feel all the colder just for looking at the crashing waves. But the longer my gaze tracks the boards bobbing on the horizon, the more the girls tell me about different tricks and rules and a million other things that have nothing to do with surfing, the less I think about anything else but this exact moment with these specific people . . .

Well, shit. I kind of fucking agree.

I spend the morning on the beach, the afternoon in classes, and most of the evening trying my best to do my homework while Heath tries his best to distract me. The next day starts with the same ambush, and with take-out, face masks, and *How to Lose a Guy in Ten Days* with the volume down low because God forbid anyone actually wants to watch instead of chatter.

By Thursday, I've caught on – *keep Dani so busy, she doesn't think about the missed practices.* Distract me so thoroughly that I forget that this is the longest I've gone without submerging myself in a chlorinated body of water since I first started swimming. Do such a good job that I wake up on Friday morning in a cold, concerned sweat because I had a dream.

A vision, really. A fucking apparition of my dad, screaming at me from beyond the grave, berating my laziness. My carelessness. His disappointment is palpable. It still lingers hours later when Heath appears on my doorstep; it must be pretty damn visceral, because he's frowning before I even get in the car.

'Can you just drive me to the pool today, please?' I ask, before I've even settled in the passenger seat, before he can spit out any question of his own. The dark cloud above my head must be worse than I thought, because he agrees without a word.

Cranking the radio up as loud as it'll go in the hopes that'll keep the thoughts out of my head, I slump with a sigh and close my eyes. A second later, they fly open again.

My dad. My fucking dad, and his disappointed face. I think decades, *centuries* could pass and I wouldn't forget that specific twist of his expression. It's pretty fucking terrible that I can't conjure him up any other way. That that's my lasting image. That everything good about him is just . . . not forgotten, but vague and kind of nonsensical, like my few-and-far-between memories of my mom. My parents are just bedtime stories and pressure.

Fuck, that's depressing.

As that tell-tale itch sparks beneath my skin, it hits me that me and my stress rashes have been estranged for the past week. They haven't cropped up once. I haven't been stressed. I wouldn't dare to call my demeanor happy, but I've been . . . good. Better than I should've been, given the circumstances. An odd, concerning thought that deserves more attention, that I really should analyze more thoroughly, that might—

I jolt when a hand catches my wrist; again, at the intensity of the frown I find when I glance to the side; and a third time as Heath rasps, 'You're bleeding.'

Glancing down, I swallow. Sure enough, tiny scarlet drops well where my nails have dug in. 'Oh.'

His concern is so tangible I can taste it, but he doesn't voice any of it. He only squeezes my wrist gently before letting me go and getting out of the truck. It's only as I silently follow, right as I'm about to insist that I don't need a lifeguard, that I realize we aren't at the public pool.

Brow furrowing, I peer at the side entrance of the Haven Cove University pool complex. 'Why are we here?'

'You wanted a pool.'

'I've been banished, remember?'

'From team practice. Your *team*—' he snorts the word like it's the punchline to a joke, '—won't be here for another hour.'

'I don't have my keycard.'

With a flick of his fingers, Heath produces his own, tapping it to the electronic reader beside the door. When it unlocks with an audible click, he hauls it open and sweeps a dramatic arm through the air. 'After you, honey.'

The smell of chlorine hits me the second I step inside. It doesn't soothe me like I thought it would, but I guess that's just a testament to how dark and deep-rooted my mood is. Instead of dithering about what I do or don't feel, I focus on going through the motions that are like second-nature to me. Dropping my gym bag, kicking off my shoes, shedding my clothes to reveal the swimsuit beneath. I move toward the pool, toes curling around the edge as I drop to my haunches. Tucking my swim cap under a swimsuit strap for safe-keeping, I lean down to wet my goggles, splash my face. I already slicked my hair with coconut oil earlier; I just have to pin dual tight braids to my scalp before slipping on my cap, but I don't rise to grab the hair pins from my bag just yet. I stay where I am. Spine rounded, forearms braced against my straining thighs, staring at the water, and thinking . . . well, I don't really know what I'm thinking. What I'm feeling. Something's wrong, but I can't pinpoint what. It's like my brain and my body have switched frequency, and I'm not privy to the new channel.

My hand is halfway to my chest again when another engulfs it.

Crouched at my side, Heath tugs my stolen limb. Guides me to sit, legs dangling in the water, my goggles forgotten on the tile between us. 'Why did you start swimming?'

Before I actually make the conscious decision to answer, one comes pouring out. 'My dad was a swimmer. He was really good. Got a scholarship and everything, but halfway through sophomore year, my mom got pregnant so he dropped out to get a job. Stopped swimming. Tried to get Seba into it, but it never really stuck. Not like it did with me.'

Heath sits with that for a long moment before opening his mouth again. 'I wanted to be a marine biologist when I was a kid. Used to stay up late reading *National Geographic* magazines and wake up early so I could watch *The Discovery Channel* before school. I had a Shark Week-themed birthday party, like, five years in a row. I learned to swim on that beach outside my house. Learned to surf there too. Spent more of my childhood splashing in the waves than I did on land.'

'And you were an extra on *H2O: Just Add Water*,' I drawl sarcastically, though there's a distinct ping from somewhere in my chest as he details the most normal childhood, and I find myself feeling jealous. 'Do you have a point?'

'I did all of that because I loved it. Not because someone else did. Just like I swim because *I* love it.'

'You think I don't?'

'I think you love it differently to how I do.'

'And that's, what? Wrong?'

'Different,' he emphasizes. 'Just wonder if you know there's another side.'

'A fun side,' I easily piece together, and something sour curls in my belly. 'Because I don't have fun, it means less?'

'Baby, that's not what I'm saying.'

'Then what are you saying?'

'I just . . . What would you do if you didn't swim?'

'Be a princess. Obviously. I'm just getting that anthropology degree for fun.'

'*No*,' he shoots me a look, lips quivering with how hard they stifle his amusement. 'I mean, like, day-to-day, normal shit that you never do because you think you don't have time.'

I resent that *think*, but I let it go. 'I would sleep in.'

Heath feigns a yawn. '*Boring*. Pick a better one.'

'I don't know. Take more classes.'

'Oh, Daniela.'

'*Fine*. Jesus. Uh, paint. My mom was a painter.'

His face softens. 'What else?'

'Travel. Never been out of state.'

'Where'd you move here from?'

I name where I grew up, another coastal town all the way down the other end of the state, similar but not quite . . . I don't know. Real. Not a Hallmark special waiting for someone to shout *action*. 'My mom's parents moved there from Mexico when she was a kid. After she got pregnant, her and my dad moved back there.'

And after my dad died, Marisol stuck it out for a whole two years before deciding she needed a *fresh start*.

'And your dad's parents?'

'England. He grew up there. Moved here for college.' I pause, a not-quite-smile twisting my mouth. 'Y'know, he met Marisol before he ever knew my mom. He did one of those foreign exchanges in high school. Went to Spain and ended up in her hometown. Never saw her again until after Mom died and he went to an old friend's destination wedding and came back with a bride of his own.'

Heath is quiet for a long time before he asks, 'How long after?'

'A perfectly respectable fourteen months.' The lump in my throat burns. God, I remember that day like it was yesterday. I remember starting it crying into my pillow, begging God to bring my mom back, and ending it with some stranger wearing a stiff smile and too much perfume telling me I could call her *mommy* if I wanted to.

In that youthful, almost instinctive way most eight-year-olds are, I was excited, for a little while. Hopeful. My dad started to smile again. I think she liked us, at first, before she realized having two grieving children who were old enough to remember their mother, and too old for her to so easily take her place, wasn't all it was cracked up to be.

For once, Heath doesn't know what to say. A true achievement, but at what cost?

I clear my throat. 'I'd get drunk. Really, obnoxiously drunk. Like, hungover for three to five business days drunk.'

'Now we're talking. Keep going.'

'I kinda always wanted a tattoo,' I slowly admit, and, I swear, those eyes practically glow. 'But at least two weeks no swimming to let it heal . . .'

'You'd shrivel up and die, I'm sure.'

'I'd learn to cook.'

'You can't cook? At your big age?'

Rolling my eyes, I shoulder him semi-gently. He nudges me back, his warmth lingering as his side remains flush against mine. 'I'll teach you,' he promises, like he really means it. 'You still wanna get a swim in, don't you?'

I blink, shifting my gaze to the pool that I just . . . forgot. As if it isn't the very reason we're here. 'Right.'

Clambering to my feet, I reach for my googles, but Heath beats me to it. Hooked around his wrist, the plastic brushes my chest as he steals my swim cap too. The backs of his knuckles graze the scratch marks from earlier and he tuts, and I hardly have time to even register the gesture before I'm distracted by another one. By him securing my braids with the pins he must've pilfered from my bag. Tucking my hair securely beneath the cap. Slipping my goggles over my head, adjusting them perfectly as if he has a sixth sense for my comfort.

My mumbled gratitude is paltry. My cheeks, flushed. Skin hot because he isn't looking at me like you should look at someone in a swim cap and fucking goggles. I would laugh if that look wasn't so . . . whatever it is.

'Go on.' He pats my hip. 'Assume your true form.'

At that, I do laugh. With a deep breath, I dive in.

Strangely, it doesn't feel nearly as good as I thought it would.

THIRTEEN

THE DAY OF THE COVE COLLEGE AND HCU MEET starts out the same way every other meet does – likely the same way every meet ever will.

Early start. Stretching. A light workout that does more for my head than my body. Oatmeal made with soy milk, and a banana and peanut butter, and some of the caramel-flavored protein powder I actually like, the kind that makes me hate all the more the bland shit my dad used to force into my diet. A teaspoon of salt, a habit that was Dad's doing too, one I've never quite been able to kick. Coconut water for electrolytes.

Green tea for anxiety.

Paolo Nutini blares in my headphones as I leave my apartment earlier than I really need to, the swimsuit I wouldn't dare to call lucky hidden by a hoodie and sweats, the day's impending races running through my head, the rosary beads that used to belong to my mother, and now live on my keychain, clutched between my fingers – a soothing comfort more than a religious tool.

It's as I'm getting into my car that the day starts to differ – when a rough hand slams the driver's side door shut right as I open it, causing me my very first heart attack.

With a screech I'm not entirely proud of, I whirl around, keys swishing through the air and damn near gouging a chunk out of a very pretty face.

'Goddamn, honey.' A lazy hand fends off my attack, a lazier laugh teasing me. 'It's just me.'

'What're you doing here?'

'We're picking you up.'

'We?' I ask, approximately a millisecond before getting my answer.

It's hard not to notice the rustbucket old Volkswagen van that I think used to be some shade of orange, especially when the driver is laying on the horn like it isn't still the murky hours of right before sunrise, and a redhead hangs out the passenger side window, exuberantly beckoning me over. 'Let's go, Phelps.'

'She's had three espressos already,' Heath murmurs in warning, as he prods gently at the small of my back, pushing me toward the van. Louder, he teasingly chides, 'Inside voice, Matty.'

While she flicks her middle finger at Heath, Matilda is all smiles for me. 'Didn't you get my text?'

I didn't even know she had my number. 'Sorry. I didn't check.'

Unbothered, she waves off my apology and jerks her thumb toward the open back door with a cheery command to get in. I don't quite wrinkle my nose at the bench seat already occupied by Brendan and Imani, but I must make some kind of a face because a quiet chuckle brushes the curve of my ear. 'Already tried to get you out of this. Didn't work.'

'We'll leave you alone,' Imani calls, as she leans over Brendan to grin at me – a grin that wobbles, ever-so-slightly, when pale fingers sweep her braids over her shoulder, out of her face. 'We promise.'

Though doubtful, I climb into the van with a sigh. Surprisingly, as I settle in with my headphones on and my eyes closed, no one so much as attempts to disturb me. Maybe it has something to do with the wall of redheaded, freckled silence right beside me acting as a sound barrier, but it's like someone took the mute button to the headphone-penetrating decibels this group usually puts out. I don't hear a peep the whole ride, and when a gentle tap to my shoulder coaxes my eyes open, it's only to confirm that we've arrived.

'Thanks,' I mumble, as I push my headphones down around my neck, aiming a half-smile at Brendan and trying not to look so surprised when he does more than just return it.

'I'm the same before games,' he tells me quietly. 'Gotta get in the zone, right?'

So caught up trying to mentally confirm if that is actually the first real thing he's ever said to me – or at least the first full sentence – I miss my chance to ask what he means by *games*. The van door opens with an ear-splitting screech, and my attention shifts elsewhere.

All week, Heath has been dropping oh-so-subtle hints. Completely off-hand, totally casual suggestions of having a little fun this weekend. Doing some of the travelling I've never done. Taking a road-trip up the coast to some surfing spot they all love.

Briefly, as I recognize half a dozen of the faces that looked oh-so-delighted at the news of my suspension, I wish I'd found it in me to screw my team, miss the meet, teach everyone a fucking lesson. See how much they revel in my absence when it leads to them losing.

But I couldn't. I don't even know why. The ache in my

stomach, rooted deep in my chest, thrumming between my shoulder blades, makes it abundantly clear that I do not want to be here. Yet here I am. Here, I feel like I have to be. Here, I stand tall and lift my chin and pray that I look even half as unbothered, as confident as I am so desperately trying to be as I stride toward the meet venue.

Only Heath follows me, the others calling well wishes and encouragements to slaughter the competition in our wake. As if he senses my stress, he folds his hand around mine. Squeezes it comfortingly. Lifts it to kiss the curve of my knuckles. Keeps holding it as we both check in, and practically cuts off my circulation as he marches me to the women's locker rooms.

When we're within a foot of the door and he still hasn't let me go, I snicker quietly. 'You coming in with me, Mommy?'

'Don't tempt me,' he huffs. 'You okay?'

'Uh-huh. Are *you* okay?'

'I hate your school.'

'*No.*' I pretend to gasp. '*What?* Since when?'

'Funny girl.' Narrowed eyes contradict an upturned mouth and the genuine offer it murmurs. 'I really will come in there with you.'

'How about I come to the men's with you?'

'Ah, yes. And then *I* get suspended for mass murder.'

An eye roll makes him grin and sigh, and kiss me so quickly, so fleetingly, that I don't even register his lips being pressed to mine until they're gone – until *he's* going, backing up with stiff, stilted steps as if he has to force himself away. 'Get in there before I change my mind.'

Again, I laugh. 'Go. I'll be fine.'

He doesn't believe me. I don't believe me. But he goes, and I breathe deep before forcing myself into the changing room.

I know everyone notices my arrival; I feel a dozen gazes lock on me. Instantly, the snickers and the whispers and the discomfort starts, but I push it all out of my mind. I tell myself it's just part of the routine, filtering out all of the fuckery. Over and over again, I silently chant three little words – *they don't matter.*

It helps. Like a cool wave washing over my temper.

Somehow, I manage to keep my mouth shut and my head down, and the latter only changes when I'm poolside – when my own name catches my attention, hollered from the stands where Imani waves and flashes a thumbs-up. Beside her, Matilda makes me snicker as she drags a finger across her throat before flipping her own thumb downwards. Brendan, sandwiched between the girls, tips his chin and mouths what I think is a 'good luck'.

I'm still smiling when I dive into the water.

I'm smiling when I haul myself out, and it isn't because I won – I laugh as I glance at the stands and catch sight of a big fucking glittery sign with my name on it.

I stop smiling, rather abruptly, when it strikes me that I can't remember the last time I finished a race and actually felt good about it.

'Question,' Imani muses, a couple of hours later when I finally have enough time to join them in the stands. A smirk playing across her pretty face, she shifts until she's practically siting in Brendan's lap – something neither of them seem all that disturbed by, I can't help but notice – and pats the empty space made beside her. 'Is that pool salty?'

Taking a seat on the bench, I go from grimacing as the cold metal seeps through my sweatpants and damp swimsuit to frowning at her question. 'No?'

'Really? You don't taste the tears of your competitors at all?'

Caught off guard by the quip, I snort as I flick my hood up over my head – shielding my wet hair from the cool air as much as hiding my pink cheeks.

'Seriously,' Matilda chimes in, leaning forward to peer around her twin. 'Why do they even try? I would literally disintegrate if I had to compete against you.'

I shift and shrug, unsettled by the praise for some reason. It's not like I haven't heard something similar before – it's not like I don't know how good I am. It just sounds . . . different, coming from the girls. Better. *Not* bitter. It makes my stomach feel weird, so I swiftly shift the conversation elsewhere. 'Heath's up now, right?'

Both girls confirm what I already know. When I double-checked the schedule this morning, I made a mental note of his too. Because that's what girlfriends do, right? They watch their boyfriends compete. They want to watch, and I would be lying if I said I don't, because I like seeing Heath swim.

I like that when I spot him lining up along the pool's edge, tanned and half-naked and somehow still outrageously attractive even in his swimming cap, with goggles hanging around his neck, he's already looking at me.

I like that I'm so consumed with returning the wave he offers me, with watching the flex of his biceps as he stretches, with wondering if that cocky smile means he knows exactly what I'm doing, that I don't even notice Ben stewing down the far end of the line-up. Not until I hear a snicker beside me, and Imani pokes my thigh. 'You think the water's gonna start boiling when he jumps in?'

As I glance at my ex, I can't help but smile at the scowl on his stupid, cheating face. 'I think the salinity of that water might come into question again when he loses.'

'I feel bad for his girlfriend,' Matilda murmurs, and I follow her gaze to where Sienna lurks on the sideline, chewing on her thumbnail as she stares at her boyfriend, who is so obviously staring at me. 'He's clearly not over you.'

I laugh at that, shaking my head. 'Oh, trust me, he is. He just doesn't want me to be over him.'

'Are you?' a quiet voice asks, and it takes me a second to realize it was Brendan.

'Completely,' I respond, without hesitation, momentarily floored by how much of a relief it is to not have to lie about something, to offer them this one, true thing. 'Honestly, I think I've been over him for a while.'

'Why didn't you break up with him?'

'Easier not to.'

'That's sad.'

I shrug, shifting uncomfortably, grateful when a klaxon sounds, signaling the swimmers to get ready. And with another, they set off.

I've seen Heath swim before. I know he's good. But I didn't

realize I'd always watched with a certain kind of detachment before until right now, when every facet of my concentration is focused on him as he flies through the water with clear, powerful butterfly strokes, leaving everyone else in his wake.

I shift again – for different reasons this time. Experience a different kind of discomfort. The unnerving kind. The kind that makes me want to slap myself upside the head, the kind that I imagine would inspire mockery and jeering and judgment because it is, undoubtedly, a little weird to get turned on by a man's aquatic prowess.

Yet here I am. Hot and bothered by the sight of my fake boyfriend cutting through the water like a knife through butter. Securing a win so easily, it's thoroughly embarrassing for everyone else.

It's over quick – too quick, I find myself lamenting, find myself thinking I could watch him go all day – and as the men pull themselves out of the water, I turn to the others. 'Is that what people look like when I beat them?'

Both girls burst into laughter. 'I think they look worse, actually.'

'Huh.' Well, I almost feel bad now.

I face forward again, and immediately lock eyes with Heath. Jerking a little in surprise, I quickly compose myself, lifting my hands high enough for him to see my little clap of congratulations.

My mouth quirks when he bows dramatically. My cheeks heat when he winks. My eyes roll when he blows me a fucking kiss, but I'm smiling, damn it. Hard enough to fucking hurt.

And then, my perpetual frown is slipping into place when a hand grips the back of my head and turns it to the side, to where a group of swimmers in my division are taking up space on the bleachers, scowling as their gazes flit between me and Heath.

'*That's* what they look like.'

'Huh,' I say again, spine straightening, a little . . . not sure. 'Sucks to be them.'

I don't see him again until my last event of the day – his too. We're both warming up poolside, him with his team, me more than a stone's throw away from mine because my team consists of a guy I've barely spoken to, the girl who fucked my boyfriend while he was still my boyfriend, and the former boyfriend in question.

I ignore them as I stretch, but the piercing eyes at the other end of the pool aren't so easy to dismiss.

Heath has his own stretching to do, but he isn't. There are at least three different people trying to talk to him, but he doesn't do that either. He just looks at me. Drags those eyes over every inch of my body, lingering on my bare legs, bare shoulders, bare arms.

I cock my head, eyes narrowing, and he just grins. Unbothered. Unashamed by his perusal. And, shit, if he's going to do it, I guess I have every right to too.

He's ridiculous, is all I can think. Absolutely ridiculous, because no one should look like that. A sculpted torso, strong shoulders, every inch of him lean and honed and powerful. And the tattoos. Jesus, the tattoos. One thigh completely covered in intricate work, a longhorn on the other, smaller ink scattered along his calves and arms, that jellyfish spanning one firm pec and curling over the same shoulder, and another piece nestled amongst the defined lines of his right oblique. I've noticed them before, of course I have, but I've never *noticed* them. Not with any kind of real interest. Now, though, I wish I was a lot closer, capable of proper scrutiny, of deciphering what each one is.

When it registers that my gaze has lingered for far too long on the ink peeking out from below the waistband of his Speedo, I have to look away. Shaking my head, trying to shake him out of it, except he's kind of stuck. As is this weird, all-consuming need to impress. To do even better than usual. To win, but not just because I want to beat him.

I want to show off for him.

I'm mentally grabbing that ridiculous notion with both hands and choking it when real hands curl over my shoulders. I jolt, surprised, and I'm not sure what to think about the way I instantly relax when I glance back and find Heath right behind me, barely a couple of inches between us, the warmth of his body bleeding into me. I'm even less sure about the goosebumps that spring up as his thumbs dig into the tired muscles between my shoulder blades, soothing the aches of a busy day, and the shiver that tickles my spine when his mouth brushes my earlobe. 'How you feeling, baby?'

Watchful eyes burn the side of my face, but not as potently as calloused fingertips scald the skin they skate over. 'Fine.'

'Heard you've been killing it today.'

'Obviously.'

A husky laugh warms the curve of my neck, and something pulses in my lower stomach. 'Sorry I missed it.'

'Wasn't anything special.'

'Beg to differ.'

'How would you know? You weren't watching.'

'Because it was you.'

My entire body goes lax. I think, if I didn't catch myself in time, I would end up nothing but a puddle on the floor. As it is, I don't feel entirely solid as I roll my shoulders back until that overwhelming touch falls away. 'Go away now,' I flick my fingers dismissively and pray I don't look quite as dopey as I feel. 'You're distracting me.'

Another laugh brushes my shoulder – warm, smiling lips do too. 'Yes, ma'am.'

Dutifully, he starts to walk away, leaving me to marvel over how easy that was. Establishing a boundary, and having it respected. Asking for what I wanted and getting it without the guilt trip.

'Heath?' I find myself calling out before he gets too far.

He pauses instantly, quick to glance over one broad shoulder.

I swallow. 'You were pretty special yourself.'

Perfect white teeth flash. 'Thanks, baby.'

Something hot curls at the base of my spine. 'But I'm better.'

His bark of laughter fills the entire room. 'Oh, I know.'

'Are you . . .' I pause, cock my head, half-joke, half-actually-ask, 'Are you gonna be mad when I beat you?'

That smile falls away. Head shaking, he drags a palm over his buzzcut, and then, a second later, that palm is cupping my hip. He closes the distance between us in the literal blink of an eye, so sudden I instinctively take a step back. But I don't go anywhere, he doesn't let me, his fingertips curl beneath the tight elastic of my swimsuit, hold me in place, make me shiver.

'No, Daniela,' he says, firm and deep and unwavering. 'I will not be mad when you beat me.'

I swallow again, finding it a lot harder than I did a minute ago. 'You sure?'

'Anyone with half a brain would be turned the fuck on by how good you are. And I've got a whole one.'

I swear I hear the distinct clunk of my jaw hitting the tiles.

I'm sure I'm bright red, sure I visibly tremble when he snaps my swimsuit against the sensitive skin where my hipbone curves, sure I'm losing my fucking mind, because when he walks away for a final time, I want to chase after him like a needy puppy.

I don't, though. I stay exactly where I am. I curl my hands into fists, I mentally slap myself across the face, and I demand that my good sense comes the fuck back to me.

'You're such a fucking idiot, you know that?'

Yup.

That'll do that.

With a sigh, I brace my hands on hips and paste on my best, bored expression. 'Talking to yourself, Ben?'

My ex scowls. And then he winces because I guess such a fierce expression pulls at the bruise still mottling his cheekbone, at the tiny split in his top lip. 'You see what he's doing, right?'

God, I can't wait to hear this. 'Enlighten me.'

'He's distracting you, Dani.'

I bristle at the accusation. 'I'm not distracted.'

'Yes, you are, and you're gonna fuck up the race.'

I scoff at the audacity, laughing at how ludicrous he is.

'He wants to win,' the freaking devil on my shoulder sneers.

'Then he'll win, and it won't be because of me.'

'You're delusional.'

'You're one insult away from drowning.'

Ben's nostrils flare, but I'm saved from any more of his temper tantrum by a whistle blowing, leaving him no choice but to stomp toward the starting blocks because he's the leader in our relay.

Sienna lines up behind him. She tries to talk to him, but he straight up ignores her – I spend a split second feeling sorry for her before imaginary scarlet letters spelling *fucked my boyfriend* flash above her head. Third in our relay, I take my time slotting in line, leaving a healthy amount of space so the blind rage I consider synonymous with the duo in front of me makes way for my focus to snap into place.

Almost into place. It cracks for a second, letting through a tiny sliver of indulgence that guides my gaze sideways. To Heath, first in his line, no longer smiling. Locked in. He lowers himself into the pool, ready to launch into that unbeatable backstroke, and even though my intense stare must be pretty freaking close to tangible, he doesn't look my way. He's completely focused.

Anyone with half a brain would be turned the fuck on by how good you are.

I swallow thickly.

Yeah, I get that.

FOURTEEN

A POINTY BLACK HAT SETTLED CROOKEDLY ON HER head, Imani holds a long, black dress to her chest and assesses herself in the mirror opposite her. 'This is too lazy, right?'

I shrug. I have no idea. I am not the authority on appropriate Halloween costumes; for almost every haunted holiday of my childhood, I wore the same pair of cat ears and called it a day. A tradition that, as quickly becomes clear, is not going to fly this year.

Trailing my fingers over one of the many clothes racks in this store, all of which are stuffed to the brim with every costume you could think of, I wrestle out a sweeping, high-collared cloak. 'If witch is too lazy, then I'm guessing vampire is too?'

Sighing, Imani drops her unsatisfactory loot. 'Find anything?'

'Nah.' Not that I'm really looking. I don't really understand why we're dressing up in the first place, but I've already made the mistake of questioning whether it's entirely necessary. Apparently, Halloween is not just for children. And according to Imani, it is absolutely vital that one is properly, spookily adorned for the occasion – according to Imani, it's the most important holiday of the year, and I think that, if I dared not join them on whatever mysterious venture she has yet to properly detail, the consequences could be dire.

Clumsily swishing a flimsy styrofoam sword through the air, she sidles up to my side. 'You wanna crash at mine after?'

Unsurprisingly, my first instinct is *no*.

Surprisingly, the initial impulse to refuse is fleeting. Chased away by something oddly needy. I've never been one to fear missing out, but as I imagine being alone in my apartment while the festivities continue on without me, I kind of get what FOMO is all about. 'Uh, yeah. If that's okay.'

'More than.' She flashes me a warm smile, giving me a nudge. 'Anyone you wanna invite out with us?'

Belatedly, I realize that I probably say *no* a little too quickly.

Too nonchalant, Imani presses, 'No one at all?'

'Nope.'

'Really?'

'Keep going,' I drawl, with some exaggerated nonchalance of my own, as if this line of inquiry doesn't make my stomach hurt. 'There are at least three more ways you can call me a friendless loser.'

Slender fingers flick the curve of my shoulder. 'Hey, I have it on good authority that you have at least five friends.'

'Oh, yeah?' I muse absent-mindedly, distracted by a gorilla costume that smells like it might've actually been peeled off a gorilla. 'Who?'

Silence falls. When I glance at Imani, I find her brows high, her expression twisted by some combination of pity and amusement and *duh*.

Flushing a little, I look away. 'Oh. Right.'

Her, and her friends. *Duh*, indeed.

With another gentle nudge, she moves around the clothes rack until we're face-to-face. 'Can I ask you something that might sound really shitty and judgy, but I'm honestly just curious?'

Hesitantly, against my better judgment, I nod.

'Why don't you have any other friends?'

The question hits me like a punch to the gut – more so, the realization that no one's ever actually asked me that before. I don't think anyone's ever even thought it. It's just . . . assumed. Like the answer is obvious. There's always a *this is* before the *why*, and it's never a question, never a doubt. 'I'm not a very friendly person.'

'Oh, *bull*.'

'I'm just . . . not very good at relationships. Talking to people. I don't really *like* talking to people. Plus, I barely have time to, like, be alive, so I don't think I would be great at nurturing friendships.'

'You're doing just fine right now.'

I start to smile, only to stop when I remember that we're not actually friends, are we? She's Heath's friend. They're all Heath's friends. I'm just a temporary addition. When this whole fake-dating deal thing comes to its inevitable end, it'll just be me again.

Good, I force myself to think. *Everything will go back to normal*.

In a bid to distract myself from that surprisingly sobering realization, I hold up a blue-checkered dress stuffed in a clear plastic bag. 'What about this?'

With a dramatic gasp, Imani snatches the Dorothy costume right out of my hands, and I swear a lightbulb goes off above her head. Loudly deeming it perfect, she sets off toward the cashier, throwing a comment over her shoulder about how Matilda has the perfect pair of red heels for her to borrow, about how her friend would be the perfect Glinda – *you can be Elphaba,* she practically squeals, and I work real fucking hard to stop my face from showing just how much I detest that offer.

Because I have a sneaking suspicion that if I don't leave this store with a costume of my own finding, that witch hat will find its way to my apartment, I renew my efforts tenfold. I swear, I've damn near gone through everything in the store before something catches my eye.

Head crooked thoughtfully, I pick up the lone starfish hair clip from a huge pile of random accessories. The slightest shift of my gaze, and a stack of stencils suddenly makes itself obvious. Snagging one, I flag down Imani and hold up my meager finds, hoping she gets where I'm going, and she likes it.

I take another squeal as emphatic approval.

I thought that the Haven Cove University library would actually provide some semblance of peace and privacy.

Oh, how dare I.

Slouched in an armchair with my knees tucked to my chest, an open textbook balanced on my thighs, and a highlighter poised above the relevant paragraph, my vision suddenly goes dark.

I don't even startle – I recognize the scent wafting around me even before a voice croons, 'I've got a bone to pick with you, young lady.'

Peeling a pair of calloused hands away from my face, I tilt my head back and feign a concerned frown. 'Is this some kind of foreplay?'

I swear Heath's cheeks go a little pink. 'No.'

'Hey,' recapping my highlighter, I hold my hands up, *'I'm* hardly gonna judge you for *your* sexual preferences.'

Slowly, Heath drops to a crouch at my side, his forearms stacked against the arm of my chair, his head cocking at a cheeky angle. 'You wanna talk about sexual preferences, baby?'

Unfortunately, I definitely go a *lot* pink. *Anyway.* 'You mentioned a bone?'

I literally watch a dirty joke flash through his brain.

'Heath.'

He sighs, but he spares me. He gives my ponytail a tug before rising and circling around to stand in front of me, towering over me, making a dirty fucking joke flash through my own damn brain.

Long fingers twitch where they settle on trim hips, but, again, Heath cuts me a break. 'Heard you went shopping for Halloween costumes.'

Spoken like an accusation, yet I fail to see the crime. 'Yeah?'

'You didn't consult me.'

Consult? As if I need his permission? My eyes narrow. 'I would choose your next words very carefully, young man.'

Knuckles turning white, Heath swallows. 'Huh. Maybe this *is* one of my sexual—'

'Oh my God, *Heath.*'

Again, he shows me a little mercy, and I wonder if this is some kind of self-control record for him. 'I thought we could match,' he tells me, almost whining. 'Y'know, a *couple's* costume.'

I barely restrain a shiver. 'I think I'm morally opposed to doing that.'

'*Wow.*' Jesus, if I didn't know any better, I'd think he actually looks offended. 'You ever match with Ben?'

'God, no.' I never dressed up with him at all. Strangely enough, none of his suggestions – including, but not limited to, slutty nurse, slutty nun, or, ironically, slutty Glinda the Good Witch – ever took my fancy.

Moderately consoled, Heath's frown lessens ever-so-slightly, but that indignant pout remains.

I roll my eyes – and have to try so freaking hard not to smile. 'I'm sure Kiki would match with you if you asked nicely.'

With an exaggerated scoff, Heath drops to sit on the low table in front of me. 'Well? What did you get?'

'I'm not telling you.' I laugh, stretching out to kick him playfully. 'You'll probably turn up in the same thing.'

'Would not,' he grumbles. Catching my offending leg, he holds it hostage on his lap, fingers locked around my ankle, thumb tracing the protruding bone. 'I don't get a hint?'

'No.' It's hardly a revolutionary costume, and he's too smart for a hint. Plus, Halloween is, like, two weeks away; he can wait. 'Patience, *cariño*.'

He sighs again, but the noise is sated this time. His eyes flutter shut for a moment, heavy-lidded when they lock on me again. 'Now, that's definitely one of them.'

It takes me too many seconds to realize we've circled back to the whole sexual preferences thing. When I do, I choke on my next breath, digging my heel into his thigh until he lets me go. 'You're distracting me.' I kick his shin gently, retreating quickly before he can catch me again. 'Get out of here before someone sees you. This is enemy territory, y'know.'

His mocking laugh echoes around the empty library. 'I'm shaking in my boots, Dani.'

'*I'm* busy.'

'Good God, woman. I come here to thank you for all your wisdom and this is the response I get?'

'What?'

He fiddles quickly with his phone. When he shows me the screen, the Cove College student portal is pulled up. 'Got that practice essay I submitted last week back.'

More invested than I have any right to be, I snatch his phone so I can get a better look at the little box stamped with his name and a grade. '*Heath*,' I all but screech, entirely too loud for a library setting. 'That's a B!'

He smiles. 'That's a B, baby.'

A little excited noise I don't dare to call a giggle escapes me. I warble his name again. I'm practically bouncing in my seat. It's a practice essay, for fuck's sake, that has no actual bearing on his final grade, yet I throw myself at him like he's just won a fucking gold medal. 'I'm so proud of you.'

With zero hesitation, he wraps me up in his arms, something like satisfaction warming the skin of my neck where he nestles. 'It was all you, really.'

'Shut up.' I pinch the sliver of lower back exposed by his shirt riding up – I briefly lament our current position preventing me from being able to get a peek at the tanned, toned skin. '*You* wrote it.'

'Using *your* notes.'

'Oh my God.' Groaning, I reel back. I swear I mean to gently slap a little sense into him – somehow, I end up cupping his face instead. 'Stop that. You did good. Let a girl be proud of her boyfriend.'

Pretty eyes blink and widen.

'Fake,' I rush to spit out, to amend. '*Fake* boyfriend.'

'Right.' Something flashes across his face, gone before I can decipher it, forgotten when he twists to kiss my palm. 'Thank you, Daniela.'

I swallow thickly, my gaze fixed on the spot where his lips meet my skin. 'You're welcome.'

'Got you something.' Barely leaving my grip, he reaches for his bag. A second of blind rustling later, something dangles in my peripheral vision. 'Well, *made* you something, technically.'

Head turning, my lips part with entirely too sharp an inhale. God, I'm embarrassed by how gingerly I take the little item from him, how reverently my thumb traces the smooth edge of a cornflower-blue miniature surfboard, how hard I laugh at the tiny letters carved onto the nose, encircled in a crooked heart. '*Death*?'

'Dani and Heath,' he informs me, as if it's obvious.

I laugh again. I love it. I don't think I've ever loved anything more. I grin like a loser as I snag my keys and, using the chain drilled into the tail between two teeny fins, attach it to my key-ring. 'You really made this?'

'I am a man of many talents.'

Do I hallucinate the sly, seductive note to his tone? Probably. All this smiling is making me downright silly. 'I can't wait to see what you get me when you pass this class.'

'A full-size one,' he promises, and I don't even get the chance to delve further into that little nugget of information, because, abruptly, I realize that my hand is still on his face. Because I feel the pull of his muscles as his mouth curves upwards, feel that dimple form, feel the weight of his head just a little more heavily. 'But this is for something else, actually.'

'What?'

'You forgot about our one-month anniversary? I'm wounded.'

'It's been a month? Really?'

'Time flies when you're having fun, huh?' He kisses me again, my wrist this time, before standing. 'You doing anything tonight?'

Dropping to my lap, my hand feels so very warm as it curls into a ball. Toying with my little present, I try to remember the last time something made me feel so *fuzzy* – I fail to recall *ever* feeling fucking fuzzy. 'I have practice.'

'After?'

I shake my head.

'Wrong. We're having dinner. My place.'

'Shouldn't we, like, go out? Be seen?'

'Do you wanna go out?'

'No.'

With a smug little brow pump, he repeats, 'My place. We'll take pictures. The internet will disintegrate with jealousy.'

My head ducks, hiding a too-big smile. 'You cooking?'

His mouth quirks. 'Actually—'

An abrupt yell cuts him off. Yell*ing*, I should I say. Lots of it. A hell of a commotion coming from somewhere within the shelves.

'Is that who I think it is?'

Nose scrunched, I grin. God knows I would recognize Ben's disapproving tone anywhere – Sienna's shrill squawk is pretty recognizable too. Their argument, on the other hand, isn't so clear. But even though I can't hear exactly what they're saying, it doesn't take a genius to figure out the furious gist.

'Damn.' Heath lets loose a short whistle. 'That doesn't sound good.'

'Sounds pretty good to me.'

He shakes his head, tutting. 'Reveling in their misery. Shame on you.'

'Oh, you'll *hate* to see me when they break up.'

'You're rooting for that?'

His crumpled brow causes me pause. 'Of course I am.'

That frown of his gets even harsher. Jesus, I better not ever let it slip that sometimes, occasionally, I hope they fucking die. Peacefully, of course, like, in their sleep or something, but still.

'Did you forget that, at my core, I am a bitter witch?'

'Can't forget something I never thought in the first place,' he corrects, so smooth, all honest. 'Just forget sometimes that you care about him.'

'Cared,' I correct, nose crinkling. 'Don't anymore. Wish I never did.'

Heath doesn't quite look like he believes me. He looks . . . worried, almost. He tries so valiantly to hide it, though, that I pretend I don't notice.

Hot breath brushes my neck, commanding me to go, 'Harder.'

Huffing hard enough to displace the loose hair around my face, I really put my weight into the smooth, methodical movements.

Inked, ring-adorned fingers sweep my hair back, tug on the tail of my fishtail braid. 'Too hard.'

'Do it yourself, then,' I snap over my shoulder, and a low laugh pimples my skin with goosebumps.

Heath moves from my back to my side, arms crossed as he leans against his kitchen island. Wearing a boyish, goofy smile, he dips a hand into the open bag of flour on the counter and flicks his white-stained fingertips at me. 'Then it wouldn't be you learning to cook, now would it?'

Deadpan, I contemplate lobbing the entire ball of yet-to-be-properly-kneaded dough at his head. 'This is why you've never had a girlfriend,' I grumble, and not for the first time in the past hour. 'Because you invite women over for dinner, and then you make them make it.'

'Hey, baby, this is your bucket list.'

'It's not a bucket list.' It's not even a list. It was just . . . *thoughts*. Throwaway ideas, coaxed out by him, now being used by him for his own personal freaking gain.

While I'm hard at work perfecting my dough – my third batch because I already made pasta, and my first garlic rosemary focaccia . . . well, I maintain that Heath set me up by handing me sugar instead of salt on purpose – he leisurely sips wine. Stirs the simple tomato sauce bubbling on the stove every so often. Instructs me like he's the fucking Barefoot Contessa. Granted, my own wine glass is regularly refilled. Sure, every dirty dish I create is promptly washed. Yes, we both wear aprons, *matching* fucking aprons, two stained swathes of fabric printed with commands to *kiss the cook*. And I swear that when I put my pasta in the pantry to rest, I spotted a suspicious oiled, covered bowl that could definitely be some kind of back-up, but still. I feel obligated to point out, 'This is a very old-fashioned picture.'

As he knocks back merlot, Heath laughs over the rim of his glass. 'Yeah, I'm practically a caveman. Man teach woman cook. Grunt grunt.'

I elbow him, fighting a smile. I've been fighting smiles since I found a freaking cooking show waiting for me, ingredients neatly laid out and a damn *mirepoix* – said in a very sorry rendition of a French accent, I have to note – already sautéing. Because despite all my grumbling, I'm enjoying myself. The cooking and the wine and the banter, the soundtrack Heath had no reservations informing me was *painfully curated* – I can admit that I like it.

It's *how much* that's the problem.

It's a date, I said earlier, without even thinking about it, and, shit, that's exactly what it feels like. There isn't any motive. No one to make jealous. Nothing to study. It's just us. Hanging out. Alone.

It's intimate – that's my real issue. Even as I finish with my bread and Heath whisks it away to rest, and we move onto making meatballs. I'm fucking massaging raw meat with fingertips that reek of garlic, Heath is laughing at the faces I'm pulling, I'm kicking his shins, we aren't even actually dating, and there's a silly little parasite in my cerebrum thinking *teehee. How romantic.*

It's not a date, yet it's the best date I've ever been on – that's the fucking root of it. And a pretty sobering thought too. Something I'm sure I'll pick over relentlessly the minute I'm alone.

'So,' Heath pulls himself up to sit on the counter. 'How was your day, honey?'

I let a greedy gulp of wine speak for me.

'Your team giving you shit?'

If *shit* is a synonym for *cold shoulder,* then sure. Plenty. But I'd rather not get into it, so I shrug. The second his mouth opens again, I slap a hand over it. 'Can we please talk about something else?'

A whine heats my palm, but Heath nods. Nipping me hard enough that I pull away with a laughed curse, he snags my hand within his own and rubs soothing circles over the imprint of his damn canines. '*Fine*. Ask me how my day was.'

Stifling an eye roll, I oblige. 'How was your day?'

A pale brow crooks expectantly.

This time, I don't stifle anything. '*Honey.*'

His sigh is so pleased, it makes my stomach hurt. 'My day was fine.'

'Just fine?'

'Hm. Sucks when being a college student means you actually have to go to classes, hey?'

'That's the best part of my day.'

'My little freak,' he croons softly, so obviously joking, but it still pokes at a sore spot.

I snatch my hand away, curling it into a fist behind my back while the other tightens around my wine glass so much, I half-expect the stem to snap. 'God forbid I worked my ass off to get a scholarship and I actually wanna keep it, *hey*?'

'Woah, baby.' Heath lunges for me before I even make it two steps away, pulling me close again and trapping me between his spread thighs. 'I was kidding.'

'I like school,' I snap, I *defend*; I'm so used to having to do it, it comes naturally. 'You like taking on the ocean and hoping you won't drown. But I'm the freak?'

'You're not a freak. I'm sorry. I shouldn't have said that.'

Arms crossed, I tuck my chin to my chest and stay quiet.

'Is there anything about you,' he says quietly, so cautious, 'that Ben didn't rip to fucking shreds?'

I inhale sharply. Jesus, it isn't fair, how he can not only see right through me, but fucking crawl inside my head and sift through my thoughts until he finds exactly what he wants to know. 'He used to get irritated,' I quietly start, and, I swear to God, it's as if he's pulling the words out of me, 'when I didn't wanna, like, let loose and party in the off-season. When I wanted to stay in and study instead. Always asked why I bothered studying when I had swimming, like he couldn't fathom that I just liked doing it. Sometimes I think I like it more than I like swimming because it doesn't feel as hard. I'm just good at it. Like you're good at—'

'Everything?'

Deadpan, I peek up at from beneath my lashes. 'Being an egotistical dick.'

Heath clunks his forehead against mine. 'All I just heard was *good* and *dick*.'

I make up for the laugh that sneaks out against my will by digging my knuckles into his solar plexus. I try to push off him, away from him, but those muscular thighs tighten, keep me exactly where I am. 'I thought you had a sports scholarship.'

'And I thought you knew everything,' I toss back. 'No. Academic.'

His fingers dance up my arm, chuck beneath my chin. 'My little *genius*.'

The praise flushes me hot. Burns the attitude right out of me. The instinctual defensiveness holding me taut slowly subsides, and as the steel rod in my spine melts, my body does too. I wish I could blame the wine for how completely I slump against Heath, but I would be lying. It isn't alcohol making me drunk, but the sincere apologies and sweet praise. Such a damn novelty, they make me dizzy.

As my cheek finds the hard plane of his chest, his touch curls around to my nape. Flutters down my spine to the very base, where it dips beneath the waistband of my pants to palm bare skin. 'I just don't get it, Dani,' he murmurs against the top of my head. 'Why you stayed with him for so long.'

I offer the same, paltry excuse I gave his friends. 'It was easier.'

'Than?'

'Breaking up,' I say, my tongue working of its own volition, spilling secrets. 'Being alone.'

His heart thumps beneath my cheek. A rapid staccato, such a contrast to his smooth, rumbling, 'You lonely, Daniela?'

'I like being alone.'

'Not what I asked.'

I don't really know the answer. I do know that it's complicated. And I know that when I reel back just enough to peer up at him, to meet the gaze already trained on me, I'm telling the truth when I say, 'I'm not right now.'

'Good.' Fingers slip beneath my shirt and drag a slow path to the curve of my ribcage, blunt nails tickling my sides. 'Am I making you uncomfortable?'

'I don't think anyone has ever made me more comfortable,' I admit. Because it's the truth, and I think he deserves to know it.

A rough noise rumbles deep in his chest.

'What?'

'Nothing. Just . . . thinking.'

'About?'

His gaze zones in on my mouth. He swallows. 'Dark hallways.'

My breath catches. 'Oh.'

With laser focus, he watches the unsteady rise and fall of my chest. He touches it, his palm pressing between my collarbones, fingers splayed wide. 'I have a theory.'

Keep it to yourself, my common sense urges. Every other part of me is responsible for a low 'Go on.'

His hum is a frustrating denial. 'You're gonna spook.'

'Don't bring things up, Belfort, if you're not brave enough to follow through.'

'You know how many times I watched Ben kiss you?'

'Considering your stalker tendencies, I'm gonna go with a lot.'

He grunts. 'I watched *Ben,*' he repeats, he emphasizes, 'kiss *you.* It was never you kissing him.'

My cheeks flush, and his thumb swipes over one of them, like he's trying to rub the crimson stain away. 'It wasn't *never.*'

'It was barely ever. And you never kissed him like you kiss me.'

'I was never putting on a show.'

'See, I don't think that's it. I don't think – no, I *know,* there isn't anything wrong with you. You're not the problem.'

'So my subconsciousness was so repulsed by Ben, it sabotaged my libido? That's your theory?'

'Just saying it didn't feel very sabotaged with me.'

'Sounds like an egotistical theory.'

'I'd call it wishful thinking.'

'What're you wishing for, exactly?'

He looks at my mouth again – I'm already staring at his. It holds all of my attention, is the focal point of my thoughts. I wish I could blame the wine, I wish I could blame anything other than plain old human want, but I *want* that mouth.

I think, if not for the sound of the front door slamming shut, I might've taken it.

Instead, as dual feminine voices call out greetings, I try

valiantly to get the hell away from that mouth. But, once again, Heath won't let me go anywhere.

'Your sister's gonna think we were doing something,' I protest, as I try to wriggle free, casting a panicked glance at the doorway, waiting for the sounds of Saylor and Lyla shedding their outdoor layers to become the sounds of them walking down the hall.

Heath grunts, hands vice-like on my hips. 'She's gonna *know* we were doing something if you don't cover me.'

'We *weren't*—' My mouth snaps shut so fast, my teeth clink together. Before I can stop myself, I look down. Briefly. Barely. Just long enough to get an eyeful of the bulge tenting his sweats, and then I'm looking literally anywhere else.

The ceiling is getting a pretty healthy dose of my attention when Heath chuckles roughly. 'Nothing sabotaged about my libido either, Williams. Not when it comes to you.'

A sick little thread of satisfaction makes a mess out of me – it dies a painful death the moment Saylor saunters into the kitchen, a knowing quirk to her mouth, her hands braced against her daughter's shoulders, holding her back. 'Are we interrupting something?'

Maybe my squeaky 'nope' would be more convincing if it wasn't contending with a massive shit-eating grin. When I pinch the crook of his elbow, Heath sobers. 'Dani wants you to know we weren't doing anything.'

Silently, I plead with the ground to open up and swallow me whole. Not that much louder, I hiss, 'I hate you.'

Lips pursing to stem a smile, he smacks a kiss on my cheek.

Perhaps a touch childishly, I wipe it off. Definitely a little maliciously, I pull away enough for panic to flare in those sea-glass irises, but it's just so I can turn around, so I can flash a small smile at Lyla as she wriggles free of her mother's grip and skids toward us.

Head angled curiously, the kid hits us with a level of scrutiny far beyond her years. 'Uncle Heath, why does your girlfriend hate you?'

The arms wrapped tightly around my middle constrict playfully. 'It's her love language.'

'Uncle Heath, why is your girlfriend so red?'

'She's just so full of love.'

The five-year-old looks dubious. 'Is it because you were kissing?'

I choke.

'Jesus, Lala.' Muffling a chuckle against my ear, Heath shakes his head at his niece. 'You're gonna kill her.'

'How—'

'*Okay.*' Coughing to disguise a laugh of her own, Saylor grabs her daughter again and steers her out of the room. 'Let's go, little one. Bath time.'

While Heath promises leftovers in their wake, I just barely resist the urge to beg them to stay. Because they leave, and my embarrassment at getting caught goes with them – my embarrassment at what we got caught *almost* doing sets up shop. What *I* almost did.

Clearing my throat, I cautiously peel Heath off of me. This time, he lets me go. Physically, at least. I move out of his reach, not even looking at him, and yet still the mere low, casual gravel of his voice has me standing to attention. 'If you ever wanna test that theory.'

I hold my breath.

'Test it with me.'

My lungs deflate with loud, bemused noise. 'What's in it for you?'

'What do you think?'

I think lots of things. Silly things. Presumptuous, impossible things that are ridiculous notions compared to the very obvious reality. 'One-upping Ben really does it for you, huh?'

His smile falters. I almost think I might've gotten it wrong – I might've gotten it right in other ways.

And then he nods. 'Exactly.'

FIFTEEN

THE GIRLS SCREAM WHEN THEY SEE ME.

Wincing, I thank my past self for pre-emptively finishing my costume with a pair of earplugs.

'Heath's gonna pass away,' Matilda declares, as she scurries across her kitchen, wine clumsily sloshing over the rim of a very full mug – suddenly, the barely intelligible *come in* that was just hollered at me through the front door makes sense.

Because I figured this night was going to be long and busy and socially draining enough, I declined their invitation to get ready together. Clearly, I missed some integral drinking time, and the bickering I assume ensued when Matilda decided against being Glinda. There isn't an ounce of pink to be seen on her body, but there is a whole lot of body bared by her costume – a pixie? A woodland deity? Something winged and floral and almost naked that makes me feel a lot better about being so scantily clad myself.

Shimmying excitedly, Matilda the Drunk Fairy emphasizes her friend's apparently imminent demise. 'He is literally going to die, Dani.'

'Huh. Fitting for the occasion, I guess.' Half-smiling, I fiddle with the straps of my . . . well, I wouldn't really call it a top. More of a bra adorned with beading and shells that hang down and string across my stomach, which is otherwise completely bared by a low, slinky skirt that flows down to my calves. Everything is in shades of blues and greens and pearlescent purples, just like the shimmering scales I painstakingly painted onto my face, my neck, and across my ribcage, using that stencil.

For so little, it's a lot. I didn't really know how far I was supposed to go. How much I should commit to embodying one of those nicknames of mine and being a siren for the night.

Toying with one of the braids I weaved the front pieces of my hair into, I try not to grimace. 'I don't look ridiculous?'

'Oh, you do. But, like, complimentary.' Imani crooks a long, red fingernail at me, brandishing the camera clutched in her other hand. 'C'mere. I need to immortalize this.'

I groan, but I go to her. Shit, I kind of want to immortalize this too. Sure, I think I look ridiculous, but not because I think I look bad. Just a little over-the-top. I am very sure that I look very hot. I'm also very sure that, wherever we're going, I'm going to be very cold, but hey. Such is life. I'll live.

I open my mouth to ask where, exactly, that is, since no one's provided me with any details beyond the fact we're going to a party, but new voices and heavy footsteps interrupt me.

'*Wait,*' Matilda calls out to the boys, and the footsteps come to an abrupt stop. Launching herself at her purse, where it's strewn on the counter, she pulls out her phone. 'I wanna record this.'

Imani hums in agreement, her camera poised too. 'Good idea.'

Resisting the urge to duck and fucking hide behind the counter, I settle for closing my eyes for a steadying beat. 'You guys are so dramatic.'

'No, we're not. You're just that hot.'

Wolf-whistling her agreement, Matilda hollers for the boys to enter.

Contrary to popular belief, Heath does not lay eyes on me and immediately perish. However, he does . . . malfunction or something. He's last in the door behind our sober designated driver for the evening and a not-so-sober Kai, and while Brendan offers vague compliments to all three of us girls – though they're spoken while staring straight at Imani – and the latter wolf-whistles shrilly enough to bust eardrums, Heath says nothing at all. He freezes in the doorway, wide-eyed and gawking right at me.

'What're you supposed to be?' I taunt, curiously taking in a backwards black baseball cap, an oversized t-shirt layered over a baggy long-sleeved top, a pair of equally loose sweats, and scuffed sneakers.

Still, he says nothing. He only snaps out of it when Kai slaps him upside the back of his head. 'Compliment her already, dickhead, or I'm gonna. Explicitly.'

Heath coughs, chokes, as if he's coming back to consciousness after a period in stasis. 'Sorry. I think I just died for a second.'

The girls cackle.

Literally stumbling, Heath makes his way toward me. His hands find my hips only to immediately retreat, only for him to hiss like my bare skin has fucking burned him, only for him to replace his grip just as quickly. 'Jesus, Dani.'

He's drunk. Not, like, *drunk* drunk, but tipsy at least. No way he would be looking at me like that, with such blatant heat, if he was in full control of his faculties.

He did the other night, my consciousness takes great pleasure in reminding me. *And it felt just as good as it does right now, didn't it?*

I punt that thought right out of my brain before it starts to fester. Before it swells to an *over*thought, and I ruin this night for myself before it even begins.

Pasting on my best attempt at an easy smile, I slink my arms around Heath's neck. 'Down, boy.'

He lets loose a canine yip that makes me laugh. His hands shift, flat against my lower back, dangerously close to caressing a different part of my anatomy entirely, 'You look . . .'

His pause lasts too long, and I cluck my tongue impatiently. 'Go on.'

'Can't.' Two thumbs dig into each of the dimples framing my lower back. 'Broken.'

God, I like this too much. 'Maybe Kai can help you.'

'Kai can die.'

I snort, the pads of my fingers scraping over short, bristled hair before touching sturdy fabric. 'Seriously,' I pull back a little, scanning his outfit once more. 'What are you?'

'Seriously,' he sighs like he's offended I don't know. 'You've never seen *Step Up*?'

A vague bell rings in my distant memory. 'Oh. You're the hot dancer guy?'

'Yes, I *am* hot. Thank you, Dani.' Heath pats the curve of my ass. 'We're adding a movie marathon to that list of yours.'

'Kinky.' Matilda waggles her brows suggestively as she hands out drinks, and admonishes everyone for *not being on her level*. 'Where were you guys?'

'Nowhere,' the trio of guys chorus too quickly, exchanging looks that have us girls frowning at each other.

'Well, that was believable,' Imani drawls. 'Try again.'

While Tweedledee and Tweedle-fucking-dum gaze at the ceiling, Brendan mumbles around the rim of his cup. 'We just had something to do.'

'Like what? Egg a house?' Matilda jokes.

None of the guys laugh.

'Oh my God. You were egging a house? Are you twelve?'

Some kind of internal alarm buried deep inside of me starts to wail. A sixth sense for fuckery. 'Who's house?'

No one answers – each of them make a really obvious effort not to look at me.

I study Heath. That gaze, cast low. The jaw, wound tight. The neck muscles beneath my palm, hard as rock. The very picture of guilt. 'It was Ben's, wasn't it?'

'We plead the fifth.'

'What the hell?' Matilda huffs, wings flapping erratically as she drops her hands to her hips. 'And you didn't invite us?'

'It was a crime of passion,' Kai insists.

'Very spur of the moment,' Brendan adds, in support of his friend's claim.

Looking me dead in the eyes, Heath nods solemnly. 'Not at all a premeditated offense.'

There's a beat of silence. And then Imani, slow and sarcastic, starts to clap. 'And the Oscar for worst acting ever goes to . . .'

Beyond flashing a trio of matching middle fingers, the guys

ignore her. Each of them are focused on me, gauging my reaction, braced for it.

I think they each have a little teeny tiny heart attack, born of complete shock, when I smile. 'I think that might be the nicest thing anyone's ever done for me.'

'Baby, that's incredibly sad.'

My head falls to one side as I sigh. 'Why do you have to ruin it?'

'Did I say sad? I meant sexy.'

'Hm.'

My eyes roll, and, God, Heath's entire fucking face lights up. He licks his fucking lips, and I would have to have the self-control of a god to resist rising up on my tiptoes and pressing my mouth to his, just for a silly, self-indulgent second. Not for show even a little. For no one but myself. Just because I want to.

'Hey.' A dramatically cleared throat draws my attention sideways, to Kai, as he waves a questioning hand between him and Brendan. 'We did it too. Where's our kiss?'

Heath literally growls. A commitment to our little arrangement, or actual, genuine jealousy, I can't quite tell. I don't get the chance to dwell because he's kissing me, hard, eyes half-open in a glare he fixes directly on his snickering best friend.

'Rein it in, you two.' A hand that does not belong to Heath whacks my ass – by the way he jolts, I'm pretty sure Imani gives him a slap too. She throws a wink over her shoulder at both of us as she saunters into the hallway, red heels clacking against the tiled floor. 'We've got trick or treating to do.'

While everyone else hoots and hollers their excitement, I frown. 'Seriously?'

'You know Bay Avenue? That street where, like, half of Cove College lives?'

My nose wrinkles as the name rings a particularly grating bell. *Cove College, and one little Haven Cove University intruder.* 'Yeah.'

'Every year, they do their own version of trick or treating.'

'Let me guess, they're not giving out candy?'

'Depends on your definition of candy,' Kai croons.

'It's usually cheap vodka Jello shots. Every house has a different flavor, you dip in, take a shot, move on to the next place, pick your favorite party, y'know.'

I don't know, but I get the gist – I cross my fingers and pray it's not quite the hellscape I'm imagining.

A warm hand engulfs mine, squeezing. 'We can leave if it gets too hectic.'

I side-eye Heath. 'Are you my boyfriend or my babysitter?'

Humming teasingly, he leans in for a quick, chaste kiss that feels too natural for my own good. 'The first one. Thank God.'

'I was wrong,' Matilda warbles into my ear as we amble down Frat – sorry, *Bay* Avenue. Our arms linked at the elbow, she bumps her hip against mine playfully. 'Heath's not gonna die. He's gonna kill someone.'

Tearing my intrigued gaze away from the couple in front of us – seriously, does no one else notice something between Imani and Brendan? – I sigh wearily as I glance over my shoulder at the pair taking up the rear of our group. Just as I did five minutes ago,

I find an uncharacteristic scowl marring Heath's face. 'What's his problem?'

'Mankind. Emphasis on the man.'

'What?'

With a sweep of her arm, Matilda draws my attention to the gaggle of bros on the other side of the street, walking parallel to us, eyes on us. My mood instantly sours, my face contorting to match that of the man skulking a few steps behind me. Yeah, I'm not a fan of that brand of *man*kind either.

Obnoxious, cat-calling, *I scream profane commentary at women and it definitely makes them want to sleep with me* mankind.

'What?' I question again. 'One of them praise the tightness of his ass?'

'No, one of them praised yours.' Her elbow nudges my ribs. 'He's jealous, Dani.'

'Oh, no, he's not.'

'Oh, yes, he is.'

'He's not like that.'

A *ha* booms out, loud and borderline mocking. 'He is one hundred per cent like that. Are you kidding? Jesus, even when you were with Ben—'

Her mouth snaps shut.

Mine opens to a painfully intrigued gape. 'What?'

Matilda blinks. 'Huh?'

'When I was with Ben . . . *what?*'

The flimsy wings strapped to her back flutter as she shifts awkwardly. 'Did I say that?'

'Uh, *yes*.'

'Well.' She titters nervously, swishing a dismissive hand through the air. 'I'm drunk.'

'Matilda.'

'Oh, look at that.' Detangling herself from me, she gestures wildly at the nearest house. 'Last stop. We're here.'

'*Hey—*'

Shrieking something unintelligible, she takes off across the street. Like, at a dead-damn-sprint. She literally flees the conversation, leaving me gaping in her wake. I'm still there, still gaping as the others follow her, when Heath catches up to me.

'If you're gawking at those guys, I might actually lose it.'

'God, you know me so well. I *love* gross frat boys. Do you think the skinny one will call me *mamacita* again if I ask nicely?'

'He did *what*?'

'I'm joking.' *I'm so not*. 'I was gawking at Matilda.'

'Plot twist.'

I backhand his chest semi-gently. 'She said something weird.'

'Likely thing for her to do.'

'When I was with Ben—'

Heath hisses. He literally fucking hisses and makes the sign of the fucking cross, and I think that if I try to bring up my ex again, he'd pretend to faint like a stricken, offended maiden.

'There is something deeply wrong with all of you, you know that?'

Teeth playfully catch the tip of my nose, making it scrunch. 'That's why we're so fun.'

My eye roll makes him smile, makes him kiss me, before he wraps his hand around mine and tugs me in the others' wake. His grip tightens as we cross the street, and his expression does too, eyes narrowing as we near that group of guys. 'Enjoying yourself?' he mumbles without looking at me, too busy re-enacting a freaking Western showdown.

'Uh-huh,' I reply, with less enthusiasm than is warranted because I actually have been. The crowd is a lot and this street has some kind of weird barrier that traps sound and heat and amplifies both, and despite how hard I try to forget the sugar content in Jello, it never quite leaves my mind. But . . .

I'm in a group. I'm with friends. With people who know me and like me anyway. People who included me like I'm not just their friend's girlfriend. People who see my ex from a distance and screech *denied, scumbag* before he can get within ten feet of me. I've never had that before. I really, really like it.

I also really, really like when the bones in my hand are intact so, with a grunt, I wriggle myself free from Heath's constricting grip, and hook my fingers around his waistband instead. 'They're really bothering you, huh?'

'They're not bothering you?'

'Not my first day being a woman, Heath.'

He grunts, glaring as the objects of his irritation saunter inside, practically foaming at the damn mouth as he moves to follow.

Tugging firmly on his waistband, I make the wise decision to guide him elsewhere instead. 'If one of us fights someone every time we go out,' I start, as we pick across the front yard toward the side gate, 'we're gonna get a reputation.'

Heath grumbles a laugh, nudging me aside when I'm not quite tall enough to reach over the gate to unlock it from the other side. When the bolt slides free, I push it open and lead Heath into a relatively empty backyard, but that's not our final destination.

I keep walking, Heath dutifully following, all the way to the very back of the enormous yard until we reach an outbuilding that's the size of most people's actual houses.

'This is where you murder me, isn't it?'

I snort. Rising to my tiptoes, I reach for the flowerpot hanging beside the entrance, fumbling blindly in the dirt until my fingers close around a key. 'You know who owns this house?'

'Someone living with excess wealth?'

'Well, yeah,' I concede, even though that's not my point. As I push open the double doors, I don't dare to flip on the flights, but it's pretty easy to make out where we are anyway – the pungent reek of ammonia certainly gives it away. 'Letty St James. Captain of the Haven Cove University swim team.'

Owner of her very own Olympic-sized swimming pool, courtesy of her very own Daddy Warbucks.

An impressed whistle echoes off the flat water, rebounding off the high ceiling and windowed walls.

'Why are we here?'

'Being around the water always calms me down. Thought it might be the same for you.'

'*Sea*water,' he jokingly corrects, but the soft smile he shoots me is appreciative. 'You've been here before?'

'Once.' Freshman year, just after I made the team. Right

before Letty learned that I was better than her. The first meet we swam, I crushed her times, and, shockingly, I never got invited back here.

'You wanna go in?'

I laugh.

He isn't joking. 'C'mon, *sirena*. You're dressed for the occasion.'

'I can't swim in this.'

'Then take it off.'

'Excuse me?'

'Hey, I'm just tryna broaden your horizons here. Remember? Things you've never done because of swimming?'

'Yeah, I don't remember skinny-dipping being on the list.'

'Huh. Must've been on mine.'

I shove him with a huff.

He catches himself just in time to avoid plummeting into the pool fully-clothed – something he soon rectifies. His hat comes off, his tops next, and his sweats are pooling at his feet by the time I finally get myself together.

God, those abs are distracting.

When he starts plucking at his waistband, I screech his name. He holds his hands up with a sigh. 'Fine. Semi-skinny-dipping it is.'

'Have fun.'

'Please. Pretty please. For me?'

I snort.

'I'll buy you something pretty.'

Another snort, although marginally less snide this time.

'I'll race you.'

My interest piquing is literally audible. Slowly rocking back and forth on the balls of my feet, I hum thoughtfully. 'Two hundred meters?'

'Are you trying to kill me?' He scoffs. 'One hundred.'

'And I get something pretty.'

'Sold.' He seals it with a handshake and then he's gone, hauling ass toward the far end of the pool, like if I take too long, I'll change my mind.

Which I do, a little. I reach behind me and my fingers hover over the clasp of my bra, hesitating.

'Oh, come on,' Heath yells, throwing his hands up. 'We have a deal.'

'I, uh, don't have anything on under this.'

'Wear my t-shirt.'

And lose because sodden excess fabric is holding me back? That competitive little devil on my shoulder revolts.

They're just boobs. Nipples. Pectoral muscles. Heath has them too, big ol' developed ones that he flashes on the regular, that would honestly probably fill out my bra pretty damn well. It's no big deal.

You're not shy, I remind myself.

'Turn around.'

'You know my mouth—'

I shut him up with a scowl and a particularly vulgar gesture. With a wink, he turns – he even covers his eyes, earning himself another middle finger that he must sense because he laughs.

Quick, before I can over-think it, I unclasp my bra and let the material fall away. I wriggle out of my skirt and start toward the end of the pool, kicking off my heels as I go.

'You know,' he starts again, in that same teasing tone when I take my place beside him and give him the all clear to turn around. He faces forward before uncovering his eyes, not even looking at me, but I swear I feel the rake of his gaze anyway. 'I have really good peripheral vision.'

'Beat me and maybe you'll get a little full-frontal.'

I swear I hear him choke a little.

Positioning myself to dive, I grin. 'Ready?'

In my own peripheral, I watch him shake himself out before assuming the same position. 'Baby, you are so fucking on.'

I'm halfway through my first lap when I realize that there is a distinct lack of excess splashing coming from beside me – I hit the wall and turn, and I come to an abrupt stop when I realize that there is a distinct lack of *man* beside me.

'Excuse me?' I holler, treading water on one side of the pool while Heath grins at me from the other. 'I was promised a race!'

'Sorry,' he yells back, not looking very sorry at all as he lounges against the pool's edge. 'Got distracted.'

'By?'

'You. You're too fucking talented. You need to be watched.'

'I *need* to charge if you're gonna gape like that.'

'I can't see anything good from here.'

'All of me is good.'

He doesn't argue. Pushing away from the wall, he dives

underwater, swimming half the length of the pool before coming up for air. At a leisurely breaststroke, he continues his approach.

I resist the urge to retreat. The closer Heath gets, the harder my limbs have to work to keep me afloat. I'm a D1 swimmer, for God's sake, and I can barely break the surface, everything submerged but the crease of my chin and up.

Bobbing only a couple of feet away, he stares at me like there's a whole lot more than my face on show.

'You trying to burst me into flames or something?'

'I'm trying not to look at your tits.'

A good thing too, or else he might notice how hard my nipples suddenly get. 'You've looked at them before.'

As he loves to point out, they've been in his fucking mouth.

'Oh, constantly,' he finds such little shame in admitting, I can't help but laugh. 'Think of all the times you've caught me and times that by, like, ten.'

'Pervert,' I accuse.

'Man,' he corrects.

I cock my head. 'Difference?'

'*Ha ha.*'

A thick forearm swishes through the water, creating a veritable tidal wave that half-drowns me. I'm spluttering a curse and swiping chlorine from my eyes, when the air . . . shifts. Warms. *I* warm, from the tips of my ears right down to my toes, and especially the curve of my hips where submerged hands suddenly hover. Even before I open my eyes, I know how close I'm going to find Heath – not quite inescapable, but unavoidable all the same. 'Is this how you normally pick up women?'

Wide eyes blink in a poor attempt at innocence. 'Other women exist?'

God, I hate how hard that makes me smile. 'Cute.'

Beneath the water, short fingernails graze the underside of my ribcage. Barely a touch, yet my back arches. 'I prefer ruggedly handsome, but thank you.'

'You take everything as a compliment, don't you?'

'I take what I can get from you.'

That is not dirty, I chide what must be my faulty hypothalamus. *You cannot make that dirty.*

'You're doing it again.'

I can barely swallow. 'Doing what?'

A thumb swipes beneath my eye. He doesn't say it, but I hear it nonetheless – *you look like you want to kiss me.*

My lips part, but a denial does not come out.

Gentle pressure urges me through the water until my back meets the pool wall. While Heath braces a hand against the edge, I brace mine against his chest. Fingers curled, nails pinching skin. 'Daniela.'

'Heath.'

'I'm gonna kiss you now.'

'Why?'

'Because I really, really want to.'

I repeat, 'Why?'

He groans, his forehead falling to my collarbone, and I swear I feel his tongue dart out to taste my skin. 'I take it *because I do* is not an acceptable answer?'

'It's too complicated.'

'It's just a kiss, honey.'

'No, it isn't.'

He doesn't disagree – he doesn't back off either. 'Ten seconds, Daniela. Brace yourself or get out.'

I do neither. I don't move. I cling to the pool's edge like a limpet, tense and barely breathing and so utterly unprepared for something I know damn well is going to happen, for something I let happen. Willingly.

More than.

Later, when I look back on this moment, if I even dare to, I might just admit that I'm the one who obliterates that last inch of space between us, and kisses him.

It's the same as always – *always*. Like this is a regular occurrence, as if I'm used to it already. It's messy and a little frantic, like neither of us are entirely sure it'll happen again, like neither of us want that to be the case. We kiss each other like we're each equally sure that the other might realize this is a monumentally terrible idea and change their mind at any minute. We're desperate, and it's so fucking *good*.

As his teeth sink into my lower lip, Heath cops a greedy handful of my ass. He cradles the curve of my neck while lapping wet kisses on the opposite slope. I don't fight him, I fucking encourage him, my damn legs lock around his waist, yet still, I pant, 'This is not very friendly.'

'Who says?'

So true. *So. True*. Plus, how would I know? I don't have friends. I'm not friendly. Maybe friends kiss each other's necks all the time. Maybe heavy petting is just a prerequisite of friendship.

Maybe this is how you're supposed to feel when wrapped around your friend – maybe you're supposed to wrap yourself around your friend in the first place.

'Oh, God.' He laps at a particularly sensitive spot and I shiver. My legs tighten, drag him a little closer, and, *God,* he's hard. He's so fucking hard. Hard and perfectly slotted between my thighs at just the right angle, nudging just the right place. 'Fuck, *Heath.*'

With a groan that makes me tremble, he takes my mouth again, our tongues a rough tangle. While my fingernails gouge marks in his shoulders, his fingertips leave bruises on my ass-cheeks as he guides my hips into maddening rolls that he meets with eager thrusts of his own.

I need to stop. I need to *still.* My entire body is throbbing, my skin *hurts*, and if he keeps grinding on me like that . . .

An orgasm hits me before I even recognize that's the sensation I'm rapidly hurtling toward. A choked moan ripping out of my throat, I lose the ability to do anything but writhe and pant and *come.*

It's not until my body goes slack that I realize Heath has gone completely still. Not until the pleasured fog clears do I clock the slack-jawed, deer-in-fucking-headlights look on his face. 'Did you just—'

'No.' Flushed so hot I'm surprised the water around me doesn't start bubbling, I scramble for a grip on the wall behind me, clumsily hoisting myself up and out. 'Nothing happened.'

Heath says my name, and nothing else. He makes no move to follow me. Every part of him is frozen, except his eyes; they track me as I use his t-shirt to roughly dry myself off. Carefully. Intently. Tangible and too much.

I snap, '*What?*'

'Nothing,' he lies, taking pity on me. Or maybe he senses that if he even thinks about making a single joke, *God,* I actually might drown him.

Fuck, I might drown myself. This is . . . *fuck,* me and humiliation have developed quite the repertoire after the past few months, but this has to take the cake. Coming all over the guy I begged to pretend to be my boyfriend after only a few minutes of *barely* third base activity.

I would laugh at the universe's cruel sense of humor, if I wasn't on the brink of fucking tears.

Dropping to a crouch next to our stuff, my hand shakes as I pluck my bra from the pile. 'Then get out and get dressed.'

'I, uh, can't right now.'

'Why not?'

'Because I'm one wrong move away from coming in my boxers like a fucking teenager.'

I still. My clothes flutter to the ground as my grip goes slack, my entire body does. He . . .

I swallow. Lick incredibly dry lips. Slowly turn toward him and quietly rasp, 'Really?'

Face contorted in a wince, he nods.

The muscles in my lower stomach constrict. 'Did you . . .' *Don't ask, Dani. Do not ask*. 'Did you want to?'

Without hesitation, he nods.

Don't, I command myself again, but it's not my mouth I'm

talking to this time. It's my brain. My silly, hormonal brain thinking silly, hormonal things. Entertaining silly, hormonal fanatics. Conjuring up silly, hormonal ideas.

Like what if we didn't stop. What if I didn't get out of the pool. What if I . . .

I stand up. Heath looks down almost immediately, something akin to misery flashing across his face. My legs tremble as I walk toward him and resume my crouch poolside, and my voice isn't all that steady either. 'Do you still want to?'

His breath hitches. 'Can I?'

I wobble as I move to sit with my legs dangling in the pool, the cool water a welcome balm to my overheated flesh. 'Fair is fair.'

It will make you feel better, I tell myself. *It'll be even then. The scales will be balanced.*

That's why you want it to happen.

Heath parrots my words beneath his breath, an odd tone to them, like he can't believe he's saying them, or that I did.

I don't actually know what I'm expecting to happen. If I just . . . *offered* something, or if he's going to take matters into his own hands.

I would laugh at my word choice, if I wasn't so busy trying to remember how to breathe as he does exactly that.

My view is distorted by the water, but I'm sure the image of his hand slipping into his boxers will be clearly imprinted in my brain for the rest of my life. I can't see the most intimate of details, but the muscles working in his biceps, the veins bulging beneath his skin as he . . . and his face . . . and his hand on my thigh, digging desperately into my skin . . .

Fuck.

I squirm, and his grip tightens. He pulls my legs apart. Stares at the space between them that only aches worse under his fevered gaze.

'Please let me touch you.'

'I don't think that's a good idea.'

He lets out a frustrated groan. His cheek falls to my thigh. Pants wash over my skin, heavy-lidded eyes flutter, and, Jesus, I don't think I need him to touch me. I think I might get there all on my own.

I reason that it's fine for me to touch him. It's safe. But my fingers ghost the back of his head and his groan doesn't feel very safe at all. I swear it reverberates right down to my bones as he buries his whole face against my thigh, lasting all of five seconds like that before he's tilting his chin to gaze up at me again.

My hand slips to his nape, curves around his shoulder, cups his neck. I feel his pulse, his rapid breath, him leaning into my touch, shifting toward my palm so my hand brackets his throat, so I'm—

My first instinct is that he's making fun of me. But, no, his eyes are so bright, he's groaning so loudly, he's writhing beneath the water, making the surface ripple with how hard he fucks his hand.

My grip tightens.

After that, it doesn't last very long. *He* doesn't last very long, and he blames me. He chants my name as he accuses me of making him lose his mind, he sinks his teeth into my thigh and punishes me for the inconvenience, he thanks me as he licks a path all the way up to the crease of my pelvis where he collapses, groaning, shivering, spent.

For a long while, he doesn't move. He pants, collecting himself, nuzzling me gently and mumbling things I don't hear – or rather that I don't comprehend because a family of bees have suddenly set up camp between my ears and they won't stop *buzzing*.

His head flops to the side. He looks up at me, he just looks, that's all he does, yet my whole body seizes because, while I'm one wrong move away from disintegrating, he's the picture of serenity. He's not freaking out. This is a regular occurrence for him. For him, casual intimacy is not an issue; I've heard the locker-room stories.

'Fuck,' he breathes an exhausted laugh. 'That was—'

'An experiment,' I butt in. It's the first thing that comes to mind. He said it himself – college is for experimenting. It's a great excuse. It's the only thing I can get past the pure panic clawing up my throat. That, and 'Testing the theory.'

'Right.' His teeth grind together as his jaw locks. 'Results?'

'Inconclusive.'

'Right,' he says again. 'Dani—'

'Can we not?' I beg, my voice a rough rasp as genuine dread claws up my throat again. 'Can we just . . . can we pretend that never happened?'

He tries so hard to hide it, to keep a blank face, but, nevertheless, the flicker of hurt that echoes across his features is glaringly loud. 'What?'

'I just . . .' I struggle for the right words. 'I feel like we just did something that we can't take back and it's gonna change things, and I really like how things are right now.'

The water ripples as he pushes away from me. Goosebumps race to cover my skin as he lets go. For a horrifying second, I'm sure he's pissed; I grip the edge of the pool hard enough to hurt, bracing for him to hurl the frigid, heartless accusations I've heard more than once before.

When he doesn't, I'm disappointed – not in him, but in myself for forgetting, for a split second, that Heath is good. Heath is kind. Heath smiles – a little wan, a little reserved, but warm nonetheless – and so easily nods. 'Nothing is different,' he rasps, and relief has my entire body going slack. 'Nothing happened.'

SIXTEEN

'GOT A LITTLE WET TONIGHT, HUH?'

In the middle of dragging yet another wipe over the fake scales making a mess of my skin, I freeze. Steeling myself, I look away from my reflection in the small mirror I hold a few inches from my face, and tilt my chin toward the man sprawled on Imani's bedroom floor beside me. 'What?'

'Your hair.' Kai reaches for me, twirling a still-damp strand around his finger and tugging. 'You go for a swim?'

'Oh. Uh. Yeah.'

It's literally tangible – the shift of mild curiosity to much stronger, mischievous intrigue. 'What did you think I meant?'

Though my mouth remains shut, I fear my flaming cheeks give me away.

Luckily, an interruption saves me from an interrogation.

Knuckles rap against the door a second before Brendan peeks around the edge, his Chucky costume gone and replaced with pajamas, though fake blood still stains his red hair. 'Heath in here?'

'Said he had to go home,' Imani replies from the en suite, yelling to be heard over the running shower.

Blue eyes drop to the checkered dress discarded on the floor.

Brendan swallows. With a sharp nod, he disappears, leaving me with the acrid tang of guilt coating my tongue.

I didn't know Heath had left. We all walked here together; I figured he was staying over too. I'd resigned myself to a sleepless, fretful night spent thinking myself in circles and avoiding his gaze – which I'll probably still have anyway. Without that last part, but with the added knowledge that I drove him away from his friends.

'Lover's quarrel?'

The shake of my head is slow, and not anything close to convincing.

'Are you—'

'Leave her alone, Kai.' Emerging from the bathroom wrapped in a silky bathrobe, Imani kicks her inquisitive friend as she walks past us on her way to her wardrobe. 'Go make yourself useful. I want a large Hawaiian pizza on my doorstep by the time I'm dressed.'

Though he gags at her choice, Kai dutifully climbs to his feet. On his way out the door, he makes sure to shoot me a look that promises *this isn't over*.

'And a Veggie Lover for Dani,' Imani calls in his wake, bent at the waist as she shimmies into a pair of boxers. 'Light on the cheese.'

I don't get the chance to insist that I'm not hungry – or to marvel at the odd, simple loveliness of someone knowing my fucking pizza order. Quickly pulling on a t-shirt, Imani drops to sit cross-legged opposite me. 'Okay.' She claps her hands together before clasping them in her lap. 'Spill. What happened?'

Too quickly, I blurt, 'Nothing.'

Brows high, Imani snorts.

'Y'know, it's not really any of your business.'

'It's not,' she agrees. 'But I think you should tell me anyway.'

Her hand lands on my knee, and I swear to God, it plucks the fight right out of my body. Rasping an exhale, I close the mirror still in my grip with a snap, my fingers closing tightly around it. 'I—' I start and fail, and try again. 'I like Heath.'

Imani's gasp is a gentle tease, not quite mocking. 'I know, babe,' comes out genuine, soft. 'I have eyes.'

I huff, frustrated. She doesn't get it, she doesn't know, she thinks I'm a real girlfriend confessing feelings for a real boyfriend, she thinks I'm allowed to have feelings, she thinks I just go around having feelings for people. 'I mean . . . it doesn't . . . It doesn't feel *right*,' I do a piss-poor job of trying to explain. 'It feels like too much.'

Sympathy marks soft lines in her expression. 'Oh, Dani.'

As my fingers rise to rake over itchy skin, my gaze drops to the floor. 'And tonight we, uh, hooked-up.'

'Did he . . . did he do something you didn't want?'

'*No*. God, no. I, uh, wanted it.' My ears burn so hot, they fucking ring. 'I really wanted it. I liked it.'

'That's good,' she almost questions. 'You're supposed to.'

'I know, but *I* don't. Not all the time, not usually. I'm not, like, interested.'

A soft *ah* makes my stomach hurt. 'It freaked you out.'

Barely, I nod.

Floorboards creaking beneath her, Imani shifts closer until

our knees touch. A cleared throat is an obvious demand, and when I begrudgingly look up, I realize I was wrong. That isn't *sympathy* she's wearing – it's *empathy*.

'I'm like that too, kind of,' she admits, with none of the shame that plagues me. 'Can't get off with strangers, can't relax enough. It only feels good when it's someone I really know.' Imani looks down, watching her fingers as they fiddle with the hem of her t-shirt, a faint smile twisting like a frown. 'Someone I care about.'

Like Brendan? I almost ask, but I don't dare. Whatever's going on between them is not something I should be wading into – I do, just for a second, let myself dwell on the fact that I *want* to.

And then I move on.

'I think,' I slowly mouth, 'that's what it is for me too. Kind of.'

'With Ben,' Imani starts, and the mere mention of the man is enough to make us both grimace. 'What was it like?'

'Good at first,' I say, and I mean it. Because it *was* good, the beginning of things between me and him. It wasn't always bad. 'Then fine. Then . . .' I trail off, hoping a wave of my hand is an adequate replacement for the right words. 'He used to . . .'

'Make you feel like it was your fault?' Imani rightly assumes. 'It wasn't. I would say it's no one's fault, however I do have this weird instinctive urge to blame Ben for literally anything and everything.'

I snort – God, do I share that urge.

'Have you talked to Heath about it?'

'A little.'

'And?'

There's nothing wrong with you, Daniela, echoes around my skull. *Not a single thing.*

I picture him last night, recall the awe in his eyes as he gazed up at me, the erratic flutter of his pulse beneath my fingertips. Flushing, I tuck my knees up to my chest and hide behind the curves of them. 'You were right. He's a really good guy.'

'Yeah.' Pride stretches her mouth wide. 'Matty and I trained him well.'

For a split second, I feel that weird almost-grief again as the *what could've been* of it all hits me. As I imagine what it would be like to have friends you grew up with, friends you can't remember ever not knowing; what it would've been like to have *these* friends, specifically. 'I didn't mean to chase him off tonight.'

'You're not responsible for things he does of his own free will, Dani. He wanted to give you space, so he did. Simple.'

Simple, she claims, but it doesn't feel so to me. 'I just feel guilty.'

'Well, stop it.' She playfully reprimands me with a backhand to the shin. 'He's a big boy. He can survive one night on his lonesome. Although,' her mouth crooks, momentarily wicked. 'I guess he's got some pretty good memories to keep him company, huh?'

I choke on a shocked, scandalized squeal of her name.

She only smiles wider. 'Long night ahead of him, I bet.'

My hands slap over my face, hiding my mortified flush, muffling a strangled laugh. '*Shut up.*'

'He's gonna show up looking like Popeye tomorrow.'

I laugh so hard, my stomach hurts. Hands dropping, I shift my weight so I can free the pillow lodged beneath my butt and use it as a weapon rather than a cushy seat.

Yelping, Imani bats off my attack. It takes her a second to grab a pillow of her own and retaliate, getting in a hard thwap to my ribcage that I return.

'Aren't you supposed to be naked for that?'

Pausing, we both turn to the doorway – we both roll our eyes at Kai, who leans against the doorjamb, pumping his brows suggestively.

With outraged noises, we launch our pillows at him. He catches them easily before tossing them back, *ha ha'ing* mockingly when he hits us both square in the face. 'Your abominations to Italy are here,' he calls, as he disappears again, footsteps taking him back down the hall, 'and you have five seconds before I feed them to the rats.'

Clambering to her feet, Imani suggests he do something a lot more vulgar with them. As she drags me up too, I make a face. 'You guys have rats?'

She shakes her head, snorting. 'Our neighbor has a Chihuahua pack.'

'Ah.' I snicker, sobering quickly when Imani moves to leave the room. 'Hey.' I grab her, gently pulling her to a stop. 'Thank you. For listening.'

Without missing a beat, she throws an arm around my shoulders and squeezes me tight. 'Thank you for talking.'

I wake up rather abruptly when someone, unwelcome and unceremonious, sits on me.

'Morning,' Kai sing-songs, clearly unperturbed by my

grunt-slash-growl and the vicious scowl one half-cracked eye shoots his way. Tilting a deep, plastic bowl toward me, he shakes it so the wrapped candy within rustles. 'Want some?'

My nose literally turns up. 'It's—' I reach for my phone where it sits face-down on the coffee table and check the time, '*—eleven?*'

'Is that a question?'

No, it's an anomaly. I am, and I always have been, a natural early riser. I can't remember the last time I slept until eleven. I don't think I've ever slept until eleven. I know I had a late night – how people who spend almost every waking hour together still have so much to talk about at two in the morning, I'll never understand – but still. Sleeping until almost midday?

As if a fire is lit under my ass, I buck Kai off and scramble off the sofa that served as my bed last night. I might not actually have anything I need to do today, no class or practice, but I never just waste a morning like this. I get in a few laps or I run or I study, I find something productive to do, I never just do *nothing.*

'Good God, woman.' Snagging my wrist, Kai yanks me back down. 'Stop moving. You're making me nauseous.'

'I think that's the Tootsie Roll you're having for breakfast.'

'Don't be ridiculous.' He scoffs. 'I had Twizzlers for breakfast.'

I'm one hundred per cent sure that the look on my face is nothing short of horrified. Kind of like how Kai looked at me last night when he discovered my apparently criminal lack of a sweet tooth – Mounds bars being the exception to that genuinely had him reconsidering our friendship.

Snorting, he elbows me. 'Heath's in the kitchen making real breakfast. Strictly protein powder and egg whites.'

I flick him on the forehead as I get up again, sticking my tongue out as I stoop to steal a Snickers bar just to irk him. So busy snickering at the boyish outrage that follows me out of the room, I'm already in the kitchen by the time what Kai said actually registers.

I'm already freezing at the sight of Heath standing in front of the stove.

Silent and still, I stare. Almost against my own fucking will, as if it's some intrinsic, unnegotiable instinct, I gape at the gray compression shirt molded to his upper body, perfectly showcasing every muscular flex as he stirs something in a pan and sways to low music. He croons along, and I flinch when I don't hear the lyrics, but instead the dirty praise he rasped against my thigh last night. One arm rises and his bicep flexes, and I remember how every vein and tendon and muscle jumped in tortured pleasure. When he scratches the back of his neck, his body twitches in something I only recognize as a wince once I notice the thin red scratches marring his nape.

Little half-moon shapes that, if I had to guess, are the exact width and thickness of my fingernails.

Talk to him again, Imani had quietly urged me before we turned in for the night, when too much pizza was sitting heavy in my stomach, fatigue and comfort weighing down the rest of me. *Trust me, you'll feel so much better.*

I might've agreed last night. I might've even thought about calling him before I went to bed – that might've been the last thought on my mind before I drifted off to sleep.

Last night, I wasn't a coward. Evidently, right now, I am.

A brisk draft draws my attention to a sliding door left open. A second later, I'm slipping outside, shivering as winter proves it has well and truly arrived. Ominous clouds contribute a drizzle that threatens to be more, and my borrowed pajamas provide very little protection, but the cold feels nice. Calming. Clarifying.

Not quite so much that I realize hiding in the rain is entirely pathetic, but enough to temper the anxious rash already wreaking a little havoc.

Mindlessly scratching my chest, I scan the yard in search of somewhere semi-private to collect myself – I refuse to call it a hiding spot. Almost immediately, my gaze snags on something suitable, and on bare feet, I pad across the grass to the hammock strung up between two trees. One pear, one apple, Matilda's pride and joy, I vaguely remember being told.

The sparse branches don't provide much shelter, the rope is frayed and the fabric ever-dampening, but as I clumsily roll into the cotton cocoon, I sigh with relief. I settle in the center, and the excess material comes up high either side of me, creating makeshift walls that block everything but the gloomy sky above me.

Under different circumstances, I would like this a lot; find it peaceful. Except, right now, my racing mind won't allow that. My relief is only fleeting. I can only be a little coward for so long.

I just need a second to gather my thoughts. Think up what I'm going to say. How to properly convey these silly little feelings of mine. My crush. Because that's all it is, right? A crush. Confusion, really, in its basest form. I'm simply not used to being treated the way Heath treats me, and it's fucking with my head. I'm fucking with my own damn head. I—

'Morning.'

'*Jesus.*' As my little sanctuary gives a dangerous rock, I scowl at the face suddenly blocking my view. 'That's it. You're getting a bell.'

Heath snickers, the sound more reserved than it should be. No suggestive remarks leave his lips – just a soft little sigh. 'Gotta say,' he muses, fingers curling around the hammock as he drops to a crouch, tugging the material down with him, and the movement forces me to roll onto my side, to roll closer to him. 'Not a fan of this sneaking-out thing.'

In lieu of denying it, I just shrug.

'How are you?' comes out stilted, careful, too formal, and I don't like it, and how hypocritical of me is that, huh? Considering his caution is only born of my panic? 'Sleep okay?'

Again, I shrug. 'You?'

He shakes his head.

Long night ahead of him, I bet.

Of their own volition, my thighs squeeze together tightly. *Fucking Imani.*

Heath cocks his head curiously. 'What?'

'Nothing,' I rasp.

Tutting quietly, Heath taps my temple. 'Let me in.'

'No.' I lick my lips, and his gaze drops to watch. 'It's for your own good. You'd crumple like a leaf.'

With a weary sigh, he stands.

Just as I'm wondering if a bad night's sleep is all it takes for him to finally reach the limits of his tolerance for me, the hammock jerks roughly as Heath fucking throws himself into it. I curse as I'm almost sent to a grassy demise, and again when my comfortable sprawl becomes a lot tighter of a squeeze. 'Excuse me,' I grunt, as an abnormally large foot comes entirely too close to kicking me in the face. 'Can I help you?'

'Yeah, by moving over a little.' Heath shifts too enthusiastically, almost upending our precariously rocking perch again. 'Jesus, how did you look so comfortable? This is awful.'

'Well, I wasn't sharing it with *you*.'

'Save all that contempt for the bedroom, baby.'

My wriggling comes to an abrupt stop.

As if anticipating an escape attempt, long fingers lock around my ankle. 'Smooth segue, huh?'

'Like sandpaper.'

His laugh is just as rough.

One last adjustment and then he stills too, curled on his side to face me, the curves and contours of his body perfectly molded to my own. 'Hypothetically,' he starts quietly, hand sneaking beneath the cuff of my borrowed pajama pants to draw mindless patterns on my calf. 'If I hooked up with a girl last night—'

'Heath—'

'And,' he cuts me off, voice firm while his eyes cast a soft plea, 'she wants to act like it never happened, what am I supposed to do?'

'Act like it never happened, probably.'

'Probably. Thing is, I'm not much of an actor. But this girl . . .'

'What about her?'

'Well, I obviously upset her last night, and I'm not real fond of that. And if I upset her some more, if she decides she's had enough and leaves me in the dust . . . well, shit, Dani, I think I would just die.'

Eyes rolling, I dig my knee into the stomach pressed against it. 'Little dramatic.'

'You haven't met this girl.'

'She kinda sounds like a mess.'

'No one's perfect.'

I pinch the thin skin above his ankle bone. Cautiously, I roll onto my back because it's a lot easier to talk to the sky than it is to him. 'Maybe she's scared.'

'Oh, she definitely is.'

'Maybe,' I continue with a huff, 'this girl doesn't hook up often. Ever.'

'She doesn't.'

'Do you wanna have this conversation by yourself? Since you know all the answers?'

Silence settles. An encouraging squeeze is bestowed upon my ankle.

'Maybe you and her are already in a really complicated situation. Maybe she panicked a little, a lot, because . . . well, maybe things have been really good lately, but there's an expiration date on these things, and she's scared of getting in any deeper than she already has because she's already pretty sure it'll hurt like hell when it ends.'

'Just because it ends doesn't mean it *ends*. Even if we're not dating, Dani, we'll still be friends.'

If, my brain vaguely catches, *not when*. 'Really?'

'You can't honestly think that everything that's happened in the past month has been for Ben's benefit.'

'Obviously not,' I grumble, glowering. 'For his *detriment*.'

'Oh, silly, beautiful woman.' Heath groans. There's a rasping sound as he rakes both hands over his head and down his face. The hammock rocks again as he half sits up, just enough to loom over me. 'Very little of what we do is because of Ben. Last night is at the top of that list, by the way, in case that crossed your mind.'

I look away, a little ashamed that it did. 'We have a deal.'

'Yeah, we do, but we also have a relationship. A *friendship,*' he clarifies, almost like he's correcting himself, like he needs the reminder. 'I like being around you, Daniela. I like *you*. I've always liked you.'

My heart jumps. 'What?'

At my disbelief, Heath shakes his head. 'C'mon, Dani. You don't think that, if it wasn't for Ben, we would've been friends a long time ago?'

Just like that, I plummet back down to earth. *Friends*. Right. Silently, I laugh at myself for even briefly assuming anything different. 'I've never thought about it.'

'I have. A lot. And I think that we would've been,' he hesitates for a split second, making me think that he was going to say something other than 'best fucking friends'.

I can't imagine it. Not because it's so unimaginable – God, it's almost too easy to imagine – but because it hurts. It's fucking painful to think that if I'd just stayed single, my life might've been a little better. A little easier. A little friendlier. 'Why?'

His smile is sweet enough to make my teeth hurt. 'Because we are now, aren't we?'

'I mean,' I somehow manage to correct around the sudden lump in my throat, 'why do you like me?'

His face twists like the question baffles him. 'Why wouldn't I?'

'People don't like me.'

'People don't *get* you.'

'And you do?'

'God, no.' He smiles crookedly. 'But I like the challenge.'

My gaze drops to his throat as a rough swallow scratches my own. 'Is that what last night was? A challenge?'

'No. Fuck, Dani, *no*.'

The raw panic fueling his denial makes my lips twitch. 'So I'm easy.'

'*No*—' His vehement refusal comes up short. His eyes narrow, zone in on the subtle upward curve to my mouth. 'You fucking with me?'

'Maybe.'

'Unlikeable, my ass.' *My* ass, meanwhile, he almost freaking slaps, just missing it to catch the curve of my thigh instead. 'Enough. You're getting me off track. Last night—' Long fingers wrap around my calf and squeeze. 'It happened. I don't think we should pretend it didn't because it wasn't a bad thing, okay? We did nothing wrong, nothing to be ashamed or embarrassed about. We just had some fun.'

Fun. Right. Exactly. We did have fun. I had fun. I enjoyed it before my head got so involved. God, he makes it sound so easy.

So normal. Which I guess it is. We're hardly the first friends to ever hook up on a drunken night out, right? I'm probably not the first that he's—

Nope. Not going there.

Following the stroke of a calloused thumb along my Achilles tendon, I rasp, 'Yeah.'

'It was . . .' His movements stutter for a second as he clears his throat. 'Good? For you?'

My cheeks flush as I nod.

'Yeah?'

'Jesus, do you need a fucking poem? You were there. You saw.'

I wait for his expression to turn smug. For that pure male satisfaction guys get when they manage to do the bare minimum. Instead, I get the very opposite. Rosy cheeks and a lowered gaze and a hand that's not quite steady as it drags over a shaved head, and a smile I wouldn't dare to call shy, but, fuck, that's kind of what it looks like. 'Good,' he croaks. 'So we're good?'

'We're good,' I confirm, and I can't actually believe that it's the truth. Mostly. I definitely feel better.

A crooked pinky extends toward me. 'Promise?'

Laughing, I hook my finger around his. 'Promise.'

SEVENTEEN

I SPEND A LOT OF TIME RAKING THROUGH MY MEMORY, searching for more of the little moments I must've missed. Forgotten because I deemed them unimportant at the time – because I deemed *Heath* unimportant.

I've always liked you.

My bottom lip already chewed raw, I click the back of my pen against an almost blank page of my notebook relentlessly. I scan the scarce scribbles, and I laugh beneath my breath. Instead of the notes I should be taking for the lecture I'm currently more than halfway through, I wrote a list. A meager, pathetic list. The few instances I can recall that made it very clear that Heath didn't just view me as the surly girlfriend of his sworn enemy. That he didn't interact with me for the sole purpose of pissing off someone else.

The Little Prince incident tops the list. I was alone. No one around to witness our conversation. God, I was hiding, wasn't I? Tucked around the back of a building after sneaking out the service entrance. He would've had to be actively looking to find me. He had no reason to talk to me other than he just fucking wanted to.

I can recall at least half a dozen times when he was trading quips with Ben but looking at me – and quite a few more when he was looking at me, just leisurely looking, like he had all the right in the world to do it, and all the time too.

He knows my drink order. He knows what I like to eat. He knew to bring earplugs on a night out. That night on the beach, that very first night, he brought me rum, and he knew I might not want it.

Pool is etched in teeny, tiny, barely distinguishable letters. Because it doesn't count. Fondling me in a pool a couple of weeks ago provides approximately zero insight into how he's felt about me over the past couple of years. Everything that happened after, though; how he treated me, everything he told me . . . well, that's friendship, isn't it?

And then there's freshman year. The Cove College and HCU swim teams held a joint welcome mixer for prospective new members, and a buzzcut blond who smiled bright enough to blind a girl was the very first person to welcome me. My first meet, he shot me a thumbs-up from across the room – now that I'm really thinking about it, I don't even know why he was there. We weren't swimming against Cove College.

To anyone else, it would've been obvious. To me, it wasn't even noticed, and, fuck, that's *sad*. All this time, someone was in my corner, someone wanted me, and I didn't even fucking see it.

It won't do me any good to dwell, though. I definitely shouldn't be dwelling right now. I should be listening to my professor, taking notes as studiously as the rest of my class, *focusing*.

Tucking my hair behind my ears, I roll my shoulders back and resolve to do just that. Except the very second my pen touches paper, a sudden jostle to my chair sends the inky tip flying. Clucking my tongue at the skewed black line cutting a horizontal path across my page, I shoot a glare at the feet propped on the back of the seat beside me.

I don't bother turning around. I've already wasted an hour and a half thinking about a man – I'm not going to waste the extra minute it would take to reprimand whatever asshole in the row behind me desperately requires a footrest all of a sudden.

I do, however, waste a couple of seconds flipping to a fresh page with a little more vigor than necessary. I also make sure my huff is extra loud. And maybe, *maybe*, I scratch the nape of my neck with my middle finger. But after that, I re-focus on the professor as she discusses . . . *Fuck*. I have no idea.

Busy clicking through the lecture slides pulled up on my laptop until I find the one that matches my professor's warblings, I almost don't register the creak of wood as those intruding feet fall away.

I definitely do register the hand that clutches the back of my seat instead.

Without turning around, I hiss, 'Not interested.'

'God damn.' My quick rejection earns a whispered husky laugh – my brows furrows at the slightly distorted familiarity of it. 'Got a boyfriend or something?'

'Uh-huh. Big one. Real scary.'

'I'm not *scary*.'

For a split second, I freeze. Just long enough for a muttered *no fucking way* to make its way into the world, and then I whip around, jolting, not because I find the literal last person who should be in here lounging behind me, but as a last-ditch attempt to escape the flashback that comes hurtling toward me like a metaphysical fist.

Can I? Please. Fuck, Daniela.

A long moment passes before I manage to get ahold of myself, and I know it was a moment too long. A moment too obvious; a mere inch away from my face, Heath's grin reduces me to glass. Makes me feel entirely transparent, as if he can see everything, every last nasty reminiscence.

'What the hell?' I pray I don't sound quite as husky as I fear I do, glancing at the droning professor, who's apparently oblivious to the intruder invading her class – and finding a handful of students who are the very opposite of oblivious, much to their thinly veiled chagrin. 'How did you get in here?'

'It's a university, baby. Not a prison.' In my peripheral, I watch a hand rise. Calloused fingertips graze the underside of my chin, closing my gaping mouth. 'Get your stuff. We're kind of on a time crunch here.'

I shift my gaze from Heath to the professor and back again. 'I'm kind of in the middle of something.'

'Oh, please. Like you were listening.' Leaning even closer, he whispers, 'Whatcha writing?'

Flushing, I hurry to snap my notebook closed. 'Nothing.'

He stacks his forearms on the thin edge of my chair, chin propped on top of them. 'Could've sworn I saw my name.'

'Could've sworn we already talked about you needing glasses.'

'Hmm.' The corners of his mouth quirked high, he moves his chin to the palm of one hand. 'Question. What the fuck does *acephalous* mean?'

I blink. 'How long have you been in here?'

He blinks back. 'Long enough to basically have an anthropology degree.'

'This is a sociology class.'

His hand swishes dismissively. 'Same thing.'

My inner nerd screeches internally. A little externally too. 'It is *not*—'

'Am I interrupting something?'

Jolting again, I swing a guilty grimace toward my professor, my head shaking fervently. 'I'm so sorry.'

'So sorry,' Heath echoes, without even trying to sound like he means it. He stands, and if everyone in the lecture hall wasn't already looking at us, they sure are now. 'But we actually have an emergency.' Snagging my laptop with one hand, he cups the back of my neck and yanks me to my feet with the other. Like a kitten held by the scruff of their fucking neck, I'm guided out of the row and pushed up the stairs toward the exit. 'So sorry again.'

Before I know it, I'm in the hallway. Rushing down it. Skipping class for maybe the first time in my entire life, spluttering at the guy making me do it. 'I'm literally gonna murder you.'

'Later. We're busy right now.'

'I *was* busy. Now I'm being kidnapped. *Again*.'

'Yeah, and you still haven't learned to fight back.'

Goddamn it. When did I start holding his hand? Ripping mine free, I come to an abrupt stop.

Heath groans. His head flops back as he slowly turns, before it lolls to one side. 'Did I mention we're in a rush?'

Only just resisting the urge to stomp my foot like a petulant child, I cross my arms over my chest. 'Where are we going?'

'We're meeting the others at the harbor.'

'Why?'

'It's a surprise.'

'What kind of surprise?'

'A fun one.'

Shockingly, I don't believe him. 'Is it, or is it something you know I'm gonna hate so you're not gonna tell me what it is until we're actually doing it?'

His smile doesn't waver. 'It's whatever will make you come with me right now.'

'Do I get a hint?'

'I already gave you one. Keep up, darling.'

'Heath, I have class.'

'You *had* class. You're hardly gonna go back in there, are you?'

My lips thin. 'That's not the point. I don't have time for this.'

'Well, make some, my—'

'Oh my God, enough with the cutesie nicknames.'

Abruptly, Heath straightens. 'Daniela,' he drones. *'Ma'am.* Come with me, pretty please?'

Stifling a defeated sigh, I look away from the pouting mouth I briefly, involuntarily consider *tempting*. I shouldn't go with him. I should put my foot down. That little stunt wasn't okay, I can't encourage behavior like – *oh my God, I sound like my stepmother.*

And that thought alone is enough to have me conceding. *Kind of.* 'I'm not missing practice tonight.'

'Oh, my—' he cuts himself off before a *pumpkin* or a *sweetheart* or a fucking *pookie* can spill, grinning wryly. 'I would *never* do that to you.'

Haven Cove Harbor is surprisingly bustling, considering the steady drizzle of rain and the brisk November chill. Shivering as the wind nips at the skin my sweater and jeans don't hide, I begrudgingly trudge down the dock – a stark contrast to the man practically skipping along ahead of me.

'For future reference,' I grumble, when Heath eventually notices my leisurely pace and slows to match it. 'This is not my idea of a *fun surprise*.'

'Duly noted.' An arm drapes across my shoulders, stemming another tremble with its heavy warmth. 'I left extra layers for you on the boat.'

Distracted by the sweet gesture, I make it another couple of steps before abruptly coming up short. '*Boat?*'

Over the squawk of seagulls and the low keening of hulls bobbing in choppy water, a bout of snickering announces that I haven't come up short at all; I'm exactly where I'm supposed to be, stopped beside a small vessel with the white cursive words *An Gráinne Mhaol* standing out against the dark navy hull. Crouched over one of the bollards on the dock skillfully unravelling a knot, Matilda grins at me. 'The harbor didn't give it away?'

My middle fingers twitch, but I keep them at bay. After all, she does have a point. Honestly, what did I think we were doing?

How am I still surprised when Heath easily hops onboard and extends a helping hand toward me?

Mine remain firmly stuffed in my back pockets. 'Y'know, I think I really draw the line at stealing a boat.'

'We're not stealing it.' Matilda snickers again as she straightens up. Easily straddling the gap between the dock and the boat, she holds out a hand too, perfectly balanced, not even a little affected by the gentle rocking. 'It's ours. Our dad runs whale-watching tours.'

Eyeing that gap warily, I grumble, 'He's not running one today?'

'No. *We* are.'

We being not just the three of us, I finally notice. Huddled on the stern deck, I spot not only Kai, but half a dozen unfamiliar faces too. Tourists, if I had to guess, all bundled up in lifejackets layered over warm clothing. I squint through the tinted windows of the cabin, and just about make out Brendan at the helm, Imani by his side. While the latter waves excitedly, the former starts the engine. 'Is this free labor or am I getting paid?'

'Daniela.' Matilda's smile sharpens, and her extended hand becomes less of an offer, more of a threat. 'Get your pretty ass on board, please. We're running late.'

Hence why there isn't a gangway to be seen, I guess. Hence why I have to risk a very brisk dip to embark. Which I do, because what the hell else am I going to do? Refuse and watch them chug away, wave them off like a fucking lemon?

No, I take Matilda's hand and I make the damn leap, and I wheeze an exhale when I overestimate said leap just a little and go careening into Heath hard enough to have him thumping against the cabin at his back.

'Jesus, baby.' The hands encircling my waist squeeze gently. 'We're in public.'

Unimpressed, I push down on his wrists until he lets me go. 'You dragged me out of class to go *whale-watching*?'

I try to back up, but Matilda cups my shoulders and shoves me against Heath again, making room for her to slink past. 'I don't think I like your tone,' she shouts, as she rushes to the bow to do God knows what, but whatever it is must mean we're clear to leave because she flashes two thumbs-up at her brother.

As the boat edges away from the dock and the rocking gets worse, Heath takes my hand and leads me toward the stern deck where everyone is gathered. He pauses to holler greetings and a quick introduction that most definitely does not paint me in a great light, considering that we're moving now and the wind has really picked up and I was already cold before, so now I'm freezing, and I do not make the best of impressions at the best of times, let alone when I'm shivering and irritated and on a fucking boat for no good reason.

I sigh with relief when Heath herds me inside the cabin. He points out a cushion-covered bench seat and I sit, grinding out a greeting to Imani and Brendan. My ears already stinging from the cold, I cup them as I scowl and pout and mutter profanities – until I catch sight of my scowling, pouting, muttering reflection in the window opposite me and I mentally bitch-slap myself.

God. No wonder it's taken me twenty-one years to find some fucking friends. Holy fucking buzzkill.

When Heath hands me a lump of clothing, I try my best to paste on a serene smile. I try to sound polite rather than snide as I thank him. My grateful sigh isn't forced, though – I genuinely could kiss everyone on this damn boat as I shrug on a waterproof jacket, a woolen hat, and a pair of gloves too. Heath even wraps a scarf around my neck, tucking it into the neckline of my jacket and tugging the soft material high while urging my hat low, covering pretty much every inch of visible skin.

Reaching up to grab one of the lifejackets suspended from the ceiling, he slips me into that too. As he puts on his own, he steps back and sweeps his gaze over me thoroughly before nodding, satisfied. 'Happy now?'

I pluck at the scarf until my mouth is free. 'Undecided.'

Heath chuckles. Cupping the back of my head, he pulls me in so he can kiss the bridge of my nose; an affection I barely get the chance to register before he's guiding me back outside.

I don't know anything about whales, and I can't say it's exactly a burning interest, so as Matilda gathers the group and launches into an informative spiel, with Kai and Heath acting as her assistants, I peel away.

Carefully, I sidle up to the railing. Fingers curling tightly around the top rung of metal, I peer over at the choppy water. My stomach churns. God, people really think this is *fun*?

'Won't let you fall in,' a warm voice croons as warmer hands cup my biceps. 'Promise.'

I twist enough for the man looming behind me to feel the full force of my dry, unimpressed expression. 'I just think it's funny that I say *I hate the ocean* and you hear *let's go on a boat trip*.'

'You said you hate *swimming* in the ocean. We're not swimming.' Heath squeezes me gently, winking playfully. '*Today.* I'll get you in there eventually.'

'Sounds threatening. Did you forget the almost drowning?'

'I would never let you drown.'

'Okay, Aquaman.'

'*You* would never let you drown.'

'So *I'm* Aquaman?'

'*No.* I just think,' he mimics my earlier tone, 'that if you started drowning, the weight of your own failure would take you out before the water did. Death by pride.'

Jesus. Is that supposed to be a good thing? Because I'm not so sure.

Curling a hand around one of mine, Heath hooks his other around the buckle of my lifejacket. 'I'm exposure-therapying you,' he croons. 'Figured it's hard to be scared when you're having fun.'

'You thought I would find this fun?'

A hot groan warms the top of my head. 'I actually did think you might like this. Y'know, once we were actually out here.'

Swallowing down a mild dose of guilt, I cast my gaze out to sea again. 'I don't *not* like this.'

'You hate it.'

'I did not use that word. Not even in my head.'

With a laughing groan, he stoops to kiss my cheek, and I don't know why that makes me huff a little, why I consider shifting, ever-so-slightly, until his lips touch my own instead of anywhere else. 'You'll forgive me if we see orcas.'

'Oh, I will, will I?'

'Uh-huh. You'll like 'em. Remind me of you.'

My exhale is something between a scoff and a laugh. 'I remind you of a *whale*?'

'No.' That damn grin burns the patch of skin right beside my eye. 'They're dolphins, technically.'

'Don't they, like, eat the organs of other animals?'

'Exactly. You don't see the resemblance?'

Expression incredulous, I twist to face him again. 'Why so many women in this town are in love with you, I will never understand.'

Liar, my traitorous brain protests.

'Liar,' Heath's smirking mouth parrots.

Liar, I summon up just enough courage, just one tiny sliver, to quietly admit of my own accord.

We don't see orcas.

The allure of breaching gray whales is somehow tempered by screeching tourists, the underlying threat of seasickness, and the fact that I can't feel my face.

But I don't need to feel it to know I'm smiling.

'Admit it,' Heath murmurs in my ear, his fingers curled tight around mine where they clutch the railing. 'I was right.'

I admit nothing. Except for, 'This is nice.'

And he agrees, as he warms the side of my face with the side of his own. 'Yeah. It is.'

EIGHTEEN

'IS HE STILL WATCHING?'

'Huh?' As the man kissing me within an inch of my life reels back, I blink quickly, a little dazed. Gaze caught on swollen lips, on the tiny, dark freckle just slightly off the middle of the top one, it takes three tries before I even realize he's mouthing something – it's another couple before I make out a single word.

'Oh.' Glancing in the direction Heath discreetly jerks his head, I swallow harshly at the sight of my ex, exactly where he was ten minutes ago, still glaring. At the reminder that all of that kissing had an objective, I wilt, just a little. 'Yeah.'

Wriggling his left hand free from where it's trapped between the bed of his truck and my ass cheek, Heath slips beneath my sweater to palm the small of my back. His other hand, he wraps my ponytail around, stealing it from the whipping coastal whip. 'You okay?'

I nod. 'Just, uh, thinking about the meet tomorrow.'

'Damn. Not my best work then, huh?'

I drop my gaze, hiding a flush, biting my bottom lip to stop a disagreement from spilling out. As usual, his 'work' is just fine. Perfectly distracting. Too distracting. To the point where I genuinely completely forgot he wasn't kissing me just to kiss me. That, only a little while ago, we pulled into the beach parking lot and found Ben and some of his buddies already here, zipping themselves into wetsuits, presenting a perfect opportunity for some of that *getting him back* I'm supposed to be hell-bent on doing.

Except it didn't feel perfect. Heath smiled at me the same way he's smiled at me too many times to keep track of, that devious glint in his eyes, revenge written all over his face, and instead of the hundreds of other things I typically feel when bearing the brunt of his full attention, an overwhelming wave of ick washed over me.

Leaving his wetsuit stuck around his waist, he hoisted me onto the bed of his truck, one-handed. I wrapped my legs around his waist, my arms around his neck, and I kissed him, and, before his very own personal brand of anesthetic washed my common sense away, it just felt . . . wrong. Forced. Which is ridiculous, I know, because this whole thing is forced. This isn't the first time we've made out for show.

It *is* the first time it's felt so . . . obvious. It's the first time it's bothered me.

I don't blame that night. The pool incident. I refuse to. I won't be *that* girl. Unraveled by a single real taste of Heath fucking Belfort. I can like him, fine, but I can't *like* him. Not in any serious way. It'll ruin everything. Things are . . . well, like I told Heath, I really like how things are right now. I don't want anything to change; I sure as fuck don't want to be the one to change them, to *ruin* them.

I'm just in a weird mood, I guess. Seeing Ben when I wasn't expecting it, in possibly the last place I expected it, just threw me off. It was supposed to be just me and Heath, hanging out, friends, me proofreading the first draft of his final essay while he frolicked in the waves. I wasn't prepared for the whole fake relationship song and dance, and that's my problem.

Fucking Ben.

Hopping down from the truck, I cast a glare his way. 'Why is he even here?'

Heath snickers as he slips his arms through the long sleeves of his wetsuit. Turning around, he gestures for me to zip him up. 'Hmmm. I don't know. What could possibly have instilled a sudden love of surfing in your ex-boyfriend?'

Deciding not to point out he can do his own damn zip, I grab the long cord attached to the tab and drag it upwards, tucking it away before securing the Velcro at the base of his nape. 'You think this is an ego thing?'

'I think the majority of Ben's entire existence is an ego thing,' Heath quips as he faces me again, and I don't disagree. 'This, though, I think is a jealousy thing.'

I snort, arms crossed as I lean against his truck, watching him slide free a board so light blue, it's practically white. His favorite. 'You think he's jealous of your rad skills?'

'Please never say *rad* again.'

My eyes roll.

'He's jealous of us, Dani. I'm pretty sure this is him trying to win you back.'

'Well, that's just silly. How is embarrassing himself and *drowning* gonna win me back?'

'You got better suggestions? I'm sure he'd love to hear them.'

I pretend to think about it – I do not enjoy that, with each passing second, the set of Heath's jaw grows more and more stiff. 'Build a time machine,' I eventually drawl, before molars start cracking. 'So he can go back and decide not to dip his dick elsewhere.'

Surprisingly, that tension goes nowhere. 'You think you'd still be with him?'

That, I unfortunately don't need to ponder. 'Yeah, I do. Not because I loved him that much or because I was happy, but . . . I don't know. I was comfortable.'

'Comfortable,' he repeats, voice as tightly wound as the rest of him. 'Not in love?'

'I don't know. I thought I was. But if what I felt for him was love, then . . . well, I don't really know what everyone is always waxing so poetic about. Highly underwhelming. And if he really loved me, if that's what it's supposed to be like . . .' I trail off again, not sure how to explain that even if I am hard to love, my partner shouldn't have fucking told me that, without it coming out so pathetic.

For a long moment, he just stares at me. Brow crumpled, white-knuckling his surfboard. Lips parting, words start to come out, but I get the distinct feeling that 'You wanna wait here?' isn't what he was actually going to say. 'I'll leave the window cracked.'

'Like I'm a dog,' I croon, only teasing. The passenger seat of his truck or the windswept, frigid beach? *Hmm*. Tough choice. 'How sweet.'

He swats me on the ass as I climb in, waiting until I'm settled before closing the door with a playful slam. Leaning in through the open window, he kisses me, a quick peck that's barely anything, and yet it feels more real than the mauling we just indulged in.

'Be gentle with me,' he says, with a nod to the printed manuscript sitting on the dashboard, a red pen on top of it. 'Got snacks in the glovebox.'

He kisses me again, like he can't quite resist. 'Send up a smoke signal if you get bored.'

I promise I will. In the wing mirror, I watch Heath head for the truck bed again to grab his board. His spine locks when Ben comes into view, a couple of guys from our team flanking him, reeking of trouble. All that happens is a little shoulder bumping, an oh-so-coincidental slip of a board so the tail thwaps Heath's side, something Heath just laughs off, but there I go, halfway out the window, yelling in my ex's wake. 'What the fuck is your problem?'

'Not worth it, Dani.'

I huff, dropping my elbow to the roof of the truck, bracing myself with a palm against the window frame. For once, I'm eye-level with Heath. 'Yeah, you are.'

'I meant *he's* not worth it. I know I am. But thanks for the reassurance, sweetheart.'

A soft *oh* puffs out of me. Tongue poking the inside of my cheek, I slink back inside the truck. 'Go away now.'

He does it again. Dips down for a third chaste kiss, and without a soul watching. He blows another one at me as he jogs down toward the beach, and I slump low in my seat, feet on the dashboard, chin tucked to my chest, hiding in case his long list of talents includes the ability to spot bashful expressions through rain-streaked windshields from a mile a-fucking-way. Or telepathy. 'Cause, God, are there some thoughts in my head right now.

I have to remind myself, pretty damn sternly, that this isn't my real life. This isn't my new normal, and I don't want it to be. I don't. I'd be bored. Irritated, likely. The allure would wear off, once it stopped being some shiny, new experience. It's nice, for now.

For now has to be enough.

A low whistle pierces my concentration, and has me cursing as I accidentally strike a perfectly good sentence with the red pen poised between my fingertips.

'Damn.' My head whips to the side just in time to catch a group of guys in the car parked a couple of spaces over wincing. 'That looked bad.'

I sit up a little straighter. 'What did?'

One of them points out to sea. 'Wipeout.'

A couple organs in my chest simultaneously stop working for a second. 'Do you know who?'

The guys shrug.

Cursing, I lift myself half-out of the open window again, squinting into the distance in search of the right board. I find it, but there's no time for relief, because Heath isn't on it.

It takes the longest damn second of my life to find him. Bobbing in the waves what must be the full length of his lead rope away, not swimming for his board at all, and I can't tell if it's because he's fucking around, or if he's hurt.

I duck back inside. Fuck. *Fuck*.

The truck creaks with how hard I shove the door open. 'Fuck,' I repeat aloud, as I hurry across the parking lot. The black boots I slipped on this morning because I didn't think going to the beach would actually involve being *on* the beach sink into the sand, slow me down, but I keep going.

By the time I reach the shoreline, Heath is close enough to confirm a lack of missing extremities or excessive bleeding. He gets within earshot, and I don't hear any choking or coughing or pained noises – just laughter.

'What were you gonna do?' His board tucked beneath his armpit, Heath grins crookedly. 'Swim out and save me?'

I flinch, unexpectedly bothered by the teasing remark. Maybe because the group coming up behind him hear, and snicker. Kissing my teeth, I cross my arms and grunt, 'You okay?'

'His dramatic ass is fine,' someone answers for him. Some *girl*. A beautiful, eye-rolling, surfing girl, prancing through the waves and flipping her long hair like a freaking mermaid. I don't know her, I don't even know if Heath knows her, but I know damn well how she's looking at him – with snarky fucking hearts in her eyes. 'Your girlfriend can't handle a little wipeout, huh?'

'She doesn't surf.'

The girl makes a noise that has my hackles rising. 'And you put up with that? Shit, I wouldn't.'

'Did he fucking ask?'

Heath gasp-laughs my name. Twining my ponytail around his fist, he tugs. 'Claws, baby.'

I ignore him, gaze locked on fucking Merlilah, and she returns the damn favor until one of the guys she's with catches her attention.

'Who is that?'

'Hazel?' Heath asks more than answers. 'I think? Dunno. Think she's in my marketing class.'

He thinks. Yeah, right. A girl like that is in your class, you fucking know it.

'We surf together sometimes,' he adds, and I really, really don't like how that little admission makes me feel. The same way fucking *Hazel's* little comment did. Icky and incompetent and inferior.

And irrational, apparently. Impulsive too. Without my permission, my mouth asks, 'You have a spare wetsuit in your truck, right?'

'Yes,' he mouths slowly. 'Do I want to know why you're asking?'

'I just added something new to my list. I wanna learn how to surf.'

'I don't know about that.'

'What, you think I can't?'

'Oh, I'm pretty sure you can do anything.'

I simper, just for a second. Tuck my hair behind my flushed ears like some kind of shy ditz and look away – look right in Surfer Barbie's direction, and promptly snap back to my senses. 'You would teach me, right? If we were really dating?'

'Yeah,' he reluctantly admits.

Jesus, does his hesitance hit a nerve. A particularly unhinged one, fueled by jealousy I have no right feeling and whatever else the fuck is wrong with me today. 'We can make out in dark corners and lie to your friends and hump in a fucking pool, but this is where you draw the line? *This* is your boundary?'

'Did you just say *hump*?'

'That is not the point.'

'Humping should always be the point,' Heath jokes, but it's muted, falls a little flat, as wonky as that not-quite-smile. Assessing me for a long moment, he sighs. And then, without denying my request or granting it either, he drops to his haunches. 'Dani, honey, I'm not gonna take a beginner out on a day like this.'

Though I can't quite distinguish between relief and disappointment, I can pick out my confusion easily. 'What are you doing?' I ask as he starts to unlace my boots. A hand on my calf guides my foot upwards, and I brace my palms against his shoulders as he slides my shoe off. He does the same to the other foot, and then he tosses both boots further up the sand, leaving me in just my socks.

A little spark of heat rushes through me when, still holding my calf, he lifts his chin to dazzle me with sparkling eyes and a Cheshire cat grin. 'I owe you a race, remember?'

My stomach tightens – I remember what we did *after* he forfeited the last one.

Heath hitches a breath like maybe he's thinking about that too. When he rises, though, there's no heat in his expression. Just that smile, bright and encouraging and so fucking easy. Holding out a hand, he wiggles his fingers invitingly.

As if diving headfirst into the crashing waves wasn't my own damn idea, a flare of panic smacks me in the chest. 'I wanted to *surf.* Not swim.'

'A good teacher makes sure their students can swim before chucking them in the deep end.'

'I *can*—'

'In the *ocean,* Dani.'

I run my tongue over my teeth. Not quite scowling, but something close – first at Heath, then at his beloved ocean. I could change my mind. He would let me; he's looking at me like he's expecting it, like he's hoping I will.

For that reason alone, I don't.

Disregarding the ten-pound weight sitting heavy on my diaphragm, I turn to Heath, start to demand that wetsuit, coming up short when I find him closer than I expected. A mere inch away, his breath scalding my forehead before he dips to my eyeline.

'Remember,' he murmurs, eyes darting between both of mine, 'you were the one who bitched about my boundaries.'

'Wha—*Heath.*'

In the blink of an eye, I'm swept up, a strong arm banding across the small of my back and hoisting. The next, I'm in the water, so shocked by the sudden frigid deluge, it takes me a minute to even protest. By the time I start shrieking and flailing and gasping, we're waist-deep.

I'm so busy shrieking and flailing and gasping, I just . . . *forget* to panic. Sodden and shivering and swatting at every part of Heath I can reach, I only really have room for murderous intentions. '*Bitch,*' I howl, slamming my palms into broad, unflinching shoulders. 'What the hell? My *clothes.*'

'What?' Shielding his freaking delight behind an innocent smile, Heath lets me drop a couple of inches. 'I figured since you put up such a fuss about skinny-dipping, I'd try the opposite.'

'I'm gonna kill you.'

'Worth it. Not bad, huh?'

Briefly, I pause my attack. I'm about four seconds away from hypothermia, my favorite sweater is likely ruined, and I'm sure there are a whole gaggle of people laughing up a storm at the absolute picture we're providing, but . . .

It's like the shock has knocked the anxiety right out of my chest. Whitewater rumbles toward us, but it doesn't look quite as . . . formidable anymore. Not with Heath holding me tight.

I swallow. 'Not bad.'

NINETEEN

'BET SHE'S LOVING THIS.'

Though I know damn well that I'm the *she* in question, I don't look up – though my teammates are, in fact, right, I don't give them the satisfaction of knowing just how much I'm loving the shouts echoing around the changing room.

Rookies. You're supposed to air your romantic grievances in a supply closet or in the back parking lot that only staff use. Everyone knows sound carries in here.

Well, evidently, not everyone. Sienna and Ben obviously did not get the memo. Either they don't realize that the single layer of lockers separating them from the rest of the team is not all that soundproof of a barrier, or they're too incensed with each other to care.

He was late picking her up this morning. Didn't bring her breakfast. She played the radio too loud on the drive here. She spoke too much and blurred his focus. He got our relay off to a slow start. Her strokes were out of sync. He did this, and she did that, they both fucking sucked, but you don't hear me kicking up a fuss, and I was the one who carried those slackers to victory all on my damn lonesome.

'What the fuck is your deal?' I hear Ben spit.

Oh, God help him if he was using that tone with me, I briefly think, before realizing that, actually, he has. He used to all the damn time. And like Sienna does now, I just stood there and let him. Except I remember finding his anger vaguely amusing – Sienna most definitely does not.

'We won,' Ben points out, earning a vicious laugh from Sienna, a noise so at odds with that pretty blonde exterior.

'Because of *her,* right?'

I feel every eye in the room swing to me.

'What does that have to do with anything?'

Yeah, I agree with Ben, and the entire universe trembles. *What do I have to do with this?*

'I saw how you were looking at her.'

'You sound insane, Sienna.'

Every woman in the room hisses through their teeth.

'*Good job, Daniela,*' comes a poor imitation of Ben's voice. I only have to fight the urge to laugh for a second – it's soon chased away by half a dozen accusatory glares, as if no one witnessed me steadfastly ignoring the words my ex threw at me. 'What was that, huh?'

'I was just being nice.'

That swallowed laugh finally escapes. I can't help it. *Ben. Nice.* I snicker again.

'We're a *team,* Sienna,' he adds, and, God, that condescension makes even my skin crawl. It makes Sienna spew a funny noise. A ringing, metallic thump proceeds it, and if I had to guess, I'd say Ben just got pretty damn intimate with a locker, courtesy of the latest entry to the long list of women he's pissed off.

He curses loudly. A moment later, in my peripheral vision, I watch him stomp into view like a disgruntled toddler. I don't need to see him properly to know he's red-faced, practically foaming at the mouth. I hear his huffing and puffing, I feel a scowl pass over me, and then the door bangs off the wall, signaling his exit.

A bout of stuttered sniffles announce Sienna, soon drowned out by soft, sorrowful croons. As everyone rushes to crowd her, I stand and turn my back, giving myself the freedom to roll my eyes while they fuss and fret and offer baseless, vague assurances that everything will be just fine, that *they're made for each other.*

The dramatics grate on me. Turn me bitter, because no one ever fussed over me. I could be standing in front of them, bawling my damn eyes out, and none of them would give even the tiniest of fucks. We're not friends, but we're a team. There should be something between us, some kind of bond, shouldn't there?

Why can't I have that here? Why did I need a fake boyfriend and a shot at his fucking friends to find some semblance of that?

So lost in my bitterness, I don't notice the room clearing out until it's just me and one other person. Someone who hasn't quite gotten enough attention from everyone else, apparently, so she feels the need to demand mine.

'Daniela?'

I don't turn around. I don't straighten up from where I'm hunched over my duffel bag, wrestling my damp towel into it. I don't spare the voice I recognize, nor the person I know it belongs to, anything more than the energy it takes to bark a cool 'No.'

The woman who fucked my boyfriend behind my back actually has the audacity to sigh at me. 'I just wanna talk.'

'And I just don't give a fuck.'

'Please, Dani. Five minutes, that's all I want.'

I repeat myself, but it doesn't seem to penetrate that mop of blonde hair.

Determined footfalls bring her closer. A hand on my shoulder makes her impossible to ignore. A shocked expression makes me fucking laugh when I promptly bat her away before turning to face her of my own accord. 'Why now, huh? Why do you wanna talk to me? Why are you now suddenly struck with regret when it's been months? Is it because you actually feel guilty or because you feel like a fucking idiot because it's already gone to shit?'

'I do feel guilty,' she argues, she can argue all day long, I'm never going to believe her. Because guilty people don't follow up their professions of guilt with '*But*.'

I snort.

'I didn't mean to hurt you,' Sienna continues, batting those big blue eyes at me as if I'm susceptible to shit like that. 'It's just . . . the heart wants what the heart wants, y'know? You get that, right?'

Oh, she has got to be shitting me. 'Funnily enough, no. I don't.'

'But it worked out for you. You're with Heath now.'

'You don't get to take credit for that. You don't get to assuage your guilt because I ended up happy while you got the short end of the fucking stick.'

'Jesus, Dani, I'm trying to apologize.'

'That's hilarious, considering I haven't actually heard a *sorry* leave your mouth, have I?'

'I'm—'

'No, Sienna. *No*. I don't care. I don't want to hear it. I'm not gonna be the balm to your guilty soul, I am not your repentance. I am nothing to you, and you are nothing to me.'

'Well, obviously you do care or you wouldn't be so mad.'

'I care about what you *did*. I care that you humiliated me, and you kept fucking doing it, and you got a kick out of it too. I care that everyone lied and snuck around and laughed at me. I care that I wasted two years of my life with a loser. But I don't care that it was *you*. *I don't care about you*.'

'Don't you think you're being a little unreasonable? We weren't even friends.'

My head drops, shaking as I chuckle. There it is. Her absolution. We weren't friends, so it doesn't matter. Ben and I weren't happy, so it doesn't matter. They're hearts fucking aligned or whatever, so *I* don't matter.

Maybe they're right. Maybe I am being unreasonable, maybe I am being dramatic, maybe I should put a pin in it, get over it, expel that lingering taint of betrayal that flares every time I have to be in a room with them, with anyone who knew about them and helped them hide it.

Or maybe *I* can feel however the fuck *I* want about the monumentally shitty thing that happened to *me*.

Slinging my bag across my shoulders, I cling tight to the strap with both hands as I look Sienna dead in the eyes. 'I never did anything to you. I never picked on you or singled you out or treated you any differently than I treat anyone else. Yeah, we weren't friends, *but I never did anything to you*. And you did the worst fucking thing to me and then, when everyone made me the villain, you let that happen too.'

At least she has the decency to flinch.

I, on the other hand, lack the kind of decency that would probably stop me from bumping into her as I stride past – and from throwing something just a little shitty over my shoulder on my way out the door. 'If you really wanna make it up to me, tell your boyfriend to leave me the fuck alone.'

I linger just long enough to know that the comment hit home exactly the way I intended before letting the door swing shut behind me.

With a groan that comes from my damn bones, I drag my hands over my head before linking them at the base of my neck. Face tilted toward the high ceilings, I groan again. Silently, I ask if the universe is ever planning on giving me a single day off from its fuckery.

The universe laughs, right before the last voice I ever want to hear trills my name.

Marisol Castro Williams is many, many things.

Widow. Stepmother.

Terrifying.

Not visually. Visually, she's anything but. Lithe and willowy and sun-kissed, with bright green eyes and long, luscious hair and the kind of ethereal beauty that has heads turning and the sun shining and birds fucking chirping, that hasn't faded even a little bit with age.

She isn't *my* brand of terrifying. She isn't surly and scowly and mean. No, her terror is specific. Her terror tends to extend to only a couple of targets.

Her stepson, occasionally.

Her stepdaughter, almost always.

'Mari,' I choke, as I feel myself shrink at least an inch. 'What're you doing here?'

She huffs, already offended. 'You haven't been answering my calls, so I had to track you down. Your brother said you had a meet today.'

God, I fear what else my brother might've had to say. 'You were watching?'

A wrinkled nose answers that question before she does. 'I caught the end of your last race.'

And . . . nothing. No congratulations. No *good job*. Just tight-lipped mutual discomfort.

'I thought we could go for dinner.'

I have plans, is on the tip of my tongue, but it never gets the chance to spill.

An emphatic, flinch-inducing 'Mari' cuts me off. Right before my literal worst nightmare develops before my very eyes.

Straight-backed and smirking, Ben saunters up to my stepmother and wraps her in a hug she doesn't hesitate to return. She exclaims and croons and pinches his fucking cheeks, remarking on his handsomeness, suddenly giving just enough of a shit about swimming to comment on his prowess.

'Come eat with us,' she insists, wrapping herself around his arm and holding him close, with more enthusiasm than she's ever shown me. 'We can go to that place we went to last month.'

Momentarily, I malfunction. I convince myself that I must've gotten half the pool in my ears, that all that chlorine must've burned a hole in my eardrums and distorted my hearing – that must be the case because I can't possibly have heard what I think I just did.

Except when I cough out a disbelieving 'You went out together last month?' both my stepmom and my ex nod.

Marisol fucking *giggles*. 'I see your boyfriend more than I see you.'

A distinct *ping* sounds from somewhere within my brain.

My eyes snap closed; the sight of this fuckery is physically painful. Blindly, I aim my incredulity in Ben's direction. 'Are you fucking psychotic?'

'Daniela.'

I force my eyes open again, if only to make fleeing a lot easier. 'I need to change,' I claim, despite very obviously having already done so.

'Dani—' Ben chides, and oh, is he so very lucky that I am too done with this conversation to deal with him the way he deserves.

'Take him to dinner,' I throw at Marisol, as I turn back to the changing rooms. 'I don't care. But if you do, I'm not coming.'

The sighed version of my name that I am *oh*-so-intimately familiar with follows me as I storm back the way I came. I shove the changing-room door open, I fucking dare Sienna to still be in here, for anyone to try me right now, and I'm a little disappointed when it's empty. A lot more relieved that no one's around to hear my incoherent yell, to watch me launch my bag across the room and fucking kick a locker.

Or at least that's what I think.

'What did that locker ever do to you, champ?'

Momentarily, I'm convinced that chlorine has gotten to my brain too. It's rotted away whatever part is responsible for perceiving reality, it's bolstered the part that causes hallucinations, because, again, I am so unconvinced that what's happening is actually happening.

Heath is not at my meet. Heath is at his own meet.

Yet there Heath stands, there he smiles, there he stoops to kiss my cheek, and here I dodge to avoid him.

'Of course,' I breathe, with a humorless laugh, because, oh God, isn't this just perfect? 'Of course you're here.'

I'm losing my mind. Teetering on the ledge. Holding on by a thread. So, naturally, some otherworldly force demanded his presence. It always fucking does.

'Of course I'm here,' he repeats, but with none of the bitterness. 'Are you okay?'

'*Why?*' I answer his question with one of my own before shaking my head, wriggling out of his grip, continuing on my way. 'Actually, you know what, I can't talk right now.'

With a rough noise, he chases me down and catches me again. Fingers wrapping around mine, he tugs despite my groaned protests until we're sheltered by the relative privacy of the emptying bleachers. 'What's wrong?'

'Nothing.'

'Try again. Truth this time.'

Sighing, I scratch the itchy patch of hot skin rapidly spreading across my chest. 'You shouldn't be here.'

'Yeah, I'm getting that. What I don't get is why. You're seriously mad that I skipped my meet to come support you?'

I chew on the inside of my cheek. 'A little.'

'But that's not all of it, huh?'

'My stepmom's here.'

'And that's a bad thing?'

'It's not bad. It's just . . .' I sigh again. 'It's complicated.'

Heath hums understandingly, one hand rising to tuck a stray strand of wet hair behind my ear. 'Tell me about it over dinner?'

'I can't.' I knock his hand away. 'She wants to take me out.'

Maybe. Unless she decides to take Ben instead. Which is honestly more likely than the alternative.

'Okay.'

Nodding brusquely, I mumble a goodbye before walking away, and he lets me.

He *follows* me.

I frown at him over my shoulder. 'What're you doing?'

'Leaving?'

As the panicked heat in my chest flares, I turn and plant a halting hand on his. 'I don't want her to see you.'

His expression droops. 'You don't want me to meet her?'

'Obviously not.' Frowning, I assess his own crumpled brow, his cocked head, his mildly . . . offended? Disappointed? Not-quite-right expression. 'Why would I want that?'

Wrong thing to say. *Wrong, wrong, wrong.*

Heath kisses his teeth, retreating a step. 'Right. Yeah. *Why.*'

'Heath, she doesn't even know I broke up with Ben. She's already gonna give me shit about that, and I can't spring you on her too. Not when I'm gonna have to explain that break-up too in a couple of months.'

'Right,' he repeats. 'I get it.'

I don't think he does. He definitely doesn't like it. As close to sullen as he's likely to get, he nods sharply and backs up again. 'Cool. No worries.'

'Heath,' I say, and nothing else immediately follows. I can't take it back, I won't lie to him, and I'm not going to apologize for telling the truth. 'I really don't know what I'm saying wrong here. It's not that big a deal, is it?'

'You're right. It's not.'

'Okay.' Awkwardly, I shift on my feet. 'I need to go.'

'Okay,' he parrots. 'I'll see you later?'

A little tension bleeds out of me. He can't be that mad, can he, if he wants to see me later? 'Yes, please.'

Two words, and he goes from stiff and squinty to butter-soft. 'Okay,' he says again, lacking any of the previous edge. 'You were fucking incredible, by the way.'

'I know.' I hesitate, before muttering a giant *fuck it*. Rising the few inches it takes to make us eye-level, I press a kiss to the corner of his mouth. Another to his actual mouth – an impulse more than an active decision. 'Thank you for coming.'

And then, because I have bigger things to reserve my bravery for today, I scurry the fuck away.

*

Shockingly, Marisol is still waiting when I emerge from the changing room, impatient and Ben-less, and as much as the thought of her and Ben fucking conspiring makes me dry-heave, I very quickly start to think it would've been a much more tolerable alternative.

Within five minutes of being seated at a restaurant that I am extremely under-dressed for, my stepmother starts compiling a thorough, ruthless list of everything wrong with me.

I need a haircut. A couple of highlights would be nice too. My freckles are getting out of hand apparently – do I know that I need to wear sunscreen every day, not just when it's sunny? My swimsuit was unflattering, my shoulders are looking awfully broad, and, oh, sweet Jesus, do not even dare to look upon the sorry state of my fingernails.

It's so relentless, so endless, that by the time the topic shifts to the one I was dreading the most, I'm almost glad.

Almost.

'Honestly,' Marisol titters over the rim of her water glass, eyes thrown up to the sky. 'Poor Ben, hm? You could make a little effort for him.'

The segue is perfect, but I hesitate to take it. I fucking fear what might come out of her mouth if she learns the one thing she likes about me is now obsolete. But then I think about what would happen if she found out on her own, and I fear that reaction a hell of a lot more.

Real quick, like I'm ripping off a Band-Aid, I blurt, 'We broke up.'

I swear to God, she gasps. '*What?*' Her hand shakes as she

sets her glass down before palming her chest, as if the news has broken her freaking heart. 'When?'

'A few months ago.'

'Daniela,' she chastises lowly with a tut. 'You never tell me anything.'

'Sorry, Mari,' I apologize, and I really try to mean it, because she can always tell when I don't. She's always griped about the offensiveness of false regrets, claims I insult her with them, that she'd rather not hear an apology at all.

I wonder if I would share that sentiment, if she had ever actually apologized to me before.

'What did you do?'

I almost laugh. Of course she would assume the break-up was my doing. My fault. She loved Ben – or at least she thinks she did. She loved the perfect, polite version of him that he became around her. The son-in-law of her dreams to make up for the stepdaughter of her nightmares. God, I don't think she would even believe me if I told her that he cheated, and if she did, she'd probably suggest I pushed him to it. 'I didn't do anything. We just broke up.'

'Can you fix it?'

'I don't want to.'

A long, aggrieved sigh strikes whatever crevice of my heart harbors that pesky, permanent brand of guilt reserved specifically for a child disappointing their parent. 'Does this have anything to do with that other boy?'

'What other boy?'

'*El calvo*. With the,' she sighs again, '*tattoos*.'

So she saw him. *Great*. 'He isn't *bald*.' I spit a needless defense and automatically regret it when her face pinches even more. 'And it had nothing to do with him.'

'But you are seeing him?'

I hesitate. I contemplate lying – or telling the truth, I guess, depending on how you look at it. In the end, for some fucking reason, I decide to nod.

'Well? Are you going to tell me about him?'

I swallow. Pick mindlessly at the hangnail on my thumb. Mentally cycle through everything I know about *that other boy*, and wonder why, exactly, a little voice in the back of my head panics at the thought of him paling in comparison to anyone else. 'His name is Heath.'

'Wow, Daniela,' Marisol muses, her faded accent coming to life as her voice thickens with sarcasm. 'I feel like I know him already.'

'I don't know what you want me to say.'

'I want you to bring him to dinner tomorrow.'

I choke on nothing but my next breath. And a mild panic attack. 'I can't tomorrow.'

'Next week, then.'

'Mari, I don't—'

'That wasn't a suggestion, Daniela.' Smiling so deceptively sweetly, she lifts her glass in a cheers. 'Wednesday. Eight o'clock. No excuses.'

Wednesday. Eight o'clock.

Time of fucking death.

TWENTY

THE GATE IN A WHITE PICKET FENCE CREAKS AS I cautiously push it open, my body stiff, as if I'm expecting someone to chase me off the property any minute now.

'Hello?' I call out tentatively, casting my gaze around the quiet backyard. 'Heath?'

'He's in the workshop.'

'*Jesus.*' The tote bag hanging off my shoulder swings in a half-arc and slams into my stomach, winding me as I whirl toward the little girl I hadn't noticed perched amongst the flower beds, digging in the dirt with a couple of toy dinosaurs. 'Lyla,' I cough. 'Hi. I didn't see you.'

Big eyes, the same distinct color as her mom and uncle's, blink at me silently.

Shifting awkwardly, I try my best attempt at a sunny smile. 'Uh, Heath told me I could come on in.'

Pretty blonde curls bounce as Lyla tips her head to one side. 'Are you going on a date?'

'No.' I pat my bag, laden with books. 'We're studying.'

'Boring.'

No, it isn't, I almost argue, only just managing to squash the urge to defend my love of studying to a freaking five-year-old. 'You said he's in the workshop?'

Lyla nods and points toward the slightly ramshackle shed tucked down the end of the yard, shrouded in ivy and surrounded by neat, flower-studded shrubs.

'Thanks.' With an awkward little wave, I start to walk away only to come up short at the command of an exaggerated cough.

'I like your hair.'

'Oh.' I graze a hand down the French braid following the curve of my spine to the middle of my back. 'Thank you. I like your dress.'

Rosy cheeks dimple as she mutters some thanks of her own, little fingers toying with the hem of a dress the exact shade of the aster sprouting in the flower bed she kneels in. Mud stains the fabric, stains her legs and her arms too, and as I frown at the little holes dotted sporadically around her, I notice it's caked beneath her fingernails too. 'Whatcha doing?'

'Looking for bones.'

My eyebrows shoot up. 'Bones?'

Lyla nods emphatically, launching into a babbling tirade about the museum exhibit her Uncle Kiki took her to last weekend, eyes round saucers of wonder as she details the fossils he showed her, and while I feel the creeping need to pry further about what kind of relationship, exactly, Kai and her mother have, a different spark of intrigue holds dominance.

'Y'know,' I dare to sidle closer, my bag dropping to the ground with a thud as I slowly lower myself to my haunches, forearms stacked just above my knees, 'I study bones.'

Somehow, those eyes widen even more. 'Really?'

'Kinda. Sometimes. Ever heard of forensic anthropology?'

Her young, blank face makes me want to smack myself in my own.

Yes, Daniela. Kindergartens offer courses in forensic anthropology now. Dumbass.

'It's the study of people. Everything about people. And I, uh, learn about their bones too. How to tell stuff about them.'

Lyla sits up a little straighter. 'What kind of stuff?'

'Like how old they were. Where they were from. How they,' I wince as the next word leaves my mouth before I really think it through, 'died.'

'Woah.'

'Yeah. Woah.'

'That's cool.'

'It is cool. Really cool.'

I, on the other hand, am not cool at all. I am the antithesis of cool. Because *cool* is most definitely not puffing up with pride as a tiny human who's yet to hit double digits finding interest in my field of study. Nor, I suppose, is sitting cross-legged in the dirt, sifting through sediment I'm almost one hundred per cent sure does not contain anything remotely fossil-like, but I don't care so much about that . . .

'There you are,' a voice calls, after I don't even know how long – long enough for dirt to creep beneath my nails and render my jeans sufficiently ruined. Shifting my gaze from the plastic velociraptor Lyla so graciously allowed me to use as a makeshift shovel, I fight the urge to shield my eyes against the sunniest of smiles. 'Get a better offer?'

My own smile doesn't budge. I don't think it would, even if I tried to make it. 'Obviously.'

With an intrigued little hum, Heath reaches out a hand to me. 'Sorry, Lala. My turn.'

'We're *busy*.' The little girl groans, scowling.

'Too bad.' Ringed fingers wiggle insistently. 'She's mine.'

'But—'

'Maybe,' I cut in, capable of sensing the imminent tantrum brewing, even with my limited experience with children, 'we could go down to the beach sometime? Look for those ammonites I was telling you about?'

'When?'

I look to Heath – for permission, I guess, which I get. An odd, soft look and an odd, slow nod, like he can't quite believe what he's agreeing to. 'Next weekend? If that's okay with your mom.'

Scowl nowhere to be seen, Lyla jumps to her feet. 'I'll ask her right now.'

She's gone before I can take back the offer. Which I wouldn't. I like Lyla. After a single conversation, I think I like her more than I do anyone my own age.

Well, my brain points out, as my gaze shifts to her uncle. *Almost anyone.*

Heath's outstretched hand still hovers between us, and as I take it, he uses the other one to haul me up too. 'Ammonites?'

Dusting the dirt off my ass, I shrug. 'I took a paleontology class last year.'

Another one of those odd looks comes over him as he stoops

to grab my bag with the hand not still holding mine tightly before leading me across the yard.

'What?'

'Nothing.' His face flattens before brightening with one of those signature grins, pure *cheek*. 'Just didn't know having a smart girlfriend would be so *hot*.'

'That's what does it for you? Dinosaur excavation?'

'I don't know.' He squeezes my hand, swinging it gently in the narrow corridor of space between us. 'What are you wearing when you excavate?'

I snort, detaching from him so I can shove him away.

He shoves me right back – right through an open doorway and into the elusive workshop that I didn't know existed until about twenty minutes ago.

A low, impressed whistle as my gaze bounces around the room, taking in the full racks lining every available wall. 'Are there any surfboards left in the cove?'

Heath laughs. My roots pinch as he tugs on my braid. The floorboards beneath my feet creak as he drops my bag, reminding me of why I'm here in the first place.

'This doesn't look like studying, Heath.'

'Very perceptive.' He pinches my chin playfully, a hand on my lower back guiding me across the space, toward a workstation on the opposite side of the room. 'I'm just finishing something.'

I blink at the surfboard propped on a wooden table. 'You're finishing this?'

'Uh-huh.'

'You *made* this?'

Heath nods, and I swear his complexion flushes a little pink.

'You made a surfboard?'

'I've made a few.' He gestures vaguely around the space, and I think I might actually gasp a little.

'All of these?'

'Well, not all of them,' he corrects, but I know him well enough by now, and even if I didn't, I know false modesty when I hear it.

Mouth agape, I move to the nearest wall, fingertips tracing one of what must be fifty different boards. How did I not know about this? God, I am the *worst* for not knowing about this. 'Woah.'

'Stop it. You're making me blush,' he drawls sarcastically, as if he isn't actively turning pink before my very eyes. Side-stepping the unfinished board, he walks over to a different table and picks up some kind of tool before patting an empty spot on the wooden surface. 'Ten minutes. Twenty, tops. Maybe even quicker if you help me.'

'Quicker?' I scoff. 'I feel like this should already be astoundingly clear, but I do not know the first thing about making a surfboard.'

'But you know how to paint, right?'

'Not really. A little.'

'Good enough for me.'

He waves me over, and though reluctant, I go to him, as curious as I am nervous. 'What am I doing?'

Stooping to reach beneath the workbench, he comes out with a mason jar of paintbrushes and an array of colorful pots. 'Something pretty.'

'Specifics would be nice.'

'Whatever you want.'

I shift from one foot to the other. 'What if I ruin it?'

'You won't.' He nudges me gently. 'C'mon. My hot tutor only gave me twenty minutes to finish.'

I start by painstakingly, methodically penciling out a design on the nose end of the board. I decide on sprawling vines studded with flowers, partly because it's the easiest thing I can think of, and a little because I hope Heath will turn up his nose at the girly pattern.

I should've known better; I should never have doubted that firm grip he has on his masculinity – hardly defeatable by a couple of fucking daisies.

And as it turns out, the design isn't all that easy. By the time I work up the courage to even wet a damn paintbrush, I'm already concentrating hard enough to work up a sweat.

More nervous than I should be, I grasp the thinnest brush, picking a navy shade that'll stand out nicely against the light blue color of the rest of the board. And while Heath sands the other end, I try really, really hard to focus on clean, fluid strokes.

Except it is much, much harder to ignore the man at work.

Brows pinched in concentration, Heath works with practiced, methodical movements. The workshop fills with the rasp of rough paper against . . . well, whatever surfboards are made of, creating a melody, of sorts. One that guides the timing of my breathing, skates across my skin like some corporeal thing, makes each fine hair stand on end.

I don't realize I'm biting my bottom lip until the metallic taste of blood fills my mouth. I don't realize I'm squirming until the skin of my inner thighs starts to burn from the continuous friction and I make a conscious effort to be still. And I don't really realize I'm staring until it occurs to me, with a sudden face-slapping brand of clarity, that I'm not staring so much as I'm *gawking. Leering.* I would say *admiring,* if I was being romantic about it. But, God knows, I'm not a romantic.

God knows there's nothing *admirable* about the thoughts swarming my brain like pesky, persistent gnats.

Maybe my ex is right. Maybe I am a freak. No, actually, there's no *maybe* about it – I must be because only a freak would, with complete sincerity, be struck with the urge to *bite* a man. Repeatedly. Thoroughly. To sink my teeth into the forearms revealed by rolled-up sleeves. The generous stretch of thigh revealed by shorts with a truly perverted inseam. The prominent V of muscle that he flashes when he stretches his arms above his head, relieving his spine from its hunched-over position.

When knowing eyes lock on me, I only realize I'm busted a beat too late.

I drop my head so quickly, my neck cracks. Praying that the few loose strands of hair framing my face are enough to hide my raging blush, I pray even harder that he won't let fly the smarmy comment I can practically hear already.

The longest minute of my life passes before that gentle rasp picks up again. Just as I breathe a sigh of relief, his own catches, and he inhales like he's about to say something.

Before he can, I blurt, 'We're having dinner with my stepmom tomorrow.'

Momentarily, the workshop goes silent once again. 'We are?'

'She demanded it.'

'Ah.'

'I can get you out of it, though.' *In exchange for a small sliver of my sanity.*

'Thanks so much.'

At the thick sarcasm coating his words, I frown. 'What's wrong?'

'You really don't want me to meet her, huh?'

'No, Heath, I don't. Why is that so bad?'

'Because—' He huffs, incredulous. 'I don't get *why*.'

'*Because*,' I parrot, mimicking his huff. 'It's complicated, okay? Our relationship is complicated and I just don't feel like suffering through those complications with an audience.'

'I'm not an audience, Dani. I'm your—' He runs his tongue over his teeth. 'Friend. I'm your friend. And, believe it or not, I know a little something about complicated relationships. I won't judge you.'

'That's not—' I huff again, frustrated as I cut off my lie, because that's exactly what it is. That's exactly what I'm worried about. He'll see that my own stepmother can barely stand me, and he'll start to question why he even tries to. 'She just . . . stresses me out. It's not a big deal. I'll be fine. By myself.'

Heath looks skeptical. He looks *hurt*, face all scrunched as he half-heartedly goes back to his sanding, and while I try to re-focus on painting, I, once again, don't do a very good job.

'Are you mad at me?'

Heath sighs. 'No.'

I don't believe him. 'I'm sorry.'

'*Fuck.*' Shaking his head, he drops the sandpaper, idle hands curling around the workbench's edge. 'When you do that, it makes me wanna punch Ben in the face more than I already usually do.'

'What am I doing?'

'You're so fucking interesting, you know that? The angriest people pleaser in the world. You hate people, but you hate disappointing them more. You're mad at everyone, but you hate when people you care about are mad at you.'

My knuckles turn white with how hard I fist the paintbrush in my grip. 'And you think that's Ben's fault?'

'I think he did a lot more damage than you're willing to admit. Made you think his issues were actually yours. Got mad at you for fucking nothing and now we can't have a conversation without you thinking I'm gonna do the same.'

My next breath is a defeated shudder. God, I hate that he's right. I hate that he's *wrong*, in a way, because, really, the damage started long before Ben, with a different man entirely, and my ex only aggravated an existing wound. I hate that, of all people, Heath is the one to pick up on that – that he's the *only* one.

'Look,' Heath starts, sighing wearily again. 'I don't care – well, no. Actually, I do care that you don't want me and her to meet. But I care more about being there for you. Supporting you. Maybe making it a little less stressful.'

My gaze drops to my unfinished art project. For fuck's sake. How the hell am I supposed to argue with that?

'Okay,' I quietly relent. 'You can come.'

'Are you sure?'

'Nope.'

His smile is tangible, even before he presses it to my temple. 'It'll be fine. I promise.'

My gut twists.

Somehow, I know that'll be the first promise he's ever broken.

TWENTY-ONE

'YOU'RE LATE,' I GRUNT, AS I RIP OPEN THE FRONT door of my step mother's condo approximately one millisecond after knuckles wrap against it.

'Hello to you too, my dear.' Breezing inside, Heath brushes a kiss on my cheek, the flowers cradled in his arms tickling my midriff. 'It's one minute past.'

'Which is late.' I grunt again. 'What are those?'

'These are *flowers*, Daniela. For your stepmom.'

I grunt a third time. Great. Can't wait to hear how Marisol turns dahlias into a shortcoming on my part. *Bad daughter. Why didn't you bring me flowers?*

I jolt as a thumb smooths over the skin between my eyebrows, a valiant attempt to iron out the wrinkles there that only ends in failure – that only makes them worse, really. As does a cautious 'You okay?'

I've been in the presence of my stepmother with only my brother as back-up for an entire hour. Of course I'm not okay. 'Fine. Can we get this over with?'

'Hey.' Heath catches me by the wrist before I can start down the hall. Tattooed fingers tug on the hem of the stupid, pretty dress I wore for stupid, petty reasons. 'You look pretty.'

I sniff – and then I sniff again when I catch a whiff of something unfamiliar, something distinctly un-Heath. 'You're wearing cologne.'

'God forbid I actually want to impress my mother-in-law.'

'Do I need to remind you that this is fake?'

'No, Daniela. I'm well aware. What's wrong?'

'Nothing.'

'Dani.'

I shoot him a look.

He shoots me one too. Soft and curious, and as concerned as a repeated, 'Are you okay?'

'Just peachy.'

'You nervous?'

'*No.*' I scoff. *Nervous* requires a certain amount of ignorance, of blissful oblivion, of uncertainty about what's about to unfold. I, however, know exactly how this dinner is going to go. Well, I know it'll be one of two outcomes.

She'll love him, and it'll make my life miserable in the near future when our arrangement inevitably ends. Or she'll hate him, and it'll make my life miserable right now.

'C'mon.' I bat his hand away and jerk my head down the hall. 'She's waiting.'

He stops me again. 'Hey.'

'Jesus, *what*?'

A thumb and a forefinger pinch my chin, holding me in place while eyes hold mine captive, sea-green on dark brown. 'You look really pretty, Daniela.'

'You already said that.'

'Wasn't sure you heard me.'

'She doesn't listen.'

Heath's hand abruptly drops as my head whips toward the other end of the hallway, to the kitchen doorway that was empty a minute ago, but sure isn't anymore. 'Never has,' my stepmother muses, laments, and chastises all at once. 'Unless someone's talking about swimming, of course.'

'Marisol.' As if a steel bar has replaced my spine, I stand ramrod straight as I clear my throat. 'This is Heath. Heath, this is my stepmom.'

Flashing that smile, Heath hands over his floral offering as he greets Marisol enthusiastically, and is either completely oblivious to or pointedly ignores the stiff way she returns it. The tight smile. The dry way she insists he call her *Mari*.

He doesn't.

Wise boy.

He does, however, wrap his fingers around mine and holds tight as he all but drags me down the hall of the one-bedroom house my stepmom's lived in since we moved here, but I never did. I went straight into dorms before finding my studio. This isn't a home to me – it certainly doesn't feel like one, and I wonder if Heath can feel that too.

If he does, he doesn't show it. That sunny exterior doesn't falter even a little bit, and it only expands when we enter the kitchen and Seba hollers an exuberant greeting.

Heath lets go of my hand to indulge in a bro-hug, and I actively fight the urge to grab him again, to maneuver myself into that hug and the conversation that follows, because those two being occupied with each other leaves me free. Vulnerable. Susceptible to a maternal attack that comes in the form of fingers wrapping around my forearm and squeezing, of not-that-quiet Spanish sing-songed in my ear, marked by the accent of someone who grew up speaking a different dialect than the one I know.

'*Es muy guapo.*'

'*Baste.*'

'*Qué?* I can't say your boyfriend's handsome?'

'Stop.'

'Too handsome for you.' An elbow jabs my ribs. 'Lucky girl.'

'*Soy el afortunado.*'

Marisol squeaks, her wide eyes flitting to Heath. 'Dani didn't tell me you speak Spanish.'

I grumble, 'Dani tried to.'

Heath laughs. 'I spent the last few summers surfing in Sayulita.'

Me and Seba exchange a look. *Of course he did.*

'Dani told me you're from Seville,' Heath adds, and as Marisol brightens at the mention of her Spanish hometown, my brother roll his eyes and mouths *kissass* at me.

Sidling a step closer, Seba stoops to murmur in my ear. 'Did you make him study before this?'

'No.' I didn't tell him anything about Mari – I don't know how the fuck he knows that.

'How did you go from a drunken make-out to meeting the mother in a couple of months?'

'I told you, I'm charming.'

'Like a grizzly bear fresh out of hibernation.'

My elbow is halfway to my brother's gut when a throat clears, overly loud and exceptionally pointed.

'Here you go, Heath,' our stepmother coos, her saccharine tone a stark contrast to the look she shoots us. 'Since you're the only one who's hungry.'

Like two naughty kids, Seba and I smile sheepishly as we sidle toward the new best friends over by the kitchen counter. My mouth is quick to flatten, though, when I catch sight of Heath's heaping plate of food, a stifled groan rattling my bones. 'You don't have to eat all that.'

'Daniela.' Marisol tuts. 'He's a growing boy.'

A growing *athlete*, who, like me, prefers not to load up on greasy food the night before a hard practice. God, it's like she made the worst foods she could think of. 'We've talked about this, Mari. We're in season.'

Huffing, she waves me off.

'It's okay.' Cupping my elbow briefly, Heath flashes a smile on his way to sit at the kitchen table.

'It's not.' She does this every year. Every single year. It's been, what, *a decade* of me adjusting my diet when the swim season rolls around to maximize my performance, and, still, she can't wrap her head around it.

'So uptight.' Marisol tuts again. Passing me a plate that's piled just as high, she shakes her head and moves to join Heath at the table, guiding him into one seat before dropping into the one beside him. 'How do you manage her?'

A bemused noise parts Heath's lips. '*Manage* her?'

Marisol waves dismissively. 'You know what I mean.'

'No, I don't think—'

Taking a leaf out of my stepmother's book, I exaggerate a cough. *Leave it*, I mouth, as I take the seat opposite Heath, my brother beside me. And though Heath grimaces a little, he listens.

Slumping with relief, I avoid his gaze, focusing on pushing my food around my plate as if I might actually eat it.

A record-breaking sixty seconds passes before Marisol clucks her tongue. 'I made that for you, Daniela.'

'I know.'

'You're not doing *that* again, are you?'

My spine damn near cracks with how abruptly I stiffen. 'No.'

'You remember what happened last time, hm? You looked terrible. All boney.'

It isn't funny, but I find myself stifling a laugh of sorts. *That's* her concern. Not my health. Not my wellbeing. My fucking bones protruding was a little too unsightly for her – *that's* what she remembers. 'I have practice in the morning. I can't eat all of this.'

'Who says? Your father?'

Seba's fork hits the table with a clatter. '*Marisol*. What the fuck?'

'Don't swear at me,' she chides. 'Am I lying? What am I saying wrong?'

What am I saying wrong? Haven't I asked that before? God, didn't I ask that just the other day, when Heath was so perplexed as to why I didn't want him witnessing something just like this? Is this how I make people feel when suffering my social ineptitude?

Fuck. What a horrifying thought.

Even if I wanted to, I can't eat now.

Beneath the table, a foot nudges mine. Cloying bile burns my throat as I force my gaze upwards, flinching when it meets a furious one. Tongue running over his teeth, Heath jerks his head toward the door. I shake my own. Leaving will just make things worse.

Bright, narrowed eyes shift to my stepmother, and the tip of my socked feet connect with Heath's shin, another shake of my head forbidding him from opening his mouth. That won't help either. It won't change anything. Nothing will.

One of these days, I'll grow the fuck up and stop hoping otherwise.

We drive in uncomfortable, nauseating silence for just long enough to escape my stepmother's neighborhood before Heath pulls over.

We're on the outskirts of town. It's dark. It's cold. It's a long walk home. I don't even want to go home, yet still, I consider it. Anything to escape this . . . *this*. *This* is beyond description. *I* am beyond description, I'm so many things right now, there isn't a proper word to encapsulate it all. 'Humiliated' doesn't even begin to cut it.

As if the man behind the wheel can hear my thoughts, the passenger side lock suddenly engages.

'Dani,' he starts, and I flinch. 'I'm so sorry.'

Pressed close enough to the door to feel the chill leaking in from outside, I knuckle my dry, itchy eyes. 'Why?'

'I should've said something. I just didn't wanna make it worse.'

'Not your responsibility.'

'Yeah, it is. I'm your— We're friends. That wasn't okay, Dani. The way she talks to you isn't okay.'

'It's just the way she is.'

'That doesn't make it—'

'Okay?' I finish for him roughly. 'I know. *I know, Heath*. But I don't really have the luxury to be picky when it comes to family members. I don't have anyone else, and I barely fucking see her anyways so it doesn't really matter.'

'Of course it matters, Daniela. What she said—'

'Don't,' I snap and beg in equal measures.

For once, he ignores me. 'You had an eating disorder?'

'No,' I sharply correct. 'I had disordered eating habits. There's a difference. My dad had me on a pretty strict diet for a while. It caused me some problems, but I got over it.'

An understatement, maybe, but, fuck, I don't want to get into it. It's not exactly something I yearn to relive. It was a dark spot, born of my sudden emergence from puberty, of my weight naturally rising and some parts of me filling out – all detrimental to my burgeoning career, according to Dad. All completely unavoidable, thanks to genetics, but, God, that didn't stop him from trying to fix it.

It was the worst I've ever swum in my life. The worst I've ever felt in my life. I was lethargic and weak and slow, and I hated it. It was the one time I can remember feeling like my stepmom was on my side.

The memory is slightly tainted by her grievance mostly lying with how terrible I looked, but hey. Beggars can't be choosers.

'I got over it,' I state again firmly – I remind myself as much as I do anyone else. 'I'm okay now, I swear. I went to therapy and I got a nutritionist, and I don't need a fake boyfriend to psychoanalyze me too, okay?'

'Hey, I'm your *real* friend, Dani, and I fucking care about you, and just because you got better doesn't mean it's okay for anyone to throw that shit at you like that. Family or not, that's fucked up.'

'I know,' I say again, but it doesn't even sound like real words anymore.

'It's fucked-up that you let her.'

'Hey—'

'I'm not finished,' he cuts me off, firm and stern and so damn serious. 'There is no one in the fucking world that is owed the right to talk to you like that.'

'She helped raise me, Heath.'

'That was her choice. You didn't choose to lose your parents, but she chose to be one. And if she regrets it, then that's her cross to bear, not yours. That's her loss, and it's *such* a fucking loss, you hear me? Jesus, Dani, I *mourn* the twenty years I didn't know you. You don't deserve to be looked down on like that. Not by your stepmom, not by your coach, not by *yourself*—'

I flinch. 'Heath—'

'And not by Ben either.'

'What does Ben have to do with this?'

'Everything, Dani. You let him treat you like shit – don't look at me like that, baby, you know you did, you said it yourself – because it was easier. Because you were lonely. Because you thought you didn't have anyone else.'

'There was no *thinking*, Heath. I didn't have anyone else.'

'Well, you do now. You have people who care about you. People who would lose their fucking minds if they'd heard that tonight. *I'm* losing my mind. I feel fucking insane because I don't get how you, *you*, can just sit there and take it. You . . . you are so fucking wonderful, honey. Anyone who treats you otherwise does not deserve you.'

I . . . gape. Heath breathes heavily, he breathes *anger*, and I just gape at him silently, because while I'm more than familiar with people being mad at me, somebody being mad *for* me is completely new. I don't know what to do with it. How to process it. How to ease it, to make it better, and, God, do I want to.

Swallowing roughly, I breach the gap between us, my hand hesitant as it finds his nape. Squeezes. Offers comfort, and finds it tenfold when he slumps into my touch. I don't know what to say other than 'Thank you.'

I don't think it's enough, but, for now, he lets it be. He shifts until his mouth finds the delicate skin of my inner wrist, a hot breath warming my veins. 'Please don't ask me to leave you alone right now. I can't do it.'

Honestly, for once, I can't imagine anything worse. My pinky tapping a thoughtful rhythm against the dainty match inked behind his ear, I drag my thumb over shorn, blond hair as I try to piece together exactly what I want right now.

I think I surprise both of us by blurting, 'I need a drink.'

TWENTY-TWO

AS I TAKE IN THE LOUD, BUSTLING SCENE BEFORE ME, I frown. 'Do they know it's a weekday?'

Heath laughs, not nearly as perplexed by the sheer volume of students spilling out of a two-story house and onto a lawn littered with solo cups and stumbling bodies. Although, why would he be? He's used to it.

Curling his fingers around mine, he starts to tug me down the gravel driveway we stand at the end of. 'You're an eighty-year-old woman trapped in a hot young body, you know that?'

'That I have a hot young body? Uh-huh.'

Something between a groan and a laugh escapes him. 'You sure about this?'

'I can't say I am. Are *you* sure about this?'

'Oh, I've been waiting years for this.'

'Hey, I thought we were friends now. You're not supposed to bask in my inevitable ostracization.'

'Am I supposed to be turned on when you use really big words?'

With a dry laugh that hurts my throat, I wrench my hand free of his and shove him away. 'Stop that.'

Sighing as if such a command is damn near insurmountable,

he takes my hand again and gives me a tug. 'C'mon. Everyone's already inside.'

Right. Inside. Party. *Distraction*. That's what I need. A big ol' distraction. I need sensory overload until I literally have no room in my mind left to think about my stepmother. Until there's no room to think at all.

Steeling myself against the very big part of me that wholeheartedly disagrees with that plan, I speed up so that I'm the one dragging Heath inside.

Body heat hits me like a slap to the face. The stench of alcohol makes my nose scrunch, the music makes my whole face crumple, makes me want to cover my ears, makes my entire body thrum, but I welcome the sensation. Embrace it. Dive into the chaos by surging through the swaying crowd, no idea where I'm going, but hey, that's what the man on my tail is for.

A tap on my shoulder has me twisting toward him – and abruptly realizing just how close he is. Plastered to my back, a proprietary hand on my hip. The other releases the one of mine it holds, rising to shove some guy out of the way before pointing to where I guess his friends are, and then dropping to my other hip. He holds me close as he strong-arms his way through the crowd like some kind of bodyguard, and the comparison makes me snicker because, honestly, that's like giving a golden retriever a rottweiler's job.

'You're here!'

Even over the din, I recognize Matilda's joyous tone a second before one of the many bodies surrounding us shifts and the redhead comes into view. A hand stretches through the crowd, perfectly manicured fingers wrapping around my bicep, and with a tug, I break through to the inner circle.

Shooting the others a stiff smile, I let Matilda guide me – and Heath too, considering his grip doesn't let up – to stand beside her, wincing at her smile because, fuck, it's so bright it hurts my damn eyes. 'How was it?'

And there goes my chest. Hurting too. 'She likes him more than she likes me.'

Everyone laughs like I cracked a joke, and I don't bother correcting them.

'You drinking?'

'No, I'm here for the ambiance.'

Imani snickers. With a flick of her wrist, a drink materializes, and as she hands it over, she offers a shot too, both of which I accept.

The latter disappears in the blink of an eye, and while I intend on making quick work of the rum and coke too, a mouth tickling my earlobe causes me pause. 'Practice tomorrow?'

I wave Heath off, my other hand bringing my drink to my lips. 'I'll be fine.'

'This,' Matilda holds up another shot, 'is an act of humanitarianism. She's just evening the playing field so her teammates can lose a little bit to her instead of a lot.'

'Exactly.' Taking the one she offers me, I clink our glasses together. 'I'm being kind.'

Heath squeezes my hip gently. 'Doesn't suit you.'

Dropping my head back, I pout up at him. 'Ouch, baby.'

When that uber-concerned expression goes nowhere, I sigh

and turn around, rising on my tiptoes and, shit, these drinks are strong. So strong that I wobble a little, and in leaning forward to balance, my forehead winds up pressed to Heath's. Quietly, only for him, I murmur, 'Your boyfriend duties are limited to PDA, y'know. The overbearing concern for my wellbeing isn't necessary.'

'I'm a method actor.'

Snorting, I drop to my soles again. 'Try *acting* like you want me to be here then.'

'Don't have to act that at all.'

'Then stop ruining my fun.'

A dramatic exhale skates across my face as palms drag up and down the length of my biceps. 'Okay.'

'And,' I add – I blurt, more like, when his touch falls away and when he starts to fall away too, when I suffer a sudden flash of parties past. Of me by myself, searching for my boyfriend, for anyone at all to talk to, and coming up completely empty. 'Don't leave me alone.'

In the blink of an eye, all of that concern melts away. Another blink and he's as close as close can get again. Our fronts practically flush. Our pinkies linked and hovering a millimeter away from his mouth, so close that I feel him breathe, 'Promise I won't.'

Something inside me, something deep-buried and dormant, trembles ever-so-slightly.

'However.' Heath tugs and I go careening into him. 'That means you're gonna have to dance with me.'

'Over my dead body, *cariño*.'

Eyelids dropping to half-mast, a content little noise rumbles in his chest. His smile blooms even brighter. The hand still hooked around mine rises, pulling me up to my tiptoes, guiding one arm around his, then the other, while his snakes round my waist. His palms flatten against the small of my back. 'Really like when you call me that.'

'I'll stop doing it immediately.'

Heath barks a laugh and it's like a freaking sonar weapon, like some kind of manipulative soundwave that has me beaming against my will, won't let me stop.

Something clicks to my left, and I don't even register the noise until it sounds half a dozen times over.

'Sorry.' Not looking even a little bit so, Imani holds her camera aloft and shrugs. 'Couldn't resist. Y'all are *cute*.'

'Told ya.' Heath pats the curve of my ass. 'Send me those.'

Imani salutes and then she's off, wandering into the crowd, snapping as she goes, completely oblivious to the tall, ginger man who wanders in her wake. I glance at Heath, wondering if he notices Brendan's pursuit too, only to find his gaze steadfastly locked on me.

I get the distinct feeling that it never strayed.

'C'mon,' he mutters, his favorite command, providing me with the false sense of choice because I don't come anywhere so much as he tightens his grip around my waist, lifts me off the ground, and fucking carries me onto the makeshift dancefloor against my will, protests be damned.

Protests.

What protests, Daniela?

I squeal and I laugh and I holler his name, but I never

actually say *put me down*, do I? My legs swing as he spins us, knocking into a whole lot of people that don't do much protesting either – they don't *care*, they're too drunk or high or happy to give a shit about a giggling girl and the stupid, smiling boy tossing her around like a ragdoll.

No, as Heath keeps me firmly aloft and does the dancing for us, I don't actually fight to be put down at all. If anything, I cling. I lace my fingers together at the base of Heath's neck, and my own creaks backwards as I cackle at the ceiling, I laugh so hard my freaking stomach hurts, and I don't even know what's so damn funny.

I don't know the song playing. I don't know the vast majority of the sweaty bodies pulsing around me. I don't know what's in the cup Imani and Matilda take turns refilling.

For what feels like the first time in life, *I don't know.*

And I don't care either.

I dance until I'm sweaty and breathless and exhausted in a way I never have been before. And I drink until most of my senses are blessedly numb, but I don't drink enough. I don't drink myself into oblivion. I am still very much in control of my faculties, still so scaldingly aware of fleeting kisses and wandering hands and bright, warm eyes that have barely left me all night.

And that's a very big problem.

It takes me a while to figure it out. To figure out the buzz beneath my skin and the restlessness plaguing my limbs and the dull ache in my lower stomach. I think it might be inebriation at first and then I wonder if I'm sick, and then I start considering if this is just what being happy feels like. If Heath dancing with me, and only me, makes me happy. If his sole purpose for the evening seemingly being to coax laugh after laugh out of me makes me happy. If his big hands and their proprietary grip on my hips, if his fingers being so long that they almost meet at the middle of my back, *just* make me happy.

I'm tucked in the darkest corner of the living room that belongs to someone who's name I don't even know, my back pressed tightly to the front of someone I definitely do know, when I finally manage to put a name to the feeling I barely know.

I'm horny. Unmistakably, irreversibly horny. I could blame the thick air in here, tainted with hormones. I could blame the girls too, the cat-calling, the loaded comments and the kissing noises and the insistence that I am *sooooo* gonna get some tonight. I could blame proximity, friction, *so much friction*.

Except I'd be lying. Because it is all of that, and it's not. It's all of that, and it's the arm banded across my waist, holding me securely, keeping me safe. It's the pinky still locked around my own. It's the hot breath that brushes my cheeks, my forehead, the curve of my neck and contours of my mouth.

But most of all, it's the attention. The unwavering, complete attention. The feeling that this place could go up in flames, and Heath wouldn't even notice because he's so focused on me. He's looking at me the way he's been looking at me all night, and I'm hot and shaky and fucking bothered, and actively fighting the urge to make him *fix it*.

I don't get it. I really don't fucking get it. *Why?* Why *him*? I was with Ben for years, and I never . . . well, I did, but it . . . it wasn't like *this*. I didn't feel like this, so *desperate*.

The back of my neck prickles as my hair is swept away, and a warm breeze dances across my skin – a warm *breath*. 'You okay?'

No. My heart is beating too fast and my skin is too sensitive and my every movement reminds me that between my thighs is slick, and a fist is holding my hair hostage and it's *not helping*. 'I need some air,' is what I rasp over the thumping music as I move out of his orbit for the first time in hours.

It doesn't last long. I don't hear him – I can barely hear anything over the blood pounding in my ears – but I feel him follow me toward the sliding back doors that lead to the backyard. I feel him follow me outside, feel him trudge across the grass to the huddle of lounge chairs tucked away in the dark far end, and just before I collapse into one of them, I feel him stop me.

I feel a whole lot of things when he drops into one, spreads his legs, and pats a thigh.

My gaze darts around the yard. I frown when I confirm that we are relatively alone, except for the few people leaning against the back wall of the house, smoking. 'No one's watching us.'

His smile barely wavers, but I notice. The same way I notice his hand flex and curl before he raps his knuckles against his leg. 'I know. Sit with me anyway.'

I wipe my sweaty palms on my skirt. My very short, very tight denim mini skirt, that barely hides the slick proof of the horny little secret I'd rather not be revealed quite so damningly. 'I'll stand.'

Heath doesn't like that option at all. I don't get why, but I don't ask – my tongue abruptly gets all tangled up in my mouth when he leans forward and grips the back of my thighs, just above the crease of my knees, and guides me between his legs. Gentle enough, but firm. Like if I'm going to stand, it has to be right here.

'Didn't work, huh?'

'What?'

'You're all tense. Still thinking about earlier?'

I shake my head. God, I forgot there even was an earlier, that that whole thing with my stepmom even happened. Isn't that kind of fucking terrible? That a supremely shitty encounter, a meal that nearly drove me to tears, can just go *poof* because of a little male attention?

Isn't that just fucking *terrifying*?

'I am,' Heath admits. 'I should've said something. I let you down.'

No, I correct myself silently. *Not because of a little male attention. Because someone cared enough to make me feel better.*

'You didn't,' I promise. Fuck, I love that he cares so much. Makes me want to burrow inside his fucking chest, get an eyeful of that big heart just so I can see how he makes it beat so nicely. Makes me want to kiss the concern right out of him, and in my tipsy state, I can't find a reason not to do that.

But as my hands find his shoulders, my gaze finds something else. 'Oh, fuck me.'

'What?'

'Some of Ben's friends just walked in.' As he twists to look, I grip his shoulders more firmly, keeping his gaze on me. The last thing I need is for a stray fucking glance or a goading facial expression to start a pissing match. 'Don't look.'

'Do you see him?'

I peer at the new crowd a little more closely, squinting against the darkness, fighting the fine haze of alcohol and music and sensory fucking overload. 'I can't tell.'

Heath grunts.

'Maybe we should, uh, do something. Phase . . .' Four? Five? I've lost track now. Honestly, I forgot they were even a thing.

I think Heath did too.

'Got anything in mind?'

I purse my lips, thinking. Out of the corner of my eye, a flash of movement catches my attention – a guy and a girl, hand in hand, stumbling up the staircase. 'We could go upstairs.'

Heath blinks. Repeats, 'We could go upstairs.'

'Yeah.'

'And do what, Daniela?'

'Well, we wouldn't do anything. But, uh, people would think we were . . . y'know. Doing what couples do upstairs at parties.'

'Why, darling, whatever could that be?'

My cheeks heat as my eyes narrow. 'You know.'

'I'm a nice, respectable boy,' he claims, he *teases*. 'Spell it out for me.'

Eyeballing the little smirk he does a shitty job of hiding, defiance thrums in my veins. He wants to tease me? Fine. Two can play at that game. I can tease too. Surely, I can.

Humming lowly, I let my hands wander. I smooth them along rigid pectoral muscles, over broad shoulders and back again, dipping beneath that indecently unbuttoned shirt so I'm palming bare skin. Tapping the freckles dusting his collarbone, I stoop to eye-level and flash a shitty little smirk of my own. 'They fuck, Heath. People would think we're fucking.'

Beneath my palm, his heart skips. A couple of inches above my fingertips, his throat bobs dramatically. 'And you'd be okay with that?'

'Why wouldn't I be?' I question, purposely obtuse, my bravado strengthened by tequila and obstinance. 'It's just sex. Hypothetical sex, of course.'

'Right.' He swallows again. Wraps his fingers across my wrists. Reveals slick, clammy palms.

My head cocks. 'That makes you nervous.'

'Not quite the word I'd use for it.'

'Pick a better one then.'

'Daniela.'

'What?'

'Enough. Please.'

'You started it.'

'And now I'm ending it.'

'Why?'

'Dani. Baby.'

When I'm no less confused by what I can only describe as anguish darkening his gaze, he lets a ragged noise loose.

With an inhale that's just as unsteady, he curls his fingers loosely around my wrist. Moving slowly, giving me every opportunity to stop him, he moves my hand down and down and down, until it reaches his lap.

Something hard pulses beneath my knuckles, and my lungs abruptly stop working. 'Oh.'

'Yeah.' He lets me go, clearing his throat. 'Sorry.'

My hand goes nowhere.

Nor does my frown.

Sorry? He's *sorry*? He's . . . embarrassed, almost. Not ashamed, but bashful. Adorable.

Entirely oblivious to how far that sweet, pink flush goes in appeasing the anxiety roiling in my gut.

It's not just me, a tiny, timid voice in the back of my head celebrates. *He feels it too.*

He can't catch his breath either. He doesn't move when I do, when I clamber onto his lap like I have every right to be there, like I freaking straddle him all the time. He does ask, quiet and almost unsure, 'What are you doing?'

'Testing that theory again,' I offer, the same excuse as last time. Like a comfort blanket for someone so insanely out of their depth. 'The results were inconclusive, remember?'

His breath hitches again. His heart pounds in a racing beat that I imagine, if I were to press a hand to my chest, would perfectly match my own. 'Here?'

I nod. I feel brave here. I'm too scared to go anywhere else, scared I'll scare myself off. 'Is that okay?'

'*Is that okay?*' he repeats, he laughs. He drops his head back, shaking it as he fucking giggles at the sky. When he looks at me again, he's utterly serious. 'You really have no idea, do you?'

'No idea about—'

Lips, rough and desperate, abruptly press to mine, and I

forget I was even speaking – I damn near forget my own name as Heath erases the word *okay* from my vocabulary. He swallows my gasps, my thoughts, my entire fucking consciousness until I am nothing but the puddle of warmth in my gut and the goose-bumped skin he caresses so reverently. He kisses me like it is the one thing in the world he was made for, and, God, I hope I'm returning the favor.

'*Fuck*, Daniela.' He bites my bottom lip like he's mad at it. Rough in a way that makes my thighs clench, he shoves up my skirt and palms my bare ass, slapping one cheek like that's making him mad too. 'You gotta tell me to stop, baby.'

The mere suggestion makes my stomach twist. I clutch him so tightly, my nails carve half-moon marks into his shoulders. 'I don't want you to.'

His groan is as tangible, as *arousing*, as the calloused fingers digging into my flesh. Snapping the waistband of my thong, he swallows my whimper. 'What do you want?'

I think it's pretty obvious. My panties are soaked, and I know he knows it because when his fingertips graze the wet fabric, he makes an unholy fucking noise. He uses my hair to guide me backwards, to give himself a better view, and he thrusts his hips upwards, grinding the hard bulge tenting his jeans against me until my eyes roll to the back of my head.

Three thrusts. That's all I get before he tugs my hair hard enough to get my attention. A silent demand. And it's confirmed for me, all of a sudden, that I am, in fact, not broken. That there isn't anything wrong with my libido, that there never was, that it was some other factor that wasn't right. Because there is very little I wouldn't do right now to satisfy it. I'll even admit it. 'I really, really want you to make me come.'

Heath goes still. As his head shakes, it flops backwards so he can curse at the sky. He curses *me*. Almost unintelligible, he mumbles that I'm going to be the fucking death of him.

'The things I would do,' he rasps in my ear, as he follows the curve of my ass until he finds the edge of my panties, 'to get my mouth on you right now.'

My lungs all but disintegrate. I'm sure that whatever those things are, I would do much, much worse.

'But we can't do that here.' He only disappoints me for a split second. The next, he's nudging my thong aside and making me gasp with light, teasing touches. 'We don't have time. I can't wait. This cunt can't either, can it?'

'*I* can't.'

He doesn't make me. Easily, *audibly*, he slips two fingers inside of me. Just enough to stretch, to madden, to push the air out of my body and replace it with white-hot tension. 'This okay, honey?'

The second I shake my head, he freezes. With a groan, I buck my hips to try to urge him back into action. '*Not enough*.'

His exhale is pure relief and tantalizing promise. He shifts, bring his hand around to cup me from the front, and then he's sliding inside of me again, two fingers right down to the knuckles while his thumb finds my clit and stokes that swollen ache. 'Was too quick last time. You didn't get to enjoy it. I didn't get to enjoy you. Slow, honey. Like that. Use me. *Good girl*.'

I shudder. It feels so good, I forget where we are, that we're only barely in private. Heath reminds me when I moan a little too loudly, he shushes me with a gentle rumble, he guides my face to the crook of his neck, where I muffle my obscene noises, where I *bite*.

Cursing and groaning and fucking *whining*, he tells me he could come from that alone. I almost demand he prove it. I start to encourage it, pulling away enough to sneak a hand between our bodies and palm him through his jeans.

And then I make the mistake of looking up.

My body clenches, tightening around Heath's fingers. I'm not entirely sure it's another hot wave of pleasure that skyrockets my internal temperature, or an equally scalding rush of panic.

'Heath.'

He grunts, satisfied. He twists his hand just the right way, and I bite my lip hard enough to taste blood.

'Heath.'

Teeth sink into my neck, and *oh my God.*

'Ben.'

Those maddening, perfect movements come to an abrupt stop, and I almost burst into tears. Slowly, Heath reels back. 'What did you just say?'

Another man's name, I realize with a wince. 'No. Not like that, I—' *Jesus,* I can barely breathe. 'Ben is here.'

'Where?'

My gaze flicks forward. Finds my ex again where he's joined his friends – where he's already looking at me.

'He see you?'

I nod.

'He know?'

Swallowing, I assess my ex. The slack jaw and crumpled brow, the narrowed eyes that take me in, that must register the way I'm moving, that must recognize it. Even from a distance, the tight, furious twist of his features is easily seen. When I nod again, it's as shaky as the rest of me.

'What does he know, Dani? That I'm knuckle-deep inside you right now? That you're soaking my hand? That you're actually enjoying it? That if I asked nicely, you'd let me fuck you, right here, right now?'

A whimper burns my throat. Of their own accord, my hips start to rock again, and, *fuck*, does that set him off.

'Don't need anything else, do you? Just me. Someone who knows what the fuck they're doing. Someone who knows you. Mind, soul, and then fuckin' body.'

I come with a strangled noise, fingernails digging into the back of my not-boyfriend's head, eyes fixed on my ex-boyfriend, but not even seeing him.

I see black. Stars. God, briefly, I think. I say *God*, I say it a lot, *God* and *Heath* and so many curse words in all the languages I know, and maybe even some languages I don't. I'm speaking in fucking tongues, I'm sure of it, I've lost my mind in pleasure, I *am* pleasure personified.

For what feels like forever, I writhe and I buck and I cry, and Heath gently coaxes me through it all. He speaks tongues of his own except his are literal, his tongue lashes against my pulse, down my neck, everywhere he can possibly reach. He mutters his own words too, words that sounds like my name and my name and some more of my fucking name, and I think I could come again and again and again, from that alone, even if his fingers weren't still moving inside of me.

He only stops when I beg him to. When I crumble, and the wet, salty tears burning a path down my cheeks scald his neck as I bury my face there. He slips out of me, making me whine – with relief or annoyance, I'm not entirely sure, though I lean toward the latter, despite it being my insistence that made him do it in the first place – and while his slick hand grips my thigh hard, the other lightly traces the length of my spine soothingly.

When my body finally settles, when I finally settle back inside of my body, I huff a sated, smiling noise.

I'm smiling. I can't stop smiling. God, that felt so *real*. I didn't have to force it, I wasn't consumed by self-consciousness, I was just here. Enjoying myself for myself, not for the sake of anyone else.

I laugh this time. I laugh breathlessly as I pull back, as I grace Heath with the brunt of my smile, as I open my mouth to thank him or kiss him or, fuck, suggest we do that—

'Theory confirmed?'

And just like that, I drop back down to Earth a little – Heath's face drags me down. His tight expression, wiped clean of any of the pleasure or the need or the desperation that was contorting it a mere moment ago.

Abruptly, I sit back – abruptly, I remember where I'm sitting. I remember *how* I'm sitting when Heath's gaze drops to my lap and becomes pure black, turquoise irises giving way to pupils, and I scramble to stand and yank my skirt into a marginally more modest position.

Heath takes his time getting up. He adjusts himself with a wince, and my cheeks burn.

'Should I . . .'

With a faint shake of his head, Heath takes my hand with the one of his that wasn't just inside me. That one . . . well. *Well.* We walk back inside, and as we pass Ben and his horde, Heath slips that fucking hand, those glistening fingers, between his lips and licks them fucking clean. He doesn't so much as glance at my ex, but everyone and their fucking mother would know that smirk is all for him.

My pussy fucking *throbs*.

He leads me into the nearest bathroom, locking the door behind us, and all kinds of different parts of my anatomy get excited. I assume more is on the cards. I'll take care of that incredibly obvious, incredibly distracting bulge tenting his jeans, and, maybe, he'll take care of me some more.

I would like that. I would really, really like that. I'm opening my mouth to suggest that, to request it, quickly and bluntly and oh-so-pragmatically, and not at all with anything remotely related to the dreamy glimmer dancing in my eyes – in fact, I blame *that* on the cloudy bathroom mirror and shitty overhead lighting.

Heath opens his mouth first. 'We shouldn't have done that.'

My stomach drops.

My expression does too, but he doesn't see that. He's hunched over the bathroom sink, washing his hands, splashing water on his face, scrubbing away any evidence of me. 'That wasn't right.'

My knees wobble. My reflection sways, and I can't tell if it's my blurring vision or a sudden bout of unsteadiness or both. 'It wasn't right?'

He grunts. He won't look at me. Fingers curled around the edge of the sink, he glares into the basin.

For a few fleeting seconds, I allow my hurt to fester. I let it spread through my body, slump my shoulders and my spine, and gather at the back of my throat, the corners of my eyes, the pit of my stomach that was, what can't be more than five fucking minutes ago, cramping with pure, unfamiliar pleasure. I let myself . . . fuck, I let myself *grieve*. I mourn the first taste of sex that's ever felt like anything more than just body parts clumsily colliding.

But by the time he looks up, I'm glaring too.

He says my name, and I don't say a word. I don't make a single noise, don't offer any acknowledgment of what he can't possibly know was the absolute worst thing to say, because then he wouldn't have said it. He turns around, but I'm already unlocking the door and slipping into the hallway.

If he says anything else, it's lost to the music. I wouldn't stop to hear it anyway. I make a beeline for the kitchen. I grab the first alcoholic beverage I find, and I swig straight vodka, right out of the bottle.

And as it screams a burning path to my stomach, I cover my mouth with my free hand, and I scream just a little bit too.

TWENTY-THREE

I'M UNSURE HOW, EXACTLY, I END UP ON TOP OF A questionably steady table, a bottle of mystery liquor in one hand, and Imani's in the other – I just know that it happens.

I know that, any minute now, I'm likely to tumble to the ground in a heap of tangled limbs and broken furniture, but if anything good has come of this night, it's my handy new ability to not fucking care. A *timely* new ability, because imagine if I did care right now; imagine if I was dancing on a table, surrounded by strangers who are doing their best to see up my skirt, still a little buzzy from all those *not right* orgasms, and I *cared*.

'Daniela Williams,' Imani screams in my ear, her hip bumping mine in rhythm to the music, an emphatic member of the table-dancing, not-caring committee; party of three, including the headbanging redhead on my other side. 'I am so glad Heath finally grew some balls.'

I cackle. I have no idea what that means. I don't want to. I have been doing a spectacular job of not thinking about Heath at all.

If spectacular was a synonym for piss-poor.

Semantics.

What's important is I've successfully avoided him for the

better part of . . . well, however long it took to get me this drunk. I haven't checked the time in a while. I lost my phone, I think. And I have no idea where my keys are, but, again, not important. Not at all. I don't know where Heath is either, and that right there *is* important.

That's worth another swig of . . . tequila. I think. I can't tell; my tastebuds are as plastered as the rest of me.

A little bit misses my mouth and dribbles down my neck. I'm wiping it away when something grazes my leg. I tighten my grip on the neck of the bottle, ready to wield it like a weapon in case some drunk frat dipshit is trying to get handsy. Or worse, if it's Ben tugging on the hem of my skirt. Or even worse-er, if it's *Heath*.

Scowling, I drop my gaze.

My relieved sigh is almost loud enough to be heard over the ungodly techno racket.

I don't know the man smirking up at me. Or maybe I do – he's looking at me like he knows me. And he looks mildly offended when I drop to my haunches and slur, 'Do I know you?'

That slick expression momentarily falters, but the maybe-stranger recovers quickly. 'It's Ryan.'

I stare at him blankly. 'Doesn't ring a bell.'

'I'm on Heath's team.'

At the sound of his name, I wince. I take another swig of alcohol, and I don't wince at all as it burns a path down my throat because, actually, it doesn't really burn all that much anymore. A sign that I've had enough, surely, if I was coherent enough to notice it. 'Right.'

I remember now. He was there that day, the first day, the first practice Heath and I attended together, hand-in-hand. He introduced him, and he stared at me the way he's staring at me now. With that glimmer, that sheen of interest. The one that Heath always—

No.

Bad Dani.

Palms planted on the table, Ryan leans in to shout in my ear. 'You look good up there.'

I laugh. Funny how I can do so much of that with such a great big ache in my chest. Chuckling like I don't have a care in the world, I reach out a clumsy hand, swaying precariously for a moment before finding a warm, hard shoulder to steady myself on. 'Thanks, Ron.'

'*Ryan.*'

'Right.' I sling back another drink. 'Can I help you with something?'

'Wanna come down here and dance with me?'

'No,' I answer so easily, too easily, and it makes me pause. Maybe I should. Maybe that's exactly what I need; a man that isn't my ex-boyfriend or my fake boyfriend or even a friend at all, just a boy. Mindless, unimportant dancing with someone who doesn't have the capacity to break my heart.

That thought sobers me. Briefly, and only enough for the tiniest shred of common sense to wriggle through my cushy little drunken protective layer, and remind me a man is never what I need. Dancing with the girls is way more fun, and I start to get back to that, start to straighten up only for all of that alcohol to suddenly catch up with me.

A headrush has me wobbling. As my hand slips off Ryan's

shoulder, the rest of me slips off the table with a shriek. Luckily, I'm caught before my face gets intimately familiar with the floor.

Unluckily, my face gets intimately familiar with something else instead. With someone else's. With brown eyes. Not blue or green or any combination of the two either.

My eyes close for a moment as I breathe deep, and my face scrunches when an unfamiliar scent fills my lungs. They open again and I realize just how close my little fumble has brought me to Ryan, and I reel backwards. I register how firmly hands clutch the bare skin above my waistband, and I knock them away, shivering as this utterly nonsensical feeling of wrong washes over me.

'Don't touch me,' I find myself snapping, which is ridiculous. He just saved me from finding out exactly what is making the floor beneath my unsteady feet quite so sticky. He was helping me, not fondling me.

So why am I so *itchy*?

'Sorry.' Ryan holds his hands up, completely innocent, he didn't do a damn thing wrong, but I feel like I did. He holds one hand out, an invitation and, shit, that feels wrong too.

Against my will, my brain imagines the metaphorical tables turning. Heath too drunk, too touchy with someone else, too close, dancing.

My stomach roils.

Face crinkled with concern, Ryan steps forward. 'Are you alright?'

I step back, almost tripping over my own feet. 'Drink,' I oh-so-eloquently mumble, holding the bottle I clutch aloft and giving it a shake, wincing when a whole lot of liquid sloshes around inside, *lying*, 'Need a new one.'

'I'll get you one.'

'No,' another voice drawls. 'I don't think you will.'

Slowly, I turn around. Crank my neck back. Find the dark gaze of a deeply unimpressed man glowering at the one behind me.

I gulp. 'I wasn't doing anything.'

Jaw cocked, Heath grunts. 'Time to go.'

Later, tomorrow, when I've returned to my body and remember this incident, I'm sure I'll burst into flames at the memory of sticking my tongue out like a misbehaving child.

'It's late, Dani. You've got practice tomorrow. You've gotta sleep this off.'

God help me. I do it again. My middle finger makes an appearance too.

'You're gonna regret it in the morning.'

I cackle and lift my drink in a mocking *cheers* before tipping it to my lips, muttering around the rim, 'Then I guess we'll be a matching pair, huh?'

'Okay.' A hand snatches the bottle away before it makes contact. 'Enough. I'm taking you home.'

With a whine, I spin away from Heath – and then I spin some more, a dizzy spell making me stumble, but at least my stumbling brings me into the kitchen, away from most of the crowd and toward a decent replacement for my stolen maybe-tequila.

Except the very second my fingers close around a can of beer, it's snatched away from me.

'Jesus,' I huff, throwing my fucking stalker a squinty scowl. 'Back off. What are you,' I snicker, 'my boyfriend?'

If I was sober, I'd notice Heath's entire face falling. I'd see a single second of despair before he hastily covers it up with gritted teeth and a snarled mouth and a sighed 'Daniela.'

His exasperation is deafening. Provoking. It pokes me in all the wrong places, reminds me of all the wrong things, makes me think of a different man needling me about the same things, in that same fucking tone. 'Do you know I once swam a meet with an infected wisdom tooth?'

'Why would you do that?'

'My dad said dentists were for winners.'

Full lips part. I stare at that freckle on his lip as it stretches and pulls, as his mouth contorts into ugly shock, as he repeats a breathy 'Daniela.'

I crack a smile. 'Kidding.'

'Are you?'

No, but it doesn't matter. I won. I got my tooth pulled the next day, and as soon as I was coherent enough to get back in the water, I did. I didn't mean to tell him that, though. I don't mean to tell him anything at all, but my damn mouth won't stop moving. 'When I was thirteen, I got strep and couldn't go to practice, but my dad made me swim laps in the pool in our backyard anyway. I think it was the year after that – before that? I can't remember. Anyway. Our pool broke so we did drills in the ocean and—' The memory isn't even remotely a funny one, yet I find myself chuckling anyway. 'I genuinely thought I was gonna drown. But I didn't. And then, when I was sixteen, I won the state championships the day after my dad's funeral, so I think I can handle a hangover.'

His face falls again. A third quiet utterance of my name makes me sway on my feet, makes my chest fucking hurt, but I push past it. 'I'll go home when I'm ready to go home, okay, Heath? So *back*,' I press a palm to his chest and shove, '*off*.'

He doesn't move a muscle. He's like a brick wall, and the thing about brick walls is when you go smashing into one, you're the one who gets hurt. I'm the one who ends up careening backwards. I essentially shove myself. I trip over my own damn feet, and as I go down, I cackle at the utter ridiculousness of it all.

I'm still cackling when my shoulder catches against the edge of the counter hard enough for a spark of pain to actually penetrate the thick layer of alcohol clouding my senses, and when the tiles bruise my ass – I stop abruptly when I try to get up, and putting any weight on my left side sends pain so intense radiating out from deep within my shoulder that it's almost sobering.

Almost.

'Jesus, Dani.' Before I can protest, Heath hauls me to my feet. 'Are you okay?'

Swaying listlessly, I shake myself out and ignore how very wrong something feels – I shake him off, but that doesn't feel all that right either. 'What did I just say, Heath?'

He doesn't make me repeat myself. Hands up, he backs away. He leaves me be.

I don't linger long enough for him to change his mind.

My left knee is bleeding, and I'm not sure how it happened.

Maybe it was when Kai spun me a little too vigorously on the makeshift living-room dancefloor and I collided with a poorly placed coffee table. Or when Heath finally succeeded in hauling my wobbly ass outside and I got extremely familiar with the gravel cutting a pathway through the front lawn. I do vaguely remember wincing when I tripped up the steps of my apartment complex, but I remember laughing too, so, really, my injury can't be that bad.

Although, if Heath's face is anything to go by, I might not survive the night.

Crouched in front of me, he surveys my broken skin with fierce concentration, one hand cupping the back of my knee while the other swipes away dried blood and bits of debris with an antiseptic wipe.

'Is an amputation imminent?' I drawl, or at least that's what I try to drawl. I'm not sure it comes out all that coherent – I'm pretty sure it's nothing more than a mess of syllables.

My yipped *ow*, on the other hand, is perfectly clear.

Heath mumbles an apology, a calloused thumb swiping along the outside of my knee as he smooths a Band-Aid into place. His mouth a gentle upward curve, he braces both hands on his thighs and sighs softly. 'What am I gonna do with you, huh?'

Fingers curled around my bedsheets, I lick my lips. I have an idea. Many ideas. Terrible ideas. *Not right* ideas.

Internally, I slap myself across the face. Hard.

Externally, I snip, 'Leave me alone, preferably.'

'Can't. Pinky-promised otherwise.'

'Well, I free you from your promise.'

'I think *that* requires an amputation.'

Snorting a laugh, I forget, for a split second, that I'm mad at him. I lean forward on instinct, I go to kiss him on instinct, on silly, drunken instinct, and I am silly, drunken confusion when he pulls away. Like *away*. Like stands up and backs up a step and holds his hands out like he's anticipating needing to keep me at bay.

'I'm not kissing you like this.'

Of course. Why the hell would he? No one's around. My ex isn't watching. It's *not right*.

'Yeah. Sorry.' Forcing out another laugh that I pray could in any way, shape, or form be interpreted as nonchalant, I try to stand. Naturally, since gravity and I haven't been on speaking terms for quite a few hours now, I wobble something fierce, and those pesky fucking instincts kick in again. Have me bracing myself against a hard chest, fingertips smoothing over soft cotton, forehead feeling that softness too as it falls against a hard sternum with a thump.

I rest there for a second. Just for a second. A silly, indulgent second. Suck in a silly indulgent lungful of sweat and beer and Heath.

I exhale, and I get the fuck ahold of myself.

Pushing off him harder than I need to, I shake my head, and mentally shake some sense into the rest of me. 'Okay. You can go now.'

'I think I should stay.'

'*I think* I don't want you to.'

'Dani, I know you're mad—'

'I'm not mad.' *I'm upset.*

'You're upset.'

Get out of my head. 'Why would I be upset, Heath?'

His mouth opens.

An answer does not come out.

Has anyone ever laughed this much over something so painfully unfunny?

'Right,' I say again. 'Exactly. *Adiós.*'

With a dismissive flick of both hands, I take one step toward the bathroom before quickly abandoning any aspirations of showering off this whole icky night because slipping and cracking my head would *so* be the best way to end it. Instead, I drop to sit again. I flop backwards, having every intention of wriggling my way under the covers and passing out, but firm fingers wrap around my wrists and yank me upright again.

'Change first.'

I grumble something that's incomprehensible even to me. I think the words *aye aye, captain, yes sir* and *okay, daddy* are somewhere in the mix; I think tomorrow, if I remember this – *when* I remember this, because the universe would never be so kind as to let me forget – I'll add that to the list of reasons I should just go ahead and perish.

Another pull – and a wince, because, shit, what the hell did I do to my shoulder? – and I'm on my feet. I didn't see him rummage through my drawers, but he must've because one of my t-shirts is thrown over his shoulder, my softest and most-oversized, and I pout as pesky gratitude warms me.

I'm like a doll as he undresses me, stiff and unhelpful. He's the perfect fucking gentleman, eyes half-shut, and tastefully averted.

For fuck's sake. He was tickling my fucking cervix a few hours ago, but God forbid he cop an eyeful of my boobs.

'You're drunk, Daniela.'

I blink. I said that out loud. Of course I did. *Kill me. 'You're* drunk.'

'Then you're whatever comes after drunk.'

'It was on my list.' *I'd get drunk*, I told him what feels like an age ago. *Really, obnoxiously drunk.*

'I know, baby.'

With a gentle push, he sits me on the bed again, but, still, he doesn't let me curl up, he won't let oblivion take me yet. Instead, he subjects me to more of the worst kind of torture – care. Attention. He bolsters those ridiculous, drunken notions of mine. He convinces me of things that can't be true. He really makes me think that whatever is between us isn't fake, that it's more than friendship, that it's more than *like* – he makes me forget the evidence proving otherwise.

He gathers my toiletries, he does my night-time routine for me, and my heart hurts so bad, I half-expect it to stop.

He's slowly, methodically lathering moisturizer down my neck and across my collarbones when my throat starts to ache too. When words start to claw their way up it, and refuse to be swallowed no matter how hard I try.

'Did I do something wrong?' I rasp, whispering and utterly pathetic, cowardly gaze fixed on the divot in his chin. 'Earlier? Is that why you . . .'

'Oh, honey.' A pinky curls around mine. 'I promise you didn't.'

I stare at our entwined fingers, unblinking, until my vision blurs. 'Then why didn't you want me?'

'Honey,' is all he says.

He doesn't explain. He finishes my skincare in silence, and then he pulls back my sheets and guides me beneath them. He tucks me in, and he backs up. I close my eyes so I don't have to watch him leave. I keep them closed, a furrow forming between my brows, when instead of receding footsteps, I hear the creak of bedsprings, feel him settle near my hip.

'You were upset. We were both drinking. I went too far.'

'Right. Because *you* crawled onto *my* lap.'

'It was the wrong timing, Dani. Wrong reasoning. Making Ben jealous . . .'

'Right. That's what it was,' I mean to question, but somehow find myself stating instead.

'That's what it was,' Heath parrots stiffly, and, God, it sounds like *he's* questioning it. Briefly, I contemplate opening my eyes to gauge his expression, to confirm whether or not it's my own drunken, wishful thinking. Instead, I shut them tighter; let myself pretend, for a little while, that this is all as confusing for him as it is for me. 'I'm sorry, Daniela. I didn't . . . I thought you would agree. I didn't mean to upset you.'

My voice fails me, so I just nod.

A warm weight settles on the curve of my waist. Slowly, it travels upwards until it becomes the gentle brush of fingers over my cheekbone, the drag of a thumb following the curve of my ear. He smooths my hair away from my face, he strokes it reverently, he mumbles words I can't quite make out, but they're soft and warm and, somehow, I know they're sweet. They're like a lullaby, soothing me to sleep. They get a little longer, become more intelligible, so that I can make out him whispering, 'You never have to worry about me not wanting you.'

And, 'If you knew how much . . .'

And a quiet, wobbly 'Stay', that doesn't come from him at all.

I fall asleep before I can find out if he does.

TWENTY-FOUR

THERE'S A MAN FAST ASLEEP ON MY BEDROOM FLOOR, and I have no idea how he got there.

Jesus, I have no idea how *I* got here. In my bed, in my pajamas, my hair in a bun, confused by the distinct lack of that itchy discomfort one suffers after a night sleeping in mascara.

My pulse thumps an unhappy beat behind my temples as I roll onto my back with a groan, my stomach roiling in solidarity, my flushed skin crying out in relief as I kick myself free from my bedsheets and feel the cool morning air trickling in from the window someone had the good sense to crack last night.

Swallowing the bile that tickles the back of my throat with even the slightest of movements, I drop a leg over the bed's edge and unceremoniously kick the lump of muscle sprawled across my floorboards. 'Hey.'

The lump groans.

'*Heath*.' I kick a little harder. 'Wake up.'

Quicker than a half-asleep man should be capable of, my guest rolls onto his back and grabs my offending limb, strong fingers squeezing my ankle as sleepy eyes level me with an unimpressed look. 'Stop kicking me.'

I try to wriggle free only for his grip to tighten – I watch his thumb stroke the fine bones of my ankle only for it to make my head hurt worse. I shift my gaze to the heavy-lidded one fixed on me. 'Why are you on the floor?'

'For the sake of my sanity.'

I frown. 'What?'

'Never mind.' Squeezing once more, Heath releases me and pushes himself upright, the scent of him invading my senses as his upper body flops against my bed. 'How're you feeling?'

'Wonderful.'

He lifts his head enough to flash a grin. 'You look it.'

With a snort that makes my head throb, I flick him on the forehead. 'Shut up.'

A low chuckle momentarily soothes all of my aches. Shifting again, Heath struggles to his feet only to make my mattress dip as he perches beside me. I frown again as I peer up at him through squinted eyes, déjà vu tickling the back of my poor, hungover mind.

We sat like this last night, I think. Or some way similar to this. Me curled in a pathetic ball, him looming over me. He . . . he stroked my hair, I think. Said something that made me feel warm, except that doesn't really track because there's an odd, bitter ball lodged behind my ribcage, and I don't know how it got there. 'What happened last night?'

Tired eyes crinkle at the corner as they squint. 'You don't remember?'

'I remember lots of alcohol and bad dancing and Kai

attempting to rumba, and then I'm out.' I push myself upright with a loud groan and rake a trembling hand down my face. 'Why? Did something happen?'

Those green eyes suddenly find something extremely interesting on my headboard. 'Nah.'

Lie. Big fat lie. Something happened and he doesn't want me to know, and if he doesn't want me to know then it must've been—

Oh.

Oh, God. *Oh fucking God.*

It comes back to me like a slap to the face. Not a forgotten memory, but a repressed one. Deeply, deeply repressed, stuffed beneath a death-inducing dose of mortification and someone else's regret.

What does he know, Dani?

We shouldn't have done that.

I'm not kissing you like this.

Face red-hot, I quickly look away. My cringe melts into a frown when my gaze lands on red, scabbed skin. 'What happened to my knee?'

'You tripped up the stairs.'

Of course I did. 'Great.'

Heath drops to an elbow so he can stroke the curve of my knee gently, and there it is again. That pesky déjà vu. 'Does it hurt?'

'No.' I oh-so-nonchalantly shift myself out of his reach. 'Must've gotten back late if you passed out here.'

'You asked me to stay.'

'Oh.' *Fuck*. I was hoping I was mis-remembering that. But, no, this whole awkward ordeal really is my own doing. Great. *Fantastic*.

God, I'm never allowed to drink again.

Stomach bubbling at the mere thought of alcohol, I swallow hard before forcing myself out of bed. I ignore the wave of nausea that washes over me, I ignore the man who yawns and stretches and lazily gets up only to perch on the edge of my bed, I ignore everything that isn't the top left drawer of my dresser, and the plethora of swimsuits inside it.

'What're you doing?'

Plucking out a plain black one-piece, I wave it in the air with a grunt. 'Getting ready.'

'For?'

'Practice.'

'You're not seriously going.'

I half-turn to shoot him a scrunched look. 'You're not seriously surprised.'

'Dani, you can take one morning off.'

'No, I can't.'

'Yes, you can.'

'Maybe *you* can.'

'Oh, c'mon. You know you're better than me.'

'I do.' A matching sweatsuit slung over my shoulder, I hip-check my dresser drawer shut and start picking through the toiletries littering the surface. 'Because I don't take mornings off. You're that good all on your own.'

'It's a genetic gift.'

I huff, that signature sarcasm rubbing me the wrong way this morning.

'It's one practice,' he presses, and, fuck, if that doesn't jab at me too. 'It's not that serious.'

'For you, maybe.' My scalp pulls as I wrangle my hair into a too-tight ponytail, and I blame the ensuing tension headache for my next question coming out quite so snippy. 'Is anything serious for you?'

Slowly sitting up, Heath blinks. 'Woah.'

'What? It's just a question.'

'Kind of a pointy question.'

'Yeah, well, that's me. Pointy.'

'What's wrong with you?'

'Nothing is wrong with me.'

'Is this about yesterday?' he asks carefully, and my entire body locks.

I only marginally relax when he clarifies, 'Your stepmom?'

And I stiffen right back up again when he adds, 'What you told me about your dad?'

'I don't know what you're talking about.'

'You told me some fucked-up shit, Dani.'

'That wasn't fucked-up, Heath,' I snap, instinct driving me to defend my dad. To defend myself. 'That was hard work.'

'No, it wasn't.'

I scoff a mean, nasty noise. 'How would you know?'

Ever-so-slightly, Heath flinches. 'You think I don't work hard?'

'I think you don't work hard *enough*.'

'Why? Because I don't put swimming first over everything else in my life? Over my happiness? Over my health? Because, God forbid, I actually *have* a life?'

'Fuck you. I put swimming first because I have to. I have to work to be the best. I don't have all of this God-given talent, this genetic fucking gift, or the luxury to just squander it, and it's infuriating that you do. It's insulting, and it's fucking disrespectful that you don't respect what you can do, what *I* do. There are people that would kill for your talent. I would kill for it. I would kill *you*.'

'I don't believe that. I don't believe anything that just came out of your mouth. You put swimming first because someone told you that you had to. You swim because someone else wanted you to. Someone else put swimming before you, and now it's all you know how to do.'

'You don't know anything about my dad.'

'I know what you told me.'

'I was *drunk*.'

'But you weren't lying, were you?'

My breath is a sharp, painful rattle. As defensive as the arms I wrap around myself, the chin I lift high, the eye roll I pair with a suffering sigh. 'Fine, Heath, you win. He was a shitty dad with shitty parenting skills and even shittier coaching methods, but he was my dad. Everything he did was only because he wanted me to be better.'

'He should've wanted you to be happy, Dani.'

He says it so calmly, so evenly, nothing accusatory about it, just pure, sad honesty, yet I bristle like he just spat on my dad's grave. Like he just spat on me. 'You have no right to talk about him like that.'

'I have no right to care about you?'

'That—' Frustration leaves me in a huff, my scalp tingling as I rake my hands through my hair. 'I know, okay? I know it wasn't just hard work, I *knew* it wasn't, and I know it wasn't okay, but he's dead, Heath. What do you want me to do? Dig him up and make him pay? Spend the rest of my life resenting him? Because that doesn't hurt him, Heath, it hurts me. It makes me feel guilty because he gave up his life for swimming as much as I did. He never missed a meet, he spent every free second coaching me, he took out a loan so we could move to a different school district because they had a better swim team. He gave me everything I needed to succeed, and I'm supposed to hate him because he didn't ask first?'

'That's not what I'm saying, honey. I just . . . you don't owe him the rest of your life.'

Don't I? a meek, young voice in the back of my head whispers, shaky and unsure. *Don't I owe him at least a little bit of it?* 'I need to go.'

'Do you want to?'

I don't answer. I don't have one. I just repeat myself, and I lock myself in the bathroom, and by the time I come out, Heath is gone.

I'm not sure what it says about me that I'm upset he actually left.

Hours later, I storm out of the pool complex with someone humming the *Jaws* theme tune in my wake.

As the rest of my team snickers, I ignore all of them, incapable of even conjuring a withering look to shoot over my aching shoulder. Or, rather, I'm perfectly capable, I just fear I might do something worse than just look. Something murderous. Something to alleviate the unrelenting frustration bubbling beneath my skin, the fucking mortification that forms on the heels of the shittiest practice of my life.

'What the hell is wrong with you today?' my coach screeched, more than once, and I wish the answer was my hangover. I wish my poor times and languid strokes had something to do with a throbbing headache and a sensitive stomach and the fucking twinge in my shoulder that won't go away no matter how steadfastly I ignore it.

I wish more than anything in the entire world that it wasn't a boy plaguing me. A stupid fucking boy, burrowed into every single crevice of my brain, distracting me exactly the way my ex claimed he would, and, fuck, it was like Ben knew. He knew exactly what was going on in my head, and all his sideways smirks and self-satisfied huffs and a barely audible *told ya* made me want to crack his head against the pool tiles.

Even now, practice is done, but he isn't, he's still on my fucking ass, he's a step behind me, a palm planting itself against the swinging door to prevent me from slamming it in his face. 'Wow.' I don't turn to look at him, don't stop my strides, but I still feel his eyes roam the length of me. 'Rough night?'

Throat too tight to squeeze any words out, I hope my middle finger says everything I can't.

'Aw, babe.' Ben chuckles darkly, jogging to catch up with my long strides and plant himself in my path. 'Don't be mad at me. I'm not the one who kept you out all night.'

I can't articulate that nobody kept me anywhere, that my late, drunken night was all my own doing, that that's not even why I'm such a mess today, and I wouldn't even if I could. I have no energy, let alone any to waste on Ben. Even the simple act of ignoring him drains me, my whole body heaving as I shift direction, hurrying to the safety of my car before the breakdown I feel nipping at my heels finally crashes.

Except today isn't my day. The universe isn't my friend – it just had to put another obstacle in my path, and my entire body locks as my gaze lands on the Cove College swim team.

'There she is,' Kai hollers, with a playful shimmy. Mid-salsa, he stretches out a hand, two fingers crooking in an invite to join his little dance – to recreate last night, I remember with a humiliated flush.

The limb drops, as does his smile, when I completely ignore him.

I ignore all of them, every single member of the team because every single one of them hollers out some kind of greeting. As if one night partying in the vicinity of each other suddenly makes us best friends. Palpable confusion stains the air when I don't greet them back, and I don't get why they expected anything different, why they care.

I don't get why Heath doesn't take my stormy silence as a hint, why he can't tell that I'm not in the mood, why I have to very clearly, very bluntly state, 'Don't talk to me right now', for him to fucking get it.

The hand that was a mere inch away from curling around

my bicep freezes mid-reach. I'm gone before it can retract, leaving *ooohh*s and *aaahh*s and questions of trouble in paradise in my wake. I don't look back, I keep my gaze forward, a wise choice turned into a horrible mistake, because Ben is suddenly forward, Ben is leaning against his car where he parked it next to mine, Ben is staring and smirking and delighted, but I guess that's better than Heath, stunned and confused and hurt.

But what would be best, really, is to not see either of them. To not be near either of them. To not be near anyone.

My shaky hands fumble my car keys. I swear and I grunt and I yank on the stupid stuck door of my stupid old car so hard, I almost fall on my ass. Correcting myself at the last moment, I throw myself behind the wheel, well aware that I'm embarrassing myself. I'm only adding to my own humiliation, and I'm frustrated and annoyed and upset.

Fuck, I'm upset. I wasn't good enough for my stepmother yesterday and I wasn't good enough for my coach or my team or, fuck, *my dad* today, and, last night, I wasn't good enough for Heath, and I hate that that's so upsetting to me. I hate that, somewhere in my brain, a wire has gotten crossed – I let it get crossed. I let myself get upset even though I know so much better.

White-knuckling the steering wheel, I press my forehead to the plastic cover, eyes closed as I try to steady my breathing only for it to get worse, thinner, shakier, as I sniffle and liquid leaks from my eyes.

I flinch when the door opens, I flinch when I recognize the

invader by scent alone, I flinch when a hand cups my shoulder gently, and again as I bite out, 'Leave me alone.'

'Can't.'

'Try.'

'My hero complex doesn't let me leave beautiful girls crying alone in parking lots.'

'Just ugly ones, then?'

'No such thing.' Knuckles drag down my spine, and I'm not sure if I arch away from the touch because I can't stand it, or because I like it too much. 'Bad practice?'

My grip tightens even more. 'Really bad.'

'I'm sorry.'

You should be. It's all your fault.

'Listen,' I start, pausing when my voice cracks. 'I'm really not in the mood to be your girlfriend right now, so maybe you could just do me a favor and leave me the fuck alone.'

I don't mean it to come out so nasty. It sounds desperate in my head, it feels like a woeful plea, but, out loud, it sounds . . . cruel. Unnecessary. It sounds like a punch to the gut.

It must feel like one too, if a sharp, whistling inhale is anything to go by.

Heath's touch falls away. It curls around the doorframe instead, metal creaking with how hard he grips it. He clears his throat, and I wonder if he's coughing away something nasty of his own. If he's as capable of being mean as I am, but he's just better at holding his tongue. 'Later then. I'll come over.'

'I don't—'

'Did you hear a question?'

My mouth snaps shut.

'Need to talk to you, Dani.'

Shockingly, that ominous profession does very little to sway me. 'About what?'

'Nothing bad,' he promises, easily anticipating that that's the first place my mind jumps. 'You don't think we need to talk?'

'I think we talked plenty this morning. And if it's about last night—'

'It is.'

'Then I've heard it already. Really don't need to hear it again.'

'It's all brand-new information. Scout's honor.'

'You really were a Boy Scout, weren't you?'

'Eagle Scout, honey.'

Of course. Sighing, I let my head loll to one side, my temple throbbing against my knuckles while my eyes throb at that open face of his. He does nothing to hide his hurt. That frustration painting his face with harsh lines, I feel as clearly as I do my own. His desperation, I can't quite separate from my own.

'Sorry,' I say quietly, gaze homing in on the dimple that makes the briefest of appearances. 'For snapping.'

His smile is pallid. Perfunctory. Fleeting; he barely flashes it before robbing me of the sight. Quickly, almost rushed, he rises out of my eyeline. 'I'll see you later.' He bids me goodbye through the roof of my car, rapping his knuckles against it before backing up and closing my door.

Without looking at me, he takes off at a near-fucking run.

Nothing bad, he swore.

For once, I don't trust him.

*

I'm dithering in the center of my apartment, gaze flitting between the text that promises an imminent arrival and my closed front door when, finally, the doorbell rings.

Beneath a stolen Cove College hoodie, my stomach constricts. Trepidation sends a whole freaking horde of butterflies flapping wildly.

Nothing bad, I remind myself for the umpteenth time. Clinging to those two words, I do my best to believe them whilst my brain tries valiantly to convince me otherwise, and I paste on my best attempt at an easy-breezy smile.

A complete waste of energy, considering that, when I open the front door, it isn't Heath I find on the other side.

Without so much as a first thought, let alone a second one, I try to slam it shut again. When a strong hand plants against the wood and prevents that, I bark, 'What the hell are you doing here?'

Ben smiles. Like, actually. He doesn't sneer or smirk or leer, he just smiles. Normally. Sincerely. As sincere as a quiet, 'Checking on you.'

I blink. Frown. Internally cuss myself out for being so idiotic as to think that anything about Ben is ever *sincere*. Even if, right now, he does look remarkably like the guy I actually, once upon a time, really fucking liked. 'Whatever this is, I don't have time for it.'

'I'm here to apologize.'

I can't help it – I laugh out loud. In lieu of pinching myself, I roll my shoulder back until that pesky ache twinges, and once I've confirmed that I'm not dreaming, I laugh again. 'And what's brought on this sudden apology?'

His expression clouds – guilt darkens it.

'Let me guess.' I cross my arms over my chest, hip resting against the doorframe. 'You and Sienna broke up.'

Thin lips press together tightly. Of course. How utterly predictable. 'Get the fuck out of here, Ben.'

'C'mon, Dani.' He pushes the door, gaining another inch. 'I'm sorry.'

I throw all of my goddamn weight into it, but it's no use. He props a forearm against the wood and he shoves his fucking foot up against it too, and even when I kick his ankle, he doesn't back off. 'I don't care.'

'Yes, you do. I know you do.'

'You know shit.'

'I know we were good together.'

Laugh isn't a strong enough word for the level of amusement that comes out of me. 'You're delusional, and I'm with Heath now.'

'Are you? Saw you arguing today.'

'You fucked another person while we were together. I think me and him are allowed a little argument.'

'I know you don't really like him.'

'I do,' I insist, and in the back of my mind, underneath the pure rage rendering me near-blind, it registers just how much I mean that.

'You *don't*. You're only doing this, *him*, to get back at me, I know you are.'

'Go away, Ben.'

'You want to hear me say I'm jealous? Fine. I'm jealous. I hate that you're with him.'

'I—'

'Dani.' Clammy hands rise to cup my face. 'I love you. Please, baby. Give me another chance.'

Just for a second, I entertain the idea. I try to imagine giving him another chance. Forgiving him. Loving him.

The concept completely eludes me; it's unfathomable, it's *ridiculous*. I just spent the last few months being treated infinitely better by a man who isn't actually even my boyfriend. Why would I ever go back to someone who treated me like a dirty inconvenience?

'Ben,' I sigh, and he actually looks hopeful. His eyes light up, and I actually almost feel bad for him. Except I don't. I don't feel bad at all when I wrap my fingers around his wrists and yank him away, and his entire face falls. 'I would literally rather die.'

A puff of shocked air parts his lips. 'I'm being serious, Dan.'

'So am I.' I step back into my apartment, gripping the door so tightly, the edge cuts into my palm. 'There is nothing you could ever say to me that would make me want you back. Nothing. I don't want you. What you did . . . You betrayed me. You embarrassed me. But you didn't break my heart. And I deserve heart-breaking, earth-shattering love. Not some asshole who did nothing but waste my time. Not someone who only knows how to love if it hurts too.'

I slam the door in his face.

Palms braced on either side of the frame, I rest my forehead against the wood and wait for the yelling to begin. The brutal, insistent knocking. The profanity. The embarrassment as he rips me to shreds for all the block to hear.

I wait for regret. For a part of me, any part of me, to lament the finality of that rejection. Because something about this feels final. Feels different to the other times he harangued me. Feels like the tipping point, the final straw, the inevitable conclusion to a lengthy chapter.

Maybe because, for once, Ben doesn't fight. He doesn't yell. Through the flimsy barrier separating us, I hear him sigh. Twice. I flinch when knuckles connect with the concrete right beside the door, I wait some more for that aggression to fester, to swing my way, but it just . . . doesn't. He sighs again, I hear the scuff of shoe soles against concrete, and then he's gone.

And maybe I'm naive or stupid or just really fucking desperate, but it actually feels like he's *gone*.

Backing away from the door, I drag my hands through my hair. Fingers laced together at the base of my neck, I marvel at the sudden absence of *weight*. Like I've actually physically shucked him off, like he's really, truly gone.

I drag a hand down my face, and it's only as it skates over my mouth that I realize just how hard I'm smiling. Laughing into my palm, I shake my head and rush into the kitchen. As I rummage through my cabinets, I curse myself for not anticipating such a celebratory moment and buying champagne or prosecco or, shit, I'd settle for some freaking sparkling apple cider.

I grab my phone and pull up my conversation with Heath so I can tell him to pick some up only to pause midway through the sentence. Frowning, I check the time he sent his last message. He should be here by now. Like, by a long shot. Deleting my request, I type out a simple *Everything okay?* Instead.

Ten minutes pass without an answer, and I start to fidget. A half-hour, and the concern hits. An hour, and my mind has jumped to some very lofty conclusions and sent me pacing around my apartment – a minute after, I hit the call icon next to his number.

It rings so many times, I barely have any thumbnail by the time the call finally connects. 'Hey—'

'What?'

Halfway through my thousandth loop of my living room, I freeze. His voice . . . I frown. He doesn't sound right. 'Are you okay?'

'Uh-huh.' Something slams, like metal on metal. Jingles, like keys. Squeaks, like a tight grip on plastic. 'Do you want something?'

'Aren't you—' I swallow around a thick lump of dread. 'Don't we have plans?'

A pause. A deep breath. 'Oh. Right. I forgot.'

A pause of my own. A matching deep breath too. 'You forgot?'

'Uh-huh.'

'So you . . . you're not coming over?'

'Can't,' he claims, curtly. 'I'm busy.'

'Doing what?'

'I, uh, got that paper due this week.'

'Oh.' A tangled knot coils in my stomach, pulling tight like it hears the blatant lie as clearly as I do. 'I could—'

'Listen, Dani, I gotta go.'

'Right. Maybe tomorrow—'

'Yeah, I'll call you.'

With that empty promise, the line goes dead.

I stare at my phone screen until it goes dark, until my own blank expression is reflected in it. A burning sensation tickles my nose, the back of my throat too, behind my eyes. I swipe at them with the back of my hand and my knuckles come away shiny, wet, stained with cutting disappointment.

Well. Okay then.

TWENTY-FIVE

HE DOESN'T CALL TOMORROW.

He doesn't so much as text. Neither him nor Kai turn up at practice. I go to Barefoot Joe's and he isn't working. I wander around the entire fucking cove, searching for proof of life, and I come up empty. He's nowhere to be found.

Yet, somehow, he's everywhere in my apartment.

He's in the sink in the form of a dirtied mug, the bottom all gooped up with caramel fucking syrup. He's on the coffee table with the textbook he forgot the last time he was here, next to the overlays I ordered for his laptop a little while ago, those ones that are supposed to help with dyslexia. He's in my bed because I haven't changed the sheets since he slept over, and something tells me that, even if I did, my detergent might not be strong enough to wash away the scent of him.

I barely set foot past my front door after evening practice before I'm stepping back out again. I don't know what, exactly, drives me to the coast, but the second my feet hit the sand, I know it was a shitty idea.

The beach smells like him too.

Jesus, I swear the ocean *looks* like him. It doesn't look so violent to me now, so scary. It reminds me of him – how can it not? – and it reminds me of how I felt that day, when it was just the two of us, freaking frolicking in the water. Everything was so muddled in my head, but the waves just washed all of that away.

The December chill biting at my goose-bumped skin, I shed my clothes and drop them to the sand. In just my swimsuit, still a little damp from practice, my hair the same as it whips in the wind, I hurry down the near-empty shore until water laps at my toes, threatening to freeze them right off.

I welcome the cold. Need it. Need the numbing, need to chase away the cloying bitterness left lingering by a fleeting phone call that did more damage than it has any business doing. And that's exactly what it does as I duck beneath the waves, and stay under there as long as my lungs will let me. As long as it takes to feel nothing but the freeze.

I don't last very long. And I might be shivering violently as I dart back up the beach, but I feel better. I hate it, I hate that it worked, but I can't deny that it did. I feel like shit physically, like cold, quaking shit, but, mentally, I'm clearer.

Jesus. All that money on therapy after my dad died when I could've chucked myself in the ocean for some peace and clarity.

Toes burrowing in the sand in search of some semblance of warmth, I stoop to grab my discarded t-shirt, quick to dry off my upper half so my hoodie isn't entirely sodden when I shrug it back on. I wince as cold droplets from my hair trickle down my spine, gathering it in one hand while squeezing out as much frigid water as I can with the other.

As I'm fixing it into a quick braid with trembling fingers, a sudden barrage of noise catches my attention. Half-turning,

I squint at the wet-suit-clad group trudging through the sand. Their laughter floats toward me and my heart pangs, loneliness squeezing it as I think about—

I freeze. In every sense of the word. My blood runs fucking cold because I recognize that group. I recognize the guy toting a bright, almost-white board decorated with a hand-painted floral design. Barely, I recognize my own name being carried across the sand by someone else's voice.

Sluggish, almost like I'm in a trance, my gaze shifts to the figure waving me over – to Imani. When I don't move, she does, jogging across the sand with Matilda hot on her heels, and it's only when they're a handful of feet away that I finally regain control of my body.

Hot embarrassment fueling my movements, I hurry to get dressed, but I'm not quick enough. It's too late to make a break for the parking lot – right as my head pops through the neck hole of my hoodie, an arm slinks around my shoulders.

'What're you doing here?' Imani croons. 'Heath said you were sick.'

A shaky laugh escapes me. It's not a complete lie, I guess. I do feel pretty fucking sick right now.

Imani gives me a squeeze before letting me go, Matilda replacing her and giving me a gentle shove toward the boys. 'Come sit with us.'

I shake her off. I shake full-stop, shivering from far more than just the cold now. 'No, thanks.'

'Oh, c'mon.' Gentle knuckles collide with my bicep, a playfully stern look warning me. 'Don't make us bring out the big guns.'

'Don't—' I start to snap, to beg, but it's too late.

In perfect unison, the girls holler a sing-song version of Heath's name, somehow loud enough to combat the distance and the wind and the waves and the ringing in my ears.

It's too far away to really see him, but, somehow, I know the exact moment his eyes lock on me. Too far, but I can perfectly picture lips parted with surprise and high, curious brows. Suspicious, maybe. Does he think I followed him? Tracked him down because I somehow knew he was lying? Tore down here, raring for a fight?

I don't stick around to find out.

As Heath tears out of the water, I flee as fast as I'm capable of.

Which isn't as fast as him, evidently.

Cold wind bites at my bare legs, carrying an equally biting '*Daniela*' along with it.

'Fuck off.'

Low, surprised *woahs* sound from the girls.

'Will you slow down?'

'Sorry.' I turn to walk backwards, to make sure Heath can see just how *pissed* I am. 'Can't. I'm just so sick, I have to get back to my apartment before I keel over.'

'Right.' The noise that splutters out of him is genuinely, shockingly nasty – only barely tempered by the flash of guilt I watch twist his face. 'Bet someone's there waiting for you.'

My rushed retreat falters. 'Excuse me?'

'You know exactly what I mean.'

'Did you hit your fucking head out there? What are you talking about?'

'Ben,' he spits my ex's name like it's the foulest curse ever invented. 'He stay over last night?'

For a long moment, I don't respond. I can't. I lose the capacity to do anything but gape in disbelief. To laugh, because what the actual fuck? 'Please tell me you're joking.'

Heath puffs his chest and folds his arms across it, pure fucking defense – pure fucking *man* in the worst fucking way. 'I saw you.'

'Doing *what*, Heath? Fucking him on my doorstep? Because I don't really remember that happening.' I laugh again as I reel back a couple of steps, my hands going to my hair and clutching so tightly, I damn near pull a few strands out. 'Jesus Christ, I have been losing my mind, wondering what the hell I did wrong, and you're telling me the answer is *nothing*? That it was just you jumping to conclusions?'

'He—'

'He left about five fucking seconds after he arrived, unannounced and uninvited,' I snap, I yell, I all but screech like the seagulls flying above us. 'He was told, in no uncertain terms, that he would never, ever, in a million damn years, get another chance with me. And he, by the fucking way, would do something exactly like this if I dared to piss him off.'

Heath's face drops. In a millisecond, he goes from an irate, jealous idiot to a remorseful one. He literally stumbles in the sand, and I use his unsteadiness to put a little more space between us. 'Dani, I didn't . . . fuck, I'm sorry.'

'Yeah, he said that last night too. And every time he got jealous for no fucking reason. And every time he made an excuse not to see me so he could hang out with his friends without me ruining the vibe. And, every time, I just let it go.' I pause. I swallow. I don't think before blurting what I, deep down, just *know*. 'I can't do that anymore.'

'What are you saying?' Heath hesitantly asks, but he doesn't look like he wants the answer.

I want to say it even less. 'I'm saying that this was a bad idea.'

'It was *your* idea.'

God, do I know that. God, do I wish I didn't. God, do I wish I hadn't been so desperate and then gotten so confused and ended up so attached because now . . . Now, I'm acting like my heart isn't doing something that feels an awful lot like breaking as I force a nonchalant shrug. 'It's a good thing you were working so hard on that essay last night, huh? All ready to turn it in so we can be done?'

Heath jolts. He blinks a few rapid times, and then slowly, robotically, he murmurs, 'That's it?'

'That was the deal.'

'Right.' He drags a hand across his gritted jaw before planting both hands on his hips, looking out to sea briefly before looking at me once more. 'This is what you want?'

'What I wanted was for you to come over last night,' my mouth admits before my mind agrees to it. 'I . . . I know I snapped at you yesterday, I know I can be reactive and callous, but I'm never *trying* to hurt you. You knew blowing me off would hurt me, and you did it anyway. You say all the time that we're friends, we're *best friends*, but you hurt me anyway.'

'Dani . . .' What I can only describe as devastation twisting his features, he takes a tentative step toward me. 'Can we talk about this some more?'

'I don't wanna talk to you anymore.'

He says my name again, but I barely hear it. The rushing of blood in my ears is too loud, and it only gets louder as I turn on my heel and sprint across the sand as fast as my shaky legs will carry me.

Vaguely, I register someone following me. It's only once I reach the parking lot and start fumbling for my keys that, without turning around to confirm who two sets of footsteps belong to, I spit, 'Go away.'

A flash of red hair in my peripheral is my only warning before a wetsuit-clad body slips between me and the driver's side door of my car. Hands on her hips and brows high, Matilda scoffs, 'What the fuck, Daniela?'

I turn away from her only to be met with a different obstacle, an expression caught somewhere between bewildered and severe. 'What the hell just happened?'

Gaze steadfastly fixed on the horizon just to the left of Imani's head, I white-knuckle my keys. 'Ask your friend.'

'*You're* our friend,' she insists, and she reaches for me, but I dodge her touch before it makes those pesky brewing tears of mine too hard to keep at bay.

'No, I'm not.' I forgot that for a while. Tricked myself into believing otherwise, and I have no one to blame but myself.

'How can you say that?'

'You're Heath's friends. I was just his *girlfriend*,' I choke out bitterly, 'and now you're off the hook. Congratulations. Now get out of my way.'

Matilda doesn't need to be told twice. Spitting something bitter, she side-steps with her hands in the air, all those freckles swimming in a sea of angry red. When her friend doesn't move, she tries to tug her away too, but Imani hesitates.

Though I refuse to meet her gaze, I feel her seeking mine. I feel her looking at me the same way Heath so often does; like she's seeing far more than I'd prefer, past the sharp edges and the harsh lines. I feel the air shift as she gears up to say something sweet and supportive that would render me even more broken than I already feel.

'I don't know how to make myself any clearer,' I say before she can. 'We're not friends. Leave me the fuck alone.'

Both girls flinch. Matilda steels herself the quickest, she grips her friend tighter, works harder to drag her off.

In the end, I get exactly what I want. They leave me alone.

As I cry my way home, I wonder why the hell I ever wanted that.

TWENTY-SIX

I TELL MY STEPMOM I'M SPENDING THE HOLIDAYS WITH MY boyfriend.

Ironically, she calls me the day after I abruptly stop having a boyfriend. She doesn't ask how I am. Doesn't exchange a single pleasantry. She just informs me that she's made the last-minute decision to visit her parents, that Seba has his own plans, and instead of enquiring about mine, she muses, 'But I suppose you'll be with your Heath, yes?'

I hum confirmation before I even really think about it – before the hopeful note to the question has time to sink in. And less than a minute later, when I hang up after faking promises to catch up in the new year, relief and loneliness compete for dominance.

The latter lingers. It follows me around, clinging no matter how fervently I try to shuck it off. No matter how often I try to drown it.

I start swimming in the sea again. A lot. Every day for the first fortnight of winter break. I swim laps in the choppy waves, challenging every ounce of my ability as I fight the current, numbing the shoulder pain that ibuprofen no longer keeps at bay, freezing for as long as my body can stand – longer. On Christmas Day, I well and truly take the piss out of my limits, and I'm practically blue by the time I shoulder my way into my apartment.

My quiet, lonely apartment.

Despite how desperately my goose-bumped skin begs for a hot shower, I linger in the living room for a moment, scanning the bland surroundings. I didn't decorate. Didn't get a tree. What's the point? It's not like I have any presents to stash beneath it. Not like I have anything to celebrate.

Not like you have anything at all, a nasty little voice in the back of my head taunts.

I become so consumed by that depressing thought, I don't notice a knocking sound until it becomes a loud, abrasive banging. And it takes me a moment longer to realize it's someone at my door.

Swiping at my eyes, I don't bother to check the peephole before opening the door – I figure it's my neighbor, ready to ream me out for dragging half the beach onto the walkway again.

It is most definitely not my neighbor who breezes inside my apartment like he has every right to be here, and barks, 'Do you have a death wish?'

My blank stare meets an oddly enraged one. 'No.'

Kai huffs humorlessly. Jostling the tote bag straps bundled in one hand, he holds out the takeout cup clutched in the other. 'Drink this before you disintegrate.'

Too tired and confused to argue, I do as he says, and rich hot chocolate burns my tongue, warming me from the inside out. 'Thanks.'

Kai blinks at me slowly. The anger harshening his features fades, and we become a matching, disoriented pair.

'Idiot.' He tuts, but it lacks any real venom, as does the reprimanding headshake he sends my way as he saunters further into my apartment. 'Hypothermic *idiot*. Couldn't wear a wetsuit out there?'

'I don't have one.' Honestly, I'm not sure I would wear it even if I did. Kinda defeats the purpose of a cold-plunge if you're insulated against it.

'You know the currents this time of year are ridiculous, right?'

I know. Barely an hour ago, I got caught in one and almost wrenched my damn shoulder out of its socket fighting my way out. Living up to my new nickname, but I couldn't help myself. Couldn't just let myself drift until the rip spat me out.

Not in my nature.

As if hearing my thoughts, my abused rotator cuff demands attention with a nauseating throb.

Stifling a wince, I keep one eye on Kai as he drops onto my sofa and head for the kitchen. Draining the rest of my drink, I set the empty cup on the counter and rummage around in the drawers for an almost empty bottle of painkillers. One-handed, I pop the lid and shake out a couple of pills, tossing them back and swallowing them dry.

'You hurt?'

'I'm fine.' Shuffling into the living room, I drop to sit on the edge of the coffee table with a huff, right beside where my unexpected guest has propped his socked feet. 'What are you doing here, Kai?'

'I don't do Christmas,' he answers, as if that's any kind of answer, as if that's remotely what I'm asking. 'Saw you flailing around like a dead fish and figured maybe you don't either.'

'My family went out of town.' My fingers curl around the edge of the coffee table, white-knuckling the wood. 'I didn't.'

Slouched lazily against the cushions, Kai eyes me thoughtfully.

Before he can let any of those thoughts fly, I snark, 'You're telling me there's no one else around for you to bother right now?'

'I'm sure there is. No one else I wanna, though.'

'And I suppose what I want counts for shit.'

'Heath was right. You *are* smart.'

My breath hitches – my chest *hurts*. 'I don't wanna talk about him.'

So easily it damn nears pisses me off, Kai backs off. 'Sorry.' He nudges my knee with his own. 'How ya doing, Lola?'

I grunt. 'Fantastic.'

He grunts right back. 'You look sad.'

'Not in my programming.'

'Dani.'

I stand abruptly, not liking how he says my name, how much it reminds me of *him*. 'I need to shower.'

I need to kick him out yet I don't. His presence makes me cringe, but the idea of him leaving makes me want to cry.

I'm equal parts panicked and relieved when he seemingly makes the decision for me, slapping his palms against his thighs as he pushes to stand. Except he doesn't steer himself toward the front door – he takes his bag to the kitchen and starts unloading carton after carton of takeout, announcing he'll heat up our dinner while I wash away my frostbite.

I start for the shower. I really am cold. But I'm more of something else. I'm so damn curious, and I need to know, 'Why are you doing this?'

He looks at me like it's obvious. 'I miss you.'

The knowledge that no one has ever missed me before lodges in the back of my throat like a rock. 'Oh.'

'I'm your friend,' he continues, and the words warm me from the inside out. 'And I was worried about you.'

'I'm okay. Really.'

'Yeah,' he drawls dryly, shaking his head just a little. 'So is he.'

I inhale sharply.

'That was sarcasm, in case you missed it. He's a fucking mess, Dani.'

'Kai,' I half-sigh, half-sob, want to scream. 'No, he isn't. It was fake. All of it. I wanted to piss Ben off and he needed tutoring to pass a class, so we faked it.'

His complete lack of surprise peaks my interest – a too-knowing expression chases it away. 'Didn't look very fake.'

'Well.' My shoulder screams with the effort of shrugging. 'It was.'

'Does lying to yourself make you feel better?'

'Drop it, Kai.'

'Did it *feel* fake, Dani?'

A resounding *no* echoes inside my head before I even really think about it. Barely at the start, and certainly not at the end. It might've been the realest thing I've ever experienced, and isn't that a gut punch and a fucking half?

Frustrated, I grunt quietly and push off the counter with a forced, heavy shrug. 'Doesn't matter either way. It's over.'

Kai makes a face like he doesn't agree, like he knows something I don't.

I leave the room before he can share – before I can ask him to.

In the long, weird gap between Christmas and New Year, Kai spends more time in my apartment than literally anyone else ever has.

I spend more time in my apartment than I ever have. I am held hostage and force-fed three meals a day and forced to watch nearly three entire seasons of a Danish series about poisonous rain because Kai claims it's a travesty that I haven't already seen it.

'God, you must be bored,' I remark irritably, more than once, almost every day, almost every hour, on the hour. And on the last day of the year, when he struts into my home wearing a fucking party hat and blowing one of those godforsaken noisemakers, I almost scream. I almost cry. I do beg: 'Please tell me your friends are back in town soon.'

And he crooks his head to one side, the fucking pompom on the tip of his hat flopping jauntily. 'Who said they were ever out of town?'

I don't understand his frequent visits. I have no idea what spurs him on. I don't particularly enjoy the constant invasion of my space, but I don't fight it either.

So when my doorbell rings a couple of hours past that

celebratory midnight mark, I assume it's him. 'You're lucky I was still awake,' I grumble, as I wrench the door open, scrubbing at eyes gone blurry from the hours and hours of reality TV I've been using to block out my apartment building's raucous activity.

'Happy New Year, baby,' a deep, male voice slurs.

A voice that does not belong to Kai.

'I'm sorry,' the voice that is Kai mutters, and I can't tear my eyes away from a pair of unfocused blue-green ones long enough to check if he really means it. 'But he wouldn't shut the fuck up.'

About what? I don't ask. I don't have the capacity for questions. There is nothing in my brain but *Heath*.

Drunk Heath. Very drunk Heath. Like, nearly comatose Heath. Like probably does not even register it's me in front of him levels of drunk.

Except he must. Because he says my name. Quiet and content and reverent, and my chest constricts so tightly, it's a wonder that my ribs don't cave in.

He looks . . . not good. Not quite like shit, as his best friend claimed, but *not good*. And it has nothing to do with his rumpled clothing or slack, drunk features, or the fact he's leaning so heavily on Kai, he's practically horizontal.

He just doesn't look like him. He isn't smiling.

Presumably because this is the last place he'd rather be.

Presumably because of me.

I don't remember inviting them in or letting them in or even moving at all. I just know that I blink and the duo is lumbering into my apartment, one of them dropping the other's dead weight on the sofa, one of them peering at me worriedly while the other . . . gazes.

He fucking gazes.

Like I'm not standing here, silent and fidgeting, hair a mess and popcorn grease staining my fingertips, pale and skinny and sad, in sweats and a hoodie and—

Fuck.

His sweats. His hoodie.

Hurriedly crossing my arms over my chest, I pray that he's too belligerent to notice the Cove College logo etched on the soft cotton. 'Wild night?'

Heath babbles something unintelligible.

Kai grimaces. 'Pretty sure he's been drinking since Christmas.'

'And that's my problem because . . .'

He shoots me a look that I choose not to understand.

'At the risk of sounding like a broken record,' I start, pausing when Heath makes a little noise, a soft sigh that floats toward me and skates across my skin like a phantom. 'What are you doing here?'

'He lost his keys,' Kai answers, without actually answering at all, tossing his barely conscious friend a thoroughly unimpressed glower. 'And he tossed mine into a fucking drain.'

'Why?'

'Didn't wanna go home.'

'Where are the others?'

'Brendan was . . . *busy*.'

I hear the innuendo loud and clear.

Was Heath busy too? I want to ask, want to spit, hate myself for even thinking it, hate my stomach for daring to roil. *Before he consumed an entire liquor store?* 'And the girls?'

He doesn't answer, but his face does a guilty little twist.

I crook a brow.

'Bren has their keys. They're downstairs. Didn't wanna bombard you.'

Despite the glaring lack of humor to the situation, I bark a laugh. 'How thoughtful,' I call over my shoulder on the way outside, giving myself five, pathetic seconds to hover on the walkway before forcing myself into action.

The cold metal of the railing sears my palms as I lean over to peer down at the parking lot. 'Y'all planning on sleeping down there?'

Two figures, shrouded in darkness, start at the sound of my voice. Only one tilts their face in my direction. 'We thought it might be warmer.'

With another one of those empty laughs, I wave a summoning hand. 'Come up.'

I half-think they won't, just on principle. But by the time I'm back inside, they're already on the walkway, and, a second later, they shuffle across the threshold.

And bring a brand new layer of awkward tension with them.

Matilda won't look at me. Sniffing and huffing, she toys with the tip of her long, red ponytail and shifts from one heeled foot to the other, casting haughty glances at the ceiling, at the floor, never at me.

Imani won't stop looking at me. Peering at me. Her eyes bore into me, the dark depths unreadable, her entire face a careful blank slate.

It irritates me. More than any of the rest of this does. Like a fresh cut over a healing scab, itching and aching and picking at me until I snap. 'Can I help you?'

Her eyes flare before narrowing, head shaking as she croons an emphatic *nope*.

'Ladies. Come on.'

'Shut up, Kai,' three feminine voices snap in perfect, pissed unison.

Wide-eyed, he holds his hands up innocently and mimes zipping his mouth shut. Knocking Heath's legs away from where they're awkwardly strewn over the arm of the sofa, he starts to sit down only to immediately hop to his feet again when I move toward the front door again. 'Where are you going?'

I have no idea. I'll decide once I'm out of here, once I can think clearly again. Reaching for my keys where they hang on the hook beside the door, my fingers just graze that silly fucking key-ring when it's abruptly yanked away.

'Nuh-huh.' Kai holds my keys aloft. 'No way.'

'Give them back.'

'No way,' he repeats, backpedaling a few steps. 'Don't be a dumbass.'

'Don't piss me off.'

'Don't exist, you mean?'

I scowl, groaning with irritation when he twists even more out of my reach. '*Kai*.'

'Dani.' He copies my tone, bearing a remarkable existence to an extremely annoying little brother. 'No.'

A nasty noise escapes Matilda. 'You'd rather walk around in the middle of the night than spend a few hours in the same room as us?'

'Pretty much.'

Imani sighs. 'Dani.'

'What?' I snap at her, but I'm still looking at Kai, the itchy frustration pooling behind my eyeballs is all for him. 'Why are you doing this? Why can't you just leave me alone? This is mean, Kai. Coming here all the time, bringing them here, bringing *him*,' my voice cracks. 'It's fucking mean. It's *cruel* because there are a million other places you could've gone tonight and we both know it.'

'That's not—'

'Are you punishing me? Is that what it is? You're mad that I duped you, that I used Heath, that you had to be my friend for no fucking reason, so now you're throwing it all in my face? Your night got boring so you thought you'd come over and torment me a little?'

'Dani. Jesus, no.'

With a ragged huff, I make one last failed attempt to grab my keys before deciding I don't need them. I'll just walk . . . somewhere. Anywhere that's not here. Maybe I'll go for a swim just to spite the asshole gawking at me. I just need to grab my phone from where I left it on the coffee table and then—

'Don't go.'

I freeze. Slow as fucking molasses, my gaze drops. My

stomach does too as I stare at the long, tan fingers looped around my wrist. Pretty eyes blink at me sleepily. *Dreamily*. Heath repeats his quiet demand, and I feel my legs fucking obey, I feel my knees fucking lock, primed to stay right here.

It's Kai who clears his throat. 'I'll get some blankets.'

'I'll help,' Imani adds.

Matilda doesn't even offer an excuse – she just follows the other two into the tiny bathroom that's barely big enough for one person, and is not where my blankets live.

The door closes behind them with a soft click, and it's like they take all the air in the room with them.

I don't particularly want to breathe. I think, right in this very moment, drowning under a heavy, unreadable gaze, I would actually quite like to suffocate – I think it would be a far better fate than *this*.

Heath tugs on my wrist, and I close my eyes.

He murmurs my name again, and I breathe deeply through my mouth.

He tugs again, harder this time, more insistent, and as the couch rustles beneath him, I find myself with no choice but to do as he silently asks and drop down to a crouch lest he try to rise to my level and finds himself face-first in my coffee table.

I regret it immediately. Within a single split second, barely that. Because the moment I'm in real reach of his clumsy, clammy hands, they're on me. Touching me. Tracing the contours and divots of my face, like he has any right to do that.

And I don't do a damn thing to stop him.

A finger traces my bottom lip, and I suddenly so vividly

remember raking my teeth across the calloused pad. He palms the curve of my jaw and I feel the ghost of a tiny mouth-made bruise. He tucks a piece of hair behind my ear, rubs the soft strand between his thumb and forefinger, and sighs with fucking relief. 'Hi, pretty girl.'

My fingers itch with the urge to return the favor. To graze the buzzed hair that looks a little longer than normal. 'Hi, drunk boy.'

He smiles, just for a second, until the curve of his knuckle brushes beneath my left eye and comes away glistening. 'Why are you crying?'

Lips parting with surprise, I swipe at the tears I didn't even feel falling. 'I'm not.'

Too drunk to press the matter, Heath hiccups. 'You didn't show up.'

'Where?'

'The party. Kept calling you and calling you and you didn't come.'

'You didn't call me.' I stared at my phone the entire hour leading up to the countdown, until my vision went askew, wishing he would – so fucking *weak*.

'Did,' he argues, as strongly as someone in his state is capable of. 'I said your name, like, a hundred times.'

Against my will, a faint smile curves my mouth. *God, he's drunk.* 'And I didn't magically appear? How rude of me.'

Heath huffs. 'Exactly.'

I smile a little harder. *God, he's cute.* 'I'm gonna get you some water.'

When I stand, he pushes himself upright too, peering over

the back of the sofa as I make a quick trip to the kitchen. He tracks my every move with a goofy smile on his face, makes a goofy noise when I return with a full glass and painkillers for the morning because I know he'll be in a sorry state, and I guess he'll still be here – I only worry about that inevitable confrontation for a second before getting distracted.

The moment I'm in reach, Heath pulls me down again. I don't sit this time; I just crouch awkwardly at his side because it feels a little safer, a little healthier, not being quite so close.

Yet still close enough for him to invade my every sense; it only gets worse when he twines my hair around his forefinger and uses it to tug me just a little closer. 'Tried to find you.' He hiccups. 'At midnight. Was gonna tell you.'

Gently, I free myself from his grip. A millisecond later, he fists the cuff of my hoodie. 'Tell me what?'

'Too many things.' He yawns, eyes screwing shut as he seems to think hard about something. 'Can't remember them all.'

'Must not be very important, then.'

'They are.' That ever-moving grip shifts once more. He holds my hand now, so tight and so tangled, I can barely tell where he stops and I begin. 'You are. To me.'

Liar, some bitter little part of me accuses, while every other inch wishes so badly for that to be the truth. 'Time to get some rest, okay?'

He pouts. Eyes still closed, he blindly pats himself down until he finds his phone in his pocket. Almost the second he fishes it out, it falls to the ground. My lips curl upwards as I dip to fetch it.

They flatten immediately when I catch a glimpse of his lockscreen.

Weeks ago, he changed it to a picture of me. One of the many he took that night when he taught me how to make pasta; the one he posted online, along with the caption *luckiest man alive*. Me, holding a glass of wine, dusted with flour, nose scrunched, a small, real smile twisting my mouth.

That same picture stares up at me now.

Swallowing hard, I set his phone face-down on the coffee table. When he whines and makes a grab for it, I push him back down.

He protests, thrashing against my palm, too drunk to actually put up any kind of a fight. 'But I wanna show you something.'

'Show me tomorrow.' Dipping into the wicker basket under the table where my blankets actually live, I tuck one around Heath. 'Go to sleep.'

He sighs. Right before he obeys, he claims, 'I miss you.'

Maybe, if he were sober, I'd believe him.

TWENTY-SEVEN

I'M HURRIEDLY TYING MY LACES INTO A SLOPPY BOW when a throat pointedly clears.

Jolting, I cast a panicked look at the two bodies still passed out in the living room before pressing a finger to my lips, shushing the woman shuffling across my apartment.

Rubbing sleep from her eyes, Imani sighs as she takes in the athleisure wear I silently wriggled into barely ten minutes ago. 'Going somewhere?'

Finishing with my laces, I straighten up and snag the water bottle sitting on the counter. 'Yup.'

'Running?' Imani asks, as she wrenches open a cabinet at random and pouts when a whole lot of nothing greets her. 'How fitting.'

My temper simmers, but I'm too tired for it to really flare. I didn't sleep a wink last night, and it had nothing to do with the fireworks and the music and the festivities that only stopped when the sun came up a little less than an hour ago. It wasn't even the pain of my unnaturally crooked neck or the ache in my shoulder that slowly morphed into an unbearable throb the longer it remained immobile, slung across the back of the sofa.

No, it was the heavy head and the broad shoulders practically fusing me to the cushions that kept me awake. It was a hot cheek pressed to my thigh and a hot arm looped around my waist and hot breath tickling my skin because just using me as a cushion wasn't enough – Heath had to wriggle his way beneath my hoodie, smush his face against my bare stomach, and torment me just a little more ruthlessly.

He held my hand. All night. Rested our twined fingers on the leg he wasn't slobbering all over. Pressed to his chest, right where his heart thumped steadily.

No, I didn't sleep at all. And I don't have the energy to fight, I barely have anything at all. Just the sad, quiet truth. 'I can't be here when he wakes up.'

Imani's gaze bores into me. I wince when she sighs again. I slump with relief when shuffling footsteps take her back to the bedroom – only to snap to anxious attention again when she reappears towing a disheveled Matilda, still half-asleep and wearing a mismatched combination of my clothes and her own.

'Fuck your run,' Imani grumbles, her shoulder bumping mine as she edges her way outside. 'You're driving us to breakfast.'

'Why would I do that?' I grumble right back, but it isn't an argument. In fact, I don't put up a fight at all. I follow the girls outside, leaving the door unlocked behind me, and I don't take off at breakneck pace in the opposite direction. Instead, I unlock my car for them.

I get in the car with them.

I roll down the fucking windows in case the sickly redhead curled up in my backseat develops the sudden urge to spew.

I click my seatbelt into place, and Imani snickers beneath her breath, claiming, 'For the same reason you let us stay over last night.'

That makes me laugh, the noise echoed by the engine roaring to life. '*Let* is a strong word.'

'Huh. I guess I missed the part where you really tried to fight it.'

I pretend I didn't hear that. 'Where do you wanna go?'

'Barefoot Joe's,' Matilda groans, or at least I think that's what she says. I hear *foot* and *oh,* and I make an educated guess, and when the diner comes into view and dual whimpers sound, I assume they're of relief.

The full parking lot makes me cringe. An equally packed interior renders me rigid. It's only a slight solace that the girls seem equally put off by the crowd. Neither of them offer a greeting to any of the people we pass as they lead the way to the only empty table – *shockingly,* narrowed eyes and upturned noses are the only kind of acknowledgment I get – and they both slump with their hoods yanked up over their heads as they down the black coffee a waitress plants in front of us almost the second our asses hit the seats.

Palming my own mug, I wonder how long I have to sit here before they'll let me leave. I wonder why I'm even here, why they want me to be here. They certainly didn't seem like they wanted to be around me last night. Or at any point in the past couple of weeks.

It's my own fault, I know. It's silly to be bitter that they didn't even attempt to reach out once, I know that too.

But hurt, I know that I am. I yelled at them to leave me alone, I told them we were never really friends, they did nothing but hear me, and *I'm* hurt.

Holy headache.

'So . . .' It's Matilda who pops our bubble of uncomfortable silence, pausing her violent inhalation of scrambled eggs long enough to probe. 'We didn't see you out last night.'

In turn, I pause pushing a soggy piece of pancake around my plate long enough to frown. 'Why would you have?'

It's Imani who answers around a kiss of her teeth. 'We saw Ben.'

My frown persists as I try and fail to locate any correlation. 'Okay?'

The pair exchange a look I don't quite understand. 'You two aren't back together?'

Something just short of dumbfounded, I stare at them. And then, I laugh hard enough to draw more than one curious look from the surrounding tables. 'Are you kidding? *No.*'

'Are you sure?'

'Yeah, I'm pretty fucking sure.' I laugh again, gaping at their confusion. 'Why the hell would you think that?'

'Because he told Heath you were getting back together?'

'*What?* When?'

'The day you guys . . .' Imani fidgets awkwardly with the tail end of one of her braids. 'Broke up. And every time we bumped into him over the break. A lot last night.'

I lean back, another disbelieving exhale deflating my lungs. 'I'm gonna kill him.'

'Might wanna use something sharper than a butter knife.'

My gaze falls to my fingers, where they're wrapped tightly around said knife. With a sigh, I let it go and flick it out of my reach, because God knows my ex has a penchant for showing up at the most inopportune of moments, and I don't think I would actually be able to stop myself from trying to shove the dull blade somewhere vulnerable if he dared to right now.

'So you're really not back together?'

'You want me to take a polygraph or something?'

Imani holds her hands up, palms toward me, conceding. 'We believe you.'

'Thanks so much,' I snark, sullen as I slump, arms crossed and appetite nowhere to be found. 'That means a lot, considering you believed *him* first.'

'We didn't—' Imani cuts herself off with a huff. 'Yeah, okay. That's our bad. But he was pretty convincing.'

'Was he?' I question. 'Or did you really wanna be right about me using Heath to get him back?'

Neither of them respond. Soon, silence prevails again, only interrupted by the scrape of cutlery and the slurping of coffee.

I push around my food mindlessly, endlessly picking apart their accusations, desperate to know exactly what bullshit Ben has been spewing, but not quite willing to ask; smart enough not to because I know it'll reach new levels of fuckery and potentially drive me to criminal activity. I don't even begin to wonder why he's doing it, because I know *that,* his reasoning, will be nothing short of nonsense. Only logical in his shriveled little brain, and likely to make mine freaking implode with the absurdity of it all – it's already on the verge of that, as I think about Heath, and him thinking I lied to him. Him believing so easily that I did. Him thinking I was with Ben, and still having me as his phone screen-saver, still looking for me last night, still turning up at my apartment and saying sweet things.

'He's here.'

Jerking with surprise, my panicked gaze flies over my shoulder toward the front entrance. When I find a different *he* than I expected, relief and disappointment rage a silent internal battle. In the end, neither win – curiosity steals first place as, while Matilda slides out of the booth with a groan to go greet her twin, Imani goes stiff as a board.

She curls in on herself, tugging her hood further down her face, hiding, if I didn't know any better.

When I cast another look Brendan's way and finally notice the girl at his side – the one I guess was keeping him busy last night – I quickly realize I don't know any better at all.

'Sorry.'

Dark eyes narrow. 'About?'

I discreetly gesture toward the twins.

Imani huffs, arms crossing tightly over her chest. 'Why would I care about that?'

I tilt my head, brows high.

She huffs again. 'Shut up.'

'I didn't say anything.'

'Yeah, well, your face is pretty fucking loud.'

Stacking my forearms on the table, I lean as far across it as I can and lower my voice so there isn't any risk of eavesdropping. 'What's going on there?'

'Nothing.'

I throw her the same line she once used on me. 'I have eyes, Imani.'

'Congratulations. Why don't you use them to see through your own bullshit?'

'Excuse me?'

'Why did you do it, Dani?'

'What are you talking about?'

'Heath,' she clarifies, and I stiffen. 'Why did you get him to pretend to date you?'

Something like shame flushing me hot, I drop my gaze to my twisted fingers. 'Kai told you?'

She ducks into my eyeline just to give me that *duh* look again. Like I'm some kind of dumbass for assuming he could ever keep that a secret. 'You took it too far.'

'*I* took it too far?'

'You know he likes you, Dani.'

'No, I don't. He never told me.'

'He had to tell you?'

'Yeah, Imani, he did.' Frustration brews behind my ribcage, knits my fingers together in a tight, painful ball. 'I can't . . . I don't pick up on things like that, okay? I didn't know.'

'Dani, he's had a crush on you since your freshman year. He came home after that swim mixer thing and he would not shut up about this beautiful girl and her beautiful scowl and the beautiful way she walked around the room like no one there deserved to be in her presence. Jesus, he went through a fucking mourning period when you started dating Ben. It was, like, borderline concerning.'

'Why didn't he tell me?'

'Why didn't *you* tell *him*? You told me.'

'It was easy to tell you.' Pulling on my fingertips, I attempt a weak smile. 'I really liked being your friend, even if it wasn't completely real.'

A roll of dark eyes doesn't quite match the sweet, gentle way Imani tangles her fingers with mine and squeezes. 'It was real,' she insists, too firmly not to believe.

As the weight that's been constricting my chest for the last couple of weeks abruptly lessens, I realize just how much I needed to hear that. 'I'm sorry. I didn't mean for everything to get so . . . complicated.'

'Trust me.' Sympathy softens her features – *empathy*. 'I understand.'

I'm contemplating ordering another cup of coffee that I don't need just to give myself an excuse to linger a little longer when the bell above the diner's front door jingles and a haggard Kai stumbles across the threshold.

His groan reaches us before he does. My nose wrinkles when he tumbles onto the chair beside me, bringing the stale stench of alcohol with him. Whimpering, he slumps on the table and fixes a pair of pitiful brown eyes on my half-finished plate of lukewarm breakfast before flicking them up to me, making me roll my own. 'You weren't even that drunk last night.'

Kai bats those long, dark lashes and pouts. 'I'm a sensitive boy.'

'You're a drama queen,' I scoff, but I push my food his way, my full-ish mug too, and I smile a little when he thanks me with a headbutt, like a fucking cat.

I abruptly stop smiling when the door chimes again. My breath catches as my gaze flies to the person pushing inside the diner, leaving me in a low, ragged rush when I realize that, again, it's not the man I thought it would be.

'He's outside,' Kai tells me quietly, his elbow bumping mine, and I fight the urge to scowl.

So, what? He won't come in because I'm here? He's hiding out until I leave? That's seriously how it is?

'He's waiting for you.'

'To leave,' I sneer, one hand already reaching for my keys and my phone while the other grapples in my back pocket for the twenty-dollar bill I stuffed in there and tosses it on the table. 'I get it.'

'No, dummy. To talk to you.'

'Why?'

Kai shrugs. 'Go find out.'

My gaze flicks to Imani – seeking permission? Assurance? Whatever her nod means, that's obviously what I needed because I don't move until I get it.

It feels like the entire diner watches me walk outside. If I were to glance over my shoulder, I imagine I'd find a hundred faces smushed against the window. In fact, I think the only pair of eyes in the general vicinity not trained on me might belong to the man leaning against my car.

Arms crossed. Head hanging low. Last night's rumpled outfit hanging awkwardly on his athletic frame; collar popped and askew, shirt unbuttoned in a dramatic v, the hem hitched high on one side to reveal the top button of his jeans undone, the waistband slung low.

Heath doesn't look up as I approach. Nor when I ask, 'Feeling okay?'

One hand lifts to massage his temple, as if the mere sound of my voice has granted him a headache, and he doesn't say anything.

I wait, I give him a minute, and still, his mouth remains firmly shut.

Irritation tugs at the edge of mine. 'If you're not gonna talk to me, can you move?'

Heath stiffens. Discontent rumbles in his chest, but he does exactly what I asked. And even though disappointment squeezes mine, I put on my best unbothered front as I grasp the driver's side door and haul it open.

Only for a strong hand to slam it shut again.

With a scoff, my narrowed gaze meets his tired one – for a split second, and then he looks away again, squinting at the sky like he can't bear the sight of me. He inhales deeply, fucking steeling himself to look at me, and if I weren't so hurt by the dramatic display, I'd be stomping on his fucking foot.

A muscle in his jaw jumping, he runs his tongue over his teeth before levelling me with wary, reddened eyes. 'Sorry.'

I kiss my fucking teeth right back. 'For what?'

'Showing up last night.'

That's it? I want to say. Instead, I just shrug. 'Don't worry about it.'

The hand holding my car door hostage drops, and I figure that's it. That's all he's got for me – all I'm worth. Except, instead of backing up, he slumps against the frame again, his whole body now impeding my exit.

'Heath—'

'I was gonna call you.'

I blink at the abrupt interruption. The abrupt shift in his uninterested disposition. The abrupt, bewildering revelation. 'What?'

'I, uh, passed my class. The one I needed for my history minor.'

I hate that disappointment hits me first – that the first thought to cross my mind is *That's it? That's the only reason?*

I hate the wave of pride, far stronger than I have any right to feel, that punches me in the gut even more. 'You did?'

'Don't sound so surprised.'

My eyes roll – my hand squeezes the tattooed forearm I hadn't even realized I'd grabbed until right this very moment. Quickly retreating, I shove my hands in my pockets lest they do any more unsanctioned wandering. 'That's amazing, Heath. I'm so— *you* should be so proud.'

His smile is shy, as bashful as the dip of his gaze. He shakes his head once, and then, to the ground, he mumbles, 'You were the first person I wanted to tell. The only person.'

And yet, he didn't. He's so . . . God, however the fuck he feels toward me, mad or sad or entirely apathetic, that he wouldn't even pick up the phone. As tiny little needles of resentment prick my skin, I can't help but snark, 'Lose my number?'

The freckles bridging his nose collide as he pulls a face. 'Didn't wanna find out if you'd blocked it.'

And deprive myself of the endless hours spent wondering if he'd call, text, show some sign of life? God, I wish the thought had even crossed my mind. 'I didn't.'

His sigh is weighted with relief. Tattooed knuckles scrub at tired eyes. He tilts his head to the sky again, staring into space as he shifts and fidgets and sighs some more, and I'm reaching the limit of my capacity for awkward silences by the time he finally pins that gaze on me again.

'I meant what I said last night,' he surprises me by drawling – he surprises me by sounding so . . . small. Lost. *Drained.* 'I miss you, Dani.'

Three words lodge like shards of glass in my ribcage. Four more get stuck in my throat, too soft and vulnerable and scared to come out yet. I find it hard to look at him, at his drawn, unhappy face or those fucking puppy-dog eyes.

I find it even harder to look away – the notch of his throat is as far as I get. 'Surprised you remember.'

A red flush begins to crawl its way up his neck. 'Took me a second.'

What about 'pretty girl'? I silently wonder. *'Tried to find you'* and *'you're important to me'*?

'Dani.' He pushes off the car and closes all but a couple of inches of distance between us. A hesitant hand reaches for me – a stark contrast to the confident finger that crooks around my waistband, a precaution lest I try to flee. 'I'm so fucking sorry. I should've just talked to you instead of jumping to conclusions.'

'Yeah, you should've.' Maybe I over-reacted at the beach, maybe my hurt feelings were what blew everything up, but my feelings never would've been hurt if he'd given me five fucking seconds to clear things up. If he'd hesitated for a *single* second, he would've seen me shove Ben away. 'Why didn't you?'

'I . . .' A calloused thumb taps impatiently against the bare skin just above my waistband. 'Fuck. I didn't wanna know. Didn't wanna hear you say it. Didn't . . .' He pauses, swallowing hard. 'I didn't want you to end it.'

An emotion I can't quite decipher – or maybe I just don't want to – lodges in the back of my throat. Around it, I rasp a reminder. 'It was always gonna end, Heath.'

The hard set of his jaw doesn't quite agree.

'It didn't have to end like that,' he says, and at least that sentiment, we both share. 'Our friendship didn't have to end at all. I never wanted it to. I . . .' He inhales deep. Exhales slow. Tentatively shifts his grip until his pinkie is hooked around mine, holding tight. 'I don't feel right without you. I miss my Dani. My best fucking friend.'

The urge to cry slams into me so abruptly, so powerfully, I almost don't manage to stifle it. I would admit that I missed him too, that his absence was an *ache*, if I didn't fear what else might come out with that admission. If I thought that all I did was *miss* him.

If I wasn't all but positive about there being a much scarier emotion mixed in there too.

All I can do is nod. Hang on to that pinkie. Steady my knees as relief wobbles them when I'm reminded that Heath never takes my silences personally. Another deep breath tickles my scalp when he drops his face to the top of my head, lips brushing my hairline.

'Gonna hug you now,' he warns, but I don't need it. My hands already found his hip and tugged him close. His arms wrap around me, and my bones all but melt. The anxiety flees my body. It's the best I've felt in weeks. It's the most *still* I've felt in weeks.

The calm before the storm, I might recognize in hindsight.

TWENTY-EIGHT

COACH MICHAELS STANDS BENEATH THE BANNER strung up over the hotel reception desk, welcoming everyone to the NCAA Division One swimming conference, and holds aloft a stack of white envelopes.

As he hands them out, I tune out the accompanying drone of strict instructions – no drinking, curfew is at ten, no leaving the hotel or staying in any room that isn't your own. I know the drill. Just like I know there'll be two names scrawled on the back of the envelope Coach hands me, with two keys inside, yet I still sigh at the confirmation that my request for a single room has once again been denied.

What I don't know, however, is what the fuck I did to Coach to deserve the surname inked beneath my own. 'You've got to be fucking kidding me.'

'Don't start, Williams.' Coach scowls at me, and I wonder if this is punishment for my lackluster performance lately – I wonder if it matters even a little that me at half-power is still better than ninety per cent of the people at this damn meet. 'You have bigger things to worry about than your roommate.'

Actually, I don't. This weekend is nothing but an additional practice for me. A dress rehearsal of sorts. Unlike a lot of the students gearing up for a win, I've already qualified for the national championships next month. I could swim blind folded, backwards, wearing a fucking corset to hinder my every move, and it wouldn't matter a bit. I'm only here for the relay.

So I have plenty of mental capacity to doom spiral about me and my ex's ex sharing a confined space.

After casting a withering glare at Coach, I scan the hotel lobby in search of my new fucking roomie. A high ponytail calls to me from across the room, twirled around a slender finger as its owner chats to someone I can't see, and as I huff and puff my way over there, I wonder how much trouble I would get in if I *accidentally* took her out with a suitcase to the ankle.

'Hey,' I bark, thrusting my key at Sienna without so much as glancing at whoever she's talking to – and downright relishing the flicker of genuine fear that flashes in her wide blue eyes. 'Don't touch my shit, and don't let anyone else in the room.'

Sienna gulps. Glossy pink lips part, but a baffled scoff most definitely does not come from her.

'This is a joke, right?'

My head snaps toward . . .

Heath. She's chatting to Heath. Chatting *up* Heath, if that twirly ponytail maneuver was anything to go by.

Heath, who gapes at me, slack-jawed. Expression pinched. Brows high and mouth a contortion of confusion. 'You can't be roommates.'

'Why?' I snap, my narrowed gaze flicking between him and Sienna. *What were you talking about? Why are you talking to her? Was that fucking hair move working for you?* 'Am I messing up your plans?'

'You caught me,' comes his dry explanation, and I try not to flinch. I know he's joking. It's just friendly teasing because that's what we are now – friends. Friends who exchange awkward, stilted texts. Friends who haven't quite figured out how to slot back into each other's lives yet.

Friends who joke about hooking up with other people, apparently.

Yay.

I turn back to Sienna. 'Be in the room by nine or you're sleeping in the hallway.'

Heath says my name and my roomie starts spluttering about curfew, but I don't hang around to listen to either of them. I turn on my heel and elbow my way through the crowd toward the elevators, slamming the button repeatedly until finally, it arrives to whisk me up a handful of floors.

The doors close and my own reflection glares at me in the mirrored surface. With a huff, I try to straighten out my expression, but that doesn't work. It makes it worse. No matter how hard I try, my mouth remains downturned and my forehead still wrinkles in distress, but my eyes, they change. They go from bright with fury to clouded and . . . sad.

By the time I reach my floor, my eyes are itchy and the back of my throat is itchy, and the rest of my body is itchy too. I need to get in my room, get in the shower, get out of my damn head, get *him* out of my head, by . . . I don't know. Meditating. Banging my head against the bathroom wall a couple of times. Raiding the minibar because the last time I got drunk sure did work out well.

Wincing at the mere thought, I yank my suitcase down the carpeted hallway. It takes me three tries to get the damn keycard to work so I can get in my room, and then I can't slam the damn door behind me because it's one of those stupid non-slammable doors, and God forbid a girl wants to slam something every once in a while. Groaning, I settle for a feeble kick to my suitcase before rifling through the contents in search of pajamas, and mumbling a big *fuck you* to the dinner I'm supposed to have with the rest of my teammates. God knows I'm not attending that – God knows no one will miss me.

I'll just shower and change and order room service, and I'll eat that room service on Sienna's fucking bed while I watch the second season of *The Rain,* because Kai was right, and it *is* a travesty that I've never seen it before.

And that's exactly what I do.

Robe-clad and sitting cross-legged on the twin bed besides the one I've claimed as my own, I'm demolishing a Caesar salad, salmon, and a side of fries when there's a knock on the door. Grumbling something derogatory about silly little mistresses and their apparent inability to open doors, I stomp across the room, wearing a particularly vicious scowl as I open the door.

Only it's not Sienna lingering on the other side.

Jesus. How many times is the universe going to have me asking 'What are you doing here?'

'Room service,' Imani quips, with a wry smile, not asking for permission before pushing past me.

Matilda bounces in behind her, giving me a squeeze with the hand not cradling an abundance of . . . face masks? I think? And a bunch of other stuff. Nail polish bottles clank together as she dumps the whole lot on the bed, and I spy a bunch of hair products from the brand I like rolling around too. Flopping onto her side, she props herself up on an elbow and steals a couple of fries. 'We heard about your roommate.'

Hip-checking the door shut, I lean back against it, the nervous knot of my hands digging into my lower spine. 'So you're here to help me dispose of the body.'

Snorting, Imani snags a bottle of nail polish remover from the pile and gives it a shake. 'Thought this might help with the bloodstains.'

I snicker, and they do too. Tentatively, I push off the door and join them on the bed, perching awkwardly on the edge. 'I don't need bodyguards.'

'Just accomplices.'

Another laugh sneaks out of me.

'We saw your team downstairs having dinner,' Imani explains, surveying a bright pink gel polish, 'and noticed you were missing, and we figured we'd save your ceiling from that glare.'

I can't even deny it – I was, in fact, one finished meal away from crawling beneath the covers and glaring at the ceiling until sleep took over. 'Nothing better to do?'

'Nope,' they answer, in perfect, sincere unison.

'I didn't know you guys were here.'

'We're always here. Kai's convinced if we miss a single one, he'll suddenly suck.'

'You're his lucky charms.'

'Exactly.' Matilda snickers. A second later, her eyes go wide and she thwaps Imani on the forearm. 'Speaking of. Give her the thing.'

'Right.' Snapping her fingers, Imani shifts to dig around in her back pocket, coming out with something that she tosses at me. I catch it mid-air, frowning for the split second it takes me to figure out what it is. My face falls as my heart does the reverse, leaping to my throat and lodging there, throbbing.

'He says good luck,' one of the girls tells me. I can't distinguish which one, too much of my focus stolen by an orca with a wonky fin and a crooked tail and a mediocre paint job, a little too big for the keychain it's hanging from.

Made from the same material as a surfboard, if I had to guess.

My swallow is dry – a stark contrast to my burning eyes. 'Couldn't give it to me himself?'

'He didn't wanna mess with your mojo or whatever.'

'But you guys can.'

'Nuh-uh. Lucky charms, remember?'

My smile is feeble, at best. Rendered entirely too emotional by a freaking keychain, I allow myself a single moment longer of what I can only describe as *swooning* before closing my fist around my new good luck charm. Out of sight, but not out of mind, not even when I tuck it away in my suitcase, locking it behind a zipper. 'Tell him I say thanks.'

'We will,' Matilda promises. She looks like she wants to say more – she glances at Imani, and I swear it's like she's asking for permission to unzip her tightly pressed lips – but she doesn't.

Not because Imani denies her permission or because she restrains the urge, but because the beep of a scanning keycard interrupts her.

Freaking *activates* her. Like a dog hearing a whistle.

Before the door even swings open, she's on her feet and halfway across the room – before Sienna even trudges across the threshold, she's practically being forced back out. Popping a hip, she crosses her arms with a haughty little huff. 'What happened to *no people in the room*?'

Beside me, Imani mimics that noise, that indignant tone too. 'What happened to *don't fuck other people's boyfriends*?'

Sun-kissed skin flushes bright red. 'I—'

'Not interested.' Matilda cuts her off with a dismissive flick of her hand. 'Find somewhere else to sleep tonight.'

Sienna splutters. 'Excuse me?'

Without even looking at the girl, Imani offers her a wave. 'You're excused. Bye bye.'

'Dani.'

In perfect unison, the girls on either side of me kiss their teeth. 'Dani isn't here right now. Dani doesn't exist to you.'

'Dani says fuck off,' I grumble beneath my breath.

Louder, Imani repeats, 'Dani says fuck off. And I second that.'

'I third it,' Matilda adds. She barely even taps Sienna, but the girl is so dumbfounded, she goes stumbling backwards anyway. She doesn't even argue when Matilda plucks the keycard right out of her hand, only letting out a strangled noise right before the door slams in her face.

'God.' Matilda sighs happily as she skips back to the bed, smiling so brightly, it practically gives off heat. 'That was fun.'

Insistent dinging and a chorus of groans drag me out of the fitful sleep I feel like I only just fell into.

With a groan of my own, I roll onto my back. Slipping the pillow out from beneath my head, I blindly toss it in the vague direction of the bed my surprise roommates share. A couple of grunts confirm I hit my target – a loud curse has me pushing upright and blinking groggily at Imani as she throws off her duvet in a flurry. 'What's wrong?'

'*Boys*,' is all she grumbles. A flailing hand whacks Matilda on the stomach, who shoots upright with a shriek. Through a frowning yawn, I watch as she takes one look at her friend's phone screen and hurriedly rolls out of bed, both of them shuffling toward the door in nothing but socks and pajamas without a word of explanation.

I have one foot in a Birkenstock when they pause and look back at me. 'I don't think you should come.'

I fix Matilda with a grimace, the most threatening expression I can manage in my current hazy state. 'You woke me up. Wherever you're going, I'm coming.'

The pair exchange looks and sighs, but they don't protest any further. They don't exactly wait for me either, though – they're halfway down the hall by the time I've covered my pajamas with a hoodie, and they sigh again as if they were hoping to lose me. And they sigh some more on the elevator ride up to the floor I know the guys on my team are staying on, their little huffs punctuated by the never-ending influx of text messages and the thud of Imani's fingers tapping the screen aggressively.

'Should I have brought the nail polish remover?'

That earns me a couple of tight laughs, but any humor is abruptly erased when the doors peel apart, and chaos greets us.

Listen, I'm not oblivious. I know away meets and secret after-hour hotel parties are kind of synonymous, never mind the fact I've never been invited to one. I picture a clandestine affair, red solo cups and too many bodies rammed in one room and low lights, low music, low voices too. Y'know, surreptitious or whatever.

The very antithesis of the huddle of bodies crowding the corridor, begging for the attention of one of the real adults scattered across the floors. My nose wrinkles as the smell of smoke wafts toward me, as I fight the urge to remind everyone in the general vicinity that we are athletes, for fuck's sake, with a particular reliance on our respiratory system. My eardrums thrum with the too-loud rhythm of the music spilling out of an open door. A bunch of people spill out of it too. And my eyes narrow as they zone in on something raucous occurring at the other end of the hall, something that looks like . . .

A fight. A fucking fight. Or the beginnings of one at least. Two bodies squaring up to each other, practically forehead to forehead, four fists balled tight. I start to laugh at the testosterone-fueled dramatics, start to turn to the girls to ask what the hell we're doing up here, only to freeze when my sleepy brain kicks into gear and I abruptly realize that I know both of those bodies.

Pretty damn well.

I blink rapidly in the hopes my eyes are mistaken. 'Please tell me I'm hallucinating.'

A sideways glance and matching grimaces confirm otherwise.

'Kai said everything was fine,' Imani starts, pausing to throw a protective elbow at the drunk buffoon who knocks into me on his stumbling quest for the elevator. 'And then they just lost their shit.'

As if summoned by the mention of his name, Kai is suddenly bashing his hip against mine, a drink in hand and a crooked grin on his mouth. 'This is all your fault, you know. They're fighting over you.'

'It's true,' Brendan chimes in as he appears out of fucking nowhere. 'Ben was talking shit and Heath . . . well, he didn't like it.'

I scoff, shaking my head and laughing some rendition of *ha ha, good one, you got me*.

No one laughs back. In fact, everyone looks uncharacteristically grim – a stoic Kai has my gut twisting.

With a groan and a curse, I stride down the hall.

'Boys,' I mimic Imani's earlier grumble, except mine is more of a shout, more of a call to attention – still a synonym for *dipshits* – as I shove my way through the raucous crowd. 'If you're gonna kiss, get it over with. You're fucking up my eight hours.'

At the sound of my voice, both guys bristle.

Sea-green eyes snap toward me instantly. Anger sparks in them, so fierce that I have to fight the urge to back up a step.

Ben doesn't look at me at all. He's too busy sneering, and he sneers a little harder when he clocks Heath's look. He uses it to his advantage – he plants both hands on his chest and shoves. 'Here she is. Right on fucking time.'

That oceanic gaze lingers a second longer before finding their arch fucking nemesis again. 'Watch your tone, Pullman.'

Snorting his amusement, Ben parrots the warning in a high-pitched, childish tone. 'You're such a fucking pussy.'

Beyond a huffed exhale, Heath doesn't react.

Ben's expression pinches even more. 'All well-behaved now your owner's here, huh? You bring his leash, Dani?'

Heath fucking woofs.

And I can't decide whether to strangle him for being such a dumbass instigator or . . . well, *kiss him* is the other fleeting instinct that comes to mind, but I check that one pretty fucking sharpish.

Hands on my hips, I look between the two boys. 'This is a joke, right? A skit? You're both really into improv comedy all of a sudden?'

'Your boyfriend's a psychopath,' Ben spits, barking a laugh a second later. 'Oh, sorry. *Ex*-boyfriend, right?'

I just about manage to stifle a flinch. 'Shut up, Ben.'

'We should start a club, huh, Heath? *Men who survived Daniela Williams.*'

There are a handful of inches between Heath and me yet I still feel him go taut as a bowstring. As a threatening noise rumbles in his chest, my fingers lock around his wrist and keep him from pouncing.

'You're hilarious.' I cast Ben a brief blank look that suggests the complete opposite before returning my attention to Heath. 'Let's go.'

He does no such thing. Though his pulse thumps an erratic beat beneath my fingertips, his voice is utterly, off-puttingly calm as he stabs a finger at my ex. 'Use that fucking tone when you're talking about her again. I dare you.'

'Enough.' I lean back on my heels and try to tug that big, stupid body away. 'Jesus. What is wrong with you?'

'I didn't start it.'

'Yeah, of course you didn't,' Ben scoffs. 'The perfect little prince has never done anything wrong in his life.'

'*Shut up, Ben.*'

'Go fuck yourself, Daniela.'

One minute, I have Heath in my grasp.

The next, he's carefully peeled me off of him and not-so-carefully pinned Ben to the wall, damn near frothing at the mouth. 'What did I just say?'

'Oh my God.' I rush to his side and grab him with both hands this time, ten fingers curled around one bicep. 'This is pathetic. *Stop it.*'

'You didn't hear what he was saying about you.'

'Oh, I'm sure I've heard it before.' I grip him tight enough to disrupt his tan with bruising imprints, and he doesn't even flinch. '*Enough*. I'm serious.'

He doesn't budge.

'Heath.' I tug again, putting my whole damn body weight into it, putting my whole damn *irritation* into my tone. 'Come on.

You're making me nauseous. This is literally the most unattractive thing I've ever witnessed in my entire life.'

That, of all fucking things, actually causes him pause. Earns me some squinted side-eye. '*Nauseous?*'

'The whole cavemen thing really does not do it for me.'

A choked, snarky noise sounds from Tweedle-fucking-dee. 'Nobody ask her what does.'

Those eyes flash, a muscle in that tattooed neck jumps, that shorn head starts to turn.

Pinching that strong, dimpled chin between my thumb and forefinger, I keep his gaze on me. 'Seriously. I'm gagging. This is disgusting.'

'Oh, I'm disgusting?'

'Exactly.' I give his chin a squeeze before coasting my grip lower, down the arm not currently holding my ex at bay. Hesitantly, I unfurl his clenched fingers – even more hesitant, I lace them with my own. 'That's the root of the issue here. You are so disgusting and you really shouldn't be in public, so *let's go*.'

For a long, breathless second, he simply stares at me. Acts like we don't have an audience straight out of my nightmares, like my ex isn't struggling against his grip, spitting insults. His gaze is leisurely, like he has all the damn time in the world, and only when he apparently gets his fill does he deign to nod sharply.

Relief leaves me with a deep exhale as the veins in his forearms stop bulging quite so prominently, as he lessens the weight on Ben's chest. He doesn't entirely retreat, though – he holds him firmly in place, and I wait impatiently as he leans in to murmur something inaudible in my ex's ear – sweet nothings? Death threats? An explicit rendition of how *not* nauseous I've found him in the past?

I don't know. I just know that he's smirking when he backs up. Ben harrumphs and shakes himself out, big mouth opening to spew something else *delightful*, I'm sure, but I don't stick around to find out – or, rather, Heath doesn't let us stick around.

The tables turn, *he's* suddenly the one dragging *me* away, *he's* gripping *me* tightly, *I* feel like *I'm* the one fleeing the scene of a crime. 'I didn't mean to drag you into this,' he says quietly, his apologetic cringe quite the contrast to the vitriol my ex is throwing in our wake. 'Are you okay?'

'Am *I* okay?' I scoff, stabbing repeatedly at the call button of the slowest fucking elevator in the world. 'Are you okay? Like, in the head? What the fuck is wrong with you? Why are you even up here? Why are you looking at me like that?'

He blinks, but that dreamy look in his eyes goes nowhere. *Dreamy*. I'm screaming at him, and he's *dreamy*.

'Are you high or something?'

'No, baby. Just looking at you.'

'Well, stop it.'

'Can't.'

'Jesus.' Rolling my eyes, I cover his with my hand. Long lashes only tickle my palm for a split second before he catches me by the wrist, kissing the curve of my thumb as he peels it away.

As my heart swells, I snatch my hand away. 'Don't do that.'

'Sorry.' He flexes his fingers before tucking them in his pocket. 'Dani, can we—'

'No. We can't do anything because I'm going to bed, and so are you, and I swear to fucking God, if you don't . . .' I leave the threat open-ended, up to his imagination, mostly because the elevator finally dings and I just want to get the hell out of here. The second the doors open, I step inside, half-turning to snap at that dreamy fucking bastard to do the same thing.

It happens so fast. I barely have the time to form a scowl at the sight of Ben rushing up behind Heath. Certainly don't have time to holler a warning before the former plants two hands on the latter's back and shoves.

There definitely isn't time to brace myself when a tall, hard body collides with me. Or to right myself so that my shoulder, the one I twinged over the holidays, doesn't slam into the mirrored elevator wall hard enough for it to crack.

For *me* to crack. An audible, painful crack.

Fuck.

TWENTY-NINE

'NO.'

Eyes fixed on the pool in front of me, I finish tucking my braided hair into my swim cap and try to ignore the palpable fury pouring off the dripping man looming over me. I get a flashback, briefly, to hours earlier, when I was witnessing that same fury, except I wasn't bearing the brunt of it like I am now.

'Daniela.' Wet fingers wrap around my wrist and squeeze. *'No.'*

The shoulder that bore the brunt of my entire dead body weight far too few hours ago screams a similar objection, but I ignore that too. 'I don't recall asking for your permission.'

'You have nothing to prove to anyone.'

'I'm not trying to prove anything.'

'You cannot swim with a dislocated shoulder.'

'Shut up,' I hiss, head whipping from side to side to check my coach isn't within earshot. 'It's not dislocated.'

Anymore. It barely even left the socket. I gave my arm a shake and it popped right back in. I've had papercuts more painful – I've slept funny and caused more damage. 'It's fine, Heath. I'm fine.'

'No, you're an idiot.'

'Thanks, baby.'

'Don't. Don't do that shit with me right now.'

My lips press together tightly. 'It's just the relay. I have to do it.'

'No, you don't. That's what alternates are for.'

'Our alternate sucks.'

A few feet away, someone scoffs, '*Hey.*'

Heath doesn't look away from me for even a second. 'Everyone sucks compared to you, Dani, but it doesn't fucking matter.'

'It matters to me.'

'Well, *you* matter to *me*. And this is not good for you.'

'Jesus, Belfort.' A haughty snort draws my gaze, and I tense at the sight of my sneering ex. 'It's a few laps. She'll live.'

Heath ignores him. He keeps his gaze locked on me, stepping closer and stooping to murmur, for my ears only, 'Are you doing this for him?'

I shake my head. I'm not, I know I'm not.

What I don't know is who I *am* doing it for.

'Just think for a second, Dani. Think. Is this actually worth it?'

I don't need to think about it. The answer comes to me instantly – *no*. It isn't worth it. It's a damn relay with zero consequences for me, swum with people I fucking despise. It doesn't matter, not in any real way, except that, to me, it does. I'm not a quitter. I don't just give up. I don't let my team down. I don't sit on the freaking sidelines and watch other people succeed.

A voice in the back of my head echoes what Heath says – *this is a bad idea. Don't do it. Sit it out. The world won't end.*

Louder, a voice I haven't heard since I was sixteen contradicts – *Buck up, Daniela. Not good enough, Daniela. Not you, Daniela.*

That second voice drowns everything out, the same way it did when it was real, when my dad was still alive. It has panic flaring across my chest and my head dipping low with something not quite shameful, but close, and my tongue working to spill robotic words. 'Better get to your block, Heath. Race is about to start.'

The noise Heath makes is pure disappointment. His next words; pure desperation. 'I'll tell your coach.'

That panic swells and damn near chokes me. Renders me near-incapable of threatening, 'I'll never talk to you again.'

That has him reeling back. Kissing his teeth and rumbling a rough laugh. 'That's what I get for caring, huh?'

I swallow an instinctive comeback; I don't gripe that nobody's asking him to care because, God, a part of me is begging for that. A part of me almost bursts into tears when he stops caring and walks over to his own team – a really, really big part. So big that when I stuff it away into a mental box reinforced with freaking chains, there's barely anything left. Just the booming void that sounds like my dad and looks like my dad and feels like my dad too.

His presence thrums throughout every crevice of my brain as that whistle blows, signaling the lead-off swimmers to step up to the block and the rest of us to lock in. It's his voice that barks at me to focus when my turn comes around. But it's me, entirely me, nothing but my all-consuming panic, as I position myself to dive.

And when I hit the water and know with absolute, searing

clarity that I have monumentally fucked up, there's only me to blame.

The mere act of breaking the surface sets my shoulder on fire. It burns as I dolphin kick a mere quarter of the length I'm usually capable of. And as I wrench it into butterfly stroke after butterfly stroke, tears blur my vision and fill my goggles with saltwater. I'm struggling to breathe, fighting not to scream instead, and this is wrong, this is so fucking *wrong*.

I mess up my count. I don't even think I started counting. I know I've fucked the turn even before I hit, and, fuck, do I hit it – my palms slam into the poolwall, sending shockwaves up both arms.

It's so quick. A second of my life yet I swear I see the whole thing flash before my eyes. I'm swimming, and then I'm not.

The distinctive pop of my shoulder leaving its joint is deafening. The grind of bone against bone – *sickening*. The pain turns my vision black. Underwater, I scream. Above water, I scream a little too. Panicked and pained, I struggle to keep myself afloat with only one arm, the other hanging uselessly. I hear splashing and commotion and yelling – *I'm* yelling. Pure agony rips through me, but I manage to hook my good arm over the side of the pool. I try to hoist myself up, but I slip, and my chin cracks against the concrete. Another pained cry scratches my throat as I dip beneath the surface again.

Disoriented, I just . . . sink. Useless.

And then hands hook under my armpits and dead-lift me out of the water.

I scream again, the pain something north of unbearable.

Someone else is screaming too; my name riddled with high-pitched desperation.

'Fuck,' Heath says again and again and again.

Fuck, every inch of me echoes.

The emergency-room resident who sees me on arrival, the intern who winces at the bulging bone stretching the skin of my shoulder thin, the orthopedic surgeon who recommends surgery and a minimum of three months recovery, *and* two different nurses all tell me to get some rest.

An impossible feat, no matter how hard I try.

It isn't the pain keeping me awake – the steady stream of painkillers flowing from an IV bag and into the back of my hand are doing a stellar job of keeping that at bay. Hunger pangs make my stomach cramp and I'm forbidden from eating until after my joint damage is hopefully proved temporary, but I don't think I'd be able to keep anything down anyway. I'm tired. I'm so exhausted, I know it would be so easy to fall asleep.

If it wasn't for the bone-deep ache of failure acting as the caffeine from the nightmares I can't have because I can't fucking sleep.

I've fucked it. I've completely and utterly fucked it. I'm out for the rest of the season, at least. I have surgery and recovery and months of rehab after that. I'll be lucky if my stroke is ever the same again, I'll be lucky if I have the same mobility at all.

Lucky.

The doctor actually used that word. *He's* lucky I didn't dislocate *his* fucking shoulder for that.

My life is ruined, and I'm lucky. My life is nothing now, but I'm lucky. Everything I've worked for, everything I've done, everything I've not done, *means nothing*. And I have no one to blame but myself.

My eyes itch something fierce, but I don't dare blink the burgeoning tears away. I don't dare open them. I don't want the man curled up in the chair beside my bed to know I'm wide awake, ignoring some more medical advice.

Heath has been in this room as long as I have. He's heard all the same medical jargon, all the consequences of my actions, all the reprimands too. He asked all the questions while I sat there, silent and pale and counting the floor tiles, and when they delivered my fatal sentence, he tried to hold my hand.

And he didn't say a word when I jerked away.

I still feel the sting of my fingernails digging into my thighs as I resisted the urge to take that hand, to hold it, hold him. But I just . . . couldn't. Can't. I'm barely holding it together. There is a single, thin thread wrapped around my sanity, keeping it contained, and I know, I just *know*, that with one comforting touch, it will snap.

I don't want comfort. I don't deserve comfort. I did this. His train of thought should be a continuous chant of *told you so told you so told you so*, not pity or sorrow or the same kind of bone-deep grief I feel for myself that I feel pouring out of him.

'I know you're awake.'

I stiffen. Just to be stubborn, I keep my eyes shut for a minute longer before opening them to a narrow squint, pushing myself upright with my good arm. 'Why are you still here?'

The answer is incredibly obvious, the look he gives me says. *You are a dumbass for not knowing.*

I slump with a groan, wincing when my shoulder stretches the limit of that liquid pain relief. 'I don't want you here.'

His expression transforms. *Liar.*

'I'm serious.' I groan some more, wincing some more too when I try to cross my arms, and *whoops, oh look, another thing I can't fucking do.* 'I don't.'

Legs stretched out in front of him and crossed at the ankle, Heath is the epitome of calm as his head lolls gently to one side. 'Tell me to leave then.'

I try. I really, really try, but the words won't fucking come out. Instead, I seethe. 'This is your fault, you know.'

'How's that?'

'You distracted me. You fucked with my head. I wasn't focused because of you. I was at that fucking party because of *you*.'

'I know.' Regret slopes his brow, crinkling the corner of his eyes. 'I'm—'

'Don't.' I don't want to hear his apology, I can't take it. I don't need it, it's unnecessary, it's not his fault, I know it isn't, but, fuck, I need someone to blame, just a little, that isn't me, so this weight on my chest lifts and I can *breathe*. Besides, 'It won't make anything better, it won't change this.'

Bracing his hands against the armrests, Heath pushes himself upright with a sad little sigh. 'Dani . . .'

'Don't.' I'm panicking. I'm trapped. I scramble to the other

side of the bed, except this damn bed is barely wider than my body, and there is nowhere to scramble as Heath stations himself at my bedside. 'I mean it.'

'Mean what, Daniela? You haven't told me to do anything.'

'I . . .' *Fuck*. 'Just . . .' A warble escapes me in place of anything intelligible. As words elude me, my bottom lip starts to tremble. Frustration bubbles up and wells behind my eyes, and no matter how furiously I swipe the tears away, no matter how hard I press my knuckles into my eye sockets to try stem the leakage, it doesn't fucking *stop*. As pure and utter misery swallows me alive, my will gives out. My head drops, my forehead finds a hard sternum, my fingers curl around a waistband, and I all but wail, '*Heath*.'

I blink, and he's wrapped himself around me. A careful hand settles along my ribcage, just beneath where my useless arm is strapped tightly to my chest in a sling, and he angles us so only my good side slumps against him. He settles his hand on the back of my head, fingers moving in soothing strokes down my hair.

'Shhh.' His mouth brushes my hairline. 'I got you. It's okay. Everything's gonna be okay.'

'No, it's not,' I sob, soaking his t-shirt so thoroughly, the white material turns transparent. 'Nothing is okay.'

'It will be. I know it feels like the end of the world—'

'Feels like?' I pull away, wide-eyed and gasping and distraught. 'Heath, this *is* the end of the world to me. This is the end of *my* world. Swimming is literally all I have. It's all I am. And now I just . . . I can't do it anymore, and *I am nothing without it*.'

Firmly, Heath refutes, 'That's not true.'

'The only reason anyone knows who I am is because of swimming. It's the only reason anyone notices me. It's why Ben liked me, it's why *you* liked me.'

Heath makes a noise that's partly a laugh, and entirely furious. 'You can't honestly believe that the quality of your fucking butterfly is the most important thing to me.'

Except I can. Because I do. He says it all the time, he loves to watch me swim. He loves how good I am. He wouldn't be interested in me if I wasn't so good, he wouldn't even *know* me.

'That's not true,' isn't any more convincing the second time I hear it, no matter how valiantly it's spat. 'Dani, you know it isn't.'

'I don't *know* anything, Heath. You don't tell me anything. You, everyone, just expect me to know or to guess or—'

'You don't wanna hear it,' he cuts me off sharply. Near rabid with frustration, yet still so gentle as he presses a hand to my sternum. 'You don't wanna hear that I wanted you the fucking second I laid eyes on you. You don't wanna know that the main reason I hate Ben is because *he* was your boyfriend and I wasn't. You don't wanna know that *I love you*.'

Three words hit me like a punch to the fucking face. Instinctively, a *no* leaves my mouth.

Heath . . . buffers. Gapes at me blankly like he can't compute my refutal. 'No?'

'No,' I repeat blankly. 'That's . . . *no*.'

'You don't believe me? Why do you think I hate Ben so much? Because of *you*, Dani. Because something about him appealed to you. Something that I don't have. Because two years ago, he got the girl I couldn't stop thinking about. And for two fucking years, I had to watch this unbelievable asshole fucking squander this unbelievable girl.'

Frozen, I wait for it to hit me. That elation, you know. The *oh my God he loves me* euphoric joy.

It doesn't come. I think it would, under any other circumstances. If I wasn't in a hospital room, five seconds post hearing the worst fucking news of my life, I think knowing Heath Belfort loved me would make me feel pretty damn joyful. I think I might even say it back.

Instead, all that comes out of my mouth is a cold 'Get out.'

That mouth droops, lips parting with a disbelieving noise as he gives his head a minute shake. Light brows pitch inwards ever-so-slightly. Long fingers scratch behind one ear as if he's suddenly doubting its efficiency. 'What?'

Louder, but no more firm, no more sure, I repeat, 'Get. Out.'

'I'm not going anywhere, Daniela.'

'Why? Because you love me?' My laugh is so bitter, it burns. '*Wow*. Great. Someone's going to wheel me into surgery any minute now, my career is over before it's even really started, but, fuck, who cares? No worries. A boy loves me.

'Jesus,' I practically scream, my free hand finding the center of his chest and shoving him as far away as he's willing to go. 'What is this? My consolation prize? My silver lining? Instead of devoting my life to swimming, I devote it to you?'

'That is not—'

'Why now? Why couldn't you say this a month ago? Two

fucking years ago? If you love me, how could you just *wait*? You say all the time that I deserved more, but you didn't love me enough to make sure I got it? To give it to me?'

Vaguely, in the back of my mind, I recognize that I'm lashing out. That not everything I'm saying is entirely deserved. But . . . fuck? His timing isn't just abysmal; it's downright cruel.

'Fuck you,' I spit. I'm crying again. I bracket the base of my throat with my hand in the hope I can physically hold my sobs at bay. 'What is wrong with you?'

For as long as I live, I don't think I'll ever forget the look on Heath's face. I don't think I'll ever get over causing that level of *crushed* – I won't ever forgive myself for it.

But as he backs up a step, I don't move. He half-turns to the door, frosted gaze still locked on me, and my own eyes burn as they forget how to blink. With a low, humorless laugh, he straightens and shows me his tense, rigid back.

And even though the overwhelming sense of *wrong* that preceded me ending up in this room in the first place floods me once more, I don't do a single damn thing as he walks out the door.

THIRTY

'IT'S ALIVE,' MY BROTHER DRAMATICALLY PROCLAIMS the very moment my heavy eyes peel open. Rising from his slouched perch in the chair beside my hospital bed, Sebastian looms over me. Despite his jovial tone, concern pinches his face. 'How ya feeling, *tormentita*?'

Nausea clogs the back of my throat. Groggy, I try to sit up only for my head to swim with the effort, sharp pain exploding in my shoulder when I fall back down a little too roughly. 'Like shit.'

A finger pokes my wrinkled forehead. 'I told them to slip you a little Botox, but apparently that's unethical.'

I laugh, and I immediately regret it. Not because it makes my head hurt something fierce, but because it jogs my memory. Reminds me where I am, why I'm here, why I shouldn't be laughing at all. I try to sit up again, and, this time, Sebastian is there to help me, a gentle hand on my non-ruined shoulder guiding me upright. 'How long've you been here?'

'Centuries. Your recovery time is abysmal.'

That ball of nausea pulses.

Sebastian winces. 'Sorry. I didn't mean—'

'It's fine. Did Coach call you?'

'Heath did.'

Briefly, the pain in my chest drowns out everything else. My eyes squeeze shut again.

'Did you tell Marisol?'

There's a loaded pause. In my mind's eye, I picture his face, all scrunched and reluctant and woefully unsurprised. 'She sends her love.'

Yeah. I'm sure she does.

I feel pressure on my leg before the mattress dips, Sebastian's lean body carefully settling by my feet. Just as he does, the door opens, and a doctor saunters in with a nurse on his tail.

I know before he even opens his mouth that it isn't good news – or at least not the news I wanted. He didn't grossly overestimate my injuries. I'm not magically healed. It's exactly the outcome he expected.

My season is done. My next season too. I have six weeks in a sling, a minimum of six months of physiotherapy, a year before I get anywhere close to my full strength back. He talks about limited mobility and recovery periods and rehabilitation, and I sit there, silent and numb, once again letting someone else take it all in for me. Pinching myself in the hope I might wake up for real this time. That this is all a nightmare.

The doctor asks if I'm in pain, and I shake my head. My shoulder throbs, but I can't even feel it. Medicine won't do anything for the type of pain I'm really in.

I'm examined and given a referral for the best physical therapist in the state, who specializes in athletic injuries – and another therapist who specializes in the same thing, just a vastly different kind of recovery – and promised a prompt early-morning discharge, and then they're gone, leaving me and Sebastian alone again.

For once, my brother is lost for words. For once, he can't wriggle his way out of an awkward situation with humor and charm. For once, he's off-kilter, nervous fingers tapping an erratic rhythm on the bedsheet. 'Dani . . .'

He reaches for my ankle and I shift, sluggish as I bend my knees up toward my chest. 'Don't.'

'This isn't the worst outcome.'

I know that. Why does everyone think I don't? Why does it have to be the worst outcome for me to be upset, why isn't this monumentally shitty outcome enough? 'Did you hear him? I can't swim.'

'Did *you* hear him?' he volleys right back at me. 'Yes, you can. Not like you used to, I know, but—'

'Then what's the fucking point?'

'Dani, come on. I know—'

'No, you don't know. You don't know anything. You don't care about anything, you don't love anything.'

'And you love swimming?'

I answer without thinking. With pure, angry instinct, 'Of course I do.'

'Then it shouldn't fucking matter that you won't be the best anymore.'

'Of course it matters, Sebastian. What the fuck? You know how hard I've worked. I wasn't a D1 fucking athlete for fun.'

'You *are* a D1 *fucking* athlete, Daniela. An injury does not take away everything you've done.'

'No, just anything more I *could* do.'

'Oh, please. You could've been a fucking Olympian already by now, if you really wanted it.'

'What is that supposed to mean?'

'You've had scouts up your ass since you were *twelve*. You set records, Dani. I know you turned down a fuck-ton of professional teams after you graduated high school, and for what? To swim on a college team with people who don't even like you?'

'I needed the time. I needed the training. Mom wanted—'

'Mom is *dead*, Dani. She doesn't want anything. Neither does Dad, and neither do you, because your entire life is a ghost of theirs. You went to college because of Mom, you swim because of Dad. When the fuck are you gonna do something because of *you*?'

'That's not fair.'

'That's the truth.'

'So what? I'm just a puppet? I wasted my entire life doing everything for people who aren't even here to see it?'

'God, Daniela, do you hear yourself? You're twenty-one. You haven't had a life yet. Just *think* for a second, okay? Think about whether or not you actually enjoy competing. Fuck, Dani, think about whether or not you actually enjoy *swimming* anymore, genuinely think about it instead of getting all defensive. Ask yourself why you picked a degree you're actually interested in, that you need a PhD to really do anything with, while every other student athlete is doing Business or Communications or Sports fucking Management.'

I start to protest, to refute every last one of his silly little points, except something stops me at the last minute. My gut doesn't agree.

'You hate your team,' Seba continues tentatively. Just as cautiously, he moves to sit beside me, a bent leg propped on the bed while an arm stretches across the pillow keeping me upright, so careful not to touch me. 'You scratch yourself raw before every competition. You don't get out of the pool satisfied or proud of yourself. So why do you do it?'

'I like how I feel when I win.'

'Do you? Or did you like how Dad made you feel when you won, and that's never gone away?'

I don't confirm or deny. I can't bring myself to.

God, my head hurts.

'I know swimming and training and competing is all you've ever known, but it doesn't have to be all you ever know. Just think about it.' He kisses my temple, smirking against it. 'Don't have anything else to do, do you?'

My laugh is raw and guttural, my fingers harsh where they pinch thin skin. 'I worked so hard. It can't all be for nothing.'

'It wasn't. And your accomplishments aren't just null and void now. Nothing you've done changes.' He pauses – he dares to fucking smirk. 'And you met Heath.'

I can't help but laugh, though it's a pained, broken rendition. 'So it was all for a boy. Great.'

'It was all for whatever you want it to be for. Look, you don't have to figure it out now. You don't have to be okay with it. But you will be okay.'

A choked whimper escaping me, my head falls to my brother's shoulder. 'It's not fair.'

'I know it isn't. And I'm so sorry, Daniela, I really am. I just don't think it's the catastrophe you think it is. I think . . . fuck, don't kill me for saying this, okay? But I think it might be really good for you.'

What he's saying makes sense, I'm sure, but right now, to me, it doesn't. Right now, I can't hear anything but the doctor's damning words. Right now, I . . . I just can't. I'm too tired. My heart fucking hurts. *Everything* hurts. I just want to curl up in a ball and not exist for a little while.

A quiet sigh skates across my forehead as gentle fingers comb through my hair. 'Do you need anything? Heath brought your stuff over while you were doing your Sleeping Beauty impersonation.'

'You saw him?'

'He was here when I got here. Still here. All your friends are. They're in the waiting room.'

My stomach revolts at the mere concept. 'I can't right now.'

'That's okay. Visiting hours are over anyway. They just wanted to wait until you woke up. Make sure you're okay.'

My throat tightens.

'A shiny new boyfriend and a bunch of friends too. Lucky girl.'

'He's not my boyfriend.'

'What did lover boy do?'

God, I don't think I've ever loved my brother more than I do right now, just for the simple act of not assuming it was all my fault.

I give him the Cliff's Notes version, skipping over the whole fake aspect of it. I just say that we had a fight about a month ago, we fought some more last night too, and he just stood there. Loving me.

'Well, duh,' Sebastian scoffs, throwing his eyes up to the ceiling. 'He's had a crush on you for, like, *years*.'

'How do you know that?'

'*Uh*, because I have eyes.'

'You could've said something.'

'My bad. I assumed you weren't interested in the nice, happy, pretty man, considering Satan was your boyfriend.'

My nose scrunches. Can't exactly fault him for that – I wasn't interested. I was barely interested in Ben. The majority of my interest lay with swimming. Just swimming. *Always* swimming.

That doesn't just go away. Can't be changed with a single speech. I can't be told that's so wrong and just, suddenly, immediately believe it.

But . . . I can think about it. I *will* think about it. Later. Tomorrow.

If it doesn't hurt so fucking much.

Birds are still chirping the next morning when Sebastian wheels me out of the hospital, clutching a prescription I have no intention of filling and a pamphlet I don't need to read; my brother has already narrated a dramatic rendition of proper post-operative care, and he provides more than one encore performance on the long, torturous drive home.

It slipped my mind, in all the chaos, that we're several hours away from Haven Cove. That I would have so much time to sit with my thoughts, no distractions other than what Sebastian is willing to provide – the license plate game can only get a girl so far.

Food for thought, however, he provides in spades. His little speech at the hospital runs through my head on a constant loop. The *what if*s and the *why*s and the *think*s of it all.

By the time we pull up outside my building, I'm well and truly knee-deep in an existential crisis. I dismiss Sebastian's attempts to help me out of his car, to come upstairs with me, to keep me company. 'I really just want to be alone right now,' I tell him, and he accepts that. He leaves me alone.

It's someone else who doesn't.

My apartment smells like chicken soup and warmth and the ocean. Frozen in the doorway, I allow myself a single self-indulgent moment to breathe the scent in. To watch the man in my kitchen, who either didn't hear me come in or just doesn't care to turn around, tending to a pot on the stove.

Such an oddly familiar sight. Yet so unexpected it makes my heart pulse and crack and do a hundred other things that can't be good for someone fresh out of surgery.

Nor is, I'm sure, my temper rising against my will, fueled by exhausted frustration, and undoubtedly bringing my blood pressure up with it. 'How did you get in here?'

Heath doesn't so much as twitch. He doesn't turn around either, only gracing me with his side profile as he twists slightly to reach into an upper cabinet and pull out a bowl. 'Sebastian gave me his key.'

Of course he did.

'Why are you here?'

'Because I love you.'

I flinch. 'Heath, I can't do this right now.'

'Are you in pain?'

I shake my head.

He purses his lips like he knows damn well I'm lying. 'Hungry?'

I lie again, and he sighs. 'Let me guess. Not tired either?'

That, I don't even try to deny. I'm dead on my feet, and I'm sure I look it. I'm not actually entirely certain my eyes are even open right now. Honestly, for all I know, I could still be knocked out, under the knife, dreaming this all up.

'Bed,' Heath gently commands, and I don't even bristle. I'm glad to be told what to do – it eliminates the need to decide for myself. 'I'll bring you something to eat and then you can sleep, okay?'

I nod, listless. I do as he says, dragging myself to my bedroom. Except once I'm in there, staring at the clean sheets, my bed freshly made, most definitely not how I left it, I itch at the thought of tainting them with that hospital stench. Instead, I hurry into the bathroom, shutting the door behind me before a reprimand can follow, turn on the shower, and clumsily undo my braid, one-handed. I'm wincing at the straw-like texture to my hair, a consequence of not rinsing out the chlorine, when I realize the fatal flaw in my plan.

My arm is still confined to a sling. Even if I take it off, I can't straighten it properly, let alone lift it above my head. I could barely get dressed this morning – a nurse had to help me. No way am I getting undressed on my own. Plus, there's a three-inch long incision I can't get wet.

Tears burn my eyes. I am little more than pure, complete frustration. I can do little more than stare at the running water filling the room with steam and try so fucking hard to do what my brother said, to go easy on myself, to stop the catastrophizing, to consider that my life isn't over – just one little part of it is. Eyes scrunched shut, I mumble that aloud because maybe hearing it repeatedly will help it sink in.

It starts to work – or maybe it's just the steady monotony of my new mantra that helps lower my racing heartbeat – until a hand landing on my shoulder erases all my effort. Because it lands on my good shoulder, I think of it as my *good* shoulder, I think about my *bad* shoulder, and by the time Heath dips into my line of sight, tears are spilling free, burning my cheeks.

'I knocked.'

'I can't—' My voice cracks. 'I can't even shower.'

'Oh, honey.' Forehead to my temple, Heath mouths a gentle *shush* against my damp cheek. 'Please let me help.'

A croaked *okay* has his breath hitching.

So carefully, he undresses me. Apologizing all the while because, as gently as he helps me out of my t-shirt and sweats, every incidental movement ignites sharp, stabbing pain. He strips me completely bare, entirely clinical about it, too concentrated on perfecting the water temperature to even glance at my naked body.

'Okay.' He holds out a hand toward me, the other shifting the showerhead so the spray hits the wall. 'C'mere.'

Of their own volition, my fingers lace with his and cling hard enough to break freaking bone. As if driven by the one, deeply buried part of me that's capable of admitting how much I need him.

He doesn't complain. Doesn't break free. One-handed, he wets a wash cloth, soaps it up, cleans every inch of me with methodical, gentle strokes until that antiseptic reek is replaced by sweet vanilla, warm almond. He takes his time washing my hair, lathering it up twice with coconut-scented shampoo and doing the same with my conditioner, meticulously combing it through until every strand is silky smooth.

The whole time, I try my best to stop crying. Fail miserably, feel miserable. My favorite cleanser washes away my tears, but they just keep coming, silent and endless. By the time Heath has dried me off and checked my wound and bundled me into the loosest clothing I own, I'm sobbing.

And still, through my tears, still clutching his hand, as Heath tucks me into bed, I shakily insist, 'You don't have to stay.'

His scoff is just as gentle as the rest of him, but firmly dismissive. 'I'm staying.'

I whimper. Relieved and embarrassed and miserable.

Stroking my damp hair reverently, Heath kisses my forehead. Then the back of my hand, almost in apology, before he lets me go so he can shed the clothes that got wet while he was taking care of me. He changes into a new pair plucked from the duffel bag tucked in the corner while I blankly stare with heavy, wet eyes.

He rushes to get dressed and then he rushes into the kitchen, rushing right back to me with that bowl of soup he promised, a glass of water, a bottle of paracetamol. He makes me take two, makes me down every last drop, and when I only get through half the soup before my twisted-up stomach protests, he sighs, but doesn't push.

Propped semi-upright by a mountain of cushions, I watch as he slips another beneath my injured shoulder, supporting it. As he tucks the comforter carefully around me before sliding beneath it too. As he turns off the light before taking my hand again, kissing my knuckles.

Into the darkness, I whisper, 'Because you love me?'

'Yeah, Daniela. Because I love you.'

THIRTY-ONE

BLEARY-EYED, I SIT CROSS-LEGGED IN THE MIDDLE of my bed, bracketed by long, tattooed legs, gentle fingers detangling my sleep-mussed hair and weaving it into a loose braid.

Tying the end off with an elastic band, Heath gives it a tug. 'All done.'

My gratitude is quiet. Strained. So very tired, like the rest of me.

Heath has already done my whole typical hair routine for me. He guides me into the bathroom, and he does my skincare too. He changes me into a fresh pair of pajamas, and while I do the rest of my business that only over my dead body would I let him assist with, he makes me breakfast.

It's my exact routine, and it isn't. I shouldn't need help getting ready. I should be out the door by now.

I feel useless. Beyond it. I feel like nothing, which is ironic, because I feel so far from nothing. I feel so much, I can't make out one emotion from the other, can't untangle the messy, nauseating knot.

Except for grief. That, I can distinguish just fine. That, I feel with knee-wobbling intensity, especially when I peel off the surgical bandage covering a sore, ugly incision.

When I emerge from the bathroom, Heath doesn't ask about the tears. He kisses my forehead like he can see the ugly thoughts lurking behind it, settles me on the sofa, tucks me under a blanket and tells me to sleep some more.

I can't. Could barely sleep last night. Alternated between staring at the ceiling and staring at Heath and pretending to be asleep when an alarm jolted him awake at regular intervals, pretended to be all groggy and confused when he tipped pain medication and water down my throat.

I try, though. Because he asks me to, I try. Because I was upset and horrible and, still, he's here. Still, he's nice. Still, he's taking care of me as if it isn't an enormous inconvenience, and he doesn't even have to, he has no obligation, so I can shut my damn eyes and at least pretend to nap.

A knock on the front door has him swearing. I keep my eyes closed, breathing slow, as light footsteps creep toward me. His presence hovers for a moment before moving to the front door.

The lock clicks. Hinges creak. A hushed curse precedes a half-whispered, half-hissed '*Go away*.'

A chorus of disgruntled whines harmonize briefly before being promptly, emphatically shushed.

'We just wanna see if she's okay,' a familiar voice quietly insists, and I conjure up a perfect mental image of Imani – arms crossed, face set with determination.

Heath grunts. 'Of course she's not okay.'

Someone whimpers. Matilda. That high-pitch is pretty unmistakable.

'She's fine,' Heath amends. 'But I don't think she wants company right now, okay?'

'*You're* here.'

'I'm her boyfriend.'

'You broke up,' someone points out – Brendan, I think. The voice is too quiet to properly distinguish, so it must be.

'No, they *fake* broke up,' I recognize Kai's *spirited* tone easily. 'Are you fake back together?'

'I'm gonna real punch you in the dick if you wake her up.'

A weak laugh blows my cover. When I awkwardly prop myself upright and peer over the arm of the sofa, I find five gazes already on me. 'I'm awake. Cover your dick.'

Kai grins, bright and wide, and oh-so-oddly relieving. 'Now there's something no woman has ever said to me before.'

I roll my eyes as I swing my leg over the side of the sofa, although any attempt to get up is immediately proved obsolete because they come to me, crowd me, Heath barking a command to be gentle that's entirely unnecessary because nobody touches me. The girls settle on either side of me, Brendan eases himself into the armchair, Heath stands vigil at my back, a healthy distance between me and all them, hands just kind of hovering a few inches from my body, caressing the air around me.

Except Kai. Kai, perched on the coffee table, nudges his knee against mine and pats my hand where it nervously taps against my thigh. 'You're alive. Thank God. No one's been mean to me in, like, forty-eight hours and my ego's getting really heavy.'

My hand curls into a fist beneath his. 'Thought your head looked a little bigger.'

He pats me again, his smile thinner than usual. 'There she is.'

When his touch retreats, Imani's replaces it. 'How are you feeling?'

My smile is watery. It morphs into a wince when I try to shrug, and Imani winces too when Heath pinches the back of her neck, as if it's her fault.

I squeeze her hand to let her know it isn't. 'I don't really know, to be honest.'

'Does it hurt?'

Kai aims a kick at Matilda's shin. 'She just had surgery, dipshit.'

'Hence my very valid question, *Kiki*.'

'Enough, guys.'

'S'okay.' I wave Heath off. 'Sebastian said you guys were at the hospital. I'm sorry I didn't—'

With a round of tuts, my apology is dismissed. 'We weren't expecting you to. We just wanted to be there. We're here for you.'

'Thank you.'

'We brought you some stuff.'

Eyeing the enormous bags clustered by my front door, I manage another laugh. *Some*. Understatement. They brought me everything. Anything I could conceivably need. Things that make my heart hurt because no one has ever baked me a loaf of sourdough like Brendan has. I don't remember telling Matilda that irises are my favorite flowers, but there's some sitting on my kitchen counter right now. Kai can knit, apparently; the chunky navy proof is carefully draped around my shoulders. Imani borrowed, like, a hundred books from the local library that I immediately start to insist I don't have time to read, only to catch myself because I do, don't I? I have a *lot* of time now.

I push that thought away. Not the time for it. Let my throat clog with raw gratitude instead of dread.

Heath doesn't let them stay for very long. Playing the mother freaking hen, he clucks them out the front door the very second I let loose a single yawn. Locking up behind them, he aims a kick at the wood when they whine and scratch like forlorn puppies.

Sighing, he fixes me with an apologetic wince. 'I told them not to come over.'

'I'm glad they did.'

Heath looks at me like he doesn't quite think I mean it. And then he *really* looks, he must realize I actually do, and there are no adequate words for how freaking *soft* his expression gets.

Closing the distance between us again, he drags a hand down the back of my hair before joining me on the sofa. Carefully, he rearranges my feet on his lap and tucks my new blanket around them. He leans forward, flicking open my laptop where it sits on the coffee table, nestled amongst the most gifts I've ever been given in my life; smiling as he pulls up a movie that I know is supposed to make me smile too, but, instead, it just has the lump in my throat growing. Has me watching him instead of fucking *Step Up*.

'You're missing it.'

'Sorry.'

'You should be,' he reprimands softly, mindlessly twirling my hair. 'This is a good part.'

'No, Heath. About what I said at the hospital. I'm sorry'

His look is long and serious and as indecipherable as his sigh. 'I know you are, baby.'

That hand falls away. I genuinely panic when he shifts, as if he's going to get up, but he's just reaching for the laptop, pausing the movie quickly before returning to me, closer to me, tucking my hair behind my ear and holding it there. 'I'm not your consolation prize. You haven't lost anything to get me, because you already had me. Been wrapped around your finger for a long fucking time, Dani. Plan on staying there for even longer.'

My gaze snaps between those pretty, wide eyes, searching for sincerity, finding it so easily, yet I still need to make sure. To know that he knows what he's getting into, to hear it. 'You know I'm difficult.'

'I don't know that because you're not. Not to me. Not to anyone who cares enough to actually know you.'

'I'm too structured.'

'Dependable,' he corrects easily.

'I'm anti-social.'

'You're awkward, Dani. Might even dare to call you shy. And I fucking love it.'

'What if . . .' The lump in my throat throbs. Swallowing hard, I catch Heath by the wrist, settle my thumb above his pulse, wait for his steady heartbeat to settle my own. 'What if I can't swim?'

'Daniela,' he almost laughs my name. 'Honey. I don't know how many times I have to say it, but I'll keep saying it until you believe me. My love for you is not dependent on your fucking aquatic skills. It isn't dependent on anything. I love you. Mean and grumpy, sweet and shy, literally everything in between, I love you.'

'Okay.' I swallow again, and that lump, it feels different now. Its shape has changed. Feels an awful lot like three words, clumped together, stuck and unspeakable, too scary, too *much*. 'What now?'

'Now we watch a movie.'

'You know who your boyfriend looks like?'

Pausing halfway through a set of pendulum swings, I follow the gaze of my new physical therapist to the other side of the rehab clinic's gym – to the small waiting area for family members, where Heath has set himself the challenge of reading every single one of the pamphlets from a very extensive wall display.

'Not my boyfriend,' I waste no time correcting. Quietly. Guilty. As if I'm doing something wrong. 'And if you're gonna say someone hot, can you say it really, really quietly? He has freaky good hearing and his ego does not need the boost.'

Imogen – *Immy,* she tells me to call her, she says that's what her friends call her, and apparently spending three days a week together for the foreseeable future makes us that – laughs. Clicking her pen against the little clipboard scribbled with notes about my recovery, she hits me with a sunny smile. She drops her chin, all conspiratorial as she mumbles a barely audible comparison to a young Channing Tatum that makes me groan.

'Fuck, don't tell him that. Seriously. I'll never hear the end of it.'

Imogen snickers, shooting Heath another sideways glance as she signals for me to continue the exercise. She waits until I'm done this round and icing my shoulder before we move on to the next before oh-so-casually musing, 'He's here a lot for a not-boyfriend.'

That, I can't dispute. There isn't a single session in the two weeks since I started therapy that I've attended and he hasn't. If I'm here, so is he. And he leaves me lists, schedules, tick-the-box Post-it routines that make every day seem a little less insurmountable, eases the ever-present anxiety lodged behind my ribcage. He barely leaves my apartment unless it's for work or class, he acts as my personal chauffeur, he lives out of a fucking duffel bag. He provides round-the-clock care that I don't really need, but I'm not brave enough to put a stop to it. I like it too much. He's the only thing keeping me sane, and, God, do I get the irony in that. All that bitching in the hospital only for Heath to be the singular bright spot in my life.

Well, not the singular. Just the brightest.

'Is chit-chat part of my rehab?'

'As a matter of fact, *yes*. It is.' Removing the ice-pack from my shoulder, Imogen takes me gently by the elbow and guides my stiff joint through as big a rotation as it's capable of. Which isn't a whole lot. But before my frustration can really fester, she continues, 'He a swimmer too?'

'Uh-huh.'

'Hm. Can tell. It's the shoulders, y'know?'

'Shouldn't you be paying attention to *my* shoulder, not his?'

'But his are so pretty,' she jokes, long fingers gliding up my arm to carefully palpate my shoulder. 'Must be hard for you.'

I don't answer. I don't have an answer. Not a good one, anyway. Certainly not a simple one. Because, yeah, it's hard. Every time Heath walks out of my apartment and I know he's going to practice, it physically hurts. But every time he tries not to, every time he comes up with some excuse as to why he should skip a meet, the fact that he's skipped his last two meets, well, that fills me with genuine rage because how fucking dare he, right? How dare he waste what he can do. Resentment might rot my chest every morning when he slips out of bed, but I know it isn't fair to feel it, to hold my injury against him, to expect him to stop swimming just because I have to, to deprive him of something while he's giving me everything.

'You know what's funny about you, Daniela?'

'So many things, I'm sure.'

'I see thirty clients a week. Almost all of them are injured college athletes. Most of them are D1. Most of them will never compete again at the same level. I have heard every variation of the stolen dream speech. But not from you.'

'Your point?'

'What was the plan? Olympics? World Aquatics?'

'I don't know.' Discomfort that goes far beyond the physical kind makes me fidget. 'I still have a year of college left.'

'You hadn't thought about it?'

'I was focused on my student career.'

'Ah.'

'What's wrong with that?'

'Nothing.'

But. There's a *but*. Everyone has a fucking but – I'm starting to have a but. I'm pretty sure I've had a *but* all along, and it's been hiding. Repressed. Hidden under a thick, impenetrable layer of learned compliance and a fear of inadequacy and a desperate need for validation.

As if warded off by the thoughtful glare that creases my expression, Imogen doesn't press the matter any further. She just leaves the suggestion lingering in the air, just like everyone has been doing, and I don't know what's so special about her little remark, but something just . . . clicks. Like it's the final puzzle piece slotting into place, or like a crack in my metaphorical pair of glasses has been mended and I can finally see clearly.

My session finishes, and, on autopilot, I find Heath. He flashes me the same proud smile he always does, but, apparently, my expression is twisted enough to cow him too. He frowns and he glances at my shoulder, then over at Imogen, and he asks very carefully, very hesitantly, if everything is alright.

I only answer once I'm outside the clinic, collapsed on the curb, staring blankly at the parking lot asphalt. 'I didn't think about it.'

Heath crouches in front of me. Palms on my knees, emanating comforting warmth. 'Hey?'

'Swimming after college. You asked me once if I was gonna swim professionally, and I said, *Why else would I be doing it?* I didn't . . . That was the wrong answer, huh?'

Heath just sighs. He swipes a thumb beneath my eye, and the pad comes away wet.

'It's not supposed to be an obligation.' I summarize what everyone has been telling me, screaming at me. I get it now, finally. Like a shroud lifted, clarifying my senses. 'I'm supposed to just love it. I tried to, I really did, I really wanted to. And I'm not okay with this,' I curl a hand around my shoulder, and he settles one of his own on top of it, 'but I think I might be relieved.'

'Oh, honey.' A gentle tug guides me into his arms. A palm glides along my spine, rubbing soothing circles at the base. 'That's okay. You're okay.'

Stifling a sob, I nestle my forehead against the notch of his throat. When a tear slips free, it's for me; the tiny, younger version who bounced into her first swim class, overflowing with excitement, so eager to experience what her dad always waxed poetic about. Another one, I shed for the barely older Daniela who started approaching the pool with trepidation – who knew that if she didn't swim the best, there wasn't any point. Both eyes start to stream, and that's for a grieving sixteen-year-old carrying the weight of her dead father's expectations.

The torrent that follows, those are all for me too. For the time I'm not sure will ever stop feeling so wasted, and for what I could've done with it. For everything I put myself through because I never gave myself a choice. For the part of me that still, and always will, mourns the water because, even putting my injury aside, I don't think it'll ever feel the same.

I just . . . cry. For a long time. Spill the full range of my emotions on the sidewalk, guilt and regret and devastation and my confusion and *hope*.

And the next time Heath murmurs that I'm okay, I almost kind of believe him.

THIRTY-TWO

BREAKFAST IS UNDERLINED THREE TIMES TODAY. *GET some fresh air*, the same. The word *project*, just once. A reminder to do my physiotherapist-approved exercises is unembellished and entirely unnecessary – Heath doesn't usually bother to write it down, considering they're the first thing I do every morning, usually when he's still in bed beside me, watching me, but he was out the door at the crack of dawn this morning.

Because he has a meet today. A meet that we didn't discuss beyond me quietly, tentatively wishing him luck on his way out. A meet just like the one I should be swimming today. I don't quite know how I feel about it – at least not in any kind of intelligible specifics. I just . . . feel. A lot. Mixed emotions. I'm okay and I'm not and I'm kind of, and that's okay too. I'm not pressuring myself to figure it out.

I'm putting one foot in front of the other, and those feet bring me to the kitchen, to the fridge where I peel off today's Post-it. My fingers itch to flip the note over and reveal the postscript I know is scribbled on the back, but I force myself to take in the rest of my to-do list first. I sigh at the word *'ASSIGNMENTS'* in all block letters, followed by an exclamation mark, and hurriedly move on from the unintentional reminder that my professors will only email me my course work for so long; I have to start going to class again eventually.

The last item makes me tense. Not something I need to do, but another unwelcome reminder.

Coach Michaels called.

Resentment bubbles up again, fiercer and a whole lot angrier, because seriously? I dedicate two and a half years of my life to the man, and it takes him fucking weeks to reach out? Just a single phone call, no voicemail, not even a follow-up message?

About the same amount of concern my stepmother has shown, I compare bitterly.

The sound of paper crinkling has me swearing. Unclenching my fist, I smooth out the Post-it almost apologetically before flipping it over.

All of that resentment leaves me in a single, fluttering exhale. There it is. Messy handwriting, lovely words.

You said my name in your sleep, you called me and my alarm a bitch, and it took me ten minutes to peel you off of me this morning.

It took days before I realized what he was doing. Listing things he loves about me that have nothing to do with swimming. Things I probably wouldn't hear if said aloud or that I'd convince myself I misheard, so he immortalizes them for me.

Cheeks warm, I skim my thumb over the writing a few times as I absorb the words, then stick it back on the fridge. Later, before I go to bed, I'll carefully fold it up and slip it into my bedside drawer where a handful of others live. For now, I focus on ticking off the first thing on the list – I carry my fruit and a glass

Tupperware of overnight oats to the island, where I find number three on the list.

At first, I thought the little projects he's been leaving me were just to distract my mind, to stop it from going down that doomed, pessimistic path. When they quickly got very specific, I started thinking otherwise.

Yesterday, it was a cookbook, and a written demand to have a three-course meal ready by the time he came home that he made sure I knew was in jest, but I did it anyway. Today, it's a pile of those beginner watercolor paint pads.

By the time Heath walks in the door, the counter is covered in ripped-out, painted pages, watercolor smudges, the curve of my thumb is covered in watercolor smudges, and my eyes are a bit askew from concentrating on keeping within the lines so hard.

And I'm smiling. Wider, when my eyes land on him. I'm murmuring *Welcome home* without a trace of sarcasm, as if this is actually his home, and he's twirling my spare key around his finger as if it's actually his key. He comes up behind me, kissing the back of my head. He doesn't ask how my day was. He just checks the Post-it – I get another peck for the things I crossed off, a quietly grunted reprimand for what I didn't.

Sighing, I pinch the back of the hand sifting through my completed paintings. 'I'll go for a walk later.'

Another grunt. Marginally satisfied, a little threatening. *Yeah, you will, because I'll take you on a damn walk, because I'm convinced if you don't get at least ten minutes of fresh air a day, you'll disintegrate.* 'Did you call your coach?'

I shake my head.

'Are you going to?'

'No. I don't really ever wanna see him again.' I look down, watching myself pick at my fingernails. 'Don't really wanna see any of them ever again.'

Heath waits a moment before gently pressing. 'Finish that thought, honey.'

Easier said than done; I've barely finished it in my head, let alone aloud. 'I was thinking I, uh, might try to transfer.'

'To Cove College?'

I nod slightly. My forehead aches with how hard I frown, that familiar upset turning my stomach. I lift a hand to ease the burgeoning itch plaguing my chest only for Heath to catch me, lace our fingers together, squeeze gently.

'Not a single person from HCU has reached out to me,' I quietly admit, and his grip tightens. 'No one on my team, no one in any of my classes, none of them care. But *your* coach emailed me. *Your* team sent me flowers, and a bunch of them texted. Your friends—'

Heath grunts. '*Your* friends.'

'*Our* friends,' I amend. 'They come over at least once a day. I just . . . I didn't realize how bad it was at HCU, y'know? How isolated I was. Or maybe I did and I didn't care, or I just worked really hard at not caring. And I know it was my own doing, just like I know you and Imani and Kai are graduating, so it's not like you'll be on campus, but the twins will be there. And, uh, I looked it up and I'm pretty sure I can transfer my scholarship.'

'I think that's a really good idea.'

Yet he's frowning. Just short of fierce.

I drag my thumb over the creases in his brow, trying to smooth them out. 'Mad you didn't think of it first?'

'Oh, I did. Dreamed it. Just should've opened my mouth sooner.'

I blink at him, silent. He stares at me, intense in a way I'm slowly getting used to, because he looks at me like that a lot lately, like he's trying to tell me something through freaking osmosis, so we can avoid the conversation we've been skirting around all week. He loves me, we're practically living together, but neither of us can bear to ask the other what it actually means.

Proving my point, he flows around my kitchen like he's lived here as long as I have, decimating the pantry in his post-race hunger. 'You wanna go out for dinner?'

'No.'

'Let me rephrase that – *where* do you wanna go for dinner? Because we are going out.'

'Why?' I ask slowly, tentatively, not entirely sure if I want the answer. 'We celebrating a big win today?'

The cocky tilt to his head abruptly straightens. Putting down a half-eaten tub of peanut butter pretzels, he pushes off the counter and moves to stand in front of me again. One hand on my thigh, the other twirls my hair. 'We don't have to talk about it.'

'I want to,' I choke out, and I almost manage to sound like I mean it. 'How was it?'

Heath coughs awkwardly, rubbing the back of his neck. 'Good.'

'You were the best?'

'Yeah, honey.'

'Good,' I say, and that, I mean. I really do. I hate that he thinks I don't, that it pains him to admit he did well. I want nothing more than to alleviate all of that burdening concern, so I joke, 'If I can't be the best, might as well date him.'

I only realize what I've said, that I've basically kicked the elephant in the room, after the fact. *Date*. Heath stiffens, those light brows hopping a mile. Rigid too, I try to backtrack. 'I didn' t—'

'I know.' He pats my thigh lightly. 'It's okay. Don't have to talk about that either.'

'Talk about what, Heath? What are we doing?'

'You're recovering. I'm helping.'

'That's it?'

'What do you want it to be, Daniela?'

My mouth opens. Nothing comes out – just a sigh when his brows inch a little higher, twist a little more expectantly, and he teases, 'Hard question, honey?'

'Yes.' I cluck my tongue. Jesus, he has to know that it is. A hard, tangled, thorned question that I need more than a damn moment to contemplate. 'Gimme a sec.'

'Working up the nerve to break my heart?'

The back of my hand smacks his chest. He catches my by the wrist and brings my hand up to his face, kisses the curve of my thumb and repeats, 'It's okay. We don't—'

'I have a proposal for you,' I blurt, as quickly as I can, the sentence practically becoming a single word in my haste. Ineloquent and rushed and not entirely thought through, but that's my problem. I think too much. I need to just . . . *do*.

Humoured curiosity sparks those pretty eyes. 'How big is the ring?'

'About as big as your ego.'

'Then it's a yes.'

God, I hope so. 'There's this guy,' I continue slowly, and the mirth slips from his face.

He clears his throat, yet a soft 'Oh?' still comes out a rasp.

'I wanna get him back.'

'And you heard I know how to egg a house, huh?'

'No.' Tentatively, I take both of his hands in mine. Play with his fingers, trace the tattooed lines, not quite ready to see his face yet, to see whatever expression it wears, whatever thoughts he's doing a shit job at hiding. 'Not revenge.'

'Oh,' he says again. Barely audible. No less confused.

'I think we should date.'

Those beautiful eyes narrow – like he's bracing for something, almost. 'Pretend?'

'Really fucking real, actually.'

'What's in it for me, exactly?'

'You get to date me.'

He doesn't even pretend to think about it. 'Sold.'

'Heath.'

'I'm being serious.'

I know he is. I wasn't admonishing him; just making sure I have his attention. Making sure he really hears me when I say: 'I love you.'

He short circuits. Like, he literally freezes, and I swear I see the light go out in his eyes for a second. 'What?'

'I know I don't show it—'

'Honey—'

'Stop. Let me get this out, okay? I'm not good at expressing things, and I don't have all this easy affection. I'm not easy, I know that, but I don't lie. Not about important things, you know I don't. I don't lie and I don't protect people's feelings and I don't embellish, so I know you know that when I say I love you, I really fucking mean it. I really want you to be my boyfriend. For real this time.'

With a big spluttering breath, he melts. He buries his face in the crook of my neck, peppering sweet kisses there, whispering sweet words that are incomprehensible beyond their ability to make me feel so fucking *good.*

'Is that a yes?'

He laughs like the question is beyond ridiculous. Looks at me like I'm a fool for asking it. 'Baby, we've been dating for real since the first time you walked into the diner and commandeered me.'

'That's a big word.'

'I have a really good tutor.'

'Oh, yeah?'

'Hm. Really hot too.'

'She's blushing, wherever she is, I'm sure.'

'God, I hope so.' He kisses my cheek, nuzzles the flushed skin. 'So pretty when she does.'

I laugh, and it's half delirious. I shift to find his mouth, to kiss him, and the moment our lips connect, my whole body just . . . well, at the risk of sound fucking dramatic, it rejoices. It weeps. I damn near weep at the rush of comfort, at the familiarity, at this undeniable sense that this is right. Like a piece of me has been missing all along, and he's safely returning it.

Groaning, Heath cups my face and tilts it upwards, angling me the way he wants me, to kiss me as deeply as possible. So urgent, it makes my whole body buzz. I try to return his eagerness, but I'm lost, swept up in sensation, so out of my mind that my injury is even less than an afterthought; I only remember my limitations when I try to wrap my arms around his neck, and the healing muscle twinges.

My tiny hiss sends Heath reeling backwards. He curses and lets me go, stumbles back, clutches the nape of his neck desperately as if he's physically fighting the urge to touch me again. 'Fuck. Sorry. I forgot.'

Slipping off the stool and onto wobbly legs, I reach for him. 'Forget again.'

It's his turn to hiss. Like a feral fucking cat, he bats me away. 'We can't. I'll hurt you.'

I laugh, groan and whine all at once – the building heat between my thighs fucking *aches*. 'You're hurting me right now.'

'*Fuck*.' His bottom lip disappears between his teeth. Like he can't help himself, he staggers forward again. That bruising grip returns to my hips; his mouth returns to mine. Against it, he groans, 'I don't wanna hurt you.'

'So don't. Fuck me.'

I swear to God, his whole body trembles. 'Are you sure?' His forehead falls to mine, those perfect eyes flitting between both of my mine, seeking the truth. 'We don't have to. You don't have to want to. I swear to God, I'm not expecting anything.'

'I want to.' I can't believe how much I want to, how much I need to. It must be written all over me, it must be so obvious in my clenched thighs and my raspy breath and my fingernails carving marks into his nape.

Yet still, he repeats, 'Are you *sure*?'

'I'm sure I'm gonna get pissed off if you keep asking me.'

'In that case, are you sure?'

Scoffing, I lean in to nip his lip. 'Yes.'

'If you want me to stop—'

'Then I'll say it, and you will.'

God, does that make him groan. Deep and satisfied and so fucking hot. When he kisses me again, it's different. Slower. Less urgent. Lazy, as if we have all the time in the world, and he wants to use every last minute just doing this.

His fingers graze my chest, and my breath hitches. Just as leisurely, he takes his time unbuttoning my shirt. Every button that pops free makes him kiss me harder. When he undoes the last one and the fabric gapes revealingly, his kisses move to follow the fabric as he slips it off, lingering over my scar and dragging down my arm and nipping at the thin skin of the crook of my elbow. As my shirt falls to the floor, my head falls back. My fingers dig into the nape of his neck as he bestows that same gentle, thorough affection across my chest, nips the swell of my cleavage, drags the cups of my bra down, the image of my spilled tits just as obscene as the things his mouth does to them.

I'm panting by the time he gets rid of my bra and drops to his knees. I cry out as his tongue circles my bellybutton and traces the curve of either hip bone – I almost cry fat, pathetic, desperate tears when he takes his sweet time licking the length of my waistband, teeth catching on the soft fabric and pulling it down an inch before his hands help. Breathless, mindless, barely functioning, I peer down at him as he strips me completely naked.

Dazed eyes catch my stare. Holds it as he drags wet, hot kisses up my inner thigh. Loses it briefly when our eyes flutter shut in unison at the first swipe of his tongue through my cunt, and we both groan.

One hand gripping the counter, the other grips his crown, holds him where he is – as if I have to. As if he isn't more than happy to be there. Licking and nipping and wasting no fucking time, eating me out like his fucking life depends on it, making me feel things I can't even describe, I can't quantify, I just fucking can't.

I'm riding his damn mouth, right on the cusp of coming, when he pulls away. 'Need you on the edge,' he drowns out my groan with one of his own, he hoists me up, and the next thing I know, I'm on my bed, on my back, writhing and whining and watching him strip. 'Need you there. Too fucking close already.'

His clothes hit the floor, and I see exactly what he means. His cock is so hard, so red, already leaking from the tip, and he grimaces as he fists the base. I start to sit up, to reach for him, to return the favor, but he bats off my attempts. Instead, he shifts us so he's on his back and I'm straddling his hips, I'm—

'*Fuck*.' His cock slides so perfectly through my wet cunt, hits my clit just right, and it makes me buckle. Spine arched, I brace one hand on his chest and slip the other between my thighs, holding him in place as I start a slow, mindless grind. Vaguely, I'm aware of Heath bucking, of him swearing, of him watching me intently while blindly reaching for something – a condom, I recognize when it hovers in my line of sight.

Wasting no time, I rip it open and roll it on, and that alone has Heath arching off the bed. 'Jesus, Daniela.' Teeth gritted, he grips my waist hard enough to bruise. 'Please, baby. Put it in. Fucking *please*.'

I do. Slowly. Adjusting to the stretch and the sting and the fullness, *God*, the *fullness*. Grasping clumsily at his wrists for stability, I ride him slowly, getting used to it, feeling it out, finding the perfect angle and all but screaming when I do. All the while, he just gapes at me. Slack-jawed and incoherent, and the second I speed up, he swears and begs for more. He begs me to come. He begs me to make him come, to let him come, and, God, that does me in.

I break with a cry, and he's barely a second behind me.

I'm sobbing as I collapse on his chest. Honest-to-God tears drip down my cheeks and pool in the contour of his collarbone, the bone so prominent as he strains against the pleasure wringing him dry.

I cry because it feels so good. I cry because it feels so right. I cry because I grieve, just a little, for all the times it wasn't like this and I thought it was my fault. And as I slowly come down from that lovely, sense-obliterating high, I kiss Heath's throat, his jaw, as far as my limp, exhausted body can reach, and I repeat the three words I have never meant quite as much as I do right now.

The hands scalding my lower back, pressing our pelvises as flush as they can possibly be, creep upwards. One cups my nape, the other sweeping my sweat-dampened hair away from my face, crooking my chin until our lips meet.

Heath's cheeks are damp too. Salty when my mouth finds one. Dimpled with a blinding, wonderful smile. 'This was all an elaborate plan to get out of going for dinner, wasn't it?' he jokes, and I laugh.

I sound a little delirious. Raspy. Happy. I am so happy that I forget about my shoulder, and when I roll onto it like a dumbass, Heath rectifies my pained hiss by cuddling me to his chest again. So careful – always so careful with me – he wraps his arms around my middle, palms coasting the curve of my ass.

He breathes in deep. Exhales even deeper. Pure relief. The kind of sound you make when you finally sit down after a long, hard day. 'I can't believe this is real.'

Neither can I.

But, fuck, I am so glad it is.

EPILOGUE

HE ISN'T THE ONLY PERSON HOLLERING THE NAME OF the prettiest graduating student in all of Cove College, but he makes damn sure he's the loudest.

He'll pay for it later, he knows. Narrowed eyes – the richest, most beautiful brown – promise retribution for being so obnoxious. The ceremony's almost done, barely twenty people in the master's program to cycle through, barely double that in the crowd. She'll be on him any second, and, God, he hopes that second comes soon. Hopes it's a long, leisurely second.

A long, leisurely lifetime would be preferable.

His mom is the first person to hug her. He is literally shoved out of the way, the same way he was shoved down the hierarchy of Belfort children pretty much the very second they met, at his own graduation three years ago, when his mom overheard Dani gripping something snarky, snapping his ego into check, and declared very loudly, so unashamedly, that Dani was her new favorite child.

He didn't care then. He doesn't care now. How could he, when the easy open affection makes the woman he loves light up so prettily?

She doesn't dodge the affection anymore. Doesn't look surprised when it happens. She leans into it, unabashed. She lets his mother squeeze the life out of her, lets his sisters and his dad and his niece and their friends do the same, and by the time her brother is finished ruffling her hair and pissing her off, she still has enough tolerance left for him.

She *saved* some for him. She amps it up a notch for him. She fucking *glows* for him as she wraps her arms around his neck, presses that perfect smile against his own.

'God.' He groans, his palms finding their favorite spot at the base of her back, thumbs finding those dimples even through several flowing layers. 'You look good in a cap and gown.'

Her snicker is music to his damn ears. 'Need a picture? Might be a while before you see it again.'

'I'll survive.' Burying his face in the notch of her throat, he inhales greedily until that familiar scent makes him dizzy. 'Delayed gratification.'

He feels her blush. Knows her eyes roll, knows it's his favorite kind – hiding a sweet, bashful reaction. Drags his mouth across the scar that didn't ruin her life so much as gave her permission to start it, up the curve of her neck, along her jaw, until he finds a warm cheek to kiss. 'Congratulations, baby.'

'Thank you.' That freckled nose scrunches. 'I didn't know everyone was coming.'

'Well, with deductive reasoning like that, I don't know how the hell you're gonna get a PhD.'

'Good thing I've got a year to hone it then,' she snarks, shoving him away, only to pull him right back by a fistful of his shirt, to kiss him again, to incite a round of childish, garish croons.

A year, he croons quietly to himself. An entire year, just him and her, doing some of that travelling she's always wanted to do. She's been planning since Christmas, since she plucked a pair of open-ended plane tickets out of her stocking, scribbled a hundred different itineraries in the notebook he got her too.

The ring safely stowed in his backpack, that's for next Christmas. Wherever they are. Doesn't matter. As long as it's the two of them, just them. Together. In love. Happy.

God, there's nothing better.

ACKNOWLEDGMENTS

To Soraya, without whom this book would not exist.

To Ki, Hannah and Becka, without whom I would not exist.

To my agents, Alyssa and Maddalena, for endless support and encouragement.

To the team at Headline Eternal, for making a childhood dream come true.

To Summer, for the cover of my dreams.

To the many, many artists who've brought Death to life.

And to Dani, and everyone just like her. May we find our best fucking friend :)

RAISING READERS

Books Build Bright Futures

Dear Reader,

We'd love your attention for one more page to tell you about the crisis in children's reading, and what we can all do.

Studies have shown that reading for fun is the **single biggest predictor of a child's future life chances** – more than family circumstance, parents' educational background or income. It improves academic results, mental health, wealth, communication skills, ambition and happiness.[1]

The number of children reading for fun is in rapid decline. Young people have a lot of competition for their time. In 2024, 1 in 10 children and young people in the UK aged 5 to 18 did not own a single book at home.[2]

Hachette works extensively with schools, libraries and literacy charities, but here are some ways we can all raise more readers:

- Reading to children for just 10 minutes a day makes a difference
- Don't give up if children aren't regular readers – there will be books for them!
- Visit bookshops and libraries to get recommendations
- Encourage them to listen to audiobooks
- Support school libraries
- Give books as gifts

There's a lot more information about how to encourage children to read on our website: **www.RaisingReaders.co.uk**

Thank you for reading.

hachette UK

---

[1] OECD, '21st-Century Readers: Developing Literacy Skills in a Digital World', 2021, https://www.oecd.org/en/publications/21st-century-readers_a83d84cb-en.html

[2] National Literacy Trust, 'Book Ownership in 2024', November 2024, https://literacytrust.org.uk/research-services/research-reports/book-ownership-in-2024